A TRILOGY
Three Homes for the Heart
Book 2

The Bamboo
House

By

Dorothy Minchin-Comm

 www.trafford.com

North America & international
toll-free: 1 888 232 4444 (USA & Canada)
phone: 250 383 6864 ✦ fax: 812 355 4082

Dedication

To All of My Students

who shared forty-eight classroom years with me,

who taught me at least as much as I taught them, and

who remain a companionable part of my life.

Table of Contents

By the same author ...

BOOKS

1. Yesterday's Tears (1968)
2. To Persia with Love (1980)
3. A Modern Mosaic: The Story of Arts (1981)
4. His Compassions Fail Not (1982)
5. Encore (1988)
6. Gates of Promise (1989)
7. A Desire Completed (1991)
8. Curtain Call (1999)
9. Glimpses of God (1999)
10. The Winter of Their Discontent (2004)
11. Health to the People (2006, with P. William Dysinger)
12. The Book of Minchin (2006)
13. The Celt and the Christ (2008)
14. An Ordered Life (2011)
15. The Paper House (1990, 2012)
16. The Bamboo House (2012)
17. The Gazebo (2012)
18. The Trials of Patience Dunn (2012, in progress)
19. A Song for David (2012, in progress)

20-24. My World: A Personal View [Travel journals, 4 volumes]
    I. The Far East Revisited: A Term of Service (1970-1974)
    II. Return to Service in the Far East (1974-1978)
    III. Home Base: Southern California (1978-1988)
    IV. Retirement and Other Adventures (1989-2010)

ACADEMIC RESEARCH AND BOOK-LENGTH SYLLABI

1. The Changing Concepts of the West Indian Plantocracy in English Poetry and Drama, 1740-1850. [Doctoral dissertation, 1971]
2. The Bible and the Arts (1974, 2001)

3-4. Studies in the Humanities (1977, 1979). [2 volumes]
5. Discovering Ourselves Through the Arts (1981)
6. Christianity in India. [Monograph, 1992, 1995, 1996]
7. Archdeacon Thomas Parnell. [Monograph, 1992, 1995, 1996]

OTHER

Miscellaneous articles, news stories, biographical sketches, multi-media scripts, and editing assignments.

Introduction

The Metaphor of the Bamboo House

If life is to have meaning, we need to assemble our experience so that we can arrive at some basic truths. For that reason I want my reader to be able to nod his or her head and say, "Yes, that's how it is. I've been there too."

In its own way, a Bamboo House has much more stability than a Paper House. Even so, it is still lightweight and very flexible. It can be, if necessary, abandoned in the jungle and rebuilt in another place.

Living there means major—sometimes frequent—transitions. People occupying bamboo houses can expect five things.

First, they must be adaptable. The changes mean that you must be able to assimilate new ideas. You have to know how to change your mind.

Second, you may have to move, physically. Not just from one house to another. It may be to another country and culture.

Third, the Bamboo House, wherever it is, rises above ground level. You have to climb up steps to get into it. That means that you will grow.

Then, through the open windows, high up there, you catch fresh, cooling breezes. Your spirit soars. In that airy atmosphere the life of your soul begins to flourish. God's grace enfolds you.

Last, nothing in the plant world is more lovely than a graceful stand of bamboo. Green and alive. It's tough—hard to root out—but beautiful.

Dorothy Minchin-Comm, PhD
Professor of English *(Retired)*
La Sierra University
Riverside, California
2012

Acknowledgements

Cover Design: At twenty-four years old, Kara Lewis had graduated with a master's degree in Interdisciplinary Studies from the Southern Oregon University (2009). While developing her skills in photography, painting, and drawing, she works in her family's art business, Lewis Enterprises (http://lewisenterprises. blogspot.com).

Kara Lewis

Fern Sandness-Penstock

Chapter Illustration: Fern Sandness-Penstock has been a lifelong friend of Dorothy Minchin-Comm, ever since they first met as juniors in high school in Canada. She has traveled worldwide with her husband, Floyd, a teacher and school administrator. Because of her multiple artistic interests, Fern's sketch book has never been far from her side. She was well qualified to read the three manuscripts for *Three Homes for the Heart* and distill out of each chapter one image that captured the essence of that stage of the story.

Layout and Design: Larry Kidder, has worked in the Office of University Relations at Loma Linda University for close to 20 years as a writer, editor, and publication designer. After about 100 years of seclusion, some of the old pictures had virtually perished. Applying his technical expertise, Larry resurrected them. **Barbara Howe-Djordjevic** also contributed her time and artistic talent to improving a large group of the derelict photographs and Kodachrome slides used in this book.

Larry Kidder

CHAPTER 1

Rites of Passage

To all appearances, my family and that of my Australian cousins were thoroughly settled on our respective continents. I in Canada and they in Australia. That was in 1946. Still mourning our separation, even after almost four years, we wrote earnest letters to one another, desperately trying to keep the joyous days of our childhood alive.

Meanwhile, Canada had been a "Good Thing" for my immediate family. After a short sojourn in one of the oldest apartments on campus, we moved into a new house, finished up just for us. Next door, in an equally new house, lived the Balharries. Dad now chaired the Department of Religion with Gordon Balharrie as his associate. He had, indeed, made his transition from English into Bible teaching. Eileen flourished in Grade 2, with Jeannie next door for her best friend.

Me? I thoroughly embedded myself in Grade 11, not missing any event, either in or out of the classroom. I now had concentric circles of friends. A handful of special, committed-for-life companions and then widening circles of others, way out to the far reaches of acquaintance. At last, I "belonged." I was never sure just how it had all happened. Rather I sort of bathed in the warmth of being part of everything. I didn't spend a lot of time on introspection simply because I was too busy just "being."

The girls' dormitory at the time featured an oddity, "double bunk beds" capable of sleeping four people. Thus, whenever I wanted a taste of dorm life (something of which I had been perpetually deprived) I could spend a Saturday night with Fern Sandness and her two roommates, Hazel Dopher and Doris Bolton.

Usually those occasions resulted in little more than a lot of giggling and a few hours of girl-talk. One Saturday night, however, we over-reached our-selves a little. Miss Verda Deer, a tall, angular lady, was Dean of Women. She was also our geometry teacher.

Our gang had just climbed up the hill from the skating rink when Lucille asked a favor of us. "I'll get in before the door's locked. I just want to have a little more time with_____."

Arguably the most strikingly beautiful girl on campus at the time, she had a serious boyfriend. Actually, far more serious than either her youth or the school policy could permit. Still, they were such a dashingly romantic pair that I, along with the others, was more than willing to help. "Just keep Miss Deer busy so that I can get through the door when the time comes," Lucille urged.

So we hung around the dorm lobby, watching the door. At the crucial moment, we pressed into Miss Deer's office, solemnly asking about our latest geometry assignment. Miss Deer looked right over our heads and saw the miscreant slip through the front door. "You know that none of you cares a thing about geometry." She fixed us with a cold stare. "And certainly not on Saturday night!"

Stepping around our earnest little group of inquirers, she called Lucille

Winter at Canadian Union College. Beautiful but violently cold. Inset. Eileen sets out for school. Warm pants were not yet a common option, even for very little girls.

back down off the staircase that she was ascending in considerable haste.

Miss Deer lectured us roundly on our deplorable—maybe even felonious—behavior. Yes, I was embarrassed. Even as I faced my crime, however, I felt secure. I remembered how cheerfully my cousin Kelvin and his friend Cleve used to go off to their punishment in the headmaster's office back in Australia. Even though I might be on the path to perdition, I had a delicious sense of actually being part of the network.

Flooded with water to create natural ice, the homemade skating rink was the center of our social life. (Eileen actually learned to ice skate faster and better than I did.) To be sure, neither Singapore nor Australia had been optimal locations for me to learn any kind of skating.

I found the Canadian men, one and all, to be magnificent skaters. A girl had three good prospects. One of the boys might offer to lace her skates onto her feet while everyone huddled around the potbellied stove in the rink-side shack. Then, any number of them might offer to whirl her around the rink while her breath froze onto the edge of her parka hood. A special male person might offer to climb the hill with her and carry her skates up to the top. In a time and place of strictly enforced social limitations, all of these opportunities were to be played out for all they were worth.

I had a major problem. When I was on the arm of one of those strong, tall Canadians, I would sail around the circle, gulping down the frosty blue night-air and listening to the hiss of the blades on the ice. At those moments, I actually believed that I could skate.

On the other hand, I knew better. I was tipsy as a drunk and clung to the fence whenever I was left on my own. When the boys I admired would ask me to skate, I would decline and give some inane excuse. I didn't want them to find out how bad I really was. Then I had to sit on the sidelines and watch my current hero skate with some other girl.

I allowed myself to accept skating offers only from the dopey boys. I didn't care what the "rejects" thought of me. Meanwhile, the good ones I had a crush on would look at me, wholly unable to understand why I had refused to skate with them. Although this kind of "bi-polar" attitude prevailed only on the skating rink, it was a painful leftover from my former, unsettled life.

As a matter of fact, another round of chaos lay just ahead. It would be such a potent mixture of happiness and loss that I wonder, even now, how I survived.

That summer the unimaginable happened. The session of the General Conference of Seventh-day Adventists convened in Washington D.C. Uncle Len Minchin was a delegate from Australia. Although my dad wasn't an official delegate, he and Mum found the journey from Alberta to Washington well worth the effort. The two brothers could visit with one another for a few days. All of their lives they had so much enjoyed one another's company. Inevitably, we children had also become addicted to one another.

During our parents' absence little sister Eileen was left in the care of the Gordon Balharrie family next door. One of the older college girls moved into the house with me. At fifteen years old, I was not about to admit that I needed babysitting any more. Doris Bolton understood this, and we enjoyed a very adult companionship. Indeed, during that time, I began to acquire a whole new grip on seeing myself as a grown-up.

I immediately reverted to childhood, however, when the news came in from Washington. Dad and Uncle Len had both received invitations to work in England. The prospect drove us kids out to the far edges of sanity. Up to that time, probably nothing had ever excited us that much in our whole lives. England here we come!

Most certainly I loved Canadian Union College. I'd made so many good friends. The prospect of England, however, was absolutely heart-stopping. Entirely new. Surely, there couldn't be a downside to this prospect. Could there?

So we packed up our freight shipment and dispatched it to New York. We then spent a month with my mother's parents in Southern California. As the train headed east, I watched my American grandparents standing on the platform in Riverside—Grandma in tears, of course. At the moment, however, I could scarcely give the separation even one backward thought. Next, we spent two or three incredibly hot nights at my Uncle Jimmy's place in Keene, Texas.

Still sweating we arrived in Washington DC to prepare for our departure to England. Employees under overseas appointment—like our family—were

Eileen and Dorothy aboard ship, headed to England (November, 1946). The New York shipping strike had *finally* ended.

royally entertained. We had free meals at any one of three very tasty cafeterias. All we had to do was walk there and eat.

Meanwhile, we had to wait for a shipping strike in New York to end. After a month's delay, however, the glamour of "living out" had become somewhat diminished. My Australian cousins were still in the future, and my Canadian friends were in the past. The very recent past. The present situation really began to vex all of us.

The opening of the school year approached, and still we couldn't move. Besides, it was not at all clear where our freight shipment had gone. It could be anywhere between the Canadian prairies and the New York docks. No one seemed to know. Therefore, in a time when air travel was used for emergencies only, my Dad flew to London—alone. On September 19, 1946, he left us.

I don't remember thinking so much about his unusual flight as I did about my own keenly felt detachment. An all too familiar feeling began to engulf me.

Mum, Eileen, and I were duly installed on the eighth floor of the Times Square Hotel. Right after Dad left, I bought some navy-blue wool and started knitting a cardigan sweater for him. It helped keep my mind off what was beginning to feel like a huge, gaping gash in my soul. I could hardly comprehend what was wrong. Every day, I knitted furiously on Dad's sweater trying to calm my sorrows. By now I was beginning really to grieve for the friends I'd left behind in Canada.

Finding food in New York was certainly not as pleasurable as the cafete-

Left. Quaint old Moor Close has always been the showpiece of Newbold College, Berkshire, England, since the post-World War II years. **Right.** The circle window lends an air of charm to the garden view. **Below right.** Among the ruins of Sylvia's Garden.

rias in Takoma Park. We patronized Horn and Hardart, the forerunner, I suppose, of vending machines. The queues were long, people waiting to plug their coin into the slot and take out the piece of pie or hamburger when the little door popped open.

Tempers often ran short. One day, a bleached, wrinkled woman swung back on the rather fat man behind her. "Don't you touch me!" she yelled.

"Well," the grumpy fellow in his baseball cap bawled back, "What did you come here for then, if you don't want to be touched?" Thus, the anxious, sticky crowd inched along past the ranks of little postoffice-type cubbyholes, each containing a food item.

Nearing the end of making the sweater, I realized that I might be short one skein of yarn. One hot night, while Mum was in the shower, seven-year-old Eileen, in a fit of sheer boredom, was cavorting back and forth over the beds. Accidentally, she kicked my last ball of wool out of the open window.

Frustrated, I had a fleeting desire to throw her out after it. Why did she have to do that?

I leaned out, looking down to the street far below. Well, I'd simply have to go and find the ball of wool. When I got down to the ground-level, however, I had not the faintest idea which side our room was on. I walked around the enormous building twice. Everything looked the same. It was all New York. A couple of times fellows emerged out of the dark doorways as if to follow me. Too pre-occupied even to be afraid, I kept on, eyes fixed on the gutters. Nothing.

Eventually, I did get back into the hotel and upstairs, only to find Mum in an absolute panic worrying about me. Too naïve to realize that I had done something mortally dangerous, I grieved mainly over not finding the wool.

The next day we went over to Macy's where I bought another skein. Not the same dye lot, and that annoyed me. (When all was said and done, I didn't need it anyway!) I always seemed to have an uncanny ability to focus fiercely on whatever project was at hand and to cast away both caution and temperance. Besides, I was getting very tired of New York anyway.

In due course, our household stuff had been found, and the shipping strike ended. Before we could leave New York, however, another difficulty loomed large over us.

A letter came from Dad. In making his mid-life transition from English teaching to theology, he had not, apparently made a good move. As it turned out, Newbold College was already served by two Bible teachers and one English teacher. Somewhere communication had broken down. His teaching assignments bordered on the bizarre. Ancient History—no problem. But Physiology?

We had, indeed, been impaled on a dilemma with two very distinct horns. "I've thought of telling you not to come over." Mum read part of Dad's letter to us. "I am not sure how this will turn out."

"Then let's go back to Canada!" Eileen and I shouted in chorus. She was jumping on the bed again, so I closed the window to contain her. Why couldn't we go back to Canada?

"But I've decided," Mum went on with the letter, "that this is somehow for the best, and we must stick to our commitment."

Therefore, two days later, the three of us boarded an east-bound ship and sailed out past the Statue of Liberty. Now I had leisure to think again of England and the cousins. I felt almost guilty for my temporary disloyalty. The stress of New York had brought it on. Nonetheless, I look back now and marvel at the turbulence of teenage emotions. No wonder we're counseled not to make life-changing commitments while still in that condition!

On Monday morning, November 18, 1946, Dad was waiting on the dock in Southampton to meet us. Having the family all together again helped a great deal, and we were right jolly on the train going up to Berkshire.

So this was England. I looked out the window, not realizing how little I was going to see of it in the coming ten months.

Newbold College, near Bracknell, had, in addition to the main building, Moor Close, four other large country homes: Farley Copse, Binfield Hall, Egremont, and Popeswood Lodge. We were allotted the second floor in Popeswood. As is usual with incoming faculty, living quarters are never quite ready for occupancy. So we stayed in the girls' dormitory portion of Moor Close, our windows above the Dean's flat looking out over the lawns toward the ruins of Sylvia's Garden.

The end of World War II was but a single year behind us. Part of the Close gardens had been planted in cabbages, and living in general was still lean. The grand old mansion housed almost everything: The girls, the classrooms, the chapel, the administrative offices, the library, and the kitchen and dining room. While we waited for our flat (apartment) to be ready, we patronized the college dining room three times a day. Food rationing still prevailed, and the meals were very limited in both flavor and variety.

On occasion, a student could go rather mad under the pressure. One of my classmates, Brian Jacques, worked in the kitchen. One day he had a dispute with the matron, a woman of inflexible temperament. Perhaps he became crazed from eating too many gluten steaks. "I don't know what happened," he mused. "My hand just flew out and hit her."

In return, she smacked him for cheekiness. Immediately suspended for two weeks, he grieved appropriately over his crime. "But she's so cranky," he told me when he came back. "I just can't keep out of trouble."

In due course, our family moved into Popeswood Lodge. The three-story mansion took its name from the family to which it once belonged, that of Alexander Pope. Being Roman Catholic, they were excluded from both universities (Oxford and Cambridge) as well as many London activities. So the young poet walked these lovely lanes around Binfield Village, the place to which the Pope family retreated.

To be sure, we lived only in the Lodge, not in the Popes' Great House, but the building still fired my imagination. I could look out upon the same green meadows that had greeted Alexander, one of the wittiest English minds of the 18th-century. In addition to the grand sweep of spacious lawns and ornamental trees around the big house, two items remained from more affluent days, a high-walled squash court and a large tennis court. A very old wisteria vine covered the entrance to the plaster-white house with its black shutters.

The Lodge sheltered four faculty families. Dr. E. E. White, the college president, and his wife occupied the first floor. The bay windows of their ballroom-turned-living-room framed the front garden. An ambitious entryway under the arbor of wisteria vines ushered us into a spacious reception hall. There a fine, curved staircase took us up to our floor, which, in more prosperous days, would have been the bedrooms for the family. A small tributary to the grand staircase curved to the right, directly into a delicious, light room where a wide rank of lead-paned windows overlooked the broken slate steps up to the front door. The Whites' niece, Kathryn Hargreaves, occupied this choice little spot. Being about my age, she became my first friend in England.

A much more ordinary staircase led up to the smaller rooms on the top floor. The Marters, lately from South Africa, lived up there in the former servants' quarters. Finally, at the end of the building was the three-tiered apartment of the English teacher, John Dunnett. The youngest of the Lodge's residents, he and his wife were deemed fully capable of living simultaneously on three floors. If need be, they would be able to run up and down the tortuous circular staircase all day with their two babies.

Each of our high-ceilinged bedrooms had a stingy little fireplace. The only exception was a tiny room about four steps above the rest of the floor, perhaps a butler's room. We accessed it by a dark, mysterious hallway, no more than two elbows wide. Dad designated this place as his study, a retreat from the three females in his house.

A dismal little kitchen had been carved out of the landing at the top of our staircase. Wartime rationing still prevailed, however, so we didn't have any exotic variety of foods to bring home and set on the narrow pantry shelves. Nothing in the whole kitchen encouraged either contentment or appetite.

The next room was a purely functional bathroom, an afterthought to the original house. It had two doors, neither of which locked. A perpetually Arctic climate prevailed within. Nothing we could do improved that situation. Mum had to do all the family laundry on her knees at the bathtub. Afterwards she had two options for drying. To smoke the clothes dry in front of a coal fireplace. Or to hang them in front of the vine-framed windows for an entire damp, gray week before they could dry enough to be serviceable again. Yes, Popeswood Lodge provided many curious experiences.

I encountered two vignettes of life that could have occurred, I believe, only in England. The first came in late December, 1946. I awoke early on Christmas morning to find that snow had fallen again in the night. Indeed, 1946-1947 turned out to be a record cold winter in England.

I sat up in bed and looked over the now-winterized wisteria vines, the lawn, the brick wall and on into the tree-lined lane. In the still air, every leaf and twig stood dusted with white. Suddenly a bugle sounded and a fox hunting party swept around the bend. The horses feathered the dry snow under their feet. The men sat tall upon their mounts, elegant in red coats and attended by the bugler with a long, curved horn. Trotting along among the horses, a cheerful pack of hounds—at least twenty of them—pressed forward. The dogs had perfectly matched markings, as if they'd all come off a copy machine. Picturesque as the scene might be, at that moment the horror of the killing totally eluded me.

Had I entered into a time warp and awakened somewhere back in Alexander Pope's 18th-century? Or had a painted scene off the cover of a biscuit tin somehow come to life? After The Hunt passed the house, I finally drew my first breath in at least five minutes! Then I got up to dress. We had to get on with our commonplace 20th-century Christmas, after all. Still, that vision has never left me. This, indeed, was elemental England, and it touched something in the very heart of my heritage!

The second gift would come in the very early spring. In those days when mornings and evenings were edged with light mists. When a cool, conservative sun picked out the black patches that frost had abandoned. That's when the miracle happened, out there beyond the back lawn and around the tennis court.

Suddenly one morning we had an enormous field of daffodils, golden and endless, stretching away to the thatched cottage and stream down at the end of the Popeswood property. The flowers craned their heads to look through the fence, as if hoping to see a tennis game. Surely, the show was enough to have prompted Wordsworth to yet another poem, had he been able to come back and see what we saw that day. That picture of the daffodils, framed in the window above the sink, brightened our depressing kitchen for many days.

Popeswood Lodge has left me with these two priceless memories, one man-made, the other God-made. Both remain so vivid that the scenes would come back to refresh me at odd times and in strange places. Perhaps in the heat of a western desert. On the beach of a Caribbean island. Or on a Los Angeles freeway.

An English Heritage

On their first journey to Britain, Dorothy and her family had only a vague understanding of their English heritage. All of that would come much later when she would become seriously involved in assembling the history of her father's family. The shortness of their stay in England and its limitations notwithstanding, they felt an innate attachment to that lovely, ancient island. For 16-year-old Dorothy, it was the beginning of a life-long love affair with English.

In the heart of the beautiful Cotswolds, with its dozens of arched stone bridges, Bourton-on-the-Water (River Windrush), Gloucestershire, has become a major tourist destination.

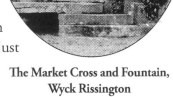

The cross on the village green is all that remains of the market place in the tiny village of Wyck Rissington, just 1½ miles from Bourton-on-the-Water. Over 600 years ago—and probably long before that—

The Market Cross and Fountain, Wyck Rissington

Dorothy's Anglo-Saxon ancestors lived here. Through the generations many of them must have come to this public fountain to draw water.

See Dorothy Minchin-Comm, *The Book of Minchin: A Family for All Seasons* (Victoria, BC, Canada: Trafford Publishing, 2006). Illustrated, 670 pages.

CHAPTER 2

A Gallery of English Pictures

Uncle Len Minchin,[1] Auntie May and the five cousins: Kelvin (17), Joan (16), Yvonne (14), and the twins, Valmae and Leona (12) arrived on February 2, 1947. After four weeks at sea, the *Empire Clarendon* reached London. Our uproariously joyful reunion took place down on Tilbury Docks. The sailing out of Fremantle, Western Australia, had been unexpectedly delayed for six weeks, giving ample time for the family to get acquainted with all of the cousins and the ancestral homes of our forbears.

Our great-great-great grandfather James Minchin had set out from Southampton, England on the *Caroline* with his five children to pioneer in the Swan River Colony of Western Australia in 1829. Of course, we realized none of this at the time. Real knowledge of our family history would come much later. Instead, for us teenagers another glorious "present" was about to begin.

Not surprisingly, Uncle Len's house in Stanborough Park was not ready, so the whole family moved in with us at Popeswood Lodge. We kids, of course, thought this to be a fine arrangement.

A sheet was hung down the middle of Mum's and Dad's big, high-ceilinged bedroom, and all of our parents slept in that room. The four girls joined Eileen and me in our bedroom over the entranceway to the mansion. Enjoying total privacy in Dad's little study, Kelvin never failed to remind us of his exclusive privileges and his personal superiority, up in the "high place." Immediately we cousins all fell back into our old patterns, obviously not advanced much beyond what we'd been back in Australia five years earlier.

Together Mum and Auntie May did the laundry in the bathtub, managed the food-ration books, and cooked in the dark little kitchen.

Although our mothers did their best, meals, of necessity, had a certain sameness about them. To offset the boredom, we sometimes made the best of it by pretending to be nobility, dining in great state. Living in a "mansion," naturally fired out imaginations. What reality failed to give us, fantasy often provided. On occasion we assumed a lordly manner, calling upon one another—the maids and the butler—to bring on the food.

Together, we elevated the local "Welsh Rarebit" to the level of gourmet cuisine. While the public recipe called for a half-cup of porter beer, everything else fit our family tastes. Registered as vegetarians, we had extra cheese coupons in our ration books. What we called the "Welsh Rabbit" used huge quantities of cheese. Full of silliness, we dipped our bread into the tastily flavored sauce. Tea with King George VI himself could not have brought us more pleasure than we had among ourselves, eating the "Rabbit" together in front of one of Popeswood Lodge's smoky fireplaces.

During World War II and in the years immediately following, the colonies sent special foodstuffs to Britain. Dairy products came from New Zealand. When we had lived there, we had enjoyed (for almost a year) a large, five-gallon tin of hard, white honey. In England we'd secured another one. It stood by our kitchen door at Popeswood. "Please get us some honey for breakfast, Yvonne." My Mum handed her a small dish and a big spoon.

Obediently Yvonne pried off the lid and reached down. How we all loved the creamy sweetness of that whipped honey. A huge treat in food-rationed England. "Oh! Oh! No!" Yvonne stared down at a fuzzy brown spot on top of the honey. An over-eager mouse had perished in its effort to share the good life that we had.

No one today is clear about what happened next. Excitement prevailed. Poor Yvonne was marked for life. Knowing my mother, however, I know that she would have struggled between two impulses—thriftiness and an absolute horror of germs. On the one hand, she could have removed the mouse and scraped off the top layer of honey. Or she could have thrown the whole tin away. Who knows?

What really fascinated us all were the dried bananas, Jamaica's contribution to wartime England. We'd never seen them before. About the size, shape, and color of cigars, their chewy sweetness reminded us of dates, figs and raisins all at once. We took to presenting the plate of dried bananas to one another with sweeping curtsies. "My dear Madam! May I press you into another dried banana?"

The ambience of Popeswood Lodge indeed had a peculiar effect upon us. About this time, our parents must have despaired of our ever attaining any kind of rational maturity. Nonetheless, this period in Popeswood, I believe, was our last stand for childhood. After all, I was a high-school senior, with Kelvin and Joan only a year behind. The rest came along in order. Even Eileen, the baby, was already in Grade 3.

In early March flu struck our household. For weeks, a depressing gray drizzle descended upon us, both physically and emotionally. All seven of us kids became sick at one time. A doctor from nearby Bracknell made several house calls to tend to us. None of us liked him.

When we were ambulatory again, we had to go for a check-up at his office. We girls were instinctively reluctant to see him again. I realize now that he had, in his "treatments," overstepped the boundaries of legitimate cures for flu. He could have been charged with molestation. But we didn't know the word and were too naïve and too shy to complain. Indeed, we would hardly have known where to complain. Unwilling to tell our mothers, we just had to "get over it" by ourselves.

The even more serious outcome of the flu episode was that the twins had been more ill than the rest of us put together. While Leona made a normal recovery, Valmae became severely diabetic. (This condition undermined her health to the point that she died much too soon, at just fifty-two years of age.) At the time, however, we rose up to enjoy the only Easter we would have together in England.

One frosty day, the sun finally returned. Another miracle. "Come, children. Do come quickly. Look at the sun!" Uncle Len stood at the living room window, and we rushed to him in a pack. "You must look so that you can remember what it's like." What a noteworthy event for a little batch of cold, damp (formerly sun-baked) Australians!

That Easter, something instinctive led my Dad and my Uncle to take our two families to a very special event in the Royal Albert Hall in London.

Sitting in a box (on the same level as the nobility), we had an excellent view of the stage. There we seven children heard Handel's "Messiah" for the first time. I've always wondered what it cost our impoverished fathers to give us that marvelous evening.

At seventeen years old, I understood the concert as a true rite of passage. I would never be the same again. I entered into the feelings of the composer himself when he testified that in the twenty-four days during which he wrote the oratorio, "I saw all heaven opened before me."

The huge organ and the orchestra, under the baton of Sir Malcolm Sargent (1895-1967), sent glorious sound swirling through the gilded arches and up into the tiers of balconies. I could scarcely breathe for the intensity of the happening. The bell-like soprano arias. The mellow altos. The sweet tenor recitatives. The resonant bass solos. All mingled with the orchestral instruments and then burst into anthems with storms of power.

Of course, everyone stood for the "Hallelujah Chorus." For me, however, that moment was surpassed by "For Unto Us a Child is Born," ending with all 1,000 voices of the Huddersfield Choral Society at full volume exulting again and again, "The Everlasting Father! The Prince of Peace!"

In front of Popeswood Lodge, the "Seven Australians" romped in the snowy English lane. The winter of 1947 turned out to be the harshest on record in Britain, to date.

In a daze, I left the hall. I don't remember any of us saying much as we walked to the Underground station to take the last trains back to Bracknell and Watford, respectively. Speech seemed superfluous. We kids had had our first spiritual encounter with great sacred music. Truly an epiphany.

After several weeks, the cousin family moved into their house, "Fernville," at Stanborough Park. Auntie May had to clean the place herself, along with whatever help she could solicit. The scantily insulated duplex had no heat. One morning she spilled a bucket of water on the staircase. It turned to ice before she could wipe it up.

The severity of that winter of 1947 in England enchanted the children. The adults? Not so much. Having come from Canada, however, I was not particularly entertained by the snow and sub-zero temperatures. Cold weather—anywhere— has always had a debilitating physical effect on me.

Now we were twenty miles apart, but at least we were on the same piece of ground. We could visit by train. Other times we'd borrow bicycles and ride the Berkshire lanes between Stanborough Park and Newbold College.

One special spring day, when the sun shone, we bicycled across and met at the Ascot Race Track. Habitual royal watchers, we parked by the roadside to see the Royal Family's carriages arrive from Windsor. Then, we hurried to find a place by the fence, opposite the royal pavilion. Thus, we got our fill of the fashionable nobility, the top hats, tea gowns, and all the rest.

Then we turned our attention to the horses. Incredibly beautiful, sleek animals! Halfway through, however, one of the horses hit the fence and dropped with a broken leg. Horrified, I watched men come out and shoot the horse dead, right in front of us.

Immediately, I lost interest in the whole affair, got on my bicycle, and headed for home. Broken bones can be set. Why does anyone, even a horse, have to die of a broken leg? I didn't understand then, and I really don't have it worked out even now.

A more satisfying occasion occurred a few weeks later, down at the Horse Guards Parade in London. All of us (both families) had arrived there at 4 a.m. to see the birthday parade for King George VI. We had staked out a good place on a little embankment above the pavement. Tall, gangly teenagers that we were, we could easily see over the heads of the crowd huddled together on the curb. The next rank of loyal Londoners stood along a low fence immediately in front of us. Intent on seeing our heroine, the Princess Elizabeth (she was only a couple of years older than I), we cared nothing for the group of stumpy, short old ladies by the fence.

"Why can't people leave their big children at home?" A fierce little woman with thick glasses glared up at us. "They do so get in the way, don't they?" With conviction she forthwith climbed up on the first rail of the fence to get a better view.

Then the marching regiments of the Coldstream Guards, precise as clockwork, swung into the quadrangle to the glorious brassy sounds of the bands. Trim in red-and-blue uniform, the Princess rode beside her father on a magnificent glossy brown mount. The rest of the royal ladies followed in an open carriage drawn by a matched team of Windsor greys.

Just as the Royal Family passed, not ten feet from where we enchanted Australians stood, the fence collapsed. The weight of the feisty grumbler and her companions bore it down to the ground with a thud. Scrambling about in the grass at our feet, they missed the great moment entirely.

Meanwhile, we big kids all stood in the open, free and easy under the smiling gaze of our King and our Princess. There must be, I decided, a certain kind of perverse justice at work in the universe, after all.

Always outgoing, Joan had social graces that occasionally took her a little far into left field. One day, she was walking the streets of Watford selling a health magazine. Her partner was a teenager, shorter than Joan in both height and in age. They came upon a dark, high-walled compound. A sign by the gate indicated that the place belonged to a nudist group. Joan suggested, "I think we should skip this one."

In all innocence her little friend objected. "But we're supposed to knock on every door." Truly, their mentors had trained them well. Believing that the receptionist would be fully prepared in every way, to meet the public, Joan stepped up and tapped the doorknocker.

Suddenly overwhelmed by the gloominess of the place, her partner shrank in behind her and backed down a couple of steps. The door swung open." How can we help you?" A young man, bare as the day he was born, smiled engagingly.

Ever faithful to her task, Joan fixed her eyes on a point somewhere above his head, grasped the porch rail, and began her canvass: "We have this … this health magazine, and … and we …" Her voice trailed off as her partner shrank still further into the shrubbery by the steps.

Perfectly at ease, leaning against the doorpost, the man drawled, "Ah, well! We're all pretty healthy in here." He straightened up and reached for the door. "So, we wouldn't be interested."

Thus released from responsibility, the girls rushed blindly down the path, out the gate and into the street. At least, no one could charge them with shirking their duty. They had not missed a single door.

When Joan described the episode to her family, they all had a good laugh. Very soon, however, the phone rang. The other girl's mother berated Auntie May because Joan had led her daughter into such corruption.

Alas, the tension between duty and modesty! Whose fault was it anyway that the girl didn't know the meaning of the word "nudist?"

With early spring came the expectation of the end of my school year at Newbold. I had made friends. Also, I'd had a very good time that compared favorably with my year in Canada. Unfortunately, I had studied only minimally.

One of my best friends, Erica Sturznegger from Switzerland, already knew French, German and Italian. She'd come to England to improve her English. She—not I—could afford the unmerciful persecution we inflicted upon the French professor, the bearded young Jean Buzenet.

Although he was a good man, he was never entirely in charge of his classroom. We exploited this failing. Later on, he got even with one of our rabble by marrying her!

Then I had Betty Mackett from South Africa. She was my age, but far ahead of me in poise and style. What could I ever do to match her grace in tweeds and plaids?

Amid all of these interests, I'd studied enough to get by, but certainly not enough to sustain a sudden ambition that overtook me. I decided that I wanted more than just a certificate from Newbold College. I wanted to try for Senior Matriculation at the University of London. A soul-chastening public examination that only one-third of the applicants could expect to pass. One had to be, as it were, the cream of the crop. I knew I certainly wasn't that. Still, the desire persisted.

The now-demolished Shoulder-of-Mutton pub was once a landmark in Binfield, near Newbold College.

It cost forty-two shillings to apply. As always, our family lived on such a narrow money-margin that this was an astronomical sum. I really didn't feel worthy to ask for it. After all, that money would buy a lot of cheese. Nonetheless, Dad gave me the money without protest. He didn't even lecture me about studying. Perhaps he saw a glimmer of maturity here and was more than happy to promote it.

I filled out the application form and headed down the road to the rustic old Shoulder of Mutton, the nearest pub *cum* post-office. When I left home I had the money. When I arrived, it was gone. Absolutely gone! To this day, I don't know what happened to it. In tears, I plodded back to Popeswood, searching every inch of the path I had taken.

Dad, bless him, gave me another forty-two shillings. I locked the money in my sweaty hand and ran back to the Shoulder of Mutton.

Now, having already wasted Dad's money, I prayed the most desperate prayer of my life. I wanted to pass that Senior Matric exam. In the darkness of that night a very substantial but wordless voice spoke to my mind. "If you are willing to work hard, Dottie, you will pass." Was that God talking to me? Then I fell into a contented, deep sleep.

In the morning, I woke up to what I knew to be my task. I literally fell into a frenzy of studying. For the next six weeks, I truly did nothing else but stick to my books. I had never been so motivated in my life. Actually, I really didn't understand why I was so driven. (Twenty-five years later, I would figure it out when I applied for admission to doctoral studies in Canada. I needed this particularly British achievement)

During that English spring in 1947, however, I determined not to disappoint my Dad. Perhaps for the first time I didn't want to shame myself either. I glimpsed, in fact, the ideal of excellence. Moreover, the results would be a really public exhibition, published in the newspapers. I knew now that I was in the middle of the race to the finish.

When the time came, I joined six of my Newbold friends who were bent on the same purpose. Daily, for a week, we walked to Bracknell and boarded the train down into London. The examination hall was filled with young people like us, as well as some elderly persons in their thirties and forties. The man next to me, I discovered, was trying for the twelfth time. The nun across the aisle was sitting for the third time. All or nothing. You passed all of the subjects or you automatically failed them all.

Whatever made me think that a carefree grasshopper like me would pass on the first try? Day after day, I wrung the answers out of my mind and soul—arithmetic, algebra, geometry, English language and literature, French and music. I wrote miles of essays, thousands of words.

Always poor in math, I found that those test papers virtually gave me fits. I came home every night to knock on Dr. White's door downstairs. A formidable mathematician, he patiently went over each paper with me. In the end, I found that my mistakes hadn't been as gross as I imagined. Might I then begin to hope?

By this time, a very painful fact of life had become clear to us all. My family was going to return to the United States. It hardly came as a surprise. While trying to preserve his career-change from English to religion, Dad had found himself very much adrift that year at Newbold. His teaching load was taking him nowhere, nor was any change possible.

So now we were scheduled to return to America, to Atlantic Union College, near Boston, Massachusetts. For the first year, Dad would teach English. The next year he would replace the retiring chairman of the Religion

Department. That was all good for him. Yes.

For me? For the seventh time in seven consecutive years I would start school in a new country. Adrift, again!

Having had no car, no money, and no time, we'd seen little of England. The local trains and bicycles had determined how far we could go. Before leaving England, Dad decided to go on his own private pilgrimage up to Wordsworth's Lake Country. Neither Eileen nor I could qualify for benefiting intellectually from such a trip, and Mum stayed home to look after us.

More was to come, but travel money would be spent only on those capable of appreciating the sightseeing. No money was available to lavish upon the undeserving.

A few weeks later, when Dad and Mum set off for Europe, however, I was included. Eileen was supposedly distracted by being told that she would spend two weeks with "my Twinnies," as she called Valmae and Leona. My parents hoped (mistakenly) that she wouldn't realize that she'd been left out. Still, there just wasn't enough money to take someone who was not yet sophis-ticated enough to profit from the sights of France and Switzerland. Eileen wouldn't know the difference. In fact, she did, but she held her peace and was delivered up to Uncle's house in Watford. I smugly relished the knowledge that I was included.

That diverse train journey from the port of Calais remains an oddly assorted collec-tion of sights and sounds for me. The regular tourist attractions, of course.

Gerald and Leona Minchin visited France and Switzerland briefly before returning to the United States in 1947. Considered old enough to benefit culturally from the trip and to be worthy of the hard-won travel dollars, Dorothy posed on the glacier at Chamonix, Mont Blanc.

The first evening in Paris we walked in the gardens of the Tuillieries. Mum became thirsty. "I hear a water fountain running."

We plunged through the bushes only to find a *pissoir* (men's latrine)! Paris didn't have any public drinking fountains then. "Well, there's your drink," Dad remarked placidly.

More curiosities followed. The women in Geneva scrubbed the public sidewalks before their front doors. How clean can you get? The horses wore little peaked caps on their ears, "to prevent sunstroke." As we took the boat-and-castle tour of Lake Geneva, Dad introduced me to Byron's "Prisoner of Chillon." At the top of the cog-railway, I shivered in the blue ice-caves of the Chamonix Glacier.

During our weekend at the college in Collonges, France, I joined a group of students climbing the *Saleve* (mountain). An unbelievably handsome young Frenchman undertook to escort me, and I was utterly charmed. Laboriously I tried out my classroom French on him. He listened patiently and answered slowly. After a couple of hours, while we were sheltering in a cave during a rainstorm, he said, in perfect English, "Now we can talk in your language, if you wish."

Ultimately, the White Cliffs of Dover, so recently famous in wartime England, ushered us back home. We had time now for little else, other than disposing of our household stuff and packing up to leave.

I had just one more treat left for me in England. While attending a Youth Camp down in Plymouth, I received a letter from the University of London. I stared at it, trembling. "I can't open it," I croaked.

"Here, I'll help you." Kelvin grabbed the envelope and slit it open. I sat down, paralyzed. Time stood still. Then Kel looked down, grinning. "You made it, Dottie."

Suddenly everyone was hugging me and congratulating me. A vast relief engulfed me. (Later on, to my utter astonishment, I discovered that I was the only one of the Newbold contingent who passed that year.) Dad's money hadn't been wasted after all. At least, not all of it.

We came once more to the Southampton docks. Uncle Len was traveling with us to a Youth Congress in San Francisco—all part of his work. He and Dad slept among at least 140 men in the hold of the ship, the *Marine Flasher*. Mum, Eileen and I shared a cabin with several other women.

After every meal, we stood on the deck of our "converted" troop ship and watched all of the food being thrown overboard. This vexed our frugal, ration-ridden souls, even mine. We must be on the way back to America. No one in England could dream of wasting food like that.

On Sunday, August 31, 1947, we entered New York Harbor. As we passed the Statue of Liberty (again), many of our fellow passengers wept. Immigrants from war-torn Europe, they grasped for hope.

I wept too, but for different reasons. Seeing my despondency, Uncle Len tried to cheer me up by dramatizing the Statue of Liberty as an emotional experience. In the middle of his production, a button popped off his trousers and rolled across the deck. I had to laugh then. We all did.

But the pain remained inside. For the second time, I'd lost my favorite cousins. I'd lost England too, just when I'd begun to want to know it better. Now I had to start all over again. Once more, I would fall among strangers at a new school in a new country.

I looked at all of the immigrants and felt far less hopeful than they.

[1] E. L. Minchin served as a long-time officer in the Northern European Division and later in the General Conference of Seventh-day Adventists.

CHAPTER 3

Establishing New England Roots

Our ship docked in New York on Labor Day weekend, 1947. The transition from Old England to New England had taken nine days.

All things considered, we had relatively few possessions—and those were predominantly books. Our goods were mainly contained in the six sturdy wooden crates (about the size of coffins) that Grandpa Rhoads had built for Mum and Dad back in 1936 when they shipped out to Singapore. The boxes sort of symbolized our seven-year wanderings that were now about to end on the campus of Atlantic Union College in the green forests of central Massachusetts.

For hours we sat with our stuff in the warehouse while the customs and immigration officers did their tasks, a work that they obviously despised doing on a public holiday. Many of them terrorized the immigrants who could not understand a word of their ranting.

My heart ached for an Eastern European couple. He in his cap and she in her *babushka* sat, wide-eyed, on their trunk. They clutched a huge, smelly cheese, big as a car tire, wrapped in white cloth. Even if they couldn't understand the insulting words they couldn't miss the nasty attitude.

The officers' churlishness shocked me, and I began to wonder what would happen when they reached us. When they looked at Dad's papers, however, the climate changed immediately. "Ah, yes, Reverend Minchin. And this is your family?" The sappiness of it all disgusted me.

When we finally cleared our stuff, Dad remarked, "Why were they so rude to the others and so polite to me? Just because I'm listed as a clergyman? Were they afraid that I was going to consign them to a hot place or something?"

Happily, the beauties of Massachusetts quickly dispersed the vulgarity of our arrival back in America.

We were allotted the basement and ground floor of a little brown house in the center of the campus, on Flagg Street. The Beverley Van Hornes and their little Jonnie occupied the top floor. Mrs. Rochelle Kilgore, Chairman of the English Department, was the Grand Dame of the whole college and lived next door. Dad had been her student and an English major twenty years earlier, so she became our patroness, as it were.

To be sure, we needed one. Although, Mum's ancestry traced back to the colonial days of Massachusetts and Connecticut, 300 years earlier, none of those honors transferred to us that autumn as we struggled to set ourselves up again in America. All of it was foreign territory, and we knew nothing of the ancestors.

Our tiny two-bedroom house didn't require much furniture. A good thing, for we had none to give it. The order that Dad and Mum gave to our home-making purchases indicated the family's priorities. First, came a middle-aged Chevrolet, our major concession to practicality.

I remembered sitting in the driver's seat formulating my plans. I was going to get a driver's license. Now, if not sooner. Dad came out of the house one evening and saw me sitting behind the wheel. "Well," he grinned. "Just look at the pope's wife." I was too pre-occupied with joy, too full of myself, however, to catch this bizarre twist in mainline theology. We'd never owned a car since Singapore, and the possibilities of independence made me quite dizzy with anticipation.

It happened that some new faculty friends invited us to spend a weekend up at the lodge in Camp Lawroweld in Maine. The huge fireplace warmed our evenings as surrounding trees incinerated the woods around us in blazing autumn colors. At night, raccoons regularly visited the kitchen.

Meanwhile, I persuaded Dad that he could teach me to drive that weekend. Way out there in the country, along the shores of Lake Webb, I surely wasn't going to hurt anybody. The tutoring sessions, however, were less than ideal.

We started off toward the gate, me at the wheel, Dad in the passenger seat and Mum and Eileen in the back seat. When I swayed a little over the edges of the dirt road, our back-seat passengers emitted a crescendo of loud mutterings. I found these sounds very unnerving.

Finally, Eileen stood up, thrust her head between Dad and me, and shrieked, "Make her stop! Make her stop!" With that, I lunged off the road and into the ditch.

Cries of "I told you so," erupted as Dad and I changed places. The ditch was shallow and grassy, so he easily drove out of it. Here, then, ended my first driving lesson.

Back home, I reviewed my driver's training to date. Not promising. I remained convinced, however, that I wasn't as dumb as I appeared to be. Then, Dad asked Dr. Van Horne, our upstairs neighbor, to take me out.

He did so, and we spent a couple of calm, dignified hours driving around South Lancaster. Nothing happened to anyone. A couple of days later I went to the Department of Motor Vehicles, took the test (both road and written) and passed. The pope's wife could now legitimately occupy the driver's seat.

Soon after the car, we bought a second-hand piano for $100. Somewhere along the way we bought beds and a dining room table, although I cannot recall the details. Meanwhile, a new sofa had been ordered straight from the factory. With it came a modest square of floral carpet.

We were still very much unsettled when a local entrepreneur, Bill Hutchins, appeared on the doorstep. He was, at that moment, selling Electrolux vacuum cleaners. Cheerful, round-faced and a thoroughly outgoing salesman, he gave my parents his sales pitch. He had a fantastic machine for only $100.00. We all looked around the rather barren house and wondered what we'd do with a vacuum cleaner. Apart from the floral square, the bathroom mat was about all we had for a vacuum to work on.

Then Bill eyed the new couch. "See how it can work here too?" He flipped out an attachment and started in on the cushions.

The sofa had been in the house for less than two days. "If you can get anything out of that," Dad declared, "I'll buy the thing!" Alas, he spoke to his own destruction.

Bill swished back and forth over the couch for about a minute and then dumped out a pile of stuff on a newspaper. "There. See?" Actually, he'd sucked up an impressive amount of sawdust, rather white and fresh. Certainly not dirt, in the usual sense of the word.

But Dad had said "anything," so he bought the vacuum cleaner. Many years would pass before we'd have enough carpets to make the machine really worth its keep. (It was not particularly suited to hardwood floors and linoleum.) More importantly, this event began a close friendship between my parents and the Hutchins. Over the next twelve years that they were together in South Lancaster, my father never had a more loyal or a more feisty supporter than Bill.

There were other friends too. Harold Mitzelfelt, Chairman of the Music Department, reveled in digging up second-hand furniture. His activities virtually furnished our house. Some of the pieces that we then took of necessity would today be worth a good price as antiques. But what did we know?

Next door, Mrs. Kilgore bought her clothes from the Goodwill Store. Although the very essence of a proper Southern Lady, she practiced frugalities of many kinds. Set in tradition, she had never moved a piece of furniture nor put away the possessions of her husband who had died ten years before.

So, it was rather in character for her to give my mother clothes that she thought Eileen and I could use. Mum accepted them. We had to wear the stuff, partly because of the economy we needed to practice and partly because Mrs. Kilgore would be offended if she didn't see us wearing the garments.

Although I'd never been particularly interested in fashion, I used to study the clothes allotted to me. Some of them smelled funny, even after they were washed. Yes, I had to wear them, but I made a mental note that things were not always going to be this way for me.

Nonetheless, we'd been taught good manners, if nothing else, so I bore my burden with as much grace as possible. Nine-year-old Eileen, as far as anyone could tell, had not yet developed any opinions on the issue. She took what she got.

We enjoyed our upstairs neighbors, the Van Hornes. He taught chemistry, his cute little wife, Grace, became good friends with Mum, and their three-year-old son Jon, took a shine to me. This amazed me, because I'd never had any talents with small children. On occasion, when I babysat for him, he taught me several skills I didn't know before. Male bathroom protocol, for one thing.

One of Mrs. Kilgore's earliest treats for us was a guided tour of Concord and Lexington and the sites of the Revolutionary War. We saw very precise things, like where the first shot penetrated a certain farmhouse.

When we got home, however, Dad remained silent for some time. He had been struggling with something deep within his soul. Something that accounted for the fact that to the end of his life, even after thirty-five years of residence in the Untied States, he never gave up his Australian citizenship.

That night, he summarized all that we'd seen. It was the "British this and the British that. And the "stupid British" who allowed themselves to be defeated by the famous "Minutemen" of Massachusetts.

"They were all Englishmen," he observed. "They couldn't have thought of themselves as anything else at the time. Rebels, yes, but still English."

Dad decided he didn't need ever to tour those places again, and, to the best of my knowledge, he never broke his word. Because he was ever the perfect gentleman, few people realized that he had taken this stand. He simply did not go on any future field trips featuring the cultural landscape of the Revolutionary War.

With the next school year, a migration began. Over a period of time, all of my cousins would come over from England to go to school at Atlantic Union College.

Kelvin arrived first. We fashioned a room for him down in the basement. Shortly after his arrival, Dad threw one of our "British parties," a Saturday night event attended by all of the Britishers on campus. Most of the students, of course, were Canadians. We can all remember Dad reading P. G. Wodehouse's *Jeeves* to us. We keenly appreciated that special subtle kind of English humor. Sometimes Dad would almost fall out of his chair laughing. The rest of us did likewise.

Those British parties also became the foundation of some of the closest friendships of my life. That's where I met Lynne Kennedy, Lorrayne Philbrick and Olivine Nadeau, Anne Lastine and others, my forever companions. I sensed a certain deprivation not being able to live in the dormitory, but every week or so I'd sleep over there in Rachel Preston Hall with my friends and partake of the pleasure of girl society. Much the same as I had done as a high-schooler back at Canadian Union College.

For my birthday party that October, I was given Chips, a mixed-collie puppy. She satisfied my perennial "dog-need." Also, she had to replace our black cat, Socks (Socrates) who, to my great grief, had committed suicide up on Main Street a few days earlier. Chips became the center of that Saturday night, and she utterly delighted Eileen and me. And Dad too, if the truth must be known.

Mum, on the other hand, had grown up in fear of dogs. In her childhood the neighbors kept several fierce animals that terrorized the community. There-fore, she decreed that Chips would have to live in the basement with Kelvin. In good faith, Kel built a doghouse for the puppy. I can't recall that Chips ever slept in it, even for one night.

Next, the pup was up in the kitchen. "All right, " Mum conceded. "In the kitchen, but nowhere else." Soon the dog made herself at home in the living room. "Certainly not the bedrooms." Mum took a last stand.

Almost immediately, Chips decided she had to sleep in Eileen's and my bedroom. Shortly thereafter, she slept by our parents' bed. From the time I moved away from home, Chips always slept beside Mum and Dad's bed. We

In 1948, the ground floor of this old house in the middle of the campus of Atlantic Union College proved very small for the growing Minchin household. Right. They filled it to the limit. Seated (L-R). Joan, Eileen, Dorothy. Standing. Gerald Minchin, Leona Minchin, and Kelvin.

had, by then, completely broken down Mum's resistance. She never had a chance. To the day she died, no dogs ever had more loving care than did the ones who attended Mum.

Every day I made the hasty ten-minute walk between classes from the main campus down to Thayer Hall, a mansion in the grand style. It housed the college administration, the library and several departments and offices. Walking the road, sitting in classrooms furnished with marble fireplaces, ascending the wide-sweeping staircase, and admiring the pair of priceless tapestries framed in the entryway. It all appealed to my rapidly developing appreciation for beauty, history, and the arts.

I still didn't have the least idea, however, what I should choose for a major. That decision would have to evolve over time.

For the next school year (1948) Joan came over from England to join our family. Now, our house really did become too small. The Mitzelfelts were leaving, so we inherited their half of the brick duplex over on George Hill Road. The house had been well used. Kelvin's little bedroom had footprints on the walls and a burn-mark in the middle of the hardwood floor where a bonfire must have been lit. The basement was full of furniture, including a complete set of pulpit chairs with faded blue velvet upholstery. Somehow we fitted in and around all of the stuff.

Eileen, Joan and I occupied the large bedroom over the garage. This put only one thin wall between us and our neighbors, the Harry Taylors. Prof Taylor, an English teacher, turned out to be a professional insomniac. The first night we slept in the house, Dad put Chips out, at bedtime. The dog delivered a single bark and came back into the house. The next morning our agitated neighbor complained to Dad that he'd not slept all night, waiting for another bark to come. And it didn't. Sleeping in that room, we three girls had little opportunity even to giggle. If we breathed heavily, Mum would rush in. "Be quiet. Don't disturb Mr. Taylor."

Then Kelvin, Joan and I joined the college band, playing—respectively— the tenor horn, drums, and clarinet. Eileen started violin lessons with Prof Taylor's wife, and we all had piano lessons. After a while we had to stop worrying about our neighbor's sleep-problems. We kids really didn't care any more. We had to get on with our own living. When the Taylors moved to Andrews University, in Michigan, he asked for a house isolated in the woods. We all wished him well.

Dr. George Shankel, the Academic Dean, and his family lived one house up the street. Our family immediately became en-

All four teenagers played in the Atlantic Union College band, which did not make for a quiet house. L-R. Eileen (clarinet), Joan (drums), Kelvin (tenor horn), Dorothy (clarinet).

meshed in the exciting music life sponsored by his wife and his already-famous musician daughter, Virginia-Gene [Rittenhouse]. I took piano lessons from both of them.

Virginia-Gene had acquired a kitten she named Piccolo. Early one morning, she and her mother stood under the big tree in our front yard. Chips had run Piccolo up into the high branches. Dr. Shankel and Dad had to be consulted. Finally, with the help of a ladder and advice from all of the women, Dr. Shankel plucked the kitten out of the tree.

While we all rejoiced, he trudged home, grumbling. "Why can't everyone make pets of the same kind of animal?" No one could give him an answer. Virginia-Gene scooped up Piccolo and went home. We'd already confined the distraught Chips to our house.

Our second summer in New England, Dad decided that even if it had to be on a strict budget, the family should have a vacation in Canada. Actually, what he needed was a "British fix."

By that time we had acquired a secondhand Fleetwood Chevrolet coupe. Being streamlined it looked somewhat ahead of its time in design. The backseat was, therefore, a little cramped.

Of course, there would be no way that we could sleep in hotels or eat in restaurants. Envision, then, six of us in the little car. We big kids of the London days hadn't grown any smaller. Joan, Kelvin, and I sat in the back seat and Eileen wedged in between Mum and Dad in the front. The tent rode on a roof rack. Our Tucker (food) Box took up about one-third of the trunk space.

Bent on at least getting through the back roads of Upper New York State the first day, we set out in the morning. Or we thought we did. At the end of George Hill Road, Mum remembered the sandwiches she'd left in the refrigerator. Return. Next time we got almost as far as the girls' dormitory when someone else remembered something.

After three returns to the house, Dad himself realized he hadn't brought his little pen-and-pencil kit he always carried in his shirt pocket. That was a symbol of his intense intellectual interests that nothing could divert. When he switched on the ignition for the fourth time, however, he muttered, "I'm not going back again. Not even if I see the place burning down."

"I wonder what the neighbors are thinking," Mum mused. "If they're watching us."

It must be a testimony to the cohesiveness of our family that, under those crowded and primitive conditions, we didn't have one moment of argument during the entire journey. We packed and repacked our camping gear, morning and evening. The organization of the stuff was regulated down to the last pair of shoes. No room for the misplacement of a single toothbrush.

At night we built fires to roast potatoes and marshmallows. Once in a while, germ-sensitive Mum became anxious about eating the potatoes we dug out of the ashes.

"No worries," Dad replied. "There can't be any bugs left in all of that charcoal." Then, we'd settle down to laugh, tell stories, and watch the moon rise over the Canadian lakes.

Chips was the much-beloved family dog in the Massachusetts years.

I believe no tourists have ever visited Niagara Falls or the Thousand Islands in more peace and tranquility. We have pictures to prove it. To say nothing of the memories.

We came home to Massachusetts with everyone still loving everyone else as much as ever. How do you put a price on a family like that?

Above. The family enjoyed a rustic campout in the Maine woods en route to Canada (Summer, 1950). The tent, the clothesline, the fire-pit. Self-contained all of the way. They spent no money and relied on no public services. Below. Four young Minchins went boating at the Thousand Islands, Ontario, Canada. L-R. Kelvin, Joan, Dorothy, Eileen. Some of the islands supported a single house. One of the smallest had just one tree and two bushes.

CHAPTER 4

The Shape of a Career

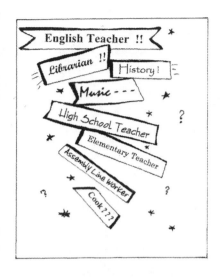

Academically, I fared rather well upon my arrival at Atlantic Union College. Dean George Shankel, a Canadian, had years of administrative experience in South Africa. Therefore, he knew that matriculation examinations at a British university far outweighed the demands of a senior year in an American high school. When I presented my document certifying my passing the Senior Matriculation at the University of London, he was able to give me credit for almost my entire freshman year.

Thus, I entered college as a sophomore. Great day! I took basic classes and enjoyed being a college co-ed. This acceleration, however, had both an up-side and a down-side. I was too naïve to understand all of the implications. I didn't have to worry yet that I would become a way-too-young college graduate. Or that I would have to do some very swift growing-up when I would be cast out upon the world just three years later.

As a probable English major, I entered Mrs. Kilgore's Survey of English Literature class two weeks late. I slid into the back row where I found Jack Bohner. "We're in Chaucer's 'Canterbury Tales'." He leaned over confidentially. "It's the 'Wife of Bath's Tale.' You can learn all about the birds and the bees here."

Indeed, Jack was not far off the mark. An incurable romantic, Mrs. Rochelle Philmon-Kilgore favored men. A boy could get an "A" doing virtually nothing. A girl could study herself blind and still never make a good grade. The only reason I was able to score an occasional B was because she had liked my Dad—ever since he, the exotic Australian, had shown up in her class at Union College, Nebraska, back in 1927.

Mrs. Kilgore knew the love story of every famous man we knew. She told the tales in such a hushed voice that we had to be quiet or we'd miss the punch line. In her classroom I even heard an account of my own parents' courtship. If nothing else, we did learn to "appreciate" literature on a very large scale. Later on, however, as several of us moved on to graduate work, we had to admit that Mrs. Kilgore, bless her, had taught us nothing that would help us toward advanced degrees. At the time I didn't mind. The realities of post-graduate study remained a distant, unvisited country for me.

That year, Jack Bohner and Olivine Nadeau (who married the next summer) along with Lynne Kennedy and I formed an innocuous little gang. Over time, sundry other friends joined us. Ostensibly, we went to the library to study, somewhat to the distress of the diligent librarian, Alfred Brandon. Still, behind the weak façade of our textbooks, we bonded in friendships that would last a lifetime.

In my junior year, I made my peace with Mr. Brandon when I went to work in the library. In fact, both Joan and I secured this rather prestigious appointment. At first, I had started out at the College Press with Olivine. Most of the time she worked as a proofreader, an elevation to which I never attained. Instead, I spent long, mindless hours punching out cardboard circles for the Bay State Company. I can't recall what they were for, but the task went on eternally and was a crashing bore. Only chatting with co-workers made the sit-uation bearable. The work being sufficiently brainless, the forewoman didn't deny us girls the privilege of talking.

Housed in three elegant, paneled ballrooms in Thayer Mansion, the library was a very different place. The first room contained the checkout desk, journals, and newspapers. The second room, to the left, was every scholar's dream. Solemn as a cathedral, it attracted very serious people and entertained high-level committee meetings. A wonderful Edwardian fireplace of Italian marble dominated the third room. In there, large study tables interspersed themselves among the open bookshelves. Less committed students (like some of us) made that our favorite venue. Recalling the old days of dignity, the ornate brass sconces on the walls still offered to provide light. Heavily draped in green velvet, each of the tall windows arose from cozy, padded seats in the bays.

Hildegarde Reinhart was Mr. Brandon's private secretary. My job, however, varied from the checkout desk to doing random chores for our boss. I liked the days when I worked in the back room with Bea Jensen accessioning books. Occasionally, her boyfriend, Al Smith, visited us in the dungeon-like accessioning room.

One afternoon Bea arrived laughing, "You know the song, 'The Night is Young and You are So Beautiful.'" Well, of course! We all kept up with the hit parade. "Al said the most romantic, funny thing I've ever heard in my life."

Bea was crippled from an early bout with polio, and she had one blue eye and one green. To know her, however, was pure inspiration. "We said goodnight out in the circle driveway," Bea went on. "And he whispered, 'Ah. The night is beautiful, and you are so young!'" A future professor of physics, Al knew a good thing when he found it. (They married immediately after graduation.)

In 1949 expectations in AUC's little library must have been low. Having all the books visible and available to all of the students all of time did not, for some reason, seem peculiar to us. Any of us who worked in the library could, at any moment, be assigned to the tedious task of "reading stacks." That is, determining that each book stood precisely in its right place. The job went on eternally, relieved only by the fact that occasionally we could stop to greet any friends who might be at the tables.

In the early spring, a new hardback arrived in the AUC library, *The Engaged Couple Has the Right to Know: A Modern Guide to Happy Marriage*. A modest gray cover with thin red lettering, but the contents were quite explicit. It also had anatomical line drawings. Therefore, as soon as *The Engaged Couple* took its place on the shelf, it mysteriously began to disappear for days at a time.

We stack-readers followed the book's career with enthusiasm. In a matter of weeks, the book began to wear out. The gray cover loosened, blackened with fingerprints and full of dog-eared pages. Yet no one had ever signed it out. The card inside the back cover remained pristine. Finally, the spine broke.

Even Joan and I took it home for a few days. Although neither of us had any legal claims on anyone and were not in immediate need of the instruction, we were fascinated. When I think of what engaged couples know today compared to what we knew in 1949, I stand amazed at our innocence.

By this time, Hildegarde had actually become engaged to Don Sandstrom. She wanted the book, naturally, but did not wish to put her name on the card. A loyal Canadian, she wrote "Princess Elizabeth" at the top of the card. "I suppose," she mused, "that the princess must need this information by now." (The royal wedding with Prince Philip of Greece was, indeed, imminent.)

When the library closed that evening, Mr. Brandon made his usual rounds, looking through the cards to see what books had gone out that day. "Ah, so Princess Elizabeth has taken this book out. … Hmm." None of us at the checkout counter said a word. Hildegarde's virtue, as a library employee, outstripped all of the rest of us put together, so we couldn't betray her.

When *The Engaged Couple* returned, Brandon placed its fragile remains on a high shelf in the closet behind his desk. It was rumored that he had a copy of the *Kinsey Report* in there also. As paid library workers, we could assure the public that the rumor was correct. Anyone wishing a book out of that closet, however, practically had to secure FBI clearance.

Although I worked at least twenty hours a week on campus during my three years in college, all of my earnings went onto my tuition bill. By summer I'd begun to lust after the feel of real money. Money in my hand. I found work at Van Brodies in Clinton, two miles away. Basically a cereal company, they, at that time, had a military contract for packing field rations to be sent to Korea, where the current war was in progress.

Now, for eight hours a day, I sat on an assembly line picking up greasy cans of Spam and packages of biscuits and putting them into each of the millions of open boxes that passed by me on the conveyor belt. Bay State was a white-collar job compared to this apparently moronic employment. Moreover, I could find no one there able to hold a conversation with me. The women and girls had not a thought in their heads beyond their ratty husbands or magnificent boyfriends. Neither subject interested me.

Still, I did have the novel experience of receiving a paycheck every week, and I often got to drive the family car to work. So I stuck it out at Van Brodies for the whole summer. Returning to college in the fall, however, I vowed to do whatever it took to keep myself out of a factory for the rest of my life. I made this stand neither from prejudice nor from elitism. It was simply a case of survival. I knew, for sure, that I would die if I had to give my life over to assembly-line work. The library job was very much to my taste, and I knew when I was well off.

Meanwhile, what was I actually going to do for a career? Having been propelled into college early, it became obvious that I was also going to emerge from it prematurely. Actually, in the mid-20th-century, girls had limited career options. Given my "druthers," I might have been an archaeologist. That work, however, was nowhere to be found on my radar in those days.

Many of my friends were going to nursing. In fact, most of the boys on campus seemed to gravitate automatically over to the New England Sanitarium in Stoneham (near Boston). There a rich field of young ladies awaited them. I gave this option only a cursive glance, despite its impressive social possibilities. Knowing what I know now, I realize that one of the best things that ever happened to the medical profession was the fact that I did not enter it.

I loved music, of course. With the parents I had, how could I not? I sang in the girls Glee Club, played second clarinet in the band and orchestra, and took piano lessons from the Shankels. Our family never willingly missed the frequent *soirees* that Mrs. Shankel and Virginia-Gene staged. These elegant evenings were a major, civilizing influence upon us teenagers. In fact, they grounded me in my lifelong love of classical music.

Decorations for festive occasions and flowery elegance for everyday times—it was all a lesson-book in gracious living. Mother Shankel set out the big punch bowl and plates of sweet goodies. All of us piano students played for one another. Sadly, my childhood preference for books over music practice still prevailed.

Still, Virginia-Gene had this knack—and she proved it over a lifetime—of inspiring her students to do their best. Indeed far beyond their best. Many of us performed music that we shouldn't have been able to play at all! At one recital, I played Chopin's "Butterfly Etude." It was far too difficult for me, and I was far from note-perfect. Somehow, the brilliance of the piece that I so loved, swept me away. I played with a gusto that astonished me, to say nothing of the audience. Alas! Who knows what "might have been!"

Yes, I had a music minor, but I didn't practice hard enough to carry it off. My interests were seriously divided. I enjoyed writing and found myself producing scripts for various campus events. I always liked the privacy of writing much better than the publicity of going on stage to act out what I'd written. So, I kept floundering. I entered my junior year without a declared major.

While doing a research paper for Dr. Shankel's course in English History, I discovered that I thoroughly enjoyed digging stuff out of a library. I simply wrote an essay about what I'd discovered concerning the history of Oxford University. Having missed the disciplines of Freshman English, I provided neither footnotes nor bibliography. No one had ever disclosed anything about research techniques to me.

In shock—but also feeling some mercy—Dr. Shankel gave me a "B" on the paper. He expressed the wish, however, that the documentation had been done and that he could have made it an "A." My ineptitude, however, was even worse than he imagined. Actually, I didn't have the faintest idea about how to take notes. Copy machines had not yet been invented. You couldn't bring swatches of material out of the library to be used at leisure at home.

Earnest in my ignorance, I took notes on my regular notebook paper,

In 1950 the annual "Hour of Charm" turned the college girls into Southern belles with a lavish stage set and well-rehearsed music. Dorothy participated in her favorite behind-the-scenes roles, writing the script that held the program together.

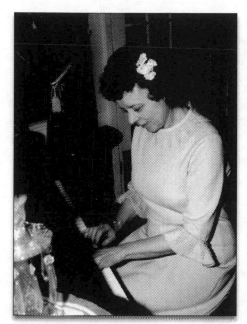

Virginia-Gene Shankel (Rittenhouse), later the founder of the New England Youth Ensemble, was the center of music life on the campus of Atlantic Union College. She inspired some of us to perform at a higher level than our innate abilities should have allowed.

thriftily utilizing both sides of each page. After supper on the last night before the assignment was due, a fearful reality burst upon me. How could I put it all together? I ended up cutting my notes into strips, sometimes having to copy what was being lost on the other side of the page. Then I pasted the pieces on a newspaper that I'd spread out on the living-room floor. By midnight I'd finished the arranging. By 7 o'clock the next morning I had finished a final typing.

At 8 a.m. I was on the road to Thayer Hall to give my paper to Dr. Shankel. "There's got to be an easier way to do this," I thought to myself. Of course, there is. One uses note-cards. From this point on, I had to be, essentially, self-taught.

Halfway through my junior year, I arrived at my "calling." By the process of elimination, I decided that I would have to be an English major. When I considered all of the things I didn't want to do, along with many more that I couldn't do, nothing remained but English. I realize now that I made the choice by default. It was certainly not an inspired or noble way to discover one's life work.

Even so, I remained uncommitted to serious study. Interested in a multitude of life adventures, I did as little as possible. For instance, Joan and I enrolled in Dr. Willis King's Educational Psychology class. The professor was aloof and shortsighted. He used to amble across campus, eyes fixed on the ground. His black spaniel followed him in a straight line, looking neither left nor right. Unlike any other dog I ever knew, he had not the least interest in investigating all of the "dog news" available along the way.

At the college bookstore we purchased the large, hardcover textbook for $10.00. It was securely sealed in a brown-paper wrapper. After attending the first class, Joan and I decided not to open the book. It turned out that Dr. King never did take attendance. Rumor had it, in fact, that once, when Dean Shankel confronted him on this omission, he said, "It doesn't matter. I wouldn't go there myself if I didn't have to."

At first, Joan and I sat in the front. Even with his thick glasses, however, the teacher simply couldn't see beyond the first couple of rows. We decided there was no point in both of us attending the long lectures. The weeks went by. Toward the end of the term neither one of us attended class regularly. As spring came on, the boys in the back row even brought a portable radio to class and listened to the ball games. The professor's hearing must have also been impaired.

Finally, we all came to the final exam. (Joan's and my textbook remained in pristine condition in its wrapper.) The test was made up of True/False and multiple-choice questions. I concentrated very hard that day, simply applying common sense. To be sure, I had nothing else to go on. At the end, both Joan and I got "Bs." I was well pleased.

I realize now, of course, that it should not be possible for such an outcome to be awarded to such undeserving students. We returned our textbook to the bookstore for a full refund.

Ultimately, as graduation approached, I had to face the reality of what to do next. I had qualified myself for secondary teaching and had done my practice teaching in the academy. There the children of my parents' faculty friends populated the classrooms—kids very little younger than I. I had weathered all of this, only to receive a succession of six invitations to teach elementary school. I knew in my inmost soul that I was not the person for that kind of teaching. I had less-than-average skills with small children.

As a last resort, without having any very clear idea about graduate study, I applied to enter the master's program at Boston University. Because my grades weren't high enough, I was turned down. Although I'd enjoyed my three years in college, I really couldn't be accused of heavy-duty studying at any time. So was there going to be a price to pay now? I wondered.

Young and with the world before me, I didn't worry for long. Yet, an undercurrent of desperation must have been running through my life. That's why I accepted a position at Philadelphia Junior Academy teaching English. Okay. But American History? In my many years in the British school system, I'd missed that course. Not good. Worst of all, I was to be "matron" of the dining room, providing a noon meal for all of the students. I, who could scarcely succeed in boiling an egg!

Nonetheless, I'd said "Yes." Sheer need of employment drove me to that insanity. Of course, I knew I'd have to have a car so that I could go home on weekends. One plus, at least.

During the summer of 1950, things changed. Quite miraculously, in fact. Suddenly I had the opportunity to return to Canadian Union College, the veritable Paradise of my adolescent imagination.

While in San Francisco for a session of the General Conference, Mum, Dad, Eileen, and I were walking from the Civic Auditorium to our hotel. In mid-journey, we met Emil Beitz, president of Canadian Union College since my Dad's days there. Right there on the sidewalk, he asked me if I'd like to bring my new English major back to Canada and teach in the high-school

Left. Four seniors (AUC Class of 1950) on a picnic. Momentarily reverting to teenage nonsense, they turned out in matching red-and-white dresses. L-R. Ann Lastine, Gloria Nash, Viola Brooks, Dorothy Minchin. Right. Out of the fifty-seven members of the Atlantic Union College graduating class of 1950, only fourteen were girls. We seven English majors made up half of that contingent. L-R. Ruth Fatscher, Ann Lastine, Lorrayne Philbrick, Beatrice Jensen, Adeline Schiffbauer, Dorothy Minchin, Joyce Harper.

division of the institution.

Would I? Supposing that I knew something about English, I found this a task much better suited to my limited abilities. I accepted on the spot as the San Francisco traffic flowed around us.

With great humility, (verbal) regret, and pleasure, I withdrew from the Philadelphia appointment. The principal and conference president never knew how grateful I was for my deliverance. Nor did they realize how lucky they'd been to avoid my service. When I think of the matter now, I believe it had to be the direct intervention of Providence. That job could have been nothing but disaster. Me, cooking meals and teaching American history? My utter madness amazes me to this day.

The Senior Class of 1950 at Atlantic Union College had fifty-seven members. Only fourteen of them were girls, and half of those were English majors. Perhaps that exclusiveness is what had enabled twelve of us to start a chain letter of friendship and keep it going for the past sixty-two years.

If the photographs that day are authentic, I was the only girl in the receiving line who got flowers. The big bouquet of red carnations came from Cal Thurlow, one of Kelvin's friends. A friend and nothing more. Still he stood at about 6-foot 5-inches, and I found any kind of recognition comforting. At 5-foot 9-inches myself, I'd decided already that I would never find a sensible man who was also tall enough. I'd already observed, morosely, that the really tall fellows wasted themselves on petite girls. Throughout my three years at college, the men who seemed interested in me barely came to my shoulder and/or were uniformly stupid.

Of course, there had been that huge Scandinavian war-veteran, fresh out of the army. He'd been through a divorce, something uncommon on campuses in those days. Harold, however, had managed to secure his "Social Privileges Card." Without that documentation, no one in college could date anyone else. This "qualifying" for the pursuit of a social life, will, no doubt, strike most readers now as eccentric, to say the least.

Even though nothing else seemed to be available on my horizon, I couldn't manage to accept his invitation. One day, he approached the library table where I sat with my gang of schoolmates almost every day. Without preamble, he pushed a note under my nose. It read: "Are you engaged? Will you go to Vespers with me next Friday night?"

I stared at him. He really was too much. I explained that I would be going with some other friends. He retreated, lumbering out of the door like an earthmover. I turned to Lynne and Olivine. "We *are* going to Vespers together, aren't we?"

Not one to despair, our Harold even invited Virginia-Gene Shankel to eat leftovers at lunch with him at the college cafeteria on a Sunday. She also declined, as did many other girls.

Finally, he went to the girls' dorm one Saturday night and presented his Social Privileges Card. "Whom shall I call," Dean Mary McConaughy inquired.

"This card entitles me to go out with a girl." Harold shoved his card across the counter. "Just call someone."

I—along with several of my friends—was thankful that I'd never been seen in any public place with him. I wasn't that frantic. After all, I was still only eighteen.

Now, at age twenty, I was heading off to Canada, unencumbered and leaving home for the first time. Maybe there was still someone out there for me.

CHAPTER 5

A Chick Hatches

At the end of the summer of 1950 I was, simultaneously "sprung" from both college and home. All of my life I'd enjoyed a school campus while still being sheltered in the security of my parents' house. Nonetheless, for at least the past three years I'd anticipated freedom and moving out on my own. (An ambition curiously absent in many of the young ones today.) Therefore, I don't know why it all came as such a shock.

I stood there in the doorway at the end of the coach as the train dragged me out of the Boston Railway Station, bound for Montreal. From there I would be transported to Western Canada and Canadian Union College. Not a strange place. After all, that's where I'd emerged from my adolescent cocoon only four years earlier.

Still, as I looked down at my family strung out along the platform waving goodbye, I just knew that my heart was going to burst and splatter all over the floor around my feet. The intense knowledge of what homesickness was going to be like absolutely devoured me that September night.

Yes, I should be rejoicing. After all, I had a job that I might, conceivably, be able to do. So I honestly tried to cheer up as I stowed my luggage on the overhead rack and took my seat. I glanced at the huge box sitting across from me. I knew it was full of sandwiches Mum had made for me, enough to last my entire journey. Given our family's frugal habits, it hadn't occurred either to me or my mother that as I journeyed westward I would find food in every place that the train stopped. We'd always picnicked because that was one important way to save money. I looked at the box, sighed, and knew that over the next four days, I would have to eat all of those sandwiches.

I arrived in Lacombe, Alberta, on a nippy, Indian Summer day. Nothing had changed. The college president, Emil Bietz, and his wife were on hand to meet me, friends of our family from former years. The unpaved streets of the town again sucked my feet down into the mud. Old men still sat on the bench outside the Royal Bank. The buff-colored college buildings still crowned the hilltop at the end of the long drive onto the campus. In a sense, I could almost persuade myself that I was home. At least, I'd been here once before. Indeed, that was saying quite a bit, considering my nomadic childhood.

So Canadian Union College would be the site of my first year of teaching. In my hot little hand, I clutched my BA in English, received just three months earlier. My job description included Grades 10 and 11 English, Grade 9 Art, and a class in music appreciation. With a mixture of panic and joy I stepped into my new position. Power! Influence! I was a stranger to both.

I found a couple of my old friends still on campus. In fact, Angie Melashenko and I wanted to room together. I was going to be in the dormitory anyway. The President, however, thought this arrangement to be unseemly because I was now a teacher and she was still a student. The segregation really disappointed me, but I resigned myself to my solitary room in the basement of Maple Hall. Other single teachers had apartments here and here in the community, but I was allotted what had originally been designed as living quarters for the school nurse. Now, for the first time in my life, I would live in a dormitory.

Immediately, President Bietz called for three days of faculty meetings before the students arrived for registration. Although I'd lived on a school campus almost all of my life, I still retained the optimistic notion that faculty meetings would be interesting. That one might, occasionally, even hear about some salacious disciplinary case. I was wrong.

I looked around the room. I knew a few of the people present, but not many. President Bietz himself had been in office when my Dad had chaired the Religion Department between 1945 and 1946. At that time, we lived next door to the Gordon Balharrie family.

Besides, the morning's meeting was being held in the same room, at the same tables, where Don Neufeld had taught me chemistry four years earlier. Together, he and Balharrie now manned the Religion Department. Just ahead

of me sat Miss Louise
Dedeker with whom I now
shared faculty status. Back
in 1945 she had literally
scared me into learning
Grade 11 French.

On this first morning
of faculty meetings, I saw
Neufeld and Balharrie
sitting at the back of the
room, the latter occasionally
rocking back on the hind
legs of his chair. I sat next to
Marge Jones, the new Dean
of Women. Nearby were

On the day Dorothy graduated with her BA in English she stood with her parents. Still a casual, study-as-little-as-possible kind of student, she would not hit her academic stride for some years to come.

Annamarie Feyerabend and Jeanne Dorsett, two other single teachers with
whom I had already begun a happy friendship. All in all, things seemed
pretty good.

Up front, President Bietz presided over the meeting, hour after hour.
As I watched the advancing clock on the wall, however, I realized that I was
the only person in the room dependent on the time-bound cafeteria for
lunch. Still weary from the long train journey from Massachusetts to Alberta,
I'd skipped breakfast.

The hands on the clock measured off yet another hour. Various faculty
members began looking at their watches and then at one another. Still,
business droned on. The need for someone to make a motion for adjournment became intense. As the most junior teacher in the room, of course, I
couldn't dream of saying anything on any subject, much less making a
motion for adjournment.

Suddenly, a firm voice arose at the back of the room. "I move that …"
A thunderous crash was followed by some long, drawn-out scuffling across
the tile floor. Automatically, everyone swung around to see what had
happened.

There sat Gordon Balharrie on the floor. He clung to the table with both hands, trying to prevent his being swept out of sight altogether. His brown eyes, barely visible above the edge of the table, stared back at us in utter astonishment. Crazed by hunger, perhaps, he'd rocked back on his chair one time too often.

In any case, without further parliamentary procedure, the faculty meeting adjourned. While the rest of the faculty went home to eat their late lunches, I returned to my dormitory room to await supper hour at the cafeteria.

Are faculty meetings interesting? Occasionally, Yes, but mostly No.

Green as a spring twig and frightened as a neurotic field mouse, I faced

my first classes. Very quickly I discovered a vast, a ghastly, deficiency in my knowledge. I didn't know any grammar. Because I'd always been able to write with reasonable fluency, no one ever stopped to inquire whether or not I could tell the difference between an adverb clause and an adjective clause. I couldn't differentiate between a gerund and a participle. They looked alike, and I couldn't explain them if you were to impale me and nail me to the blackboard in the next moment.

I had immediately discerned that this kind of information was deemed important in a Canadian classroom. Moreover, the school inspector from the provincial government was scheduled to show up in my classroom any day, unannounced.

Three single teachers at Canadian Union College chose to complicate their lives by dating (and marrying) senior college students. L-R: Jeanne Dorsett, Dorothy Minchin, Marge Jones. Nonetheless, Dorothy's first year of teaching suddenly catapulted her out of her rather low-key school years into the staggering public responsibilities of the classroom. (1950)

Paralyzed with terror, I embarked on a six-week program of self-tutoring in grammar. An enterprise that well nigh destroyed me. I'd get up no later than 6 a.m., stagger through the morning frostiness to the cafeteria for breakfast, and then propel myself up to the second floor of the Administration Building for my first class. The schedule offered me no respite until after 4 p.m. Day after day, I stumbled back down to

Dorothy spent Christmas 1950 in Edmonton, Alberta with her Great-Aunt Florence Rowland-King. There she resumed one of her favorite hobbies, knitting.

my room. I would open the door, and there was my bed—spread with my new red Royal Stewart tartan blanket. The woolen one I'd bought for $10.00, out of my first little paycheck of $113.00.

Completely drained nervously, emotionally, and physically, I would lurch across the room and crash on the bed. Sleep overtook me immediately. No, it wasn't really sleep. It was more like going into a coma. Mostly, I was dead.

Sometime around midnight I'd wake up and get my books out. For the next four or five hours I'd prepare for the next day's lessons. Week after week I faced my classes no more than one day's learning ahead of my students.

In the middle of this sadistically, intense period, Marge Jones and other friends on campus made a rather magnificent event out of my twenty-first birthday. To celebrate this same occasion, Mum sent me a big, yellow fruitcake, the kind we'd always had at home ever since we'd lived in Australia. I had no cutlery, so I sliced the cake with my ruler and ate most of it while I studied in the very early morning hours. That way, I could sleep a little later because I didn't need to go to breakfast.

About this time my social life took an odd turn. Several of my students were older than I. During this pressure-cooker of a first semester, a couple of students asked me for a date. Not being particularly attracted to either proposition, I replied smugly, "I really can't date men who are my students, can I?" At the time, it seemed to be a good line, and I clung to my "teacherliness."

Meanwhile, winter set in. As usual the college men prepared the center of campus social life, the ice-skating rink. It was situated down in a hollow between two little hills on the rolling parkland. I was still not a good skater. When whirling around the rink with some tall Canadian, the ice-crystals forming on the fur of my parka, however, I could feel like "one of the girls." By now I had overcome my folly of not skating with men I might like.

Then, Christmas vacation arrived. With it came the pleasing awareness that I'd actually mastered English grammar. At last, I could relax. Therefore, when Aunt Florence King invited me spend the holidays with her family in Edmonton, I went off, walking six inches above the snowy ground. I didn't know the Kings very well, but they were my only blood-relatives in all of Canada. I was thrilled to go to them. (Aunt Florence was the youngest sister of my Grandmother Mary Rowland-Rhoads.)

Just before I left the campus a curious little event occurred, one that I wouldn't begin to unravel until after the New Year. In early November, Walter Comm had come to college. Like so many students from the western farms, he arrived two weeks late. Western Canada's short growing season meant that the harvest could not be delayed for anything. Not school, not a state visit from the Queen, not for any sickness short of death itself. Nothing.

As a high school student, I'd known Walter Comm, already one of the "big college boys." Now when the girls all began twittering about him, I remarked, "Oh, I used to know him when I was here in Grade 11."

"Oh, did you?" one cried. "Imagine that!"

"He's so tall and dark and handsome," another crowed.

I agreed with the truth of all of the above. Then the day came when the man actually arrived. "Walter Comm's here!" The buzz spread through the dormitory halls.

The next day I actually met him in the Administration Building. We were introduced by someone who had heard of my claim to his acquaintance.

But I didn't know him. I'd never seen him before. He did, however, fit the girls' description. We made small talk and then went our ways. It turned out that he and his cousin shared the same name. This was his seventh year at the college, and over the years, the two cousins had been confused in their student accounts, their grade reports, and even their laundry.

My initial profession about knowing Walter seemed to set a series of cosmic events in motion. Whenever we met and exchanged a word in the

Actually, in 1950, Dorothy was ill prepared to face her first English classes in the high-school Division of Canadian Union College. The prospect of a random visit by the Provincial School Inspector terrified her. What if he discovered that she had not yet mastered grammar! (Her English II class followed one of Professor Don Neufeld, professor of Biblical languages. Hence, the Greek on the blackboard.)

hall, the very walls seemed to lean forward to acknowledge our standing together, however briefly. Moreover, the campus, as it were, had already matched us up.

Just before the holidays, the girls held their Open House. Of course, I had no plans for opening up my room. After all, I didn't even own a bedspread, only that red tartan blanket. Walt made a point of waylaying me in the dining room. "I would like to have gone with you to Open House, but a girl I knew from last year had already asked me. I really have to go with her. You don't mind?"

Mind? Hardly. What claims could I possibly have on him? I scarcely knew him. Besides, I was going to spend Christmas with my cousins in Edmonton.

That Christmas was all that it should have been. Aunt Florence's marvelous cooking, Uncle Gilbert telling jokes around the fireplace. We younger ones going to the great Roman Catholic Cathedral for the midnight Christmas service. Snow and more snow. I left my books behind and started knitting a sweater instead, something I had done little of since I was a kid in Australia.

Just before I returned to the College, Aunt Florence made a proposal. "You are a professional person now. I think you should have a nice, dressy suit." I probably would never have arrived at this idea on my own. After years of homemade garments, hand-me-downs, and bargain basement purchases, I just didn't think that way. Nonetheless, I was intrigued.

Forthwith, we set off to downtown Edmonton. Not to the big department stores like Eatons or Woodwards, but to a little specialty shop. A boutique, we'd call it today. With my aunt's encouragement, I started trying on suits. I looked in the mirror and almost liked what I saw. Actually, I'd never seen myself like this before. Amazing! Finally, I settled on a powder-blue gabardine suit. The long jacket had a flatteringly flared peplum, all the rage at the time.

But I choked on the price tag, $50.00. "Oh, Aunt Florence! I can't do this!" Normally, $50.00 would have provided me with all of my clothes, inner and outer, for at least three years.

"Dottie dear," she soothed. "It's an investment." She fingered the smooth material. "This is excellent quality. You can wear it for a very long time." (Indeed, I might have worn it for at least thirty years, if my move to the tropics hadn't ultimately made the suit wholly irrelevant.) Okay. So I took the plunge.

The suit had an immediate and amazing effect. When I wore it to church the next weekend, I realized that I'd never quite felt that way before. Maybe I was becoming a professional, after all!

The new year geared up quickly. On the first available Saturday night, I had a date with the mysterious Walter Comm. A double date with his roommate, Wilf Liske and his fiancée, Annamarie Feyerabend, one of the elementary school teachers. That evening marked the beginning of more than fifty years of a very special friendship among the four of us.

Both men were seniors, about to graduate in theology. Remarkably, for that time and place, they each owned a car. True, they were students and we were teachers. Walt, however, seemed to be a case worth pursuing, so I rapidly overcame my reticence about dating a student. Especially not such an attractive one who was not, after all, in any of my classes. I even skated with him.

Age and position notwithstanding, we labored under the same social restrictions as the lowliest high school student in the institution. Being seen on campus as a couple was unthinkable, and off-campus events required chaperonage. In effect, we had to live as if nothing whatsoever was going on in our private lives.

One evening, under cover of darkness and the shimmering curtain of the Northern Lights, we four went to the local Chinese restaurant in town, dutifully taking Jeanne with us a chaperone. Painfully money conscious, we ordered four dishes, and then each of us donated a portion to make up a fifth plate for her. As I think of it now, that was a bad move.

Indeed, the chaperone herself recognized the condescension of our charity and firmly voiced her disapproval to Annamarie and me the next day. As for Walt and Wilf, they were accus-

A very secret picnic by the lake on the campus of Canadian Union College. Left, Wilfred Liske, with his new Pontiac in the background. Right, Jeanne Dorsett, our chaperone, dutifully laid out the food. Annamarie Feyerabend stepped out of range, Walt turned his back on the camera, and Dorothy took the picture. The three women were faculty members and the two men college students. On no account should any of the students ever know that this picnic took place. Faculty members lived under the same chaperone policies as the youngest students in the institution.

tomed to sturdy farm cooking and found the pseudo-Chinese fare that night much too light. They, we heard later, went back to the dormitory to eat peanut butter sandwiches.

The springtime crocuses on the hill overlooking Lake Barnett scarcely had a chance to push through the frosty ground before Walt and I became engaged. On March 15, he told me that he had been offered a ministerial internship in Newfoundland. "Would you like to go with me?" Mundane as it might appear at first, that was my marriage proposal. Two months later, secluded in Marge Jones' living room, he gave me a dainty little Bulova watch.

Prior to this event, Marge and I had discussed my buying a half-share in her car. I'd begun to long for the freedom of having access to a car. Then, in the middle of negotiations, I discovered that I was going to go to Newfoundland.

Now I came forth my gold engagement watch. Things had proceeded more rapidly than I expected. Marge, however, was completely taken by surprise. "I'm so happy for you." She hugged me warmly and then sniffed. "No wonder, you didn't need to share a car with me. You figured out a way to get Comm's car for free!" Well, it wouldn't exactly be free.

Up to that point, however, no one—not even our closest friends—really knew what was going on. My students, however, with all of the instincts of trained dogs and small children, had begun to stress out my life. I would arrive in the classroom to find Walt's and my names on the blackboard, encircled by a heart. I could never decide whether to ignore the logo or draw attention to it by erasing it.

One day in art class, Ron, a gnome-like ninth-grader, addressed me as "Mrs. Comm" instead of the prescribed "Miss Minchin." I banished him instantly. "Don't come back until you've seen the high school principal.

Immediately after class, I went down to my boss's office to report the misdemeanor. P. G. Miller listened carefully to my tale. "Don't worry. I'll take care of Ron."

Then, leaning back in his chair, the principal eyed me slyly. "Tell me again. What was it that you said he called you?"

The next night the dormitory monitor called me up to the lobby. There was poor little Ron, in tears. He presented me with an exercise book in which he had written 500 times, "I will not be rude to my teacher, Miss Minchin."

Meanwhile, I had even left my parents with only a foggy understanding of my social situation. Dad finally wrote, "We aren't quite sure what we are to think about your friend. About all you've told us is that he's a good skater. But we rather expect to see you come home with him tucked under your arm one of these days."

In due course, Walt wrote the proper son-in-law-to-father-in-law letter requesting permission to enter the family. Dad's response was typically warm and uncomplicated. "I'll just ask you the same questions my father-in-law asked me: 'Are you a Christian? Are you clean? Are you a gentleman?'"

No difficulties there. Later Dad reported the reaction of my thirteen-year-old sister Eileen. "You should have seen all the silly gyrations she went through when she heard that you are getting married!"

By graduation weekend, Walt and I, along with Wilf and Annamarie, had openly become the romantic toasts of the campus. Finally, we could all relax. Nor more trying to keep our secrets and pretend that we hadn't noticed each other yet.

At commencement exercises, I met, for the first time, Walt's mother, one of his four sisters, and one of his four brothers. It might all have been rather terrifying. Instead, I put on my blue suit, held my head high, and greeted everyone with grace.

For a wedding present, Dorothy's high-school juniors (whom she sponsored in 1951) gave her a silver relish tray. With the Newfoundland assignment coming up, they explained, "You can just lay the fish around the edge and put the bones in the center." *(Photo courtesy of Cindy DeMille)*

Then, I packed my possessions in two boxes (not forgetting the red tartan blanket) and left them for Walt to bring down in his car.

My first year of teaching had propelled me into a sudden, unexpected, and amazing transition. I said farewell to the College, boarded the bus, and headed home to Massachusetts. Only two weeks remained to get ready for the wedding.

CHAPTER 6

A Wedding on Fast-Forward

From time to time, I watch girls prepare for their weddings. They spend huge amounts of energy and money getting ready. Registering in their favorite stores, choosing dresses, planning dinners, having showers, furnishing a house, designing a honeymoon. Whatever. To be sure, there's plenty of work that may be done.

On the other hand, most of these tasks can be by-passed, and you'll end up just as married as if you'd actually done all of those chores. Just put the whole wedding on fast-forward, and it'll all be over in little more than ten days. In fact, in July of 1951, Walt and I did just that.

We had virtually no money. At the time of his graduation, however, we didn't actually realize how little. After I turned my grades in to the Registrar's Office at Canadian Union College, I headed home to Massachusetts on the bus, a task that took some days to accomplish. Meanwhile, Walt went north to Peace River to visit the rest of his family and conclude affairs on the farm. He had to borrow $100.00 from one of the neighbors.

Soon, we'd be off to Newfoundland, distant enough in every way to have been in another galaxy. Also, we'd be gone for a long time.

The fact that Walt's and my wedding plans fell into place with such amazing efficiency was, to a large degree, a tribute to the high regard that the community of South Lancaster had for my parents. I'd left home the previous year, a shy, twenty-year-old college graduate. Although I'd returned a bride with one year of teaching high school English on my record, I myself could hardly have been considered a major figure in the village around Atlantic Union College.

As for the wedding service, Dad, of course, would pronounce the words over us. He was, however, in studies at the Theological Seminary in Washington D.C. and could be home only for the weekend of July 22 itself. Meanwhile, Mum and I rushed headlong into all of the girl stuff.

Friends arose on every side to help. The invitations had already gone out, and they'd been donated by the Rick family. Dad insisted that we'd show the Americans "a proper wedding reception," which, in British terms, meant a sit-down meal. No fluffy white cake. Certainly not! Mum baked our favorite Australian recipe of yellow fruitcake, and the next-door neighbor, Ruth Higgins, decorated it. The rest of the meal turned into an immense feast, the origins of which I never quite comprehended.

The George Beckners stripped their garden and brought armloads of flowers to the church. With these, Mrs. Taylor Bunch transformed the old South Lancaster Church into a veritable Garden of Eden. Other friends staged a very large bridal shower. Surveying the spread, I couldn't imagine that I needed any wedding gifts beyond these bounties.

The whole matter of music, both for the church service and for the reception, had been placed in the capable hands of Virginia-Gene Shankel-Rittenhouse, my friend who had, herself, married just a year earlier.

Then came the matter of the dresses. Of course, we'd have to make our own. We couldn't consider any other alternative. I didn't mind, because I knew nothing of the temptations of bride's magazines anyway. Down at the local department store in Clinton we chose one dress pattern for us all. Then we chose three lengths of flocked organza fabric, white for me, yellow for my sister Eileen, and lavender for Cousin Joan. Mum and I had little more than two days to make the three dresses. In the crush of things and in the concern for fitting Eileen and Joan, I scarcely took time to try on my own dress. (Very soon I would repent this negligence.)

Since none of Walt's family could be present, the groomsmen had to be friends of my choice. Because of my bridegroom's family roots I picked two Canadians, John Thomsen and Fred Crump.

Walt had promised to arrive on Thursday. That would give us two whole days before the wedding. Time for him to meet my family and be assessed.

Thursday, however, passed into night. No message. The long dark hours stretched on toward morning. Still nothing. He was driving alone, and I could see his 1948 black Chevy wrapped around a tree somewhere near Chicago. I alternated between weeping and a cold paralysis, hour after hour. Sheer agony. I'd already lost him!

Although she mercifully kept her fears to herself, my mother was thinking, "He's not ever going to show up. He's one of those deceivers who has no intention of coming to his own wedding." After all, none of my family had ever seen him before.

By morning I was a total nervous wreck, barely able to keep hold of my sanity. My mother came in a close second. Eileen and Joan, in supporting roles, lurked somewhere in the shadows, wide-eyed and worrying.

Then came the phone call. Walt's weary but still-cheerful voice came on the line. "Where are you?" I screamed.

"I drove non-stop. I hadn't slept for three days, so I stopped here to clean up. Besides, I didn't want to wake you all up in the middle of the night." He'd slept in a hotel in Clinton, just two miles away! He had, after all, just driven almost 3,000 miles, alone. "I looked pretty bad last night," he admitted. In retrospect, I now believe he didn't have enough money to spend on hotels.

Wake us up, indeed! When he appeared at the front door, I collapsed in his arms in a flood of tears. No matter that his eyes looked like two burned holes in a blanket. Never again in his life would he fail to tell me where he was and what he was doing.

Of course, it was partly my fault too. Not wanting to appear too forward and burdened with some weird sense of modesty, I'd not given him my parents' telephone number. Truth to tell, I scarcely knew the man yet.

"If only I'd known ... ." He held me close and stroked my hair. "It would have helped if I'd had a phone-number, but I didn't want to stop. I just wanted to get here."

Obviously these fine points of communication were much more important in my family than they'd ever been in his. Truth to tell, Walt and I had dated under such stringent circumstances back at Canadian Union College that we were virtual strangers. Strangers going together into paradise? Well, here we were, on our way.

By noon that Friday the household started keeping vigil for my Dad, driving up from Washington. We phoned him. "We've suffered much already. Be sure to let us know, if you're going to be later than midnight." He and his passengers, Fred and Katie Crump, appeared just five minutes before the Cinderella hour.

The next day-and-a-half passed in kind of a dust storm. At church the next day, Walt was asked to take part in Sabbath School. I can't recall what. They wanted me doing something too, but I declined. It was an exhibit

Wedding of Walter O. Comm and Dorothy Minchin, July 22, 1951.

for community friends, of course. Too much was happening too fast for me. "They've all seen me before." I sank into a pew and watched Walt carry out his duties solo.

Our little half-duplex house overflowed with so many people, each one bent on the most urgent of tasks. I remember sitting down to only two meals. Walt ate everything that was set before him while the family looked on. (We held hands under the table to steady ourselves.)

Early Sunday morning, my classmate, Morris Taylor, showed up on the doorstep with a single white gladiola in his hand. "I wanted to give you more, but this one was all I had." Charmed by his tribute, I accepted the fresh white stem in full bloom. I made a place for it in my rather large, trailing bridal bouquet. As it turned out, the flowers would become an effective cover-up later in the day.

As the appointed hour of 6 p.m. approached, everyone in the house queued up for showers and primping in the only bathroom we had. After several hours they were all done and took off for the church. Suddenly, it dawned on me that I, the bride, had not yet had my turn. Dad, Mum, and I were the only ones left in the house. By now there was no hot water left for the shower.

An insanely irrelevant thought flitted through my mind. "If I get married again, I'll make sure that I get to use the bathroom first."

I did my best, gathered myself together, and we left for the church only fifteen minutes late. I looked at my scruffy shoes, powdery with a layer of white polish. They were the ones I'd had for graduation more than a year ago. Anyway, I thought, the dress is long enough. Hopefully no one will have to see the shoes.

The Village Church in South Lancaster, Massachusetts.

Thus, I stood with Dad at the back of the church waiting for the organ to burst into the march from "Scipio" and sweep us down the aisle. As I tried to take my first step forward, however, I broke into a cold sweat.

My skirt was too long. Way too long! Running around, in and out of the car, and holding the dress up, I hadn't yet noticed. Now I could see that it was going to trip me up with every step. Perhaps in my panic I'd shrunk. The whole gown hung pretty loose, everywhere. Well, what can you expect out of a garment you cut out on the living room floor and for which you paid only $12.00.

I knotted up my dress, pulling it in from the back. Backs have to look good at weddings. This raised the front hemline off the floor. With the same hand, I held my bouquet in front of me. With the other I took Dad's arm, and we headed down the aisle toward a beaming Walt, standing at the far end of the trail. Who, after all, could tell the difference? We could still get married.

When all was said and done, given all of the kindness of so many friends, our entire wedding cost less than $100. Still a major investment for us in those days.

Dad's service was beautifully personal. The "garden" within the church gracefully brought the outdoors indoors. For decades afterwards, people remembered our wedding. "Well, he really tied that knot," they'd say. "And it all looked so lovely."

At the time, however, we faced real material anxieties. Our prospects of a honeymoon were wholly controlled by the necessity of reaching Newfoundland and getting on the payroll by August 1. I doubt that I had even $5.00 in my purse. Walt confessed to borrowing $100.00 back in Alberta. That money was supposed to pay for his road trip from Peace River to Massachusetts and then get both of us onto the ferry and across Newfoundland to St. John's.

Nonetheless, we left the house Sunday night in something of a carnival mood. Although our car had been safely locked up in Dad's garage, we'd been betrayed by cousins and friends from within. The poor little black Chevy looked like a giddy chorus girl. They'd painted signs on the doors in white shoe polish. The one reading "The Pious Pair" puzzled me. I didn't feel at all pious. Rather, I was extremely young, a very human beginner in every way. Designs on the windows in red nail polish rivaled the clumps of confetti that had been

The ever-lively Mrs. Win Shankel delivered a hilarious comic reading at the Comms' wedding reception.

pasted on with honey.

Later, at the hotel I had to spend nearly thirty minutes picking the stitching out of my nightgown. The previous week Joan had inquired if I had such a garment. "Well, no," I replied. "Just the usual old junk." Truth to tell, I didn't possess a single item for a trousseau, in the usual sense of the word.

"Well, that will never do for a honeymoon, you know." Joan was the Home Economics major, and she should know.

So she'd given me this lovely white, silky gown with blue trimming. I was quite overwhelmed with her generosity. After all, she was still in college. Now, at midnight, I discovered that she'd been into my suitcase and machine-sewed the hem, the armholes and the neck shut. "Ah, well," I mused. "She isn't married yet. I'll just bide my time."

The next morning, after washing the car, Walt and I went into the market to buy food for our camping trip. We had Mum and Dad's tent and two air mattresses. We'd hang out in Pioneer Valley, on the Mohawk Trail for a couple of days. It would cost us virtually nothing.

As I picked up the food items, I tossed a couple of green peppers into the basket. Walt touched my arm gently, "Ah, for me ... I mean ... .You don't have to buy those for me."

The Comm car bore traces of the white-shoe-polish lettering embedded in the black paint to the end of its life on Bell Island, Newfoundland.

"You mean you don't like them?" I stared at him in disbelief. 'You were eating green peppers in Mum's salad just two days ago."

"Er ... yes ... I know." He was very apologetic. "But now I don't have to," he grinned.

After two days in the woods, wandering on the trails, sitting by the cold stream, blowing up our collapsing air mattresses several times a night, cooking on an open fire, and telling other campers nearby that we were "on vacation," we left the Mohawk Trail.

In our spare time, we'd sat at the picnic table writing thank-your notes for our wedding gifts. We peeled strips of paper-bark off the white birch trees. Neatly trimmed, they made a wonderfully smooth writing surface. No point trying to hide the fact that we'd spent the first two days of marriage roving the forest. We could only hope that we didn't have "honeymoon" written all over our faces.

Then we returned to South Lancaster to get ready for the Official Departure into married life. We opened the wedding presents and packed them into the car. The Chevy contained everything we owned in the world.

We headed north, up through New Hampshire and Maine, across New Brunswick and Nova Scotia and on to Cape Breton Island. During that time we began, for the first time, to get acquainted. We knew so little of one another, but, we were in love, so we assumed that all would fall in place in due time.

In Pictou, Nova Scotia, a flat-tire interrupted our hasty-but-finally private journey. Dazzled by romance, I later pasted the nasty little spike into my wedding book. At the ferry-port in North Sydney, we loaded the car and ourselves aboard for the overnight journey across the Gulf of St. Lawrence to Channel-Port-aux-Basques, Newfoundland.

Disembarking the ferry, we immediately (on August 2) began the 500-mile train journey across to St. John's on the far side of the island. It would take almost twenty-seven hours, provided we didn't hit a caribou on the narrow-gauge track or get snowed in.

Even August couldn't guarantee decent weather. Not where we were. Popular legend had it that you actually got only one day of summer in Newfoundland, and if you slept in late that morning, you might miss most of it. The chief impression of our eastward journey was that of utter isolation, untamed tundra-like wilderness, with scarcely a man-made object to be seen anywhere. We studied our map.

The vast majority of the population lived along the coast, hence the scarcity—nay, absence—of roads. The fishing villages had quaint names like

"St. Jones Within," "Push Me Through," "Hearts Content," and "Deadman's Point." The turbulent, foggy Grand Banks to the south provided some of the richest fishing grounds in the world. The bays that took bites out of nearly every mile of Newfoundland's coastline, ranged from "Confusion Bay" and "Witless Bay" to the broad "Conception Bay" which we skirted as we finally approached St. John's.

From fellow-passengers on our journey we discovered that the "Newfies" prided themselves on two things: First, being Great Britain's oldest colony, and second, having their capital of St. John's billed as the oldest city in North America. At that time, their having recently become Canada's tenth province seemed to be a matter of little interest to most of them.

At St. John's railway station, our new bosses, Phil and Doris Moores, met our train, the president and treasurer of the Newfoundland Mission, respectively. We were hustled up the hill to the big white house that served as a school, offices, Radio Station VOAR, and the Moores' home. Walt and I were given the living room and its couch as a bedroom. Thus, 106 Freshwater Road became our temporary address.

No need for elaborate housing arrangements because, momentarily, everyone was off to Junior Camp. And, after that, Walt and I would be shipped back west to the lumberjack town of Cornerbrook.

About our first Newfoundland campout. A lodge with a roaring stone fireplace? A spacious, rustic kitchen? An assembly room furnished with tables for teaching crafts? Cabins with built-in bunk beds all ready to go? Showers and toilets within easy reach? None of the above. Just forget all of that kind of frivolity.

No. Trucks deposited us out on the swampy verge of a large, cold pond a few miles out of the city. There was nothing there. Absolutely nothing. The men and older boys unloaded the goods and set up tents. We women settled the kids and their possessions into their bleak camp quarters.

For toilets—at a modest distance from the center of camp—the men dug trenches and erected "benches" made of rough pine-tree trunks. So you sat out there, in wind and rain, balancing on the slender pole, trembling in the cold and trying to remember what you'd come out there for anyway.

The "Newfie Bullet" train toiled over the 500 miles between Port-aux-Basques and St. John's, the only transportation across Newfoundland at the time. Right. Our friend and colleague, Frank Knutson (himself a railroad hobbyist), posed in front of the Newfie Bullet engine in Grand Falls.

We had a kitchen tent and a storage tent. Presiding over the cook tent, Doris Moores produced amazing quantities of good food. The kids especially loved the pancakes and always descended on them like a pack of wolf cubs.

Every night we had a blazing bonfire as a background for singing and story telling. The fire also served as an opportunity to dry out clothes and bedding, for we were subject to downpours of rain, by day and by night.

Junior Camp near St. John's, Newfoundland, in 1951. Photographed on a rare, sunny day. The mood swings in Newfie weather usually ranged between gray drizzle and heavy fog.

Although the physical deprivations were indeed memorable, even more significant was the enthusiasm of that flock of bright-eyed children and young people. For them, the camp was heaven indeed. Never before had I told stories or taught crafts to such a crowd of little zealots.

Walt was in charge of a tent full of seven boys, and I had six girls under supervision in my tent. By bedtime we were utterly exhausted and consumed in a cold dampness that never left us for the ten days that we spent out there in the wilderness. We scarcely had time to tell each other goodnight.

But, glory be, we were now on the payroll! And none too soon. We'd finished the last dime of Walt's borrowed $100 on the train, crossing the island.

So, I lay there, stiff, cold and alone, on my army cot, shushing up my over-excited girls and marveling that I should be in such a place at such a time. We'd been married just fourteen days.

Had anyone else ever thought of having a honeymoon like this one? Probably not.

CHAPTER 7

Our Home on the Humber

Walt and I spent a month in St. John's living in the Hillocks' apartment. Emmerson (principal of St. John's Academy) and Mabel happened to be on the mainland at the time. After Junior Camp ended, we did a few errands around the city.

One, however, was of such magnitude that it changed the shape of my life forever. At that time, the St. John's church was busy at the annual Harvest Ingathering. This exercise went on constantly in Newfoundland, seemingly thirteen months out of the year. It required going from door to door soliciting donations for mission work. The more talented canvassers went to businesses where they could get larger takes. Naturally, the new intern pastor and his wife (Walt and me) were expected to participate.

I knew the process well enough, but the very thought of it invariably threw me into a fit of fear and fury. At certain festive seasons through my adolescence, singing groups had gone forth to help the solicitors. Nothing, however, could really help improve my Ingathering skills. I tended to stand on the doorstep, look at my shoes and say, "You wouldn't want to donate for missions, would you?" Of course, no one wanted to.

At college, I might go out with a group for social reasons. One might occasionally get to sit in the back seat and hold hands with a boyfriend. But I simply was not made right for the job. I've always gravitated to schoolwork where I could expect, more or less, to meet the same people every day. I didn't want to go to anyone's door. Not to sell anything. Not to ask for anything. I didn't want to go to a stranger's door for any reason at all. Besides, I could now hold hands with my boyfriend any time I wished.

Nonetheless, there I stood on Signal Hill, high above St. John's harbor on that bleak September day. Eager to fulfill my wifely duty in every detail, I didn't miss one house that afternoon. I'd spent the past three hours going from door to door while Walt had taken the local business district.

Now, however, I waited in the gray fog, consumed with frustration. The cold wind whipped away my tears. For the entire afternoon I'd received exactly ten cents. One single, slim dime! Surely, a new bride and beginning teacher (age twenty-one) deserved better than that! Did I think that just because I was a minister's wife I could actually do this wretched work? I hadn't expected Ingathering to become pleasurable, of course, but I thought if I tried hard enough it would, at least, be possible. If I'd received nothing, I think I would have felt a little better that day.

When Walt drew up to the curb, I flung the car door open and cast myself upon him in a torrent of angry weeping. Having never seen me in such anguish before, he was understandably startled. Indeed, I don't think I'd ever seen myself in such a passion either. "Don't ever, ever ask me to go Ingathering again," I bawled. "I'll pay my way out, if I have to, but I will never go Ingathering again." I slumped over in my seat and wailed some more. "I will not do it. Just don't ask." Be it said to Walt's everlasting credit, he never did.

By the time I'd recovered from that trauma, it was time for us to pack up ourselves and our car and re-board the train to travel back to Corner Brook on the west coast. Crossing the island of Newfoundland was not then negotiable by road. The "Newfie Bullet" rumbled over the twenty-seven-inch-gauge railway lines for interminable hours. Exhausted passengers at either end of the journey—St. John's or Port-aux-Basques—were usually ready to testify that they believed that the miserable little train had square wheels.

Corner Brook would be our first home. The place where we could finally unpack the car and start housekeeping. Walt would serve as church pastor, and I would teach the school. I can't recall exactly what I expected, but whatever it was it could in no way match reality.

Corner Brook was a paper-mill town operated by the English company of Bowaters. From the distant interior of the island, the Humber River floated log-booms down to the town. They came like huge rafts, jostling one another into the docks and attended by skilled "pond monkeys" who had to do complex little dance steps on the slippery surface to control the grinding, rolling logs. Great pyramids of logs filled the mill yards.

Most of the residents lived above the river, in the surrounding hills. That part of the town was threaded with narrow little streets and patched with snow for most of the year. Up there, at No. 9 Carmen Avenue, lay our destination. The schoolhouse stood solidly in a barren, muddy, unfenced yard. The front steps opened into a single, large room full of double desks clustered around a pot-bellied stove in the middle. Pegs along the back held the children's snow-suits. Apart from the teacher's desk at one end and a single panel of blackboard, the only other furnishing was a very old pump organ. Violent pushing on its threadbare treads and manipulating its chipped keys resulted, intermittently, in puffs of dust mingled with a few snarling, nasal notes of music.

Behind this public space and accessible by a door in the right corner of the schoolroom was our "teacherage." The first room was a kitchen with a small table and two chairs. A hand pump brought water up into a sink, but its only outlet was a bucket that required frequent emptying. An oil-heater and a grumpy-looking, wood-burning stove stood opposite, beside the bedroom door. Lack of space forbade us a regular double bed. A three-quarter-size (halfway between a twin and a double) was all we could fit in.

Upstairs, at the top of a ladder-like staircase ascending out of the kitchen, was our spare room. Only a midget could have stood upright there. It took us hours scrubbing away decades of accumulation of soot to clean it up. In a matter of days, however, the smoke laid down yet another layer of soot.

One end of the tiny back porch had been portioned off to hold a washtub. Some days I washed clothes in it, and other days we dragged it into the kitchen for taking baths in front of the oil-heater. As for other bathroom necessities, we had to share the two outhouses with the school kids. These two-seater emporiums leaned up against the backyard fence.

The school itself proved to be an almost overwhelming challenge. I had forty-five kids occupying every level from Grade 1 to 8. Since the New-foundlanders started school at age four, I had two more pre-Grade 1 groups. I'd never had a day's training for elementary school teaching, so I just stumbled along, day-by-day, hour-by-hour. I'd always been determined to work at sec-

Left. Corner Brook was distinguished by its pulp mills. Right. The log booms crowding the banks of the Humber River gave the town of Corner Brook its character.

ondary level, and now here I was! Being the pastor's wife had propelled me into this job. An unbelievably hard one!

Walt built two sandbox tables where I could keep some of the little ones entertained for a certain amount of time. One day I was demonstrating the Joseph story to the First and Second Graders. "And Joseph had eleven brothers!" I gushed. "Wasn't that a big family?"

Brian looked at me under his mop of sandy hair, unimpressed. "Well, we got eighteen kids in our house. That ain't nothing." Clearly, I hadn't scored a point.

Then there was Eric, ten years old but still in Grade 2. Between September and Christmas he came to school every day in the same sweater. Within a month it was caked with the remains of all of his meals. He got a new shirt at Christmas and wore that until spring.

I blocked off a small corner of the blackboard and wrote "E R I C" at the top. "Now, Eric," I led him up to the front. "This is your name. I want you to copy it until you get it right." For weeks, he worked at the board—cheerfully enough—but he never mastered the task.

Then there were the three Penny children, handsome youngsters despite their dirty hands and faces. Arriving at school, they'd grin at me while they took off their frozen snowsuits. As the suits thawed out around the stove, the stench filled the room all the way to the hoar-frosted windows. They'd simply taken care of their bathroom needs as they walked to school.

These problems dominated Walt's and my lives, day and night. "The Penneys aren't paying their school-fees, are they?" Walt reminded me one day. "Let's make a home visit." Actually, we visited the homes of all of the children, but the Penneys unquestionably outdid all of the others in shock value.

We found a twenty-five-year-old mother, surrounded by ten children, sitting in a bare room. Bare except for a wooden table in the middle. On it was a sticky jar of jam and the remains of a loaf of bread that had been torn apart in some kind of a feeding frenzy. Beside the table stood a large lard bucket serving for water drainage, garbage and toilet purposes. Through an open door I could see an iron bedstead with old coats thrown on the bare springs for bedclothes.

"My husband is not often home." The woman's tired eyes haunt me to this day. She was about nine-months pregnant with her eleventh child, however, so he must have come home sometimes. "I know I haven't been paying," she sighed. "But I have no money."

Neither Walt nor I could bear to bring up the subject of school fees. "It's all right," I said. "But maybe you could wash their clothes sometimes."

"I'll try to get in some more snow to melt. It's the only water we have." I was sorry that I'd said even that much. We got into our car and drove off, feeling very fortunate, very sad, and very frustrated. What could we ever do?

Walt spent every Friday afternoon cleaning up the school, stacking the desks against the walls, scrubbing the floor, and setting out the single-board benches that we optimistically called pews. The church membership con-

The Corner Brook School (1951-1952). The horses grazed in the yard, waiting their turn to walk through the washing, as soon as Dorothy hung it out on the line. Representing the sole plumbing arrangement on the property, the double outhouse stood behind the school, to the left.

A school picnic for the children on a bare hillside, looking down on Corner Brook. We had to learn to produce interest out of the neighborhood and create entertainment out of nothing.

sisted of two elderly ladies, one middle-aged one and three kids. Occasionally visitors came, but not often. The school, as it turned out, would be our main undertaking.

Somehow, in this setting, zestful as any new bride, I tried to make a home out of all of this raw material. Many of our wedding presents, however, looked weirdly out of place. In fact, if we'd dwelt on the subject, we might have become discouraged. For instance which of the twenty-two embroidered tablecloths we received could fit on the splintery, bandy-legged table? The soft, new towels looked odd, draped over the pump handle. I remember looking at our single bone-china cup and saucer, gorgeous in spring flowers, standing beside our tough, plastic dinner plates in the dish rack. It almost seemed to mock us!

Laundry was a major task. Heating water on the stove, scrubbing on the washboard, and then hanging everything out on the two ropes strung up between the back porch and the outhouses. In winter, the sheets and towels froze almost instantly. Sometimes, however, it was not soon enough. Almost daily the neighborhood horses would walk through my washing, coating it with mud. Getting the laundry done proceeded in a series of washings and re-washings that could last for days.

By Christmas Walt had found an exceedingly old agitator washing machine. All we had to do then was pump the water, heat it on the stove, and then fill—and empty—the machine by hand. Good. But of itself the machine didn't solve the horse problem.

Yet, this is all in retrospect, because I can remember nothing but trying very hard to do everything I was supposed to do. At the same time, I suffered all winter from bronchitis, sinus infections and flu-like symptoms. It seemed that I was never warm. The first night we slept in the three-quarter-bed, we had snow on our blankets in the morning. Walt chinked all of the cracks around the windows with newspapers and rags.

Later years were to demonstrate that I actually have a chronic "allergy" to cold weather. Newfoundland's cold, damp climate certainly didn't agree with me, and it took all the will power I had, just to stay on my feet. Walt and I were contented with each other, however, and didn't know enough to complain.

We'd been in Corner Brook less than a month when Bill McQueary arrived. A tall, spare black man from Chicago, he and Walt had been in college at the same time and had sung together in a male quartet. How Bill loved to sing! Head thrown back, eyes closed, he crooned all of the old gospel songs. Since we had no other company, we welcomed him when he first came through on the train from St. John's.

He took an interest in the school and began to entertain the kids with music and singing every day. He didn't mind sleeping on the floor in the sooty attic. In fact, he seemed to like everything we had. On our exceedingly small income, however, we soon felt the strain of feeding another hearty eater three times a day. Time began to go slowly in our very small and inconvenient quarters. After all, we rather thought of ourselves as still being on our honeymoon. It had been less than two months since the wedding.

Bill, however, was perfectly at ease and complained of nothing. After ten days, I thought he'd surely be leaving soon. One week stretched into another. At the end of about six weeks, I was asking Walt to "do something about it."

He ascertained the train schedule. "If we leave here at noon," my husband told Bill, "You can get the train to Port-aux-Basques by 12.30."

"Yes, I'll have to do that," Bill would reply benignly.

Yet, I'd come in from school to make lunch every day and find him still there. "Well," he'd smile at me pleasantly, "we didn't make it today. Probably tomorrow."

Tomorrow, it seemed, would never come. After another week, he finally came in one morning to say goodbye to the kids. Walt hastened him into the car and down to the train station before he changed his mind.

We never saw Bill again. He went home to Chicago, and I understand that he was still singing gospel songs and visiting people way into his 80s.

At last, Walt and I were living by ourselves again. Now we realized that we had no friends our age and no entertainment of any kind. I'd grown up in a house full of music. True, we had a little radio, but I longed for music that I could hear by my own choice. We debated for a long time and hung around a general store at the bottom of the hill. There we found a little turntable with a tiny speaker embedded in its wooden frame. Second-hand, it cost only $14.00, but it took us a quite a while to decide that we could afford it.

Then, having purchased the machine we realized that we had nothing to play on it. We found enough money to buy a single disk. We chose a ten-inch, long-playing record of the music of Edvard Grieg. We'd have liked a twelve-inch one, but it was beyond our means. Being long-playing, it had a pretty good selection. Happily, the new LPs were rapidly replacing the more limited old 78s. We played Grieg constantly for weeks, until we could afford another record. Today, the melodies from "Peer Gynt" still give me a replay of Corner Brook. Instant recall.

Knee-deep in snow, Walt and Dorothy Comm at the door of their two-room, lean-to apartment at the back of the school house in Corner Brook, Newfoundland. Right. Thigh-high in the snow, a few of the children cluster on Teacher's car—beside the bedroom window and under the icicles.

We needed other diversions too. Since college days, I'd collected cartoons. No copy of the *Saturday Evening Post* ever got tossed out before I'd scanned it for its cartoons. A sort of insurance against "low days." We did have a few of those.

Now that I think of it, there were many Saturday nights when Walt and I sat between the two stoves in the kitchen trying to keep warm. I can still see us there, opening the shoebox of cartoons and spending an hour or so laughing over them.

We were young enough to think that Saturday nights were made for fun. But we knew we had to find the entertainment right there within our smoky little lean-to at the back of the schoolhouse.

I'd arrived at the marriage altar with little knowledge of or interest in cooking. Fortunately, I'd received two classic cookbooks as bridal shower gifts. These I studied religiously, feeling a great compulsion to make good meals for Walt, despite the immediate adverse circumstances. I think I did reasonably well, considering that I inevitably competed with the women in his German farm family back in Alberta. All of them were master cooks, and though I'd met only a couple of them, I knew instinctively that I had a high standard to attain.

I'd been basically reared as a vegetarian. On our first married day Walt announced, "We always had our own meat back home on the farm, but I don't want it now." I was happy enough. The only meat I have ever cooked in my life was butcher scraps for the dogs. So in that first year I even washed flour a few times (without indoor water service) and made gluten roast.

At Hallowe'en that year I scored a particular success. We planned a full-blown party for the kids, jack-o-lanterns, streamers, and all. I made a huge batch of individual, mini-pumpkin pies. Apparently none of the local women knew that you could do anything with pumpkin other than boil it to death. The children, thereafter, urged their mothers to come and find out how to improve pumpkin in such a tasty way. In the warm glow of success, I shared the recipe.

Soon after, however, I met a private, culinary disaster, one that I tried to hide even from Walt. I'd grown up on Marmite, a pungent, black yeast-spread that every British child knows is essential for good sandwiches. It also has other creative uses and has appeared in various incarnations: Vegemite, Sovex, Vegex, and so forth. It's definitely an acquired taste, and the uninitiated tend to refer to it rudely as "axle-grease."

My mother had a recipe for making Vegex at home. Since I'd been suffering withdrawal symptoms for several months now, I decided to make some for myself. A big batch. Whether Walt would like it or not—I didn't care one way or the other. At least, I would have it.

I laid in a large number of yeast cakes and went to work. To this day, I'm not sure what went wrong. I never gained enough courage to try again. Clearly, however, I transgressed some basic principle of chemistry there in my shabby little Corner Brook kitchen.

Using my largest kettle and stoking up the fire, I dumped in the ingredients. In a matter of minutes the lava flow began. Like an erupting volcano, the Vegex poured over the stove in a swelling stream. I grabbed every kettle and pan I owned to catch the flood. Then came the dishpans. By the time I could bring in the washtub, however, the black tide met me at the door. By now the kitchen looked like a set for a horror movie.

Eventually, the yeast wore itself out. I spent the next two hours, carrying the sludge out to the back of the schoolyard and pumping buckets of water to clean up the mess.

I was just finishing the job when Walt came home to a den smelling of soap and disinfectant. "What were you doing?" How could he understand? "Why didn't you wait for me to help you with all of this?" he inquired.

"It's all right," I mumbled. "I'm finished now."

I'd carefully covered up all traces of the episode. Somehow, this event was much too private for Walt or anyone else to know about. I only hoped that the cold weather would prevail until the Vegex had disintegrated under the snow that I'd piled on top of it. I could only pray that the horses wouldn't uncover the stuff and kill themselves eating it.

CHAPTER 8

Some New Venues

Shortly before Christmas Walt and I were suddenly bidden to a teachers' convention at headquarters in St. John's. The stress of my teaching situation had pretty well numbed me to anything other than simply surviving amid that swirling mass of forty-five kids that I faced hour after hour. Whatever lofty ideals I'd once entertained about education had sunk far beneath the physical necessities of getting through each day alive.

A trip to St. John's would at least be a diversion, so we boarded the eastbound train with at least a little enthusiasm. We might have booked sleepers but decided we shouldn't waste the money. Fortunately, we managed to find two seats facing one another. We had space enough to lie down, sort of.

Indeed, sleeping might even have been an option, except for the four men sitting across the aisle from us. Apparently they'd boarded at Port-aux-Basques already well soused. They continued to drink, sing songs and socialize with everyone in the carriage. "We Newfies." They hailed us genially. "You Newfies too?"

"No," Walt replied. "We're from Canada." Newfoundland—Britain's first colony (barring Ireland)—had become Canada's tenth province just two years earlier. Even though it meant material gain, the Newfies had not yet adjusted to what they considered a severe loss of status. Therefore, the party across the aisle immediately lost interest in us and returned to their bottles.

The odors, the noise, and the sticky heat consumed us for hours.

Finally, one of the drunks threw up voluminously on the floor between us. Walt could usually endure almost limitless hardship, but this time he went to find the conductor. "My wife should not have to put up with this," he said. Then I realized that I was the only woman in the coach. But my champion was defending me.

"Did you do this?" The conductor pointed down at the mess.

"Ya-a-a. Maybe oi ... " The tramp sighed, his bleary eyes looking up at us out of his stubbled face. "Right then, guv'ner." The fellow could hardly deny the odoriferous evidence.

"Clean it up!" The conductor backed toward the door. "Now."

"Oi sed oi'd do it." The offender cheerfully took off his jacket and mopped up the floor with it. "See?" Then he stuffed the reeking rag into the overhead compartment. He'd done his job. The conductor shrugged and walked off.

Fortunately, the quartet tottered off the train at Grand Falls and did not return. That gave us some peace for the remaining thirteen hours of the journey to St. John's.

Back in the capital city once more we found the mission-office-plus-school-building buzzing with activity. George Matthews, a church administrator from Washington D.C., was in charge of the meetings. Sitting among all of those people, teachers, church members and finding young people our own age gave both of us a heady feeling of, at last, "belonging" to something. The workshops even inspired me to feel some enthusiasm for teaching again. Having interviewed all of us personally, Matthews told Phil Moores that my situation was impossible. Something that I'd already figured out for myself. He suggested that Walt come into the schoolroom each morning and then do the rest of his work in the afternoons.

This arrangement meant that the two of us would be teaching at close quarters at the same time. Still, the great relief of having help inspired nothing but gratitude in me. In that manner, therefore, we finished out the school year in Corner Brook.

Meanwhile, a fellow pastor and his wife, Clarence and Alice Goertzen, needed help. We hadn't seen them since they'd left Canadian Union College some years earlier. They were stationed at Botwood, one of the main outports in the central north of the island. Clarence had just started building a new church when he acquired a bad case of pleurisy. "To bed," the doctor ordered. "And stay there."

As soon as school was out, we were on the road to Botwood where Walt would finish building the church. I say "road" because we needed to take our car. Little more than a wide swath cut through the trees, the unpaved way took many, many hours to negotiate. If we could just get to Grand Falls, however, we'd be all right.

Upon arrival in Botwood we became Goertzens' house guests for the next two-and-a-half months. Their entire house could be fit into many people's living rooms today. The kitchen occupied the width of the house at the back. At the front, we had the living room and a tiny bedroom, barely eight feet square. Walt and I slept there while Alice and Clarence placed their makeshift bed across the front door of the living room. It stood on stacks of unused, outdated Ingathering magazines. With some satisfaction I thought this to be a very proper use for the literature, but I said nothing aloud. The outhouse in the backyard meant that no space inside the little shack had been wasted on a bathroom.

Encircling Clarence's bed, we went about our business, carrying out his suggestions. Visitors came and went. Somehow, we four lived like that for the rest of the summer.

Alice and I tended to church and schoolwork and made the meals. One morning I got up to find a large pan of milk on the kitchen table. It smelled so obnoxious that I gagged, just sniffing at it. "This has got to be sour beyond all hope," I reasoned. So I dumped it out in the garden behind the house. Then I proceeded to make a breakfast that didn't require milk.

A short while later, Alice came in. "Where's the milk?"

"I threw it out. It was rotten."

"Rotten? Oh no! That was the goat milk that the Gills gave us." Alice looked worried.

"I'm sorry. I didn't know." Now, I wondered, what do we do? "Well," I proposed, "Let's just thank them for it and say that it was very useful." Wasn't it possible that milk would do something good for the vegetables in the garden? When Alice admitted that she hadn't been eager to drink it anyway, I felt much better.

Before the end of the summer, it became clear that Clarence needed more

In 1950 the erratic little segments of road across the island ranged between two extremes. Left. Claustrophobic trails scarcely wide enough to let the Chevy through. Right. Then wilderness vistas that swallowed up any lone vehicle attempting the island crossing.

time for recovery, so the Goertzens returned to the mainland. Frank and Carolyn Knutson (former college friends of mine at Atlantic Union College) came up from St. John's to open the new church and school and to help Walt and me stage another junior camp.

We pitched the tents north of Botwood, on Sandy Point, one of the inlets of the Bay of Exploits. Newfoundland's quaint place names still hold the seeds of ancient Norse adventurers. We kept up the usual Newfie tradition, just tents and slit-trench toilets.

I shall never forget, however, the pristine beauty of that wilderness, the Canadian North at its best. No hardship could erase the effect of the streaks of dawn-light reflecting themselves in the blindingly clear waters of the pine-fringed bay.

One afternoon Frank announced that everyone ought to go swimming. Like homesick seals, the kids immediately rushed in. Always a lover of the water, I intended to join them. I waded out to mid-calf depth, however, and was seized with such cramps that I almost collapsed. I groaned, looking at the kids cavorting just ten yards beyond me.

"I'm still young," I gasped. "But not that young!" In actual fact, we could see the icebergs floating across the entrance of our inlet. I staggered back to my tent and shivered until bedtime.

In the cook-tent Carolyn and I frequently made bushels of pancakes, as Doris Moores had taught us. An easy and filling dish. The youngsters loved them. Frank and Walt had to hang around outside, waiting their turn. "OK now!" Frank would finally say, "Dismiss the little coyotes. We're hungry too."

I never dreamed that just the companionship of other young couples could be so delightful. I realized then what we'd missed thus far in our new work, fellowship with people our own age.

In late August, we trundled back over the road to Corner Brook. Before we could begin planning another school year, however, we received a directive from headquarters. We were to move to St. John's. Walt would help in a large evangelistic campaign, and I would teach at the Academy (high school).

Leaving anywhere is hard, even Corner Brook. We left behind dear friends there who had been the soul of kindness itself during our primitive days in the old schoolhouse: Mrs. Moyst, a true Mother in Israel, along with daughter Mabel and husband Rod Dingwell.

I confess, nonetheless, that as the train rumbled northeast, past the pulp-mills and the log-booms floating on the Humber, I was not devastated. No, I sensed new opportunities ahead. Maybe my teaching now would come somewhere near what I'd trained for in college. Perhaps I could hope for that much.

Our living quarters in St. John's proved to be unique. Unlike Corner Brook where I usually did my housework clad in my snowsuit—parka and all—the top floor of Mrs. Gosse's house was measurably warmer.

We shared the bathroom with her and her very aged mother, but at least the facility was indoors. By now we regarded the use of a real bathtub as a singular privilege. We occupied two bedrooms at the back of the house. One

Left. Dishwashing chores at Sandy Point Junior Camp, north of Botwood. Right. Summertime notwithstanding, icebergs floated across the bay in front of the camp.

Dorothy's English Class at St. John's Academy (1952). Seated front: Douglas Dowden, Maxine Dowden. First row: L-R. June March, Marjory Lewis, Phyllis Hodder, Ilah Janes, Marilyn Moores, _____, Phyllis Stokes, Joyce Lucas. Back row boys: George March, Danny Harris, David Garland, Dennis Coffin, David Rodgers.

of them we fashioned into a bedroom and a study. The other had neither sink nor water supply, but, with a table, a dishpan, and an electric hotplate, we declared it to be a kitchen.

Immediately, Walt threw himself into church responsibilities while I prepared to be homeroom teacher to the Fourth Grade. Another forty kids, but at least they were all in the same grade. The bonus was that I also got to teach English in Grades 9 and 10. That, finally, approached what I'd long hoped to do with my life.

On the side, I taught a few piano lessons. My friend Virginia-Gene might well have been surprised, but just about anyone can get through the first John Thompson books and the church hymnal.

The church in St. John's sponsored a prosperous radio station called VOAR. In addition to church services we had a variety of "canned" programs, even back there in 1952. The Voice of Prophecy came on with hours of music by the King's Heralds Quartet. The station also aired some of the very first programs of "Unshackled" from the Pacific Garden Mission in Chicago.

Automatically Walt and I gravitated to the radio studio. He was a kind of disc jockey announcer and news anchor while I wrote, produced, and performed in a series of live broadcasts on the stories of hymns. I look back now and realize that all of these tasks edged me closer to the kind of work I really wanted to do. At the time, however, I could not have described to anyone the evolution I wished my professional career to take. For the moment, I was enormously busy, just getting from one day to the next.

Beyond occasionally playing the organ for meetings, I had other responsibilities in the

In Pouch Cove, beyond the stages (racks) for drying codfish, icebergs floated south along the eastern shore of Newfoundland.

church. It seemed to be generally understood that I'd renounced Harvest Ingathering, so I was asked to be leader of the Dorcas (Welfare) Society. Now sewing, needlework and crafts were solidly implanted in my heritage. No problem with that part of the assignment.

But what was I to do about all of those dear old ladies who'd been working in the Society from the time of Noah's flood, as it were? Who was I, a twenty-three-year-old novice, to be telling them what to do? "You'll be fine," the ever-optimistic Phil Moores assured me. So I went forward.

Then, an even more remarkable development occurred. Ever since that first St. John's Junior Camp eighteen months earlier, I'd acquired a substantial little group of satellites, teenage girls now in my high school English classes. "If you're going to Dorcas," they announced, "so are we!"

Thus our whole entourage of youth engulfed the staid precincts of the Society in the room at the back of the church. Mending? Fine. Quilting? Let me at it. Knitting? I've got my own needles at home.

Of course, this phenomenon lasted only while I was in office. I believe, however, that the episode was rather remarkable for what it was. The old sisters, bless them, were very patient with us.

During this time, Walt and I had an interesting relationship with our landlady. Mrs. Gosse was a midwife and had several deliveries a week in the front downstairs bedroom of her house. The Newfoundland hospitals, at the time, would not receive unwed mothers for their deliveries. With a number of military bases nearby, the need was great, and Mrs. Gosse's house became a haven for many a hapless young woman.

One day I received an unsolicited education when she called me to assist in a birthing. Only a child herself, the girl screamed pitifully. When it was over, I stumbled back upstairs to my room. In utter exhaustion, I trembled with chills and sweat while I waited to describe my Sunday afternoon to Walt when he came home.

Mrs. Gosse was invariably forthright in all of her dealings. When the boy from the shop delivered the groceries, pity help him if he brought sliced rather than un-sliced bread. She would phone the proprietor and berate him for making an error that she considered a personal affront to herself. No doubt, he had planned the insult in advance. Why couldn't he understand that she always had to have unsliced bread?

One year the ladies of the St. John's "Dorcas Society" had to make room for a tidal wave of young women from the academy who invaded their premises.

About this time, we disposed of the old Chevrolet, our honeymoon car. Some time later we heard that it had been taken out to Bell Island. It was last seen on an empty lot, housing a large family of stray cats. When Knutsons stepped up to a new Ford, we bought their gray Studebaker. Its streamlined contour with the jazzy little propeller on the front gave us a new illusion of wellbeing, at least in the matter of transportation.

Since she didn't have a car, we always taxied Mrs. Gosse to and from church and school functions. Like all of the rest of the Newfoundlanders at the time, she had not recovered from World War II. A very tangible antipathy toward Germans still prevailed.

One harshly cold night, she and I were already sitting in the car. Walt put something into the trunk and slammed the lid shut. Amplified by the frost, the sound hit us like a bomb. "Dear heavens!" Mrs. Gosse jumped and hit her head on the roof. "You'd think the Germans are behind us!" she cried.

I almost said, "They are." But not quite. I thought better of it. As far as I know, the Newfies never realized that Walt was, in fact, a full-blooded German. (The name "Komm" had become "Comm" when the family emigrated to Canada from the Old Country.)

That year-end brought us a special treat. We hadn't been home since our wedding a year-and-a-half earlier. So, on our second Christmas, Mum and Dad sent us air tickets to come spend the holiday with the family.

My first trip in an airplane. The DC-3 had just wobbled up off the frozen runway when the stewardess put the morning newspaper in our hands. Headlines: "Eighty-eight Dead in Crash at Moses Lake." I swallowed hard and watched the blue-and-white landscape slide away below us as we headed south toward Boston.

Being home was all that it should have been. Cousins planning to get married and Eileen growing out of sight. Our dear dog Chips in the middle of everything. What more could I ask? Nothing, except to be well enough to sit down to Christmas dinner with them all. Instead, I languished in bed for many days, afflicted with a massive dose of flu and all of the rest of the cold-weather stuff that constantly plagued me. After New Year's, Walt went back to Newfoundland, but I stayed home until mid-January to recover.

When I returned to St. John's, Mrs. Gosse immediately came upstairs to tell me how marvelous Walt was. He'd kept our rooms tidy. (I am sure she checked them while he was out.) He'd cooked all kinds of meals for himself and had even made potato salad. My potato salad had always interested her. "I didn't know you could do that with a potato," she once remarked. "Give me the recipe." I told I didn't have one. That potato salad is just something you "do."

Now, after intently studying Walt for two weeks, our landlady had another project in mind. "Does Walter have any brothers?"

"Yes," I replied. "Four."

"Are they married?" All business now, she tapped her fingers on the stair railing. "I would like to get one of them for my daughter, Joan."

"I'm sorry. They're all taken." I couldn't believe that we were having this conversation.

"Such a pity!" Mrs. Gosse shrugged, doggedly turning to go back down-stairs. The request amazed me because the general Newfie opinion of Western Canada is that everyone lived in log cabins and chased buffalo all day. I never found out whether or not Joan knew that her mother had these plans in mind for her.

That same year, Walt and I entertained our first guests in our home (rooms). My parents. It was their twenty-fifth wedding anniversary, and we were delighted when they chose to come celebrate with us. Of course, our facilities were limited. We gave them our bedroom, and Mrs. Gosse allowed Walt and me to sleep in the baby-delivery room. Fortunately, no distraught pregnant woman showed up at the door during the time Mum and Dad were there.

Then the sightseeing. The rugged coastline had tiny houses clinging to the rock faces, acres of racks for drying codfish, brightly painted lighthouses and friendly villagers. Actually, we were able to give them quite a tourist-worthy trip around the eastern part of this island. Occasionally to places where time stood stone still.

Summer came, and with it the desire for something resembling a "real house." Our two rather public rooms in Mrs. Gosse's home became increasingly restricting.

Frank and Carolyn Knutson had built their little dream house in Mount Pearl Park, some four miles west of the city. Walt and I wandered around the district and studied our options.

We found a thickly treed lot, 100-feet square. In the middle of it sat a tiny house still a-building, right beside the railway track. We could have it for $4,000. A huge sum, but with both of us working, we could manage it. The four rooms (living room, two bedrooms, and kitchen) were very small. There would also be a bathroom, all our own.

In order to save money, we halted the building after the basics were in. Walt, Fred Garland the shoemaker, and other friends from the church would do the painting, winterizing, and a great deal more. Plumbing also remained incomplete. (The bathtub sat there hopefully, but we'd never find the time or money to install it.) Walt bought me a piano, however, and we moved in before school opened that fall. He nailed a screen cupboard to the wall outside by the back door to serve us as a refrigerator.

Walt and Dorothy's tiny house in Mount Pearl Park, a village outside of St. John's. Never completely finished, it was, for eight months, their dream home. Purchased for $4,000, it was the first real estate they owned.

We had little knowledge of interior decorating. We painted the living room a neutral beige but for the wall around the fireplace we chose a deep maroon. Perhaps not a bad idea for a large room, but it was the equivalent of turning our little space into a dark cage.

At set times, the Newfie Bullet train virtually roared through our house. We were just inches from the railway track. Still, I can't recall that we noticed the noise much. We had our own home at last, and everything else was secondary to that joy!

Fern and Floyd Penstock, friends from high school days, had, by now, arrived in St. John's. While Walt and Floyd went Ingathering on a weekly, sometimes daily, basis, Fern and I did creative art stuff together for school. Every chance they got, my high school girls came out to the woods to visit me.

I can remember great contentment prevailing in our Mount Pearl house. Yet, if we'd thought the matter through, we could have been afraid. Sitting as we did in that dense thicket of trees with no city-water supply, we faced a potential fire hazard. Very early one morning we found out how that could happen.

Our neighbor from the big house across the track, rushed to our door screaming, "Fire! Fire! My house is on fire!" She crashed through the door and collapsed in a chair, sobbing. "I can't think. I can't look!"

Like a shot, without even putting on a sweater, Walt catapulted out of the

Left. Dorothy and her pocket-size puppy, Sandy, pose on a cliff above Heart's Content, one of the out-ports near St. John's. Right. Visitors were rare, so sharing lunch with Mum and Dad Minchin on the cliffs above Flat Rock was a high day.

house and across the tracks. He found the kitchen in flames. Inside, he also found a basket of kittens that he gently deposited outside. Then, single-handed, he put out the fire with water he had to pump from the well. Quite an exploit in itself.

The next week, the lady brought us a beautifully wrapped gift. "And you saved my kittens too!" Tears filled her eyes. Inside the box we found an elegant,

heavy silver cream-and-sugar set on an ornate little tray. A reproduction of an 18th-century design, it has never, to this day, been used. Yet, I wouldn't

The surf at Flat Rock. Remote and little known even today, the coastlines of Canada's easternmost and oldest province of New-foundland still have some of the most dramatic scenery on the continent.

dream of parting with it. It stands as a monument to my husband's courage and to a very special time in our lives. A time when the paths we were yet to walk remained unclear.

Actually, our life in St. John's seemed so predictable. We did our work in church and school. For recreation we could drive up Signal Hill to the Marconi Tower. We gazed at the icebergs jostling about the harbor. We watched the icebreakers and sealing ships come in, spattered with blood and laden with seal pelts. We socialized with our young friends. I exchanged weekly letters with my parents. We could see nothing beyond this pattern of life in our northern Canadian outpost.

In less than two months, however, all of that would change. Our lives would make a complete U-turn. As for the bathtub? Well, it would have to be installed by the next owners of our little Mount Pearl home.

Still unused after almost sixty years, the elegant silver tea set remains a monument to the day in Mount Pearl Park when Walt became a one-man fire team and saved the neighbors' big two-story house. *(Photo by Cindy DeMille)*

CHAPTER 9

The Day We Became Somebody

For the dreaming and fulfilling of dreams 1954 turned out to be our year. General Conference, the quadrennial meeting of the worldwide church of Seventh-day Adventists, was to be held, once again, at the Civic Auditorium in San Francisco.

Being such minor functionaries, of course, there was no way that Walt and I would be delegates. On the other hand, my Dad and Uncle Len (from England) were official appointees. As a matter of fact, as plans shaped up, we all realized that here we had another opportunity for our two families, complete, to be together again, however briefly.

These exciting summer possibilities virtually set our little Mount Pearl house on fire. Moreover, after the session, we could drive up to Peace River, in northern Alberta. There I could see and be seen by Walt's family for the first time. The Newfoundland Mission granted our vacation request. That, however, was only Phase One.

"Why don't we take the train to Oshawa and pick up a new Ford at the factory?" Walt mused. Why not, indeed? Phase Two. In this connection, we learned that my parents had just purchased a new pale, blue Ford for the westward journey. Somehow, a Ford seemed to be the most desirable car to own at the time. I can't remember that we even considered anything else.

Phase Three would be the cross-country journey itself, without the benefit of modern freeways. In due course, feeling unusually smart, Walt and I drove our new blue Ford virtually off the assembly line. We headed south to Massachusetts where the family was assembling. We virtually formed a "wagon train" to head west.

There was, perforce, a great gathering of the family. Kelvin and Yvonne—

in medical school and nurses' training respectively—were already in California. We'd meet them there. Uncle Len, Auntie May, and the twins had come over from England, arriving on the *Queen Mary* on April 27, 1954. Joan, Eileen and Grandpa Rhoads were already on hand at home in Massachusetts.

That made eleven people to travel in two cars, served by only three drivers, Dad, Walt, and me. Uncle Len (only half-jokingly) remarked, "I won't come to America again until I know how to drive a car." It bothered him to be unable to help us cover the long, long miles that lay ahead.

True to family form, we never went near a restaurant. Instead, we made endless meals out of boxes and bags, salvaging the last stale bread crust and hardened lump of cheese. No motel earned our patronage either. Nightly we laid down our sleeping bags in off-the-road places. It's something of a testimony to the safety of the times that we could do all of this without fear of violence.

One night we drove too late and had some difficulty finding a place to camp out. Finally, under the starless sky we found an open space. As usual, we each claimed a sleeping spot and scrambled into our sleeping bags. We fell asleep instantly.

In the morning, the first ones up discovered that we'd slept in a chicken yard that was well paved with what chickens put down in their yards.

"I thought I smelled something when we stopped," Joan wailed. "Why did we have to ... ?" No one had an answer. Well, what was done was done. We dusted ourselves off, packed the cars again and moved on.

As we approached the west coast, however, the minimalist restrictions we'd laid upon ourselves began to reveal flaws. No one had had anywhere near enough sleep since we'd left Massachusetts. Strong family traditions forbade raised voices, much less brawls. Still, tensions rose occasionally. Over trivial concerns that would not, ordinarily, merit anyone's notice.

When we stopped in Reno, Nevada, for refueling, Walt bought me a box of chocolate-covered cherries, my favorite kind of candy. Of course, I shared it around.

Most of the time the elders in the group rode in Dad and Mum's car and the younger set with Walt and me. Uncle Len happened to be in the "young car" at this point. With his usual talent for lightening gloomy moments, he pontificated. "We all know that it is very easy to get a divorce in Reno. So we must be very careful as we drive through this city. We want to be sure that we're not divorced when we come out on the other side."

He passed my box of chocolates around the second time. "Everyone must eat one or two of these for protection." With a twinkle in his eye and a mischievous grin, he popped a third (maybe fourth) chocolate into his mouth. "These are actually Anti-Reno Pills, you know. They are very effective."

Of necessity, our frugality continued. True, our parents, as delegates, had a paid trip to San Francisco. Together, Walt and I had a combined income of considerably less that $300 a month, and we had to live leanly. Grandpa, of course, could chip in a few of his pension dollars. The rest of the kids, however, had no visible means of support. If we were going to do this family thing, it would take a sacrifice. We willingly made it.

When we got to San Francisco, we left Grandpa in San Jose with his eldest daughter, Norma Youngberg. We then proceeded to look for affordable lodgings in the city. Although our parents had assigned rooms in a respectable hotel, they readily gave them up for the sake of all the indigents surrounding them.

Accustomed to wringing blood out of turnips, Walt, along with Joan, canvassed the area for a cheap hotel within walking distance of the Civic Auditorium. They succeeded when they came upon the Bay Meadows Hotel on Mason Street. "It's only $2.00 per person a night!" they crowed.

Eleven passengers and two new Ford cars on the way from Massachusetts to San Francisco. On a hot day in Utah we stopped for ice cream.

We all went in to look at it. Nothing fancy, to be sure. Despite dirty carpets and creaky floors, however, the beds appeared clean. "Just be sure to wear your shoes all the time, if we stay here," my mother worried.

Uncle Len looked over the scene and said, "We'll all just move in here so we can be together." And so we did. Walt and I shared a two-room suite with my parents on the second floor. In between, stood the bathroom full of turn-of-the century fixtures. On the third floor, Uncle Len and Auntie May shared a similar space, with the four girls occupying the second room.

Thus established, we set off for the auditorium. The place was alive with thousands of people from all over the world. The sound of hundreds of different languages floated in the air. If you stood still long enough, you'd be sure to meet someone you knew. At every turn, great music filled the air. To Walt and me, this electrifying environment made the "do-it-yourself" realities of Newfoundland seem to be part of a distant and isolated world. The atmosphere was electrifying.

That first night, however, should have given us some clue as to the nature of our hotel situation as we walked back to Bay Meadows. I was too naïve, however, to figure out why at one place a slimy kind of man tried to drag me into a doorway while at the next a nasty girl would accost Walt. After dark, the whole street seemed oddly full of brassy-looking people lurking in the shadows.

"We must all be sure to stick together," Uncle Len advised. Actually, the ten of us moving forward in a body could well have intimidated at least some would-be assailants. Most of us were near (or over) six feet tall. Even Auntie May, the shortest one, stood at 5 feet 7 inches.

I am not sure exactly how Phase Four began for Walt and me there in San Francisco. Perhaps it was from watching all the people from overseas. Having grown up just about everywhere else except in the United States, I subconsciously found the idea of a mission appointment attractive. Having never been abroad yet, Walt may not have thought much about the possibility.

We fell into that profound spiritual ambience that a General Conference session can generate. True, Newfoundland had been a mission. No one could argue that point. What I had in mind, however, had to do more with palm trees and beaches, and—above all—warm weather.

Perhaps it was when Walt met Lloyd Reile, a former Canadian acquaintance, now an officer in the Inter-American Division. Or maybe it was when I spoke to Elder W. P. Bradley, someone from my childhood days in Singapore.

By the 1950s the "Seven Little Australians" had finally grown up. Whenever and however they met, they would line up for the prescribed oldest-to-youngest photograph. L-R. Kelvin, Dorothy, Joan, Yvonne, Valmae, Leona, Eileen.

I asked him outright, "What should we do, if we wanted an overseas mission appointment?"

Somehow all of these elements combined, and by mid-week, something remarkable had begun to happen. Would we be interested in going to the Cayman Islands? We hunted up a map, and there they were, three dots just south of Cuba and diagonally northwest of Jamaica. We'd never heard of them before. As mission president, Walt would have the management of six little churches. I would be principal of a two-room, ten grade school.

Would we go? Of course. In our new role as mission appointees, we participated in the Mission Pageant at the last weekend. With an unaccustomed show of emotion, Walt seized my hand, tears in his eyes. Together we stood while Charles Brooks sang what forever became a favorite song of ours, "So Send I You." Overnight our lives accelerated into high speed.

Firstly, we had yet to get out of San Francisco. For the last weekend of the session Kelvin and the family of his bride-to-be, Joanie Lonergan, came up from the Loma Linda School of Medicine to join us. At $2.00 a night, Dr. Lester Lonergan had no trouble providing a room for himself and another for his son Tad and Kelvin. Yvonne joined her sisters.

Although Friday night passed with a relatively small increase of noise in the hotel, Saturday night was different. A company of sailors off a newly arrived ship rolled in and soon had themselves resoundingly drunk. We locked our doors and went to bed, trying to ignore the turmoil around us.

At 3 a.m., however, we awoke to a frantic knocking at our door. Uncle Len stood there in his bathrobe, pale, wide-eyed and trembling. I'd never seen him so distraught. "We've got to get out of here. Right now!"

"What's wrong?" Dad joined us at the door. Uncle's agitation aroused fearful possibilities in all of our minds.

"The girls! They're … they're not safe."

It turned out that upon hearing a scuffle in the hall, Joan and Uncle Len had simultaneously opened their doors, which stood at right angles. There they saw one of the drunken sailors, naked as a jailbird. He thought he'd arrived at the rest room. Obviously he found it confusing when the walls moved, so he desperately tried to hold both doors shut at the same time. Then he did his best to accomplish the task for which he'd come.

Walt and Dorothy had their first formal portrait together just before leaving for their first overseas assignment in the Cayman Islands.

"And … and," Uncle stuttered, "he just stood there doing … doing his wee!"

"Where is he now?" Walt inquired.

"Well, he went back down the hall, I guess." Still much agitated, Uncle Len wanted to leave the hotel immediately. Dad and Walt, however, persuaded him that packing up the family and leaving at that time of night would be virtually impossible. "We'll get out early in the morning," they promised.

The next morning, as planned, we did indeed leave Bay Meadows. For reasons no one ever understood, we learned that Dr. Lonergan patronized the hotel again, the very next time he had to go to San Francisco. Regardless of present inconvenience, he believed that every dime saved could and should be sent to the mission-field. Hence, Bay Meadows was a deal!

Uncle Len and his family went south to California for two weddings.

Kelvin and Joanie Lonergan, followed by Joan and Ron Neall. Of course, I wanted to be there, but Walt and I now had a pressing schedule of our own in preparation for going to the Caribbean.

Meanwhile, Mum, Dad, Grandpa and Eileen headed back to Massachusetts. "We're going to sleep in beds this time," Dad confided in me. "My meat is just getting too old to lay under cactus bushes at night." Bless him! He'd more than fulfilled his obligations to the family.

What would have been a leisurely family visit to Walt's home places in Western Canada now became a "we're-not-going-to-see you-again-for-a-long-time" kind of encounter.

Thus Phase Five began for us. Before heading north to Alberta, we drove south to see Walt's sister Martha in San Diego, California, where her husband was a prosperous lawyer. For me, the sight of the California palm trees and the smell of mild ocean breezes became a prelude to what was to come. A few weeks hence Walt would also understand the charm of the tropics.

Afterwards, in rapid succession, we saw cousins in Portland, old friends at Canadian Union College (where we'd met just three years earlier). Brother Ben and more cousins in Leduc, and thence north into the Peace River District.

In this demanding but fertile farming country the frigid climate and short growing season literally dared you to plant and harvest your crops successfully. I looked at the enormous combines and other farm equipment. Work never stopped, day or night. Crops and weather dominated all conversation. I watched the women turn out huge, marvelous meals—sometimes five times a day—to meet the needs of husbands, fathers, sons and farm hands. Because in mid-summer the sun never really set, I found that our visiting days stretched out almost beyond physical endurance.

For the first time, I met the whole big crop of in-laws. Mostly I looked and listened. Really, I couldn't have done any of the things that the women around me were able to accomplish. Worse still, I didn't want to learn! Despite everyone's cordiality, I often felt alien. Here, however, Walt was no longer the pastor I knew. Oh yes, he preached in church, but he was now thoroughly at home. To be sure, he'd left the farm. But I instinctively realized two things: First, the farm would never leave him, and, second, it could never really include me.

In due course, we headed back east to Newfoundland. Much work to do. One of the first needs was to get physical examinations and secure medical clearances. Neither of us had seen much of physicians up to that time.

At random, we picked a doctor in St. John's. When my turn came, I gave him the sheaf of forms that the General Conference wanted to have filled out in detail.

It's a good thing that we were young, or the results might have become self-destructive. I sat across the desk from him while he filled out the papers. "Do you want to go to this place … er … the Cayman Islands?"

"Yes," I replied.

"Okay, then. You look pretty good to me." He scrawled an illegible signature on the bottom line and shoved the papers back across the desk.

More than glad to escape, I never stopped to consider that I might have any hidden medical problem waiting to derail me. At the time, I didn't know the difference.

I noticed, however, that he'd credited me with 20/20 vision, and I wondered about that. He never even bothered with a chart-test. Eight years later (on another General Conference-induced medical examination) the doctor

Preparation for transferring to the Caribbean included Walt's visit back to his home in the farm country of the Peace River District, Alberta, Canada.

told me I should have been wearing glasses since I was four years old. That one sent me to an ophthalmologist (an old college classmate) who promptly put me into glasses with a weird prescription for severe astigmatism. It was only then that I began to figure out what the world really looked like.

Our next concern was our little house, already under snow-laden spruce trees by the time we got home. We'd been in it for just eight months. As it turned out, we possessed only two things of any value—the piano that I had acquired only a few weeks earlier and the new car. Everything else reverted to its original state as packing crates or to the junk pile whence much of it had originally derived.

Friends rallied around in so many, many ways. For instance, Fred Garland the cobbler, dear fellow, had spent hours—just a few weeks back—helping Walt paint the house. Now he said, "I want you to give me all of your shoes. Every pair." A week later we found them lined up on our doorstep, gleaming with polish and solid with new soles that would endure for years to come.

I closed out my teaching duties, and Walt finished his church responsibilities. Together, we did our last broadcast on Station VOAR. We packed all of the stuff worth saving into a couple of crates, staying up the whole of the last night to accomplish the task.

Most importantly, we'd found a buyer for our lovely sky-blue Ford, still factory-fresh. Walter Gryzbowski was a schoolteacher whom we knew slightly. Eccentric to a degree, he had recently married a fellow teacher. Now he promised to get the money out of his bride's bank account over in Corner Brook.

He took the car on a test drive down the main street of St. John's. He barely had control of the machine. "Have you ever driven a car before," Walt inquired anxiously.

"I have driven a tractor," Gryzbowski muttered as he swerved through another intersection amid a blast of angry car horns. Thankful to still be alive, Walt disembarked back at the Mission Office. Together, we watched our beautiful new car lurch down the hill and out of our lives.

On that last day in St. John's we dispatched our boxes to Tampa, Florida, where they would be picked up for shipment to Grand Cayman. As for ourselves, we were to take the train across the island, ferry over to Nova Scotia and the train again down to Massachusetts. That would conclude our month of family time before shipping out to the Caribbean.

Having enjoyed a bountiful lunch at the Moores' home that day, Walt and Phil left for the bank to collect the car money. They then would proceed directly to the train station. Doris Moores promised to see me and our luggage to the railway station for the 5 pm departure. It seemed like a plan that should work.

When I arrived at the station platform with my party of ladies, we had thirty minutes to spare. An amazing sight greeted us. Every member of the church and every kid out of the school seemed to be on hand to see us off. Indeed, a numberless sea of people stood between me and the waiting train.

Almost three years in the role of the young minister's wife should have accustomed me to public, "generic" kissing. Still, I faced the crowd with a sinking heart. All of the old ladies and several of the old men kissed me. I lost count.

Then my tall, gawky high school boys came on in a wave. "We never had a chance to do this before," they chortled. The girls clung to me back, side, and front. Slowly and clumsily the whole mass of people surged forward toward the train. At last, I managed to scramble aboard to where the mystified conductor stood, assessing the scene.

But Walt! Where was he? In the approved Old German style, he always managed everything. I was on the train, with the sickening realization that I had no tickets and no money. "My husband is going to be here." I looked at the conductor humbly. "Could you just hold the train for a minute or two?"

"Well," he replied, "perhaps we can wait a little." Good!

"Thank you. You are very kind." We both waited, looking out over the mass of well-wishers, filling the entire platform and beyond. Still, Walt didn't come.

"Ah, ma'am." The

Walt and Dorothy had to give up their spanking-new blue Ford the day they left Newfoundland for the Caribbean.

man's voice was both compassionate and business-like. "We really do have to leave. It's ten minutes past five."

I nodded dumbly. Considering the long hours lying ahead, I thought it could hardly matter whether the train was ten or thirty minutes late, could it? In despair, I considered what would become of me, a beleaguered young woman with barely enough credibility to identify herself, let alone pay for anything. Slowly the train began to move, the waving shouting crowd shifting, at first imperceptibly, to my right.

Then, oh joy, there he was! Walt had just appeared on the outermost edge of the multitude. Like a hockey-player body-checking people left and right, he crashed through the crowd. No one kissed him, but everyone shouted with relief. The train was moving rather smartly off the end of the platform when he swung himself aboard. Too weak to move, I stood trembling there at the door, just at looking at St. John's city pulling away to the east.

For at least six miles the highway paralleled the railway tracks. Suddenly an entourage of four cars appeared, keeping pace alongside the train. Out of every window hung teenagers, screaming and waving goodbye, arms flailing like windmills. Just kissing hadn't been enough for them..

We stood at the door for a while, trying to compose ourselves. Actually, we waited until we passed Mount Pearl Park. For the last time, we saw our square little house there in the woods by the track. By then, I calmed down and normal sensations began to return. Wrung out with tension, overcome with the drama of it all, and holding hands, we finally went into the coach to find our seats. All of those people cared that much? The thought completely overwhelmed us.

But we found our compartment completely occupied. We had nowhere to sit. Festively wrapped gifts were stacked on both seats and filled the floor in between. Those dear kids, their parents, and all of the others had come to the station early and left a stunning array of distinctively English presents—silver, bone china, crystal, chocolates, and much, much more. It took some time to look at them all. Lovely things that I always admired but never thought of buying for myself.

In the midst of our reorganization, I inquired, "You did get the car money, didn't you?'

"Yes." Walt heaved the last bag into the overhead rack. "Now we can buy a new, cheaper American model to take with us to Cayman."

Giving up the new blue Ford had caused a little twinge. Our first new car! Not as severe, however, as when three months later, a friend wrote from St. John's: "I hope you two don't have a sentimental attachment to your blue Ford any more. It's now got a tooled metal look at all four corners. No one will even enter the street if they see your car there. They just wait for Grizzy to move on."

Meanwhile, the conductor had been busying himself further down the carriage. When he saw that we had all of our gifts organized into bags and were finally sitting down, he came to look at our tickets. Eyeing us quizzically, he said, "Who are you anyway?"

Who indeed? I guess we'd never given the question much thought. We could have told him that we were going to live on a remote island in the West Indies for the next five years, but he wouldn't have understood.

For us, however, the evidence was in. One way and another, we must be "becoming somebody!"

CHAPTER 10

Exiled in Paradise

Our allotted time for visiting at home in Massachusetts passed more quickly than we could have imagined.

At leisure moments we tried to visualize the place where we were going, but no one seemed to know anything about the Cayman Islands, except that they were remote and lonely. The population of all three islands was less than 7,000, but there were six Seventh-day Adventist churches, five on the big island and one on Cayman Brac.

In San Francisco one of the General Conference officers had told us with enthusiasm, "Why it could be another Pitcairn Island, you know!" The whole country might come to be one church? A rather exotic, if visionary, notion that would fall rather short of the facts. Then he added, darkly, "I hope you two like each other, because when you get there you won't have anyone else."

During that unusual month in 1954, we savored all that we could of the late summer loveliness of New England. The leafy lanes and the stone walls. The roadside fruit and vegetable stands. The elegant homes standing discreetly back from the road. The steepled, white churches.

We visited old friends around the community, and more than once we went out to Kimballs' Farm, where they sold enormous servings of ice cream, in sundaes and banana splits. Customers were limited only by their ability to walk away from the counter. Of the ice-cream itself there was no end.

The five of us, Mum, Dad, Eileen and we about-to-be-missionaries (attended by the old family dog, Chips), sometimes sat out on the lawn in the evenings just being together. Storing things in our memory banks for later use. Instinctively we seemed to know that nothing would ever again be quite the same.

Walt and I had a rather heady experience with our "Outfitting Allowance." We shopped for who-knew-how-many months to come. I'd never before associated with money in quite such a lavish way. We bought extensively at Bill Hutchins' thrift store in a big garage behind his house on Mill Street. Because of his devotion to my Dad, he gave us below-thrift prices. I remember deliberating over a pale yellow blanket banded with delicate rows of flowers. "When are we ever going to need a blanket again," I mused. Yet, it was lovely and light, and I handed over the eight dollars that Bill was asking for it.

One day I bought two sets of bed sheets. As usual, the family gathered around to see what loot we'd acquired that day. Dad picked up one package of sheets. "What's this?" he sniffed. "They're '25% stronger'? Stronger than what?"

I understood immediately. I've inherited a large share of my father's aversion to illogical claims made in the name of commerce. "Stronger than tissue paper, maybe?" Dad tossed out his last sarcastic barb and set the offending sheets down.

We also bought a new Ford car, dark green and roomy, for $1,500. The American edition was so much cheaper than the Canadian that we, for once, did rather well on the deal.

Then, one early October day, just as the air was turning nippy and the trees were beginning their dress rehearsal for autumn splendor, we headed south to Florida, our possessions packed into the Ford. One of the last things to go in was Mum's old Singer sewing machine, a very old, hand-turned model that I'd grown up with in Singapore. She'd just purchased a new electric Brother machine, housed in a handsome cabinet. For me, on the other hand, I would be living with erratic electricity for the foreseeable future.

We arrived in Tampa on time to meet our appointment with the *Merco,* the chief cargo boat serving Georgetown, Grand Cayman at the time. Apart from a couple of modest crates, we had only two other items. We'd finally treated ourselves to the luxury of a refrigerator. Then, somewhere Walt found an old piano to add to our shipment. An antique and very heavy, the little piano wore a mottled varnish and had brass candleholders on the front. Everything else went into the car, packed to the windows and the roof. Somehow, back then, it never occurred to us that we might be robbed. I can't remember that we even thought much about insurance. Walt drove the car up onto the deck, locked the doors, pocketed the keys and came back down the gangplank.

The ship was a converted minesweeper from World War II. The ballast had been removed to provide cargo space. This gave the vessel an insane urge to roll, even in calm seas, and the trip around the west end of Cuba to Grand Cayman could be anything but calm. Later, we were to hear tales of certain cars that, in times of stress, had been pushed off the *Merco's* deck in order to save the ship.

During our brief stopover at the Inter-American Division office in Miami, the staff there handsomely entertained us. Here we were—young, eager and ignorant—off to one of the most difficult posts to fill in Central America.

Miami itself entranced me. The smell and humidity of the tropics was a throwback to Singapore. The palm trees, the bougainvillea, and the beaches! 'Twas everything that Newfoundland was not. For the first time in four years, I believed, I was actually going to be warm. For Walt, everything was new. He'd never before been anywhere overseas.

The prosperous Cayman Islands of today and those of 1954 have to be

Boarding the LACSA (DC-3) plane to fly from Miami, Florida, to Grand Cayman (1954).

seen in perspective. Therefore, what follows must be understood simply as a page out of history.

In due course, Walt and I were convoyed to Miami Airport to board the once-a-week flight to Georgetown, Grand Cayman. For this momentous transition point in our lives, we wanted to look our best. I wore a rather daring, sleeveless, full-skirted

dress, white with little navy polka dots. A stole of the same fabric (with navy lining) modestly covered my shoulders. A spotless (new) pair of white sandals,

An aerial photograph of contemporary Grand Cayman, with five cruise ships at anchor. It lies in the curve of the horizon, as it always has, but the pristine coral shores are now almost completely submerged in modern land development.

a white handbag and small navy-blue hat completed the ensemble. (The latter, despite my passionate aversion to hats.) The minister's wife was going to do her best here. I've never since been so well turned out for a plane flight. Having left his felt hat along with the rest of our Newfie winter clothes in storage in Massachusetts, Walt looked pretty dapper too in his new tropical gray suit.

It took almost three hours for the DC-3 to creep over the Florida Keys and Cuba and to find the hook-shaped island of Grand Cayman. Planes had been known, from time to time, not to find the island and to just keep going to Costa Rica. Rimmed with white beaches, the "hook" lay below us in a turquoise pool of ocean.

Suddenly the water gave way to the rough runway of Owen Roberts Field. We landed, and the tail of the DC-3 flopped down like a tired dog waiting for a bone. All of the way I'd been watching through cracks in the skin of the aircraft, feeling little gusts of high-altitude air. Now we descended the sloping aisle and stood at the door of the plane, blinded by the brilliant sunshine on the white marl landing strip and consumed by a blast of sultry midday heat.

We could not know at the time, of course, but the airstrip was very new.

Previously Grand Cayman's only air connection with the outside world was a sea plane that landed, from time to time, in North Sound.

There stood our welcoming party, under the thatch-roof shelter. George and Rose Merren headed the delegation. Descended from some of Cayman's first inhabitants (ship-wrecked English sailors from the early 1800s), the Merren family played a large part in the business community in Georgetown. Indeed, the *Merco,* bearing all of our worldly goods belonged to them.

As head elder of the Georgetown church, George Merren carried much responsibility, especially during the not-infrequent times when the Cayman Islands Mission lacked a president. A lively, blonde little man, George dispatched us to town in Sunbeam's taxi, one of the few private cars on the island. Walt and I sat in the back seat, as we rattled over the two miles of rutted, white marl road to the Merren's house.

Sunbeam herself was a cheerful, talkative driver, obviously pleased with the new passengers she'd acquired. The windows of the car were inoperable, leaving us open to sea breezes and dust. The rusted body shook at every joint, and I remember seeing little by way of interior upholstery. We had to place our feet carefully to avoid stepping into the large holes in the vehicle's floor. In a kind of daze, I looked down, watching the road rush by between my white shoes.

Situated behind their store, the only real department store on the island, Merrens' house was, of itself, another world. Built with every convenience for the tropics, it was also very English. We sat down to a Caribbean meal served in crystal and bone china. Every detail had been thought of. Even the mashed potatoes had been dyed blue to match the dish in which they were served. The Merren daughters, Mary and Betty Lou, were strikingly attractive young ladies. Betty, as we would learn, was still enough of a teenager to have plenty of mischief left in her. In this company, the deficiencies of Sunbeam's taxi drifted far away.

Within walking distance (the capital city was then very small) we found the house that had been rented for us. The large rambling home belonged to a sea captain, Lawrence Bodden. Across the road was the Adventist church and to the left the Town Hall, fronted by a monument commemorating the visit of King George V. A block further on was the General Post Office, and beyond that the business section of town on Church Street.

Over an embankment of jagged coral rocks, the town faced the sea and the short wharf at which the *Merco* docked once a month. Further along the waterfront, the ruins of Fort George recalled the days when pirates of the Spanish Main had once secreted their loot on this flat,

In 1954 the airport terminal at Owen Roberts Field in Grand Cayman was not quite ready yet to receive tourists. *(Photo courtesy of Mary Lawrence)*

infertile coral island. A blight had destroyed all of the coconut trees. The impossibility of any real farming activity had rendered much of the island the habitat of women and children, the men having long gone to sea to earn a living. A Caymanian sailor or ship-builder, however, even today, is a skilled person to reckon with.

Always in love with the water, I delighted in the beaches of Cayman. After the long, gray winter days of Newfoundland, the brilliance of the sky, the sea, and the shoreline was incredible. Indeed, unless you've seen Seven-Mile Beach, between Georgetown and West Bay, you really haven't seen a beach at all. Now completely clogged with hotels and resorts, those seven miles of sugar-white sand sloping off into the utterly transparent, turquoise water was then completely open.

Walt and I had very little personal recreation. The loud dance hall nearby, nicknamed (appropriately) the "Bucket of Blood," was hardly an option! But how we loved the beach. In the late afternoon we had it to ourselves. Beyond the shore the water turned turquoise, then blue, then indigo as it approached Bartlett's Deep. There the coral shelf drops off into one of the deepest spots in the ocean, anywhere in the world.

In Cayman Walt had to learn to swim. To be sure, his childhood on a farm in northern Canada had given him no opportunity to learn the art.

Although he never got beyond dog paddling, he was strong, secure and confident. Therefore, he became good at snorkeling and diving for shells.

The primeval brightness of the sun shafting the water enabled us to see schools of silver fish swimming with us, to say nothing of the occasional stingray. The latter never failed to make us jump, as the big undulating "umbrella" slithered right under our feet, staring up at us with unblinking eyes. I never wanted to leave the beach until the sun had dropped into the ocean. Sometimes we watched it go down with a passing ship silhouetted in its flaming circle.

Within a few weeks, we made a home out of the house that we shared with crabs, frogs and termites. We even acquired a young tabby cat that we called Tigger. Short for Tiglath-Pileser, the ancient Assyrian king, and not to be confused with Winnie-the-Pooh's friends.

A verandah surrounded our house on three sides. A straight path led from the front gate, up the steps, into the house and right through to the back, where a lean-to kitchen had been attached as a kind of after-thought. While the termite-eaten floors had been freshly painted, the termites were, obviously having their way. Four large rooms, two on a side and all opening onto the

The Pathfinder group in front of the old Georgetown Church was very active, with ages ranging all the way from juniors to the "20-somethings."

verandah, made up the main living quarters—living room with wicker furniture to the left, our bedroom to the right.

Our light, airy bedroom opened to the verandah on two sides. It was full of antique furniture that would be worth a fortune on the market now. In lieu of a bedstead, our mattress lay on its own packing crate.

After breakfast, our first morning, I returned to the bedroom to finish dressing. There, in front of the bowlegged vanity table stood a little boy, about eighteen months old. His happy little brown face grinned up at me, and he seemed completely at ease with the fact that he had no pants on. He'd come from the house across the street where a mother and daughter appeared to be raising a large flock of children alone. I was soon to discover that those women (and some other neighbors) saw no point in diapers. The task of putting them on, taking them off and washing them—I suppose the cycle seemed illogical. So none of their children wore pants until they became worthy of them. Thereafter, I made a point of latching the screen doors. Clearly crabs, children, and frogs—anything—could otherwise come in at will.

Walt set up his study behind the living room. An uncut piece of plywood bridged two filing cabinets for a desk. Although the mission office functioned in a tiny room at the back of the church, much of what went on for the churches had to happen in this room. Our "duplicating service" consisted of a tray full of jelly that somehow—very slowly—produced copies for both the church and the school use. I knew about mimeograph machines because back home at Atlantic Union College, my mother operated the Duplicating Department there. The possibility of a Xerox machine, however, was pure science fiction for us. Indeed, we knew nothing whatever about it. No one else on the island did either. We had no telephone. That went without saying.

The second bedroom was merely a passage into the dark little bathroom, which someone had created out of one end of the verandah. The facilities there were barely functional. Walt had to get up early to use his electric razor because we had electricity only from 5 to 8 a.m. and 6 to 9 p.m. each day. Even that was not a sure thing. Sometimes he would get half his face shaved with electricity and then had to finish up the other side with a razor and soap.

The same uncertainty prevailed everywhere. Actually, the electricity could go off at any time. When it did, you might be without service for an hour, a day, or a week. Who could tell? Hurricane season, we discovered, added even more anxiety to the situation.

At the back door stood our entire water supply, a large, roofed cement cistern. The early morning task was to pump water up into a forty-gallon drum on top of the roof. Grateful that the laws of gravity do work, we then had running water in the bathroom. A colony of frogs lived in the cistern, singing lustily by day and by night. From time to time, as the elder frogs passed on to their reward, we had to scoop them out of the water. We took care, of course, always to boil our frog-flavored water for drinking. We did so on the smoky, kerosene stove in the kitchen-shed. Really it was the only appliance that the kitchen had.

The first night we slept in the Georgetown house we discovered that the wooden walls were alive with hermit crabs. They picked up shells on the beach and then wandered about the island searching for a place to park themselves. A large family of them lived with us. As they tramped about their business, they made enough noise to provide a percussion section for a large band.

On our first night in Georgetown, a public meeting was held in the church. Some people came from afar on the back of trucks, others on bicycles, and many more walked. These were our parishioners, bless them. We could not have felt more welcome. As for the General Conference man who said we'd be alone—how very wrong he was.

Every age, every color, every financial situation was represented among them. The women were well dressed, but not because they bought things off a rack at the store. No, nothing like that. I was to find that West Indian women are among the best seamstresses in the world.

George Merren concluded the gathering by looking Walt and me in the eye and saying: "We just want you stay here with us in Cayman until Jesus comes!"

At the time, we could not imagine the implications of that statement. But surely He'd come very soon! So we said, "Yes, we hope so too."

CHAPTER 11

Settling into the Task

Because our freight shipment hadn't arrived from Tampa yet, we lived for the first month with the barest of essentials.

Nonetheless, we immediately found ourselves hosting guests. The Merrens had lent us two table-settings, plus one kettle, one bowl and one pan. For just the two of us, this equipment was perfectly adequate. Entertaining company, however, called for some ingenuity. Two Jamaicans came first, Pastors Stockhausen and Haig, president and secretary, respectively, at mission headquarters in Mandeville. Send them to the local hotel? Go out to eat at a restaurant? Not a chance.

We contrived two beds for them in our second so-called bedroom. That room was oddly situated with three doors—to the hall, to our room, and to the bathroom. No matter where you came from, you had to stumble over the bodies of visitors, literally, in order to reach the bathroom.

For the first day, I decided to make potato salad as the staple of the first meal I served. It could be prepared in stages, and I could wash each utensil as I went along.

I set the table with care, giving our guests the two plates and the two forks. I put the knives by the bread (in the pan) in the middle of the table for common use. With the two spoons, Walt ate out of the kettle and I out of the lid of the kettle. No one seemed to mind. I remember the conversation as being very warm and lively. The two men had come all the way over to Cayman to welcome us and to introduce us to our congregation. We immediately felt part of a wonderful West Indian family, a bond that has never been severed.

In due course, the *Merco* arrived with our freight. In high anticipation, we stood on the dock watching our car being hoisted off the deck. Everything in tact, just as we'd left it in Tampa. At the time, we didn't know enough to have been worried.

Now, suddenly, the old house filled with great luxuries. The fridge stood by the dining room table. If we never opened it during the hours when the electricity was off, it functioned quite well, thanks to the thick insulation installed by the Crosley Company. It never fully recovered, however, from being laid down flat on its back at some point in its southward journey. It was ever after prone to erupting in thick patches of ice in unexpected places. Whenever they appeared, these "tumors" of ice had to be scraped off quickly, without compromising the overall cooling functions of the refrigerator.

If we timed it right, we could make toast in the morning and hear the news from the outside world. We set our shortwave radio and toaster handily side by side on the table.

The little old piano took its place by the living-room arch and became the centerpiece for the Saturday-night gatherings of young as well as older people. Kind of an ongoing "social" began and never really ended. The games, singing and fun drowned out even the hermit crabs. We lovingly unpacked our books and lined them up on the shelves that Walt made out of the packing crates. Nearby we set up our portable Royal typewriter.

In addition to Saturday night socializing we sponsored at least two week-long beach campouts for the young people. We'd learned well in Newfoundland. The idea was new in Cayman and was joyfully accepted not only by the young but also by many of the not-so-young. Communal living and eating, crafts and games, worship and counseling—all beside one of the loveliest seascapes in the world. It was well worth the extra effort.

Immediately, I began teaching in the schoolhouse behind the church. Gleeda Forbes had been holding the project together for years. She retained the lower grades. Her little pupils came in clean white shirts, slates in hand, and sat on the benches in front of her. Black eyes shining, they waited for the drills.

The other room for the older students (Grades 7 to 10) was mine. The rickety double desks were too small for some of the older students, but zeal made up for deficiencies. We had exercise books instead of slates, plus a small square of blackboard. That made us somewhat elite, I think.

We had picked up an old Remington typewriter in Tampa, along with an instruction book. I cleared out a small closet off my classroom, and we put it in there. I created a key-chart and fastened it on the wall above the typewriter. One by one, kids went there for typing class. I wonder how many of them are somewhere today sitting at their computers? Do they remember how and where they first learned the keyboard?

Always practical, Walt serviced the two typewriters himself, both of which suffered in the humid climate. He always began by dunking them, whole, into a bucket of gasoline. Then he oiled and lovingly tended their inner parts until they were good as new. Even the ancient Remington.

Likewise, he serviced our car too. As the newest vehicle on the island, our Ford aroused universal interest. Unintentionally, we'd surpassed in newness even the transportation of Sir Hugh Foote over at Government House. It served primarily as the "Mission Bus," carrying smaller groups here and there when the hiring of a lorry (truck) wouldn't have been necessary.

Although we retained our Massachusetts plates, we had to

Top left. Small as Grand Cayman was, the beautiful Seven-Mile Beach was wide open for weekend campouts. The young people gathered for morning reveille around the flag. Bottom left. Games and swimming on the beach (in front of the tents). Above. Tasty meals came out of this outdoor kitchen.

Trips to Cayman Brac required an overnight boat trip until this little Cessna service began. Several times Walt traveled with this pilot who virtually flew by a pocket compass.

apply for Cayman driver's licenses. The presiding official asked us if we knew how to drive. We solemnly promised that we did and were given our documents forthwith. Later, we discovered that he himself didn't know how to drive. Driving American vehicles on the (British) left side of the road made the whole transportation situation more fluid and flexible than one would have liked anyway.

In such a leisurely place a road test would of itself have been rather fruitless. The main road (unpaved) went from West Bay, at the top of the "hook" and down to Georgetown. Then it turned east through Savannah, Boddentown, and on through a field of dead coral tossed up in the storms to East End—a distance of barely thirty miles. In places two cars couldn't pass, and stray cattle and chickens roamed the roads.

In Boddentown old guns from pirate ships interspersed the straggling fences. Everywhere, friendly people greeted us from their sandy front yards. Women kept the grounds around their cottages colorfully neat, sweeping the sand clean and lining the paths and flowerbeds with pink-lipped conch shells.

Two other hazards of the Cayman roads were the mosquitoes and the crabs. The mosquitoes used to come in a solid pack. More than one cow inhaled enough of them to kill herself. Today, grateful Caymanians will tell you that the man who began mosquito-control is worthy of sainthood. At that time, however, the work of Dr. Marco Giglioli of London was still eleven years in the future.

In season, huge dark crabs would cross the road, each one of them big enough to provide a meal for three. No way to avoid them. I recall all too well the sound of their demise—one great "splat" after another. A round trip from Georgetown to East End and back could result in more than 100 deaths as the car rolled over them.

Left. The little cargo ship *Merco*, at the pier in Georgetown, Grand Cayman. A converted minesweeper, it belonged to the H. O. Merren Company and used to link the island with the outside world. Right. The Comms' new 1954 Ford was heaved off the *Merco* by simple manpower. When the family moved to Jamaica two-and-a-half years later, the car spent the rest of its days on the white marl island roads, until it died.

Very quickly we recognized that fresh food was going to be as precious as manna. Once a month the *Merco* came in with eggs, fresh vegetables and fruit. For a few days we'd eat like royalty, and then it would all be over. I couldn't consider throwing away a single limp carrot or an over-ripe banana. Constantly, I had to think of what I could do with it to make it edible. I kept these things almost until they became toxic.

Meanwhile, at Merren's store we could buy every kind of packaged and canned food imaginable. Could we have eaten the fish, crabs and green turtle, so readily available, life would certainly have been simpler. Instead, we stuck by our decision to be vegetarian.

One day, after many months of lacking fresh food, Walt discovered a banana boat from Honduras at the dock. Over-excited, he brought home a whole stalk of green bananas. Almost breathless with anticipation, we hung it from a crossbeam in the kitchen shed and waited. Suddenly all of the bananas began to ripen at once, some 200 of them. We gorged ourselves, we gave them away, but we still couldn't keep up.

About that time Pastor Stockhausen came by on another visit. "What you want to do," he explained, "is to dry them."

"You mean so they get like black, rubbery 'cigars'?" I asked. I remembered how I loved the dried bananas we got in England after World War II.

"Yes. That was part of my family's business. We sent dried bananas to England during the war."

How small the world, after all! "But how do I do it?" I hadn't the faintest idea.

"In the sun," he replied. So Walt made an open, flat box with a screen over it. Then Alan Stockhausen, Union President, helped me peel the bananas and lay them in the box. We set it out on the cistern to soak up the sun. "Now, you just turn them over every day."

After a couple of days they looked pretty gooey and depressing. Then, behold, they transformed themselves into the sweet, exotic, chewy fruit that I'd loved as a kid in England.

Our close proximity to the Town Hall provided us with a breadth of cultural education that we otherwise might have missed. In addition to the regular activities that one might expect in a town hall, there were rather frequent weddings there.

Just as Newfoundland girls could not give birth to illegitimate babies in the regular hospitals, pregnant brides could not be married in the Established (Presbyterian) Church in Cayman. The

Left. The Turtle Crawl, North Sound, Grand Cayman (1955) Right. Evans Myles pulled a giant green turtle out of the Turtle Crawl. When Christopher Columbus sighted the islands in 1503, he named them "Las Tortugas" because of the vast quantities of sea turtles he saw on the beaches. (The Cayman Islands were named by Sir Francis Drake when he landed there in 1586—after the local *caiman* ["alligator"]).

Left. Once released, a turtle headed back into the water—to live another day. Right. Trussed up with holes bored in his flippers wired to keep them together, this turtle is carried to the dock to board ship. Lying on their backs and gasping for air for days, he and others would stay alive for the voyage. Their destination? Turtle soup.

clergy would, however, officiate in the Town Hall.

Few West Indians would settle for a small or private marriage ceremony, no matter what the circumstances. In fact, if they couldn't make the event altogether magnificent, they would not have it at all. Moreover, the women of the Caribbean have an above-average sense of high fashion. As a result, we witnessed spectacular wedding parties issuing forth from the Town Hall, the brides sometimes being very great with child but still clad in breathtakingly lovely white gowns.

One skeptical thought did occur to me. Here was a new opportunity for designers in *haute couture*—the creation of maternity bridal gowns. I recognized the basic impracticality of that notion, however, and said nothing. Instead, I settled for the more mundane and humane: You just have to make the best of whatever life hands you.

Early on I made a good friend, Cynthia Banks. She was only slightly younger than my twenty-five years. She'd been to college in Jamaica but had returned home to care for her mother. "Let me help you in the house. You're so busy with the church and the school."

Help? What a marvelous thought. But how would I pay her. It turned out that she didn't care how little the pay would be. "I'm living at home. I just want to be with you."

What a godsend she was, and how many happy hours of girl-talk we had. I remembered again. That man who said that Walt and I would have no one in Cayman except ourselves was altogether wrong.

Suddenly the laundry, ironing, cleaning all got done, leaving me more time to help Walt in the nightly meetings in the various churches. The little portable organ rode constantly in the car trunk. I walked miles, pumping on the bellows and coaxing hymn tunes out of that hard little box. As for Cynthia's cooking, she made West Indian dishes that I still long for today but seldom taste. Like cassava cake and tangy rice-and-peas.

On one occasion, a sophisticated overseas visitor registered astonishment. "You mean she sits with you at the table to eat?"

"Well, of course. She's not a servant. She's my friend."

"But it doesn't look good. You shouldn't allow it."

Befuddled by such a colonial attitude, I decided to do as I pleased in my house. No one else has ever complained to me. I made sure that Cynthia—to the day she died many years ago—never knew that the question had been raised.

Also near my age, Mary Merren was another good friend and assistant in many projects, though she was often kept busy in her family's store. Sometimes she sat in the little brass cage in the middle of the room, the focal center of the whole business operation.

At that time, Grand Cayman lacked even the most basic of "girl things." Ever since my mother had so mercilessly cut my hair short when I was a kid in Singapore, I had this real emotional need to keep long hair. right up until the time when a decent old age overtook me. Considering the unbelievably thick crop of hair I've always had, this was a rather troublesome taste. Unlike present trends, straight hair was not then acceptable. When I'd had a permanent back in Corner Brook, the poor, unsuspecting girl in the salon had no idea what she'd let herself in for. The two of us sat together from four o'clock in the afternoon until almost midnight.

Now Mary, with more generosity than any real knowledge of what lay ahead of her, gave me my first perm in Cayman. I ended up spending the better part of the whole day at Merren's house, and Mary used two complete perm kits. We could only while away the hours chatting.

George Merren, for all his business sense and zeal for church affairs, however, was quite inept in practical matters. One day he wobbled through our gate on his bicycle. The handlebars were twisted around backwards, and he almost fell off on our verandah steps. "Look what Betty Lou did to my bicycle." Anxiety furrowed his usually cheerful face. "Can you fix it?" He looked at Walt in great distress.

It took but a moment to put things right. Walt gave the wrench an extra turn. "I think she'll have a hard time moving that now."

Although we had friends in every church and in most of the village stores, we always craved news from home. Nothing could change that. Mum and Dad were faithful correspondents. Walt's family checked in less often, but he still loved news from the farm. The Alberta boy had left the farm. I already knew. But the farm never ever left him. In a hundred ways I could read it in him.

Letters reached us once a week, so long as the LACSA flight came through. Surface mail arrived on the *Merco* once a month. Walt would haul the huge mailbag in, dump it on the living room floor, and we'd sit up far into the night reading magazines, newspapers, and stale letters from people who hadn't found out yet about airmail.

Our two-and-a-half years in Cayman provided us with "ministry" experiences for which no one could have prepared us. Shortly after our arrival, we started visiting two desperately ill church members. Although Silby Coe had tuberculosis, he didn't die until long after we left the island. Percy Ally was different. He lived in a ramshackle little house not far from our place. He was bedridden with a combination of leprosy and cancer. His house had leprosy too, of the kind I believe the Bible describes in Leviticus 14. The dank, dark walls were streaked with molds and growths of a kind I've never seen before or since. His screenless windows allowed air in but couldn't keep out those dense clouds of mosquitoes for which Cayman was then so notorious.

Always cheerful and grateful for our visits, poor Brother Ally himself lay ravaged by diseases, one working from the inside out and the other from the outside in. Faithful women of the church took turns attending him, dressing his wounds and keeping his bed amazingly white and clean. For them there must surely be great reward. Percy died only a few weeks after our arrival.

Before that, however, Walt had already conducted two funerals. The first was for a stranger from Honduras whom no one really knew. The church provided the burial. At the graveside, the two gravediggers—who otherwise were employed as stevedores on the dock—proved to be drunk. They hadn't made the hole long enough. As they jostled the coffin back and forth, we could hear the body thumping around inside. It just didn't work. The grave had to be lengthened. Down in the hole, the men started arguing, each believing that he was working harder than the other one. Having finally come to blows, they both suddenly leaped out of the grave and headed back to town. It remained for Walt and the men present to finish digging the hole and filling it in afterwards.

The next funeral hadn't been quite so ludicrous, but at the crucial moment of pronouncing "dust to dust," Walt fell on top of the coffin. The cemetery was necessarily near the beach. You couldn't dig into the coral, which is what the island is made of. So, just at the last moment, the sand pile on which he was standing gave way, and he skidded down into the grave. Georgie Merren grabbed him by the arm just as his feet hit the coffin-lid.

During our time in Cayman we left the island only on infrequent and carefully specified occasions. Work always had to come first. Our initial trip to Jamaica was to attend the Union Session in the mountains of Mandeville. We couldn't know, of course, that we were previewing our next home.

Just before our second Christmas we received a fat envelope containing two air-tickets to Boston. "These," Dad wrote, "are a gift from Bill Hutchins. You are to come home for Christmas." The thought was so overwhelming that we were speechless. We'd never dreamed of such a happening in our simple little island lives and with our slim budget.

On December 23, 1955, however, we landed in Boston. As usual, Mum had thought of everything. She'd dug into our storage barrel and pulled out our winter coats, hats and gloves. She had them at the airport ready for us. Momentarily, it all felt fearfully like Newfoundland again.

That Christmas gave us all a particularly happy time. Family, friends, cousins, and a huge tree by the fireplace. It stood knee-high in presents. Of course, we all went over to see the Hutchins. Their tree was tastefully decorated, just in red, while ours was loaded haphazardly with every ornament the family had ever owned.

When we left, I remarked, "Hutchins didn't have one thing under their tree."

Dad smiled wryly. "You can't put Hammond organs and Cadillacs under a tree." That year my musically-gifted schoolmate, Ken Hutchins, received his first organ. To be sure, Bill Hutchins had become an outstanding businessman since his vacuum-cleaner days. But I didn't care. I loved all of the socks, books, and all the little economy things we had coming. It was, after all, more than enough just to be home.

Before we left the store I made a point of taking Mr. Hutchins aside. How does one say thank you for such a gift as he'd given our family." I started, and then my voice trailed off. "We just don't feel worthy of what you … "

Suspicious of sentiment, Bill clapped me on the shoulder. "Well, I don't know whether you two are worth it or not, but I know that your father is!"

Walt returned to Cayman ahead of me, giving me a few extra days with my family and my dear old dog Chips.

I arrived back on the island to find that he'd bought me a very special present. He knew that I really wanted a dog. Tigger the cat just wasn't enough.

So I found Mickey, a tiny, pedigreed Toy Manchester, kind of a very miniature Doberman. Walt had bought him in Miami and carried him home in his coat pocket. Mickey became a sort of mascot for all the youth events that we had. He went everywhere he could persuade us to take him. He especially enjoyed swimming at the Seven-Mile Beach. Coming home, he'd sit in the back window of the car, the salt drying on his glossy black hair. Although almost twice his size, Tigger had to respect the sassy pup.

Walt kept making trips to Cayman Brac to visit the church there. The little Cessna plane flew by sight and a pocket compass. I prayed for God's automatic pilot every time I saw him take off.

One morning there was a great dispute in the departure shed. Not only was the luggage weighed but also the passengers themselves. One rather hefty woman was told, "You can fly only if you leave your luggage behind."

"Not fair," she screamed. "Look at the people who aren't carrying any luggage. Look at the little people who have more luggage than I do!"

I could never fail to be fascinated with the earthiness of encounters like this. They made ordinary life in the outside world seem boring!

Our last summer in Cayman we took our vacation time in Florida, dividing our two weeks between a motel in Key Biscayne, near Miami, and another near Daytona Beach. My parents, sister Eileen, and her fiancé Roger Eckert, drove down from the north to spend time with us. We adapted well to playing Florida tourists. We got acquainted with Roger who liked to tow Eileen around the swimming pools in an inner-tube, calling her "The Faerie Queene."

Just before this vacation we'd received a potentially disturbing call. We were to go to West Indies College in Jamaica—Walt to the Religion Department and me to the chairmanship of the English Department. With pain we remembered Georgie Merren's prayer that we should stay in Cayman "until Jesus comes." Walt insisted that we should finish out our five-year term, at least. (At the same time, I couldn't help thinking how much I would enjoy teaching in a conventional school again.) So, we refused the call, at least three times.

When we arrived in Miami, however, the officers of the Inter-American Division virtually told us that we were not at liberty to refuse. That Jamaica represented a "larger need." That the people in Cayman would just have to accept the fact that we had to leave.

By the time we got back to Georgetown, we knew that we would have to move. Walt said, "I think we should both go to Cayman Brac for six weeks before we leave."

As it turned out, our time on the Brac was different from anything that had gone before it, and I was glad that we went.

We rented a tiny white cottage in a grove of coconut palms, between the beach and the high cliff that runs down the center of the island. The island must have been named by some Irish mariner, for *brac* is the Gaelic word for "bluff." Some of the loveliest shells I ever had in my collection came off that beach.

People lived near the beach but kept their gardens and cattle on top of the precipice. From time to time a cow committed suicide by falling off the cliff. Somehow, it seemed, no one had yet thought of fencing the "high pasture."

Left. During a six-week stay in Cayman Brac Walt and Dorothy drove this car, surely unique in the world. The green plywood body was built onto a Model T chassis and engine. Here, upon their departure, the new owner took possession—Anthony Leary (1956). Right. Only 45 people lived on Little Cayman at the time. Two fishermen opened pink conch shells for eager customers, declaring the meat to be delicious, even raw. Instead. Walt and Dorothy opted to swim with the sea turtles in the lovely lagoon.

We needed transportation, even for six weeks. Walt bought an old Model T Ford that had a homemade, green plywood body set on the chassis. It served us amazingly well, and we both rather enjoyed driving the old heap down the palm-lined trails.

No electricity, therefore no fan to alleviate the constant heat in the house. The little store in Stakes Bay had a generator, kept a refrigerator, and was, as it were, the Town Center. Actually, there was nowhere else we might have gone. Our big treat for Saturday night was to go there and each buy a single (very expensive) can of cold pear nectar. For some reason, no other flavor was available. To this day, whenever I drink a Kerns pear nectar, I am immediately back on the Brac, savoring my cold juice to the sound of the generator roaring outside of the door. Food being even more limited than usual, when we got back to Grand Cayman, we found that we'd each lost about twenty pounds.

One morning, we booked a ride with a local fisherman to go over to the island, Little Cayman. Even before the boat could be properly docked the people were scrambling to get their hands on the pink conch shells. They opened them right there on the beach, pulled out the big slimy snail, and ate it. This was the best dinner the island had to offer, but we had to decline their hospitality. Another food option was the big fat iguanas roaming the scrub brush.

No roads here. Only bicycles for the forty-five residents. While we were on the Brac, however, the unthinkable happened. There was actually a murder on Little Cayman. The killer was so unskilled, however, that he didn't get the body buried well enough. He left an arm sticking out of the sand. That was news enough to last a year, at least.

What was marvelous to us, however, was swimming in the lagoon of Owen Island, in the arm of Little Cayman. The fish and giant green turtles had seen so few humans that they swam along with us companionably while the red-eyed booby birds flew overhead, trying to dive-bomb us. That was a symbol of all that was so lovely and unspoiled in those islands fifty years ago.

Walt concluded our time on the Brac with a fairly large baptism. In the sea, as usual, he had to perform the rite gracefully between the crashings of the surf. People in the Brac church realized that this was a farewell visit. On our last evening, we boarded the *Caymania*, a lumber boat, while our friends stood waving on the dock. Tears on both sides.

We were the only passengers, and two crewmembers generously offered their cabin to us. No ventilation, discolored bits of underwear hanging about to dry, bed sheets used to the point of grayness. We found it to be rather much. Thanking the men for their hospitality, we went up on the deck to spend the night sleeping on the piles of lumber. A long, hard night, but it enabled us to be wide-awake and ready to see Georgetown rise over the horizon in the morning sun.

So, we began packing to leave. I

Walt and our highly pedigreed dog Mickey (Toy Manchester), Georgetown, Grand Cayman.

would fly to Jamaica to be with the English teacher whom I was replacing at the College. Esther Mote and her husband Roy were about to leave on furlough. Walt would come with our household goods aboard the *Caymania*.

Having the same pet quarantine as Britain, Jamaica would not allow us to bring Mickey into the country. He had to be sent home, solo, to live with Mum and Dad in Massachusetts. Losing him was, for me, one more cruel twist of the knife already lodged deep in my heart.

Our Caymanian parishioners clung to us, hoping for a reprieve. For a long time, we'd hoped that we could give a little more time to the islands. To no avail. Indeed, Pastor Stockhausen made a special trip to Georgetown to explain to everyone that our going was absolutely essential in the larger scheme of things. He promised that they would not be bereft of leadership for long. And they weren't.

Can you be heartbroken at leaving a place (and a dog) you've loved and, at the same time, be vibrantly eager to begin your college-teaching career? All at the same time? I was.

CHAPTER 12

Jamaica and Another Career Turnabout

I arrived on the campus of West Indies College just in time for graduation at the end of 1956. As I would learn in ensuing years, commencement always turned out to be a very grand occasion. Crowds of festively dressed people came from all over the island to swarm up and down the narrow road on the razorback-hilltop. The buildings all stood to the left, old wooden relics, except for the new auditorium flanked by classrooms, library and administrative offices.

Leftover slabs of pre-stressed concrete had been used to form a bench, at least 150 feet long. There, under the shade of the spreading poinciana trees, you could face the college buildings and watch campus traffic go by. Over time, this inviting leisure spot acquired the name of "The Seat of the Scornful." With the surging graduation crowd The Seat was more fully occupied than ever.

Also from there you could look down over the green valley with its comfortable homes scattered at polite distances from one another. Down the middle of it ran the airstrip for Earl Gardner's little Cessna plane, an emergency bit of transportation. If need be, he could take us off the mountaintop in a big hurry and get us down to Kingston.

In order to get the feel of my new work assignment, I missed none of the weekend events. For class night I sat with Esther Mote. Amid flowers and fanfare, we listened to speech after speech. The valedictorian, however, outdid them all. At the height of his oration, he proclaimed, "We must all have the turpentine of experience."

"What's that he said?" I turned to see Esther sitting with her head in her hands."I spent two hours going over his speech with him yesterday," she sighed. "And I thought we got all of that out. Now he put it back in."

"But what does he mean by the 'turpentine of experience'?" I asked, amazed. "Does he know what he means?"

"I don't know. Maybe. Maybe not." Esther leaned back in resignation as the loud "Amens" subsided and the declamation went on, full force.

That was when I realized that the challenge of teaching English in Jamaica would be different from anything I'd known before. It would not be so much a matter of searching for words to use. Rather it would be finding out how to stem the tide, to clarify the flow of language, and to direct it into coherent channels. Never before had I heard such vitality in language. Fascinating!

In due course, Walt arrived in Kingston. The *Caymania* brought him, our possessions and the five young people we'd brought to college with us from Cayman: Linford Pierson, James Innis, and Pearldean Jeffers went into the dormitories. Patsy Manderson and Francine Haylock, our West Indian foster daughters, lived with us in our new little two-bedroom house on Waltham Road, a mile from the Hilltop.

We sold our American Ford in Cayman, leaving it to rust out the rest of its days there. We bought a little red English Hillman to negotiate the narrow mountain roads. Winding, but, on the whole, paved!

Since I didn't have household help, in the usual sense of the word, Francine, Patsy and I did our own marketing. Surrounded by rusty old trucks and sturdy little donkeys, Mandeville Market offered the best that the fruitful island could produce. After the limitations of Cayman, I found the array of fresh food intoxicating. Bananas of every ilk, huge red papayas, coconuts aplenty, pineapples, mangoes in season, to say nothing of colorful mountains of vegetables.

Very quickly Walt and I learned to love that exclusively Jamaican delicacy, *ackee*. A combination of a delicious yellow heart with big shiny black seeds encased in a red and very poisonous husk. Everything we brought home had to be washed in bleach as a health-precaution.

Bargaining on prices, even in lands where it's required for survival, has always vexed me. Although Francine and Patsy had more talent than I, none of us enjoyed it. So, for the rest of my time in Mandeville, I committed myself to one single vendor, a fat, cheerful woman with a cute little donkey. She consistently gave me reasonable prices and brought me whatever I wanted. I understood, of course, that I belonged to her. I was not free to patronize any other seller on the premises. Occasionally, I saw the women come to blows, if disloyalty—however slight—had been detected.

At the same time, a small supermarket was evolving in the town. It lacked the drama and sound effects of the open marketplace, of course. True, it catered to certain tastes. I, for one, enjoyed English biscuits and fig jam from South Africa. But who really wants chocolate-covered cockroaches instead of a fresh pineapple that's been ripening in the Caribbean sun for a whole year, just for you?

Campus life engulfed us immediately. Walt taught Bible classes and also supervised the Medical Cadet Corps. For the first time, I became a department chair but still carried a full roster of English classes.

Office space for teachers being at a premium, my husband and I accounted ourselves fortunate to find a small room to share in Rose Cottage.

Despite the romantic name, the building was an original from the founding of the school back in 1919. We had two desks and two chairs, but when our students came to consult with us we could receive only one person at a time. Indeed, we scarcely had room in there to change our minds.

Earl Gardner and his little plane stood ready in any crisis to take anyone out of the Mandeville Valley.

Thus we spent our days among hundreds of lively young people, all turned out in immaculate blue-and-white uniforms. Saturday nights were given over to socializing. We spent hours marching to "Colonel Bogey" on the Paved Lawn. The latter was the cement slab between the Seat of the Scornful and the cafeteria.

True to form, students complained much about that cafeteria—and not without reason. The building was totally derelict. This fact hit home at the times when we had faculty suppers there. The food was not even visible from the tables. On one such occasion, Pastor Nation, our "Faculty Father," was asked to say the blessing. He sighed and paused uncertainly. "Well, Lord, bless this food. Uh … whatever it's going to be." Amazing how long that poor old cafeteria, only a step away from a kitchen under the trees, served the College!

Truly, Pastor Nation was an Original. In the matter of saying grace at the table, he was unequaled in his forthrightness. At one classic event, he was guest of honor at a wedding. Neither bride nor groom was a member of the Adventist church, but he officiated at the ceremony. In the feast that followed, he, naturally, was asked to say grace. The centerpiece of the table, however, was a whole roast pig. Others in his position would probably have lifted their thoughts above and beyond the animal and just closed their eyes tightly. Not our fearless pastor! Instead, he lifted up his hands and intoned: "O Lord, if Thou canst bless what Thou has cursed, then bless this food that is before us … "

When Walt's birthday came up on May 15, 1957, we were introduced to a gentle custom that, as far as I've been able to discover, was unique to West Indies College. We came home at the end of the school day to find our bed lavishly decorated. Francine and Patsy had cooperated with the others who came down from the girls' dormitory to create the tribute. A white sheet had been spread out to serve as a background to a border outlined in greenery. Over the pillows lay bouquets

West Indies Training College Administration dominated the razorback hill on which the main part of the campus was built.

of flowers, topped by a birthday-balloon. Sundry small gifts, cards, and written messages were scattered over the area. In the center, spelled out in flower petals, we read: "Happy Birthday, Dad."

Later we were to discover that Birthday Beds were a regular event in the dormitory. For the next two years Walt and I never failed to receive a bed-celebration, sometimes attended by a serenade of singers at our window, either at dawn or late night. As time passes, the importance of birthdays often fades

Left. A ping-pong table was often set up on the "Paved Lawn," a space between "The Seat of the Scornful" and the derelict cafeteria, seen here as the backdrop. Right. In season, the flame trees framed the magnificent view of the Mandeville valley, from the Hilltop.

away. In our youthful Caribbean years, however, these thoughtful little events were a kind of "vote of confidence" at a time when we often felt uncertain about the next decision we had to make.

On September 1, 1957, an event occurred that burned itself into our minds forever. At 2.45 a.m., someone was pounding on our bedroom window. "Pastor. Come. There's a train-wreck down at Kendal." One of the cadets stood outside in the quiet starlight.

I collected some first-aid supplies while Walt scrambled into his clothes. I watched him go. Just recovering from a bout of malaria, I would be more of a liability than a help down by the tracks.

Long before dawn the rescue operation had partially emptied the campus of people. Neville Gallimore, Chief Officer and his thirty-four Medical Cadets. Seventeen girls from the Home Nursing class. Uncounted volunteers and faculty members. All converged on the hillside to deal with one of the worst disasters in railroad history.

The excursion train returning from Montego Bay to Kingston had been overloaded. It took the mountain bend too fast and derailed. The old wooden coaches exploded in splinters. Some people were thrown out into the fields, some were literally ground into the gravel rail-bed, and others were rolled out flat, like ghastly cutout cookies.

At 7 a.m. Walt returned. "I think you should come. This is a bad one."

Our West Indian foster-daughters, Patsy Manderson and Francine Haylock, hung out the washing behind our first little house on Waltham Road, Mandeville.

By the time I reached the scene, the hundreds of injured had been carried up to Mandeville Hospital. Only the dead—by now stiff and grotesque—and scattered body parts remained. These were being hauled away in open trucks. School closed for days while everyone's attention turned to the injured, and dying, and the dead. The number could never be determined exactly because of the many "parts" picked up. Upwards of 700 people died that night. Along with Neville, several other cadets came in for special honors for their expert and untiring service to the community, among them Lincoln Stevens, Paul Hurst, and Ambrose Reid.

Young Gallimore, however, had another side. As a member of my Grade 12 Senior Cambridge English class, Neville kept the days lively. Particularly after he fell in love with the graceful and beautiful Angela Holgate. She was arguably the most strikingly ladylike girl in the school. She made it clear, however, that she had no use for Neville. She'd shrug him off whenever he followed her out of the room and tried to talk to her out on the breezeway.

One day, he lingered after class. "I am going to marry Angela, but she won't even look at me." His gray eyes begged me for an answer. "What do I do?"

What could I say to this exuberant, irrepressible youth? Not for nothing was his father a member of Parliament down in Kingston. Indeed, when we were looking for campus entertainment, I'd written a play called "Mechanical

Jane." I'd produced it with Neville specifically in mind. He was the voluble salesman who sold a robot maid to a couple of old spinsters. Later he had to rescue them when they let the machine get out of control. Actually, his charismatic personality became the heart of the drama.

Now, in an affair of the heart, what could I say? "Well, Neville," I ventured. "I think perhaps you come on too strong. You probably frighten her."

Although I'm not sure of the sequence of events, it must be said for Neville that he did marry Angela before he went off to study medicine. His later career in politics placed him in high office in the Jamaican government, with occasional excursions to the United Nations. She went on to earn her PhD in English and later to become a lawyer. To be sure, he and Angela have fulfilled their life-potential. He and his family all proudly remain my "children" to this day.

Faculty and students of West Indies College offered skilled assistance in the Kendal train wreck in 1957, the worst in Jamaican history. The old wooden carriages shattered into splinters and hundreds of dead and dying were strewn across the valley floor.

We had some special Canadian friends, Ed and Ethel Heisler, down in Kingston. Respectively he managed Andrews Memorial Hospital and she supervised the School of Nursing there. Then, one happy day, Wilf and Annamarie Liske came in from the Bahamas to fill positions on the Education faculty at the College. Most of our other fellow-missionaries were older than we. Given a foreign assignment, however, we found that age really makes no difference. Instead, we all enjoyed a breadth of friendship that is often hard to come by back in the homeland.

Together we became "beach bums," as often as we could. Everyone in the crowd had fins and snorkels, and we vied with one another to build the most

Left. The "Pineapple Truck" came on campus once a week. Dorothy accommodated her addiction to fresh pineapple by purchasing up to three dozen a week. Right. Fresh off the tree with its red pod, creamy yellow meat, and glossy black seeds, *ackee* is a distinctive Jamaican food.

exotic shell collection. Never content with faded, cracked beach specimens, we spent hours diving for the best. Little orange fighting conchs and tun shells from the Palisadoes, near Kingston Airport. Rainbow-hued cocina from Black River. Big, richly striped helmet shells from Bluefields. Bright, poisonous cone shells from Negril. Sand-dollars and Scotch bonnets from Discovery Bay. A smorgasbord of the natural ocean beauties of Jamaica.

Spending many hours in the water, we attached ropes to our waists and towed inner tubes with us as we swam. Provided with wooden bottoms, they served as transportation for the shells we collected. After that, of course, came the shell cleaning. I dealt with so many big slimy snails that I was permanently cured of any possible interest in seafood.

Discovery Bay was a prime vacation spot for everyone. It was so named because that is where the ships of Christopher Columbus first anchored in 1503. The college faculty

High school girls wore smart navy-blue-and-white uniforms. L-R: Pansy Gallimore, Halcyon Smith, _____, and Norma Goodlett (1958). For some years the college students distinguished themselves in academic gowns modeled on the European style.

usually went there for picnics. For fun, we sailed down the water slide into the aquamarine water. Then we'd spend hours exploring the reefs with our snorkels. Worn out with that, we could then lie on the warm sand and drink cool water from green coconuts. Often a calypso band played our requests. I shall always associate rice-and-peas and cassava cake with the sounds of "Linstead Market" and "Chi-chi Bud-o."

Another favorite resort for school picnics was Dunn's River. This breath-taking waterfall was then as unspoiled as when the island still belonged exclusively to the Arawak Indians. We swam in the ocean, played ball on the beach, ate our rice-and-peas, and climbed the falls. Cascades of fresh water splashed down the hillside, dropping into terraces of little pools. Here we finished off the day lying about in the stone "tubs" catching glimpses of the ocean among the palms below us and allowing the fresh showers of "rain" to massage our bodies, worn out with a day of pure pleasure. Finally, we bathed, shampooed the salt out of our hair, and went back home to the cool hills of Mandeville.

But that's a dream from more

Right. First "discovered" by Christopher Columbus (1484), Discovery Bay, Jamaica, was a favorite vacation destination. Usually arriving exhausted, Walt, Dorothy, and their friends tended to sleep around the clock for the first two days. Below. Then came interludes of resting on the beach. Bottom right. Finally, as strength returned, they spent hours snorkeling and exploring coral reefs.

than forty years ago. Don't count on that privilege today. Today the tourist industry has commercialized Dunn's River to a standstill. Yes, the waterfall under the canopy of trees, the stone tubs, and the showery drop off on to the sand beach all remain. Now, however, you have to walk on wooden pathways, attended by aggressive guides vying for a tip and quarreling over which tourist belongs to which man. Definitely not a change for the better. Facing this misery of meddling a visitor will altogether miss the tranquil joy we used to derive from the place.

During our Jamaica years, going to Florida for our vacation time was too expensive to become a habit. Therefore, we soon found that spending a week at Discovery Bay had wonderfully restorative powers. Two or three couples would rent a beach house for a week. We took along a girl or two to help, and then we gave ourselves up to utter sloth. No marketing, no cooking, no cleaning up.

Usually we'd spend the first two days doing nothing but sleep, barely emerging long enough to be served a meal. Most of us were still young, and we shouldn't have been that exhausted. It indicates, I suppose, that every one of us was doing, more or less, the work of two people. By the third day, however, we were usually ready to spend several hours a day swimming out over the reefs.

Although he never developed a sophisticated swim stroke, Walt became a good, dog-paddling diver. He brought up shells to make a collector drool with envy. How we loved that underwater world! It never wearied us. We spent hours watching the fish darting in and out of the living reef. Spiky black sea urchins waved at us, and lumbering sea cucumbers ejected most of their innards when we touched them with a stick.

Sometimes the remora fish took us for sharks or barracudas and tried to attach themselves to our legs. An unnerving kind of attack. Although we didn't realize it at the time, probably one of our most potentially dangerous sightings was the sea snakes. Some of them were cream colored with large blue polka dots. Very poisonous. They never paid any attention to us, though, and we kept a respectful distance.

One of my greatest personal beach discoveries was a carrier shell. I was poking along in about four feet of water off Negril Beach when, with my fin, I kicked over a little pile of dead coral. It turned out to be a large carrier shell that had disguised himself by cementing rubbish onto his upper surface. In the market of the day I discovered that the shell would have been worth at least $40.00.

Over the years, however, we never made money out of our rather superior collection. We simply reveled in the beauty of the underwater world and in the adventure of finding beautiful specimens. When I could no longer house our vast marine display, I gave it to the Natural History Museum at La Sierra University, California, where I worked for the last twenty-two years of my teaching career.

In the middle of the school year of 1957, I made a short solo trip home to Massachusetts for my sister Eileen's June 9 wedding. Only sister I had, so, of course, I had to be there. Walt stayed by the job.

I missed him immediately. We were no more than airborne above Kingston when I became fascinated with the woman seated across the aisle from me. Weighing in at maybe 400 pounds, she occupied two seats, without benefit of a seatbelt, of course. When her lunch tray was given to her, she could barely reach her mouth. The food, perforce, dribbled all the way across the vast expanse of her bosom. And Walt wasn't there to enjoy the scene with me!

Meanwhile, several other people—all of whom seemed to know one another—were making loud conversation. One of them, scruffily dressed like someone's yard-boy sat beside a very chic younger lady. He had a dreadful, gravelly voice.

Finally, the plane touched down in Havana, Cuba, and they all disembarked for the time we were on the ground. Behind me were two English women, discussing the party that had just left us. I turned to them. "Well, who is he? That man with the scratchy voice?"

"You don't know!" They stared at me in utter astonishment. "Why, that's Louis Armstrong?"

Ah well, devotion to classical music does limit one's education, I guess. To think that I'd come so close to greatness and all for nothing! Indeed, the whole encounter had been wasted on me because of my ignorance of the pop music scene.

When we arrived in Miami, I found myself in customs with the afore-mentioned large lady. She had several equally large suitcases, each one able to hold only two or three of her dresses. At that point I discovered that she was the lead singer with Armstrong's group. Everyone in the customs shed knew who she was. Except me.

So ended our first year in the little yellow house on Waltham Road. Our little family of four—Walt and me, Francine and Patsy—was about to disperse.

A big change was on the way for all of us.

CHAPTER 13

The White Witch of Jamaica Hall

Deep within Jamaican legend lies the story of the beautiful, haughty Annee Palmer, the "White Witch of Rose Hall." Daughter of Anglo-Irish parents she grew up in Haiti where she learned the arts of *voodoo*. At age eighteen she came to Jamaica and married John Palmer, the owner of the Great House of Rose Hall and its more-than-5000 acres of land near Montego Bay.

Annee soon added Jamaican witchcraft *(obeah* and *pocomania)* to her occult skills. Thus she cruelly controlled her slaves. She murdered, in succession, her three husbands and sundry other lovers. Eventually, in 1831, her slaves managed to kill her in her rose-enhanced bedroom. They dumped her body in an unmarked grave behind the house. Always a powerful symbol of plantation times, Rose Hall remained in ruins for many years. Now, however, it has been restored to become a major tourist attraction in Jamaica.

We heard the story of the White Witch almost immediately upon arriving in Jamaica, it being a staple of island legend. At the end of our first year at West Indies College, circumstances evolved that made me a potential candidate for the role of "White Witch."

Over Christmas vacation, 1957, a great new project neared completion on the campus. The ramshackle old girls' dormitory was about to be demolished in favor of a handsome new, three-story building called Jamaica Hall. At first, I couldn't guess that it would have anything to do with Walt and me directly. How wrong could I be?

We'd been living just a year in the little yellow house on Waltham Road when, on one of the rare mornings when I was at home, three members of the College Board came to call. Formalities over, Pastor Stockhausen came straight to the point. "We're asking you to become Dean of Women in the new dormitory."

Me? A dormitory dean? "But I've never lived as a student in a dormitory in my whole life. What do I know?" At twenty-eight years old I was even younger than some of the college women who would be coming in.

"That's all right. We believe you'll do a good job." The Chairman of the Board looked down on me benevolently. "What we need is good organization and discipline." He didn't quite pat me on the head, but almost. I felt like a child. Too young to protest and too confused to understand the reality of what lay before Walt and me.

Over the next few weeks, several of my jesting American friends labeled me the "White Witch of Jamaica Hall." If any of the Jamaicans said so, it was never in my presence.

As the magnitude of the undertaking began to unfold, I tasked myself to control my witch-like tendencies. I had to build an institution from the very foundation up. From the start, I staggered under the unending demands that the work made upon my strength, my mind, and my patience.

Overnight, Walt and I became embroiled in putting the finishing touches on the new building. "Touches" is too mild a word. In their infinite wisdom, the builders had chosen to lay the ceramic tiles (a different color on each floor) first. Then they pushed their wheelbarrows full of cement over the floors to finish the balconies. This meant hours on hands and knees scraping cement off the tiles.

From the North Shore resort hotel, Tower Isle, we bought enough second-hand, metal furniture to set up all of the 100 student rooms. Walt got a crew together to sand off the old surfaces and repaint them a fetchingly feminine rose-pink.

For the Dean's apartment I requested "enough cupboards"—something that, heretofore, I'd only dreamed of. In the end, we got a kitchen with enough cupboards to serve as Central Supply for the entire campus.

As the opening of the school year approached, I made two and three trips a week to Kingston to buy furnishings. Repeatedly, I loaded up the little Hillman with bolts of drapery fabric. Back on campus, we kept my old Singer

Left. Through these gates unsuspecting men came to visit the devious Annie Palmer of Rose Hall (painting by James Hakewill, 1820). Above right. For decades the notorious plantation remained in ruins. Right. Today the Great House has been restored to its former glory, becoming a major tourist destination near Montego Bay.

sewing machine hot, almost around the clock. It ran for miles to produce curtains for all of the windows and matching drapes for each of the closets.

In January, we all moved into the light, airy building overlooking the lush Mandeville Valley. Jamaica Hall had already become the campus showpiece. Indeed, it attracted visitors from all over the island.

Then came the matter of my actually becoming a dean. I had no precedents to follow. I set up the office and a monitor system, posted bulletin boards, planned worships, and attended new committees. I wrote and published a booklet entitled "Jenny Jamaica Comes to College." By presenting the rules with humor and whimsy and by mixing in some proverbial wisdom, I hoped to forestall some of the more blatant disciplinary problems that would arise.

By the time school opened, however, I was worn out. Totally. It occurred to me that I was still Chairman of the English Department with a full roster of teaching. Apparently no one had taken that matter into consideration. Either I was too weary or too dumb to ask for relief. I don't know which.

Suddenly I had three weeks of bed-rest thrust upon me.

One morning I stood on the back steps of the Dean's apartment, instructing the men as to where to put up my clothesline. For no reason that I can remember, I walked off into space and fell down the steps on my head. I woke up in bed with the campus doctor, Alwin Parchment, standing over me. "You will stay here until I tell you to get up." I couldn't argue with him. I didn't even want to.

My monitors were girls who, after that dormitory year, became lifelong friends. They came daily to take care of me. At lights-out Walt patrolled the halls, calling up the open stairwells, "Everyone in. I'm coming up." He always considered it one of the more distinguished portions of his career, those three weeks that he served as Dean of Women in Jamaica Hall.

Meanwhile, I lay abed, staring out the window at the green wall of forest beside us. As the great knot on my head gradually reduced, half of my face turned from black-and-blue to lavender, yellow and pink, with patches of green and purple.

By the time I got up to take over my own kitchen again, I'd been introduced to the sweet possibilities of the weekly visit of the pineapple truck. Then (as now) I have a passion for fresh pineapple. Having had so little fresh fruit in Cayman, we became a little drunk when we got to Jamaica. In addition to the big mangoes and red papayas from the market. I patronized the pineapple truck. Regularly I bought three dozen a week! Just for the two of us. Undoubtedly a little excessive, but, at least, we weren't on drugs.

Left. Two palm trees mark the spot where the old Girls Dormitory stood at West Indies College. To the left was the multi-purpose Rose Cottage. Right. Walt and Dorothy Comm were the first "managers" of the fine new Jamaica Hall that replaced the ramshackle women's dormitory in 1957.

From the start, I suspected (correctly) that the six community bathrooms and the laundry rooms might become a source of difficulty. Therefore, I took great care to set up a series of bins for garbage disposal, three in each bathroom. We hadn't yet heard the word "recycling," but I think I may have invented the idea right there.

While all of the girls tried to cooperate, a number of them from mountain villages had never before lived with indoor plumbing. Hence, the bathrooms remained in a constant state of crisis. I had a direct line to the plumbers. They came, literally, every day. The stress never let up. It seemed that every evening worship hour included a discourse on the use of bathrooms.

One day, Hazel Graham, one of my most faithful assistants, rushed down to my office. "He's up there in a bathroom. The plumber. He's smoking! What can we do?"

Considering the job the man had to face, I felt nothing but compassion for him. "Think of what he has to do, Hazel. We must be fair and let him enjoy whatever he must to get through the job."

Then Walt came up with an idea, one based on the very human vice/virtue of using competition to motivate behavior. On my next trip to Kingston, I bought a graceful little silver-plated vase to serve as a trophy. Each end of the three floors became a team, six in all. A small display shelf was installed in each section to hold the trophy. Three clearly labeled bins were provided in each bathroom.

Now came a daily inspection of rooms and bathrooms. We devised a point system whereby marks could be lost even if the room didn't smell satisfactory. Every day I brought in a group of men. Might as well play the sexes off against one another as well! Men from the Conference office, campus visitors from

Cecily Reece posed beside her "Birthday Bed" in Jamaica Hall.

abroad, faculty men, and occupants of the boys' (very inferior) dormitory across campus. Awestricken, the girls worked hard, and Jamaica Hall really did shine. Truly something to be proud of.

During inspection one day we entered a bathroom to find that someone had thrown a banana skin into the paper bin. Almost in tears, the monitor of that section wailed, "But I was just here, and I checked everything!" For that, unfortunately, her team lost the trophy for the week.

A group of girls, as usual, trailed the inspection party. Somehow, they found out who had eaten the banana. I left them to administer justice in

Large posters in the dormitory bathrooms about "Bathroom Messies" delineated specific sins and the ultimate fate of trangressors.

their own way, but I think they came near killing the culprit for her crime. To this day, I suspect she never eats a banana without remembering that long-ago episode.

Another associated problem appeared on campus late that year (1958). Fidel Castro had risen to power and closed colleges and universities in Cuba, scattering students all over the Caribbean. About twenty-five of them came to West Indies College.

While they didn't intentionally try to cause trouble, they did create problems. The boys couldn't understand why they didn't have free access to the girls' dormitory. Brought up in wealthy families, the girls wanted to bring in maids to clean their rooms and do their laundry. I have never spoken Spanish, and without the aid of Yolanda Paul (my monitor from Costa Rica) I would have fared badly during those days.

As it was, we had an ongoing effort to convince the girls that they could clean their own rooms. One day on inspection, I found a Cuban room looking fairly good but smelling stale as a tomb. In the closet I found two huge bundles, each large enough to conceal a body. "What are these?"

"Clothes! Our clothes."

Yolanda, at my elbow, pressed the point. Unable to do their own washing, the girls had kept on buying new garments instead of washing the soiled ones. As for dusting the room, they'd taken care of that too. Looking out the window, I saw down below the Kleenexes they had used and tossed. Of course, most of the Jamaican girls, working around the clock just to stay in college, could know nothing of Kleenex. Try as we might, the conditioning of these Cuban students proceeded at a snail-pace.

The monitors' desk in Jamaica Hall. The "control tower" to organize the lives of 300 college women at West Indies College.

The following week, Yolanda came to my rescue again when we had one of the Cuban girls up on the roof threatening suicide. She chose the back of the building where, after a three-story drop she would also have gone down another 100 feet into the ravine. Like all of the other campus buildings, Jamaica Hall sat on a sheer cliff. After she had spent several hours on the roof, we managed to coax her back inside, whole and alive.

The Jamaica girls could pose other kinds of crises. In those early weeks of residence in Jamaica Hall, we had a variety of mechanical problems—water, electricity and such. Sometimes these disabilities became channels of panic, fed by the all-too-real superstitions lodged naturally in every girl's mind.

Early one morning the word reached the campus that a half-mile down

Left. Much of the produce came to Mandeville Market by donkey. Above right. From time to time, the very useful donkey had to be taken down to the beach for a good wash and scrub down (at Bluefields, Jamaica). Right. Dorothy (second from right) with her vendor friends at Mandeville Market. The one in the middle (with the white hat) faithfully gave her a fair price and spared her the dreary task of bargaining.

the road in Knockpatrick a man had hanged himself on a tree by his front gate. "And," one wide-eyed girl told me, "his father and uncle hung themselves on the same tree already before." It occurred to me that this was a new definition of what a family tree could be. "Everyone is going down to see him" she added. "Are you going, ma'am?"

"No," I replied. The images of the Kendal train-wreck were still fresh enough in my mind. "And it would be better for you also, if you didn't go."

But, of course, she went. I supposed 99% of the people on the Hilltop went to look at the corpse. The police left him hanging there all day, until they could decide what to do with him next.

After worship that night, just as the girls were going to their rooms for study period, all of the lights in Jamaica Hall went out. To this day, no one ever knew who perpetrated the power-failure. Someone in the boys' dorm undoubtedly knew the facts of the case. Whatever that person or persons hoped to achieve, they must have felt well rewarded for their efforts.

The entire building erupted in screams of terror. Some who had already reached their rooms found the dead man in their beds. Others saw the "Rolling Calf" and the "Three-legged Horse," staples of Jamaican folklore. Those in the halls encountered *duppies* (ghosts) at every turn.

Restoration of the lights helped, but the chaos still prevailed for the better part of an hour. Walt and I, along with the monitors and whoever else still had a grip on sanity, patrolled the halls for the rest of the evening lest hysteria break out again.

Enforcing church attendance, I found, added still further dimensions to my job. Going to church was obligatory, and that meant a search-and-rescue operation every Sabbath morning. If room-check revealed any girl still lurking in her room, she had to be cross-examined on the spot.

Being "sick," of course, has always been the standard defense. Over my years of teaching, this condition has always puzzled me. Obvious signs of illness must, naturally, be dealt with. That goes without saying. There remains, however, a large (and illegitimate) area of malaise that covers endless excuses. I've always wondered why students (who are obviously younger people) will be ill in epidemic numbers. At the same time, the teacher will be present and on duty, no matter what. Until, indeed, she or he is carried out, feet first.

My predecessor as Dean of Women had had her own way of separating the truly-sick from the pseudo-sick. If the latter claimed to be too ill to go to church, she was given a large dose of castor oil. Thus, she would be unable to leave the dorm for the rest of the day. She would also miss the Saturday evening entertainment, a deprivation not to be taken lightly.

Not wanting to resort to this severe—but undeniably effective—measure, I walked the halls weekly, carefully interviewing each "patient."

Even after the girls were off to church, I could still face problems. Campus custom of the time dictated that the girls should be clad in nothing but white. Indeed, a certain kind of white. Dr. Leif Tobiassen had by now replaced the more easy-going Dr. Manuel Sorensen as college president. He instituted the European custom of having the college students (as opposed to those in high school) wear blue academic gowns to classes every day. To be sure, the academic atmosphere improved.

At the same time, however, under his watchful eye, the students' arrival in church became something of a military review. One day, he came to me just before the church service. He'd seen a girl ushering in a dress that he deemed too thin. "Send her back to the dorm to change her clothes," he barked. "I'll not have her performing in a fish-net."

I looked at the culprit. The "see-through" properties of her dress seemed to me to be fairly mild. "It may well be the only white dress she has," I ventured.

"Never mind. She must go." So, as unobtrusively as I could, I had to take her out of circulation and walk her back to the dorm. On the way, we discussed the possibility of her getting a new dress. Impossible. Alternatively, I suggested modifying the "fish-net" she already had. She humbly agreed.

My time in Jamaica Hall involved me in so many intimate problems. One had to do with hair. In contrast to my own thick mop of straight hair that I didn't want to cut, my dorm girls faced other kinds of difficulty. The majority of them were far too poor to have their hair straightened at the local Mandeville beauty parlor. They were very skillful, however, in using castor oil and metal "hot combs" heated on an electric plate. On a warm day, the scent of all of this "treated" hair in a classroom could be quite overwhelming. Rain, or water from any other source, however, immediately destroyed their efforts. For the first time I realized that their labors with their hair were more difficult than mine, only in reverse.

An added element to this issue was the fact that there was a strong school of thought that decreed that hair-straightening was sinful! Comparable, I suppose to the American arguments in the 1920s that bobbed hair and permanents were demoralizing.

Hazel told me one day, "You know that young man who is going to marry___? He believes that straightening hair is wrong."

"Well," I asked, "does she do it?" Trying to comprehend the implications of this issue always boggled my mind.

"Of course." Hazel rolled her eyes. "She's part Indian, so she doesn't need to do it so much. Still, she does it. We told him so."

"What did he say?"

"If I found out that my bride straightened her hair, I would leave her right there at the altar." I've always wondered but never heard how that affair ended.

I've always loved animals, especially the gaudy ones like tigers, leopards, cheetahs, zebras and giraffes. Throughout my nine months of deanship in Jamaica Hall I kept a handsome porcelain tiger on my desk. He gave me tangible support.

At the same time, I had experiences never to be duplicated again, before or since. The best part, however, was making friends with girls in a way that no classroom encounter could establish. Making friends for life.

As we neared the end of that summer, I finally took a stand about my workload. "But we can't find another Dean of Women anywhere," the cry went up. Doggedly, I decided to force them to find one.

We had been granted a year's furlough, beginning on December 15. We'd chosen to spend it in Washington D.C. where Walt could earn an advanced degree at the Theological Seminary. Worn out from carrying two full-time jobs, I know I felt more than twice my age.

Esther and Roy Mote had gone on furlough and had invited us to occupy their home any time or any way we wished. Therefore, I was able to say, "We're moving out of Jamaica Hall on October 1. We will stay in Motes' house until we go on study-leave in December."

Having thus stated my case, I felt better. I began to get ready to transfer the honors of the Dean's office to my successor, Verna Barclay. A very capable person, she made deaning a fine art. Given all of my other tasks, just surviving the deanship was all that I ever achieved. Verna, on the other hand was Dean of Women at La Sierra University in California when I took up my appointment there in the English Department twenty-seven years later.

At work one afternoon in my office, I received another annoying phone call. Not surprisingly, it was a man with a thick Cuban accent. He wanted to have a room in Jamaica Hall. "This is a women's dormitory," I told him.

"But," he persisted. "They tell me it's a very nice place. I want to stay there." The argument went on for some time, and I barely hung on to my temper. "You say, then, there are no men living there?"

"Right! No men. Only women." Why, I wondered, did I have to be nice to this blockhead any longer? Not only did he have this opaque foreign accent, but he seemed exceptionally stupid as well. "You can't live here," I declared. "Why can't you understand that?"

Suddenly, I heard a roar of laughter. It seemed to be echoing eerily around in an empty room. "Well, then," Walt replied. "I guess I can't come home tonight."

The Dean's office. Always encouraged by the little tiger on her desk, Dorothy Comm discussed a problem with one of her monitors, Shirley Morrison.

Now I realized that my husband was down in Motes' empty house, in quiet retreat. He'd obviously become bored and tapped into my gullibility for entertainment. I looked at my tiger. "It's too much," I told him. "It's time for me to give up."

In due course, we cleared out of the Dean's apartment and put our possessions into the dormitory storage room. Then we spent the last three months of the school year leading a relatively private life in the comfortable big house down in the valley. We needed the rest, forsooth.

Of course, we had to sell "Little Woolley." In the latter part of our term, we'd bought (second hand) an exclusive, sporty English automobile. Even Walt hadn't seen one before. From the British Motor Company of 1901, the Wolsey had evolved into a very desirable little car, with almost sensual attractiveness. We loved the leather seats and the highly polished real oak dashboard. But it had to go. We were destined to return to a big American vehicle in Miami.

On one of my last days at the Mandeville Market, a poor woman tried to give me her baby, a round, bright-eyed little tyke lying in a basket with the cassavas and yams. "Have him, missus. You take. Free!"

The offer startled me. "Thank you," I said, as kindly as I could. "I already have a baby."

This was almost the truth, though not quite. Early in 1959 we would be adopting a baby in Rhode Island. The legal process had already begun. I looked down at the little waif, wrapped in rags. I marveled at the painful discrepancies between supply and demand.

CHAPTER 14

Baby Time *Versus* Study Time

Walt and I made careful plans for the twelve months of furlough that we'd been granted. For the next year (1959) we would live in a big, one-room apartment upstairs in Uncle Len's house in Washington D. C. Walt would have to give himself over to graduate study for his Bachelor of Theology degree while I would devote all of my time to taking care of the new baby. I imagined that I would frequently counsel with Auntie May. An expert on children, she was also a registered nurse.

To the north Eileen and Roger lived in New York, almost within arm's reach. Dad, Mum and Grandpa Bert Rhoads lived still further north in Massachusetts. We had so much to look forward to. A whole year with access to our family! We'd surfeit ourselves, filling up on "togetherness." We'd make it enough to see us through our next term of service in the West Indies.

Within a single week in late December, 1958, we left our pleasant mountain home in Mandeville, Jamaica, for the steamy streets of Kingston. Just hours later we landed in Florida.

We sold our "Little Woolley" (Wolsey) car in Mandeville. Sporty with its polished wood dashboard, I watched it go with considerable sorrow. I knew that Walt would replace it with a big American something in Miami. The day after we landed he bought a second-hand Desoto, full of fancy accessories and heavily be-chromed. Far too big for my tastes.

Mum and Dad had shipped a little barrel of our winter clothes down to the Inter-American Division office in Miami, old stuff from our Newfoundland days. Whether or not the garments were still in fashion was not a consideration that we could afford to dwell upon. Promptly, we headed north to spend Christmas with Walt's family, almost 3,400 miles away. Then we'd have to streak back across the continent again to be for the arrival of our baby. Within just over two days we took a temperature drop of more than 100 degrees.

The latter part of our trip from Miami took us over 1,000 miles of black ice, covered with skiffs of snow. Hazardous to a degree! Walt, however, anticipated special pleasures. The old German traditions of Christmas still prevailed in his Canadian farm home. They included mountains of good cooking and fine baking, crates of thin-skinned mandarin oranges, and bowls of nuts that required nutcrackers. His brothers and nephews scarcely left the dinner table. Instead, they tarried for hours nibbling at nuts and oranges and telling (for the umpteenth time) stories out of the family folklore. Everyone had heard them before, but that was OK. A dozen people were all talking at the same time anyway.

Nonetheless, our holiday in the far Canadian north whizzed past in a blur. Right after Christmas Day a panicky phone call came from Massachusetts. "The baby might be born any time now," Mum exclaimed. "When are you coming?"

Within a couple of hours we hit the treacherous winter roads again. Obsessively committed to our responsibilities, we didn't sleep again until we reached Massachusetts, some forty-eight hours later. Spelling each other off driving, we plowed through endless ice and snow, visibility near zero.

We made it! In fact we had time to spare. We'd barely settled in, however, when Auntie May Minchin surprised us with a phone call from Washington. "There's going to be a baby born here at the Washington Sanitarium and Hospital very soon. Do you want another baby?"

This second mother-to-be was very particular about the kind of home her child would go to. We realized that somehow everyone involved in the case had faith that we would be a suitable family. Hence, the offer.

My first inclination was to say "Yes." Walt agreed. We'd already considered the prospects of rearing an only child. If we were to avoid that situation, this would be the way solve the problem. "There's another couple," Auntie went on, "who also want to adopt this child. But only if it's a boy."

I responded promptly. "We'll take it if it's a baby!" So that was it. Life would never be the same again.

Eileen and Roger were still in Massachusetts, so we extended celebrations well into the New Year. They were awaiting the arrival of their first baby.

Walt and I began to recover a little from our furious transcontinental travels. We'd done nearly 6,300 miles of fierce winter driving in less than ten days.

One evening Dad suggested that we celebrate the family's being together again. "Let's go and eat supper at the Old Mill before you all leave."

Anyone with even a cursory knowledge of New England will recognize the Old Mill as a favorite place for special events. We sat around listening to Dad reserving a table for the seven of us at 6.30 pm. Aware that our destination was classy, we took some pains to dress ourselves in a manner that would be worthy of the place.

When we piled into the car, Dad just circled around and drove across the campus toward the Administration Building. He parked behind it and stepped out. "Come in." The men opened the car doors for us. "I want to show you some changes they've made in the basement," Dad said.

What a peculiar time to do this kind of sightseeing when we were on our way to dinner at the Old Mill! Nonetheless, we obediently followed Dad downstairs. A door popped open, bright light flooded out, and a loud cry issued forth from the multitude of women seated inside. Something new in the basement? Yes, indeed.

Without a word, Dad, Walt, Roger, and Grandpa all vanished. Eileen and I took our seats of honor, and our triple baby shower began. For a third time the whole college community rallied around to celebrate our parents in their forthcoming role of grandparents. The first such outpouring of love and support had been at my wedding, eight years earlier, followed later by Eileen's wedding. Now this!

The next day Eileen and Roger returned to New York City where he was in the midst of his doctoral studies at Columbia University. Leaving me literally in a "waiting room," Walt drove on down to Washington to settle our apartment and get himself started with his classes at the Seminary.

We now perceived that a veritable hurricane of babies was bearing down on our family. Lorna Gene arrived first, on February 5, 1959. Because of severe jaundice, however, she tarried in Providence Memorial Hospital in Rhode Island. Through the many days of concern about her, I was secretly glad that we had another baby on the way. Finally, she was cleared to leave the hospital. Happily, her complete blood exchange transfusion had taken hold.

When Walt and I picked her up, she howled lustily for an hour or so. As we wheeled into Dad and Mum's home in South Lancaster, however, she settled down, content to stay put for the time being. As for Walt and me, we crashed on the bed and slept for many hours. What we didn't realize was that we would never know another full night's sleep for the next five years.

On February 22, we headed down to Washington. All the way to New York Lorna slept in her laundry basket between us on the front seat. As soon as we arrived at Eileen and Roger's place, however, she started non-stop crying. Roger looked down at the squalling infant with a touch of nervousness. "She does make a lot of noise, doesn't she?" he murmured. He wasn't actually complaining, but he did appear surprised.

Although unused to this kind of uproar myself, I thought, "Well, he'll soon have the same thing round-the-clock too." After supper, we drove on to our new "furlough home" in Washington.

In our apartment one end of the large upstairs room served as the kitchen, with the bathroom to the right. At the other end, beyond the stairwell, was our bed to one side. Opposite stood the second-hand crib we'd bought for Lorna.

About 8 o'clock on Sunday morning, March 1, the hospital called Walt. We were still in bed trying to make up for some of the sleep Lorna had caused us to lose in the night. In moments, Walt was bounding back up the stairs, three at a time, shouting, "We have a son!"

Of course, we rushed over to see him. A funny little red chap just eight hours old, he'd been pushed back into the corner of the nursery. Because he was going to be adopted, he was not supposed to be seen by anyone.

I'd asked Walt, "Will you mind if the other baby is a girl?"

"Not at all," he replied. I could tell that day, however, with his jubilant announcement, that this was the way he really wanted it.

Having weighed in at 6 pounds 7 ounces, Larry gained three ounces before he left the nursery on the fourth day. He came home in the same laundry basket we'd used for Lorna. We put him in Lorna's crib until we could purchase another one.

Actually, we were rather proud of our restoration work. We sanded both cribs down, repainted them—pink and blue respectively—and stenciled the babies' names on the headboards. They needed to know where they belonged, after all.

The next Friday night, March 6, Roger called us. We could hear the excitement crackling over the phone line. "Our son Kevin was born today! He's a big one, over nine pounds." Mum and Dad had been present for that affair.

The next day they arrived in Washington, at dinnertime. All of these grandchildren at once! My parents immediately rushed upstairs to see our two little toads sleeping together in the crib. Looking a little pale, Dad said, "I think I need to sit down."

"I can stay with you until Eileen gets out of the hospital," Mum offered. Another pair of hands? What a blessing that would be. Three days later, for the first time, Mum, Auntie May and I took the babies to see Dr. Cochrane, our pediatrician. (Lorna would have to have a blood-check every month for the first year.) "Everything's on course," the doctor smiled.

Mum left for New York the next day, leaving me to adjust to my new life. Walt's program hadn't changed much. He was just going to school, as usual.

I, on the other hand, didn't do one other thing in a day, other than making up twenty-four bottles of formula and washing dozens and dozens of diapers. I soused them in the toilet, before pre-washing them and dropping them into the diaper pail. Then to the washing machine and on to the clothes-line. Although disposable diapers had been invented, they were wholly out of our financial range. Weekly commercial diaper services were also available, but, for the same reason, they in no way benefited me.

I tacked a schedule to the wall to record each feeding, the only possible way to remember who ate how much and when. Everything went on to the background sounds of hours of colicky crying.

In mid-April we descended on the new grandparents in Massachusetts, picking up Roger, Eileen and Kevie on the way. As we crossed the threshold of their home, all three infants with one accord raised their voices in loud lamentation. Chaos reigned until we got them all fed and bedded down.

On the weekend we had a kind of parade to church, viewed, as it were, by the whole community. Larry

An armful of babies. Dorothy, Larry, and Lorna in Takoma Park, Maryland (Lorna, left; Larry, right).

behaved pretty well. (Among the three, he always took things most seriously.) As usual, Lorna did a lot of wriggling. Kevin burped irreverently in the solemn pauses, and then, as a grand finale, blasted his pants during the benediction

Personalities emerged early. Larry spent solemn hours concentrating on a single object. He screamed in frustration if anything distracted him. Sometimes he concentrated so intently that he'd work himself up into a frenzy wringing his hands in a most agonizing way. I'd often find him studying the figures on his crib-bumper with an intensity that would stop me in my tracks. In a single instant he could shoot from philosopher to a howling banshee. All of this forecast his future abilities in things mechanical.

When Larry discovered his "speaking" voice, he spent hours talking to himself, cooing like a whole flock of mourning doves in the dawn hours when he first woke up. For whatever reason, we called him Muffin, I suppose because of the commendable industry of the Muffin Man of nursery-rhyme fame.

Lorna, on the other hand, constantly flitted from one sound, one color, one activity to another, throwing things here and there and enjoying the effects. She seemed to have few powers of concentration. Usually smiling and on the go, she earned the title of Moonface. She often bawled and wouldn't look at strangers. Larry might often be quite friendly, even to the point of patting men on the shoulder in quite a comradely way.

When a crying jag began all civilization stood still until either one or the other of them had been tended to. Even so, we were often left clueless as to what the yelling was about. Along with the sound effects, Walt and I had a very hard time sleeping. Between the Washington heat and the two very restless babies we could do it only spasmodically. We didn't even have the fans that we so much depended on in the Caribbean.

Early on I gave the kids empty paper bags to play with. In a couple of hours they would rattle and beat the bags into the consistency of toilet paper. When one bag got too crumpled and chewed, I'd supply fresh one, and the glorious crackly game could begin all over again. Later, the pair spent hours simply banging pots and pans on the floor. Actually, we didn't acquire many toys until their first Christmas.

Together Muffin and Moonface spent hours in their red jump-chair and walker, muttering and gurgling at each other, holding hands and exchanging their rubber animals. By the time they were nine months old, however, they had really begun fighting. Because he walked earlier Larry would take away whatever Lorna had in her hands, dig at her ears, untie her bib, and generally harass her.

Beyond the world of providing entertainment, however, everyday baby stuff sometimes drove me almost insane. Meals ranged from deliberate gagging and throwing up to Larry's very annoying habit of not swallowing the food but storing it in his cheeks, like a chipmunk. Then he'd spit it all out. Still, Dr. Cochrane said, "As long as the food's getting down and they're gaining weight, you don't have to worry." Their persistent double chins testified to the fact they were getting nourishment.

A virtual flood of babies arrived in 1959 when Gerald and Len Minchin acquired an aggregate of six grandchildren within a couple of months. Here was half the crowd: L-R. Eileen Eckert and Kevin, Leona Minchin and Lorna, Dorothy Comm and Larry. The three supporting fathers stood at the back: Roger Eckert, Gerald Minchin, and Walter Comm.

Through all of these vicissitudes of my first year with two babies, I prized Auntie May's help and advice beyond measure. As the mother of five (including twins), there wasn't much she didn't know.

When Walt had time between school terms (August 14-September 16), we made a trip to Canada. It would be another five years before we'd see his family again. (In actual fact it would be less than five years, but at the time we could not foresee the circumstances that would bring us home on Permanent Return.) Mum accompanied us to Canada, providing that so-useful extra pair of hands.

Jan Thomas [a pseudonym], a friend of the family in Washington, loved our babies. In fact, all babies. A furloughing missionary and a single woman of a "certain age," she admitted that she would really like to be married. "I don't so much care about a man as I want babies." Glancing at Walt she added, "But, all of the good husbands are already taken."

Thus, on our eighth wedding anniversary, Jan stayed with the kids while Walt and I went out to dinner and a movie ("How the West Was Won"), an almost unprecedented frivolity on our part.

As the months wore on, however, neither Walt nor I realized how unraveled we'd become. While I remained on twenty-four-hour-a-day duty at home, Walt attended classes and did whatever studying he could do in the library. He could be pretty sure that he'd come home to a sleepless night. Whichever baby was screaming we'd would put it into the pram, wheel it into the bathroom, shut the door, and leave it there. This (temporarily) reduced the noise by a few decibels.

I'd hung up bed-sheets to separate our bed from the two cribs. While that gave the illusion of being separate rooms, it didn't help much otherwise. After a few months

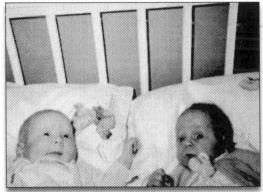

The babies had to share Lorna's crib for a few weeks, Larry's arrival having been somewhat unexpected.

the kids were tearing around among the flapping sheets in their walkers. All four of us in one room made daily living a bit heavy. Logistically, it could hardly be otherwise.

We'd just finished one of our monthly visits to the pediatrician, and he'd pronounced the children "fine." Dr. Cochrane, however, looked at us intently. "I know you're paying me to look after the babies, but now I have a recommendation for you two. You must—I repeat must—get away by yourselves. Take at least a weekend for some rest and go somewhere." I stared at him in astonishment. It showed that much?

I dully remember registering his advice and immediately dismissing it as a hopeless undertaking. The doctor went on to explain that actual twins would have some natural balance in the patterns in their behavior. Lorna and Larry shared absolutely no physical traits. That much we could understand.

Back at home Auntie May encouraged us. "I think that could work out. You know how much Jan loves your little ones. I'm sure she'd come and stay with them." So the plan evolved. Yes, Jan would be glad to help. By now she'd fully recovered from the bruises and battering she'd suffered in the recent "nose job" she'd undergone to improve her appearance.

So it turned out that we left Washington on a Friday afternoon and returned on Monday. Having heard of the beauties of Virginia, we checked into a motel in Luray. First thing we did was collapse on the bed. About eighteen hours later we woke up. So much for sightseeing. We went out for a meal and then came back and went to sleep again. We returned to Washington having seen nothing but the scenery along the highway. Anyway we'd accepted Dr. Cochrane's prescription, and we did feel alive enough to resume our duties.

Now we had to pay Jan for four days of babysitting. She was very ambivalent about it when I brought up the subject, and I didn't know how to fulfill our obligations. Finally, Auntie May admitted that what Jan wanted was for Walt to find her a husband!

We contemplated this assignment. Well, we'd have to try. Virtually every one of Walt's classmates at the Seminary was already married. Discreetly, he asked some questions among the staff. One of the secretaries gave him the name of a "nice man" she'd been dating but whom she had recently discarded.

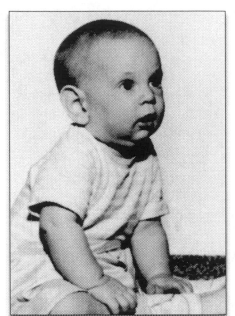 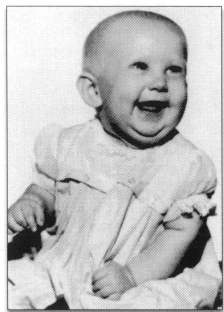

Larry and Lorna Comm, October 1, 1959.

What are we getting into? With good reason, we began to get scared. Unfortunately, we each had an over-developed sense of responsibility. The Nice Man, however, agreed to meet Jan.

In due course, we agreed to take our babysitter to an outlying Maryland church where the introductions would take place. After church she would join the young people in afternoon activities and then remain for a social gathering in the evening. Meanwhile, we would be free to gather up our babies and come home.

Not surprisingly, Jan was jubilant and made vast preparations for the coming weekend. One night she swished upstairs in a flourish to show me a new dress she'd bought for the evening function. Standing up in her walker, Lorna shrieked with joy at the sound and sight of the cherry-red dress with its sweeping full skirt. Busy twisting the legs of his rubber horse, Larry barely bothered to look up. I made a couple of quiet, congratulatory comments, and she left. For the life of me, I could imagine the dress only in a bridal procession or on a ballroom floor.

When the day came, Jan had a suitcase with her party equipment in it. We met the Chosen One after church. He appeared to be an acceptable male person. At the potluck dinner, he sat across the table from us.

We left the group for whatever missionary activities they had for the afternoon, plus the evening beyond. I headed home with a heavy heart. "But," I said to Walt, "he hardly said a word to Jan. Couldn't he have been a little bit friendly?"

My husband had more insight than I into the situation. "I think he understood where he'd been caught, and he just didn't dare give her any kind of encouragement." I still felt sad about the whole thing. "He had made up his mind," Walt continued. "No use building up any kind of false hope." Thinking of that evening dress made me blush as red as its own flaming color. Poor, poor Jan.

For our part, it went without saying, we'd done our best. Never again, however, would we take part in any kind of matchmaking. We'd pay our bills up front—with money—as we'd always done.

In early October we went to court and our two adoptions became legal. Now we could get the children on to my passport for our forthcoming trip overseas. Far more important was the fact that the proceedings were final. During the obligatory six-month "waiting period" either one (or both) of the biological mothers could have taken her baby back.

By Christmas, 1959, we were on countdown for our return to West Indies College in Jamaica. We covered much of the eastern seaboard—Massachusetts, New York and Washington D.C. While my cousins and their little ones were gravitating home to Washington, we headed north. Being New Yorkers, Eileen and Roger had not yet owned a car, so we again picked them up on our way to Massachusetts.

We burst in the door, and the three babies ran amok. Immediately, all of the adults ran hither and thither rescuing objects from the six little paws that grabbed at everything they could reach. Within the first half hour Larry had pulled the floor lamp down and broken the bowl. Instead of standing on the floor, the Christmas tree was on a table, fastened down with guy ropes.

"I guess we just need to hang everything from the ceiling," Dad sighed.

Clearly, his preliminary child proofing of the house had been quite insufficient.

Grandpa Rhoads sat on the sofa stoically watching the show. "Why not just hang the babies from the ceiling and leave everything else where it is?"

As usual we opened gifts on Christmas Eve. The youngsters received a great variety of toys, but nothing thrilled them quite so much as the wrapping paper. Lorna ate as much of it as she could. Someone gave Larry a ring of big plastic beads of different shapes and sizes. That night our "Muffin Man" found that by putting his fat little finger in the hole and pulling it out he could make a popping noise. Quickly mastering the trick, he did pops, one after another, for a couple of hours—after he'd looked around and assured himself of an audience.

On Christmas Day, Mum gave Larry his first haircut. He took it quite philosophically. The snow came by New Year's Eve. Eileen, Dad, Walt and I made three snowmen and one snow-dog in the front yard. Corralled in the

playpen inside, the kids fell into a delirium of excitement when we threw snow against the picture window. Lorna erupted in a torrent of (her own) words, her face scarlet with earnestness.

When Walt returned to Washington on January 3, he took Eileen and Kevin with him. I sorely missed him in the night vigils. By now, getting the kids to sleep at night had become a

Their first Christmas at Grandpa and Grandma's house in Massachusetts. Kevin, Larry, and Lorna were mainly interested in eating the wrapping paper.

chronic problem, and I began to dread the return journey we had to make to Jamaica.

This difficulty came to a head back in Washington on January 21. Walt came home in the middle of the morning and went to bed with chills. Half an hour later, Uncle Len came home in the same condition, both stricken down by a virulent flu.

Three days later Lorna woke up about midnight, coughing and burning hot. I gave her the cough mixture I'd bought earlier in the evening. She promptly threw it up. I took her, limp as a jelly, to the bathroom to clean her up. She didn't even cry. Her temperature registered just two points short of 106 degrees.

Frantic, I called Walt out of bed and fled downstairs to call the doctor. In my anxiety, I didn't even think of Larry, though he was standing up in his crib. Just looking. Not saying anything. His temperature was 105. I didn't argue with the doctor when he ordered both babies into the hospital immediately. Muffin never opened his eyes. Although Lorna recognized me, she couldn't raise her head. I laid them both down in a hospital crib and left them to the nurses.

The next day I phoned home to see if Mum could come down. Auntie May had fallen ill too, and I was the only one left "alive" in the house. Dear Dad! He said that they'd planned one more surprise visit before we left for Jamaica, and that they'd come now. When the babies did come home, they were irritable beyond recognition and wouldn't eat. How thankful I was for Mum and Dad's help.

Massachusetts winter. Dorothy, Eileen, and Chips attend the three babies and two snowmen.

Meanwhile I had to finish the packing because our freight shipment was to go out the next day. Once in a while Walt staggered out of bed, looked at the boxes and then stumbled back where he'd come from. Everyone in the house had shattering, wrenching coughs.

A couple of young friends dropped by to say goodbye. They both were mourning the fact that they'd been "stood up" by their boyfriends. "Ah! We envy everything you have," they told me.

Running a low fever myself, I was off to do my second washing for the evening. Lorna had thrown up again, all over everything. At the same time, Larry gave himself over to three hours of non-stop yelling. I asked them if they envied me that too. "Oh, yes! Yes! That as well."

How much I really did have to be thankful for in my home and family. I had asked for it all. And I'd received it all too.

Somehow Walt brought his academic endeavors—term papers and all—to a conclusion. At noon on Sunday, February 7 we turned the Ford's nose south toward Florida. Unlike our summer trip to Canada, this time, instead of two somewhat confinable infants, we had two jackrabbits that more than filled the car with noise and confusion.

In the late afternoon on Wednesday, we reached Miami. We had less than one day there before our final leap across the Caribbean.

With two women at the Inter-American Division office taking turns with the kids, we went out to buy a new refrigerator, pick up our air-tickets, and do last minute shopping. That night I washed two loads of diapers.

Once more, we'd made the break and said our farewells. In its own way, Jamaica had to be a home-destination too. All four of us, I think, were invigorated by the warmth, sunshine and fresh air by the sea.

By the time we boarded our flight on Thursday morning, the kids were so tired that they slept most of the way to Montego Bay. At first Larry was tremendously impressed when the propellers started up, offering his usual wide-eyed comment, "Huh! Huh!" Even so, he missed the takeoff. He fell asleep before the plane left the ground.

CHAPTER 15

Jamaica Return

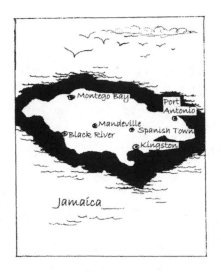

Our return to the West Indies was sandwiched between the kids' first birthdays.

We combined Lorna's day (February 5) with Uncle Len's (February 2). For one of our final social events, we had a simple little celebration with Uncle and Auntie who had been our loving, helpful land-lords for the past year. A cake, of course. Then, Lorna got to smear a lot of the frosting on her bald head. Her white-blond hair really hadn't begun to show yet.

Once more, we exchanged urban, predictable Takoma Park, Maryland, for the cool hills of Mandeville, Jamaica. Apart from leaving the family, we truly went back with no regrets.

On Thursday, February 11, 1960, Ed and Ethel Heisler met us at Kingston Airport. When their "Chickie" (Betty Lou) discovered Larry and Lorna, she squealed all the way home from the airport. She couldn't get over having playmates her own size.

When we stripped them down to their diapers, they got drunk on the fresh air and sunshine. They never did settle down for an afternoon nap.

Old Kingston Town looked and smelled the same. So much so, we could hardly believe that we'd ever been away. Early on Friday, we drove up to Mandeville, headquartering ourselves with Wilf and Annamarie Liske.

Now the mountains of Jamaica are unforgettable. The temperature is consistently mild, the rolling green hills are lovely to look at. Then the mornings! Ah, those mornings! We used to wake up to dewy sunshine and bird songs. The air we inhaled was almost Edenically pure. Above all, being with our old friends again and talking far into the night provided an almost seamless transition back into our West Indian life.

As soon as feasible, Annamarie and I took the kids up to Jamaica Hall.

An amazing number of my former students received us in triumph, as it were. The same went for the Saturday night faculty-staff supper at Tobiassens' home, our official "Welcome Home."

While Larry made himself amiable with one and all, Lorna howled and would look at nobody. That is, no one except Liskes and Heislers. They instantly became the kids' Jamaica family, a bond that has endured ever since. Moreover, Lorna was almost instantly covered with insect bites. She did have more than enough trouble to be miserable about.

The college campus perched on a razorback hilltop above an undulating green valley. Instead of fences, rolling lawns and gardens linked the homes together. I don't know of another place in the world where faculty members have lived more comfortably. At the time, however, no house was available in that area. We had to look elsewhere.

On our third day back in Mandeville we found it. A year of living all together in a single room in Washington—however comfortable and hospitable—could not have continued. Thoughts of occupying a whole house now evolved into a kind of new vision. We found a delightful, brand new home on Greenvale Drive, about three miles from the College.

Although further from the campus than we might have wished, the Greenvale house had a lot going for it. Large, airy, and floored with ceramic tiles, it stood on more than three acres of land, some 100 yards back from the road. Far and away, it was the best house we'd ever lived in. We rented it for £25 a month, the same price we'd paid three years earlier for the little Waltham Road house. Indeed, Providence provided for us wondrously well.

Moving in was much more than a day's work. The builders' debris had to be cleared away first. When our freight shipment arrived, Liskes slept at the new house to protect our unpacked stuff. We waited for the electricity to be turned on, then we moved in, exactly seventeen days after landing in Kingston. A speed record worthy of the *Guinness Book of Records.*

Certain urgent demands pressed in. Because a sprawling verandah fronted the place, Walt's first task was to break up our packing crates and enclose the porch with a white picket fence, lest Larry and Lorna fall off. A substantial drop. Secondly, he drove the car around the empty scrubby field in front three times. Thus we created a circle driveway, the configuration of which persists to this day. In time, we planted the empty field with trees and shrubs that today have grown into a little jungle.

In due course, Walt spent five shillings on an inflatable wading pool to put in the shade of the front porch. Very soon the babies had a priceless quantity of water fun in it. Cutting quite the figures in their bathing suits, they seemed to have as much (or more) fun than they did at the beach. Removing them from the little pool produced shrieks of protest.

In the tedious labors of getting our goods cleared out of customs in Kingston, our new refrigerator got left behind. Walt had to make a separate trip and haul it into the mountains. To accomplish this, he took the trunk lid off our Ford car we'd brought down from Miami. Upon arrival home he had to "un-door" both the refrigerator and the house itself to get the appliance placed. Seeing it standing fresh, tall, and capable in the kitchen, however, virtually called for the singing of the Doxology.

Within a matter of days after our arrival, Gwen Allen entered our lives. Her low-energy, seemingly unemployable, husband came around only occasionally. Our home became hers, and she occupied the maid's quarters at the back of the house. She loved the babies extravagantly, and they attached themselves to her on the spot. She also cleaned the big house and did the marketing and much of the cooking.

A week after we got into the house Lorna shot a temperature of 105 and became very ill, howling in misery. She threw up from morning to night. Three days later she broke out with measles. The rash could barely assert itself among the hundreds of sand-fly bites. At the same time, Larry, with the usual turmoil cut his fifth tooth. A week later he too had measles. All of this was hard on the little tykes following so soon after their big flu episode in Washington.

The sickness retarded Lorna's learning to walk. On the other hand, Larry, light as a coiled spring, began walking in earnest. His arrogance over his accomplishment frustrated Lorna beyond endurance. He was so proud that he could scarcely stay inside his skin. His round little face exuded pure radiance as he toddled along, occasionally bopping Lorna on the head as she sat on the sidelines, chattering. At the same time, his fussy, fickle appetite improved immeasurably.

Upon arrival, I'd told college administration that I could work only halftime. Two babies seemed a reasonable alibi. Under the policy prevailing at the time, I came in at the very bottom of the wage scale. That was half of the pay that the least educated woman on the entire college staff received. "It's all right," they explained, "because your husband is supporting you, anyway."

Much as I'd enjoyed college teaching, in 1960 I had to make a quantum leap. After a year of concentrating on runny noses and dirty diapers, I now had, instantaneously, to function again within my "intellectual harness." Although it was still at the subconscious level, I know that I really enjoyed linking up once more with the academic world.

I was expected to start teaching immediately, on a schedule that kept me away both mornings and afternoons. Therefore, I started my classes the day after we moved into the new house. Along with classroom appointments, of course, came the pestilence of committee meetings—Religious Interests and Social for Walt, Academic Policies for me, and many more.

As I set off each day looking back at the big picture window where I saw two sad little faces watching me. Behind them, however, stood the kindly, so-reliable, smiling Gwen.

At just £20 a month, I made barely enough money to pay Gwen's wages. Worse still, I soon found out that I was actually doing full time work anyway. Many nights went to class-preparation and committee work, and the weekends were often fragmented. "OK, then, put me back on full-time employment," I finally said. I was doing all of the work anyway. That's the way it stayed.

Larry's March 1 birthday gave us the opportunity to invite all of our old, pre-furlough friends out to the new house. The place filled with chat and laughter. The kids—ours as well as some other newcomers—added a new dimension to the gatherings.

We also entertained many student groups. Year after year, Liskes and we were involved as sponsors of the senior and/or junior classes. This meant even more socializing. Enjoyable, of course, but time-consuming.

Having no children himself, President Leif Tobiassen did not look with patience on any of the young ones disrupting church service. This being clear,

Walt and I spent the first year alternately staying at home with our tumultuous pair of kids.

With comforting regularity, however, Annamarie would offer to stay with Larry and Lorna so that we could be free to go to church "together and empty handed." Six-year-old Coralie (Liske) also loved playing with the babies. She believed Larry to be the little brother she'd been waiting for but who hadn't yet shown up. One looks back over long friendships such as we have had and is at a loss to find any words to describe the depth of those experiences. One can only conclude that they have been among God's best gifts to us.

On Walt's birthday in mid-year (1960) we were returning from a night committee meeting. Just a half mile from home a drunken jeep driver broadsided us. My door took the brunt of the crash, with holes punched along the whole side of the car. The largeness and heaviness of the Ford no doubt saved our lives. Neither of us slept enough that night to make it worthwhile even going to bed.

Car repairs created a long nightmare. Before the crisis ended Walt had to make several trips to Kingston himself to search out parts for this American car. Our blue Ford was laid up in Rehban's Body Shop for an indefinite time, we realized that we'd have to replace it with a smaller, local car. For the second time, we'd made the mistake of importing an American car into the Caribbean. Actually, Walt had seen our beloved "Little Woolley" on the streets of Mandeville, up for sale again. It was temptingly well-preserved, but we knew that our household could no longer fit into that carefree kind of automobile. As always, Liskes stood by and helped us manage transportation.

In early June that year Jamaica Hall had its official opening, debt free. The girls had gone to enormous effort to decorate their rooms for Open House. As I joined the inspection party I was followed by cries of "Come see my room." My mind went back to the beginnings of it all in 1958. How Walt and I had toiled to get the dormitory established. Much *déjà vu,* but I had not the least desire to return to the deanship. Happily, I didn't have to worry about anyone asking me to do it either. Now I could just have pleasure without responsibility.

Most of the time, we enjoyed our spacious estate out on Greenvale Road. We were, however, very much part of the local community. From time to time, our neighbors to the left slaughtered pigs in their front yard. Unfortunately, we had a front row seat for each event. I can still hear those doomed animals screaming.

One night at 1 a.m. we awoke to a major marital conflict traveling down the road in front of our house. In the starlight we could see a man striding along followed by a frenzied woman. Even though we knew nothing of the details of their problem, the current drama was clearly very distressing.

Apparently they'd been living together long enough to produce a quantity of children. Now, he was leaving her. She, however, had taken his shoes and had no intention of giving them back. Abandoning her with no shoes to facilitate his escape was the issue. All of this information was delivered at top volume as they straggled along the road, stopping from time to time to turn around and yell at each other, face to face.

Eventually, we were able to go back to sleep. At least we knew where our shoes were.

Much as we (and our friends) enjoyed that first year in the spacious Greenvale house, when we had the opportunity to rent the home of Shirley Greene, just below the College Hill, we decided to move. Expansively well planned, this home stood high on a hillside. A long flight of steps climbed up to the front verandah. From there we had an amazing view of the green Mandeville valley.

Now in the middle of the campus community, we began hosting small social events. By this time, pizza had long since been invented at home in the United States, but in Jamaica it remained unknown. We women, however, possessed a marvelous, made-from-scratch recipe. We cared nothing that it required a huge amount of work. For birthdays or on any other pretext we would make pizza. Loads of it. If I do say so myself, our pizza was good. As good as any I've eaten anywhere since.

At this point in time, Dr. George Shankel was coming up from Kingston to teach history classes on Mondays and Tuesday. He always slept at our house one or two nights a week. At times, his wife and their daughter, Virginia-Gene Rittenhouse, came also. As she has done ever since, Virginia-Gene had the ability to coax music out of veritable slugs. She inspired those who did play to perform better than their meager abilities could have made possible. Even I got out my clarinet and joined what she called her "Cockroach Orchestra." One member in it played a bamboo flute of his own making.

Dr. Shankel was accustomed to modest, controlled table service. At one of our pizza "fests" he ate one piece and stopped. "Oh, no," Walt urged. "You must have more."

Somewhat surprised Dr. S. took another. Eying all of those delicious strings of melted cheese linking one pizza slice to another, Walt remarked, "Well, none of the rest of us will sleep very well tonight, so why should you?"

With that, the dignified Dr. Shankel grinned, laid his ears back, and went to work. No one counted how many pieces he ate that night.

Those big Mandeville homes seemed to have been planned for entertaining. One night our house was crowded to the walls and out on to the verandah at a full faculty evening. My kitchen was not large, but mountains of good eating came forth to fill the long buffet table in the L-shaped dining area.

The end of that night's entertainment was a duet by the music teacher, Glenn Wheeler, and one of the Jamaican teachers. They played saws. Although saw playing can be well done, it can also be pretty dicey. These two were working on a Stephen Foster melody, but they never got together. Not for an instant, however, did they quit trying. I guess Glenn felt he just had to keep going so as not to betray his colleague. So together they plowed through to the end, in an agony of disharmony and general disarray.

As hostesses, Annamarie and I remained in the midst of the company. We listened in pain but graciously heard the piece to its end—wherever and whenever that might happen. Everyone in the audience held his/her ground in utter commitment, not wanting to add to the embarrassment in any way. I stood rigid in my effort not to burst out laughing.

Finally, the crowd, from old to young, dispersed. Walt and Wilf, however, were nowhere to be seen. After everyone had gone, we found them rolling around on the grass in the back yard, still roaring with drunken merriment. They couldn't stop and had almost laughed themselves sick. "Oh my!" I thought, my own hands trembling and sweaty. "I wish I had had the chance to give myself that much relief."

As far as time would allow, we kept up our beach trips and shell col-
lecting. All of our young ones learned to eat sandwiches mixed with sand and
to play in the clear, clean water that encircled our beautiful island.

In August of 1960 we made a week's vacation trip to Grand Cayman. We
still had many friends there, and we wanted Wilf and Annamarie to see our
first Caribbean roots. Although Coralie went with us, we left Larry and Lorna
at home with Gwen. This was possible because Gwen had long since proved
her skill and devotion to us all.

For a week we lounged about the Merrens' very relaxing and private
Pageant Beach Hotel. After the idyllic Mandeville climate, we found Cayman
unmercifully hot. On our first afternoon, we lay limp under fans, unable even
to consider going to the sugar-white Seven-Mile Beach until the sun had
lowered itself.

The acting mission president at the time called on us. A Caymanian,
he'd spent many years in the United States and had acquired certain northern
ideas. The soul of hospitality, he sat in our motel room, eager to welcome us
"home" to the island. He wore a thick wool suit, including a vest. It seemed
to be made of a kind of blanket cloth. I looked at his crossed legs and saw a
long ribbed kind of sock. Does he have to wear elastic support stockings too
in this heat, I wondered.

As it turned out, the dear man was simply following a tradition of the
19th-century church. One of the founders had written on health matters and
had said that the body's extremities should be carefully kept warm at all costs.
I'm sure that she had never heard of the Cayman Islands or that she had any
idea that this particular piece of advice would be carried to such an extreme.

Later in the week, I learned from another Caymanian friend that the good
pastor was actually wearing "long johns." Indeed, such garments had never
before been seen on the island. Passersby, it was said, often lingered at the fence
to view this unique underwear hanging on the clothesline in his back yard.

Although we had to slip it in between school terms, our beach week with
Liskes has remained a prized memory.

Over the next months the child-count in our overseas community

Beach time. Left. Beautiful Dunn's River gurgles down out of the Jamaica mountains toward the beach. Right. At the end of a picnic day, with his feet on the salty, sandy beach, Walt shampooed and bathed under the fresh, cool showers of Dunn's River Falls. Sadly, today a frenzy of tourism has impaired the natural loveliness we enjoyed in the 1950s.

reached eleven. Five of them were in Larry and Lorna's age group. At Christmas time, Annamarie, Evelyn (Korgan) and I bought a big bolt of red flannel featuring snowmen. We made either pajamas or nightgowns for each one of the children, including the offspring of some of our Jamaican friends. Then we threw them all into motion, as it were. We made movies as they paraded around the living room. The only one left out was seven-month-old Julie Liske, clad in white and sitting wide-eyed in the middle of the dizzy, rotating circle of kids.

Sadly, another, much darker thread had been running through our lives. As political tensions escalated so did the number of "emergency" committee meetings to which we were summoned. The word became a cliché and was used to describe almost every committee that was called. I kept telling myself that if the mighty decisions we made were followed up by action, then we should not have lived in vain. On that point, however, we had little evidence to encourage us.

In my effort to "keep up" I often hit a brick wall. Final exams might end on a Friday and our grades would be required in on Sunday. Along with several other classes, I was teaching at least two Freshman English classes with fifty students apiece in them.

More than one of the college presidents pressured me, "Of course, you require a full essay each week from all of them, don't you?"

Left. The spot where the Black River flowed into the sea provided a quiet, fresh pool where the kids could be bathed at the end of another day playing in the ocean. To counteract many hours spent in the sun, everyone wore shirts over their bathing suits. Right. On Negril Beach on Jamaica's north coast. Larry held a large helmet shell and watched Lorna chew on a starfish. Both trophies had been brought ashore by their snorkeling parents.

How little they understood of the curious aspects of Jamaican English, an odd mixture of the bad and the amazing. One day a student turned in a paragraph that I read in class—incognito, of course. Even his classmates had to smile. Every line contained at least one word that even I couldn't recognize.

He himself was the one who raised his hand. "Do you make me to understand that this is not good writing? If we don't write this way, how will people know that we're educated?" (The man went on to become a high-level church administrator.)

I rose and silently wrote in foot-high letters on the blackboard, "SIMPLICITY." That was my credo and a very difficult concept to teach in the West Indies.

From where I stand today I could argue in high court about the most effective way to teach writing courses. It would concern reasonable class-size, teachers reading papers personally, creative ways to produce essay material in "bite-sizes," and so forth. At that time, however, I didn't know enough to defend myself.

By now (1961) serious changes were at work around us. Some major difficulties were coming to the fore. Anyone who has worked in any kind of overseas assignment understands that one of the purposes of his/her service is to prepare a national to take over the task. Colonialism had its day long ago.

Since the end of World War II, the position of a missionary (or any other kind of foreign employee) has changed. He/she should stay only as long as it takes for a local person to be trained to fill the need. Logically, this is the theory. In real life, that transition can be prolonged and difficult.

On three occasions our terms of overseas service were separated by yearlong periods of study leave. In each case a distinct pattern repeated itself. Upon returning to the same place after a year's absence, you find that the institution managed pretty well to get on without you. Although you technically still have a job to do, you too often find that the second half of a double term is in many (sometimes indefinable) ways inferior to the first part. A year is a long absence.

Against this background several events were now taking place at the College. Although I was working full time, I'd been relieved of Senior Cambridge English class, a kingpin of the secondary school program. In other ways I'd been somewhat "un-chaired." One of the terms of Walt's first study leave had been the teaching of college religion, but now he had only high school classes. These various arbitrary replacements had an uneasy political flavor.

We eventually came to the point of resignation. That, however, turned out to be a bad word, and we were persuaded to give up the idea. All the same, we did begin think seriously of another study leave. This time the kids would be old enough, and I would have my chance to upgrade too.

Meanwhile, two college presidents had collapsed within the past three years. Dr. Tobiassen was currently away on sick leave, and it was the common opinion that he would return only to sell off his goods and depart. Moreover, half of the overseas workers and several of the nationals threatened to leave before the start of another school year. We ourselves hoped to hang on for one more year.

Be it said now, fifty years later, that West Indies College developed into what is the important and highly successful Northern Caribbean University. We just happened to be present in a time of painful transition. Growing pains are always just that. Pain!

Then came a joyful diversion. One day in August 1961 we stood on the observation platform at Kingston Airport and watched Mum and Dad alight from the Miami flight. What a thrill to have them with us for a couple of weeks. We had it all planned out—the sightseeing, the campus tours, and, above all, the renewal of our family time. We made sure that they saw all of our favorite beaches—Negril, Bluefields, Montego Bay, the Palisadoes, and all the rest.

On their first night in Mandeville we had occasion to see just how well adjusted we'd become to our environment. With delight Mum resumed her old role of putting the babies to bed. The rest of us had just settled into bed too, when Mum suddenly rushed out of her room. "Is one of the babies sick?" she cried.

I met her in the hall. "Well, no," I replied. "Why?"

"That noise! Someone must be throwing up."

Then I remembered. "Oh, no, that's just the donkey next door. He brays loud and long, at about ten o'clock every night." I hadn't even heard him. Welcome to Jamaica!

Over time, West Indies College produced a major field of study in English in our department. In the new year (1962), I deliberately added two new advanced classes to my teaching load, Creative Writing and English Topics. It meant a lot of work, but I looked on it as preparation for study leave when I would get my turn to sit on the other side of the teacher's desk.

Meanwhile, our newest college president (Dr. Osborne) worked in Jamaica part time. (He didn't actually ever move his family there.) When he put much pressure on us not to leave on Permanent Return, confusion prevailed for three or four months. Then he himself left.

Even though our letters to the office in Miami weren't bringing prompt replies, we decided to carry on with our plans. Morale and school spirit generally were low, as was ours. We could see little chance of improvement. Besides, if you really are going to find a place in *academe,* there comes a time when you really are too old. We needed to get on with our project.

In the midst of all the uncertainty, I chose to have some fun. I decided to go all out on Larry's third birthday cake. I shaped it into a boat, the lower deck with green icing and the upper with yellow. Lifesavers and Smarties made the portholes, with walnuts for anchors. The *piece de resistance* was a group of

Just before the family left Jamaica for the last time, Grandpa and Grandma Minchin visited. On the front veranda, Lorna and Larry "rode horsy" on Grandpa.

three fat candles for smoke-stacks. I don't think anything I've achieved in my whole career could, in his eyes, match the glory of that cake. With her meddlesome little fingers always in motion, Lorna swooped down on the cake. Larry stood his ground and would scarcely let her even look at it.

Finally, on April 5, 1962, the General Conference voted our Permanent Return, and, we would have a year's salary. Worried that we'd be departing under a cloud, we could only hope that at least some people realized our campus situation.

Our last months were more than full. Walt and Mrs. Lucille Walters sponsored the high school seniors and Annamarie and I had the college class. This responsibility increased social and financial obligations and occupied every weekend. In the midst of it all I wrote another play for the Class Night program, an adaptation of Rachel Field's "The Patchwork Quilt." That would mean drama coaching and much more. Once again, I marveled at the many jobs I kept accepting, even when I had neither training nor ability for ful-filling them.

Walt had various speaking appointments at churches, and we accrued several Kingston trips. One of the last was a weekend with Heislers and their three little girls. Between Friday and Sunday morning the kids had no more than half a dozen fights, all of which led us to hope that they might all be arriving at some more advanced level of civilization. On all of these journeys Larry and Lorna talked incessantly, and every comment had to be acknowledged.

On May 10 we had a picnic at Dunn's river, the last of our social engage-ments connected with the sponsorship of these senior classes. Plus, there was still an agenda of home entertaining. The kids thoroughly enjoyed all of the goings-on. Lorna so loved the crowds. Racing between the back and front doors, she shouted, "See all the bodies coming. Look, Mummy, more bodies are coming here."

And what a way the bodies could eat! It took Annamarie and me two whole Sundays cooking for the events. Saying grace over one of those meals, a student pastor said, "Lord, give us a good appetite and help us to do a good job."

On the man's third trip to the buffet table, someone remarked, "You're really helping to answer your own prayer, aren't you?" That, I suppose, is good theology.

We hadn't planned to

Larry's third birthday. He would scarcely let Lorna even *look* at his "Steamboat Cake" for fear of her damaging it.

break up housekeeping quite so soon, but people kept asking for this and that item, and the house was beginning to empty. The day our big buffet went, Lorna cried in the morning, "Where's Mummy's big table gone?" We suffered as we saw the household "mash up," as the Jamaicans would say.

One more full-scale faculty supper, and we gave up the catering and started packing. When again would we enjoy so much really good company as we had during our years on the Hilltop. Inevitably, we'd leave with major regrets. Every place to which you truly give yourself becomes part of the fabric of your life. But how could we stay? The College appeared to have contracted some kind of emotional disease. We could only pray that it wouldn't be terminal. (It wasn't.)

Now Walt had to put in many hours and many Kingston trips to unreel all of the red tape connected with his U. S. immigrant visa. Part of his pile of paperwork was a set of life-size chest x-rays that couldn't fit into any suitcase we possessed.

In mid-May, amid the normal departure turmoil, Lorna started ailing with a sporadic fever and a terrible cough. The doctor said it was a sinus infection. She was utterly thrilled with the visit. As we neared the Medical Center she grinned from ear to ear, "Poor Lorni sick, got a bad cough." Then, with a hilarious laugh, "Gonna see the doctor." At the same time, Larry was deeply offended. He practically ruptured an artery trying to make a bad enough cough so that he could see the doctor too.

On June 14 we flew to Nassau, Bahamas, by jet. Liskes had lived there for years, and it would have seemed very proper for them to be there to show us around as we had introduced them to Cayman. But they weren't.

Larry was jittery at take-off. Looking back down to the receding airport parking lot, he moaned, "I want to get out and walk." Then, "Go ride in the car."

"But we don't have a car anymore," I reminded him.

"Go ride in Unky's car." Larry kept up the doleful monologue all the way to Montego Bay.

We finally reached the Bahamas and enjoyed a good weekend there with friends. For sightseeing we hired a horse carriage for an advertised "romantic" tour the waterfront. The driver blithely rode the wrong way on a one-way street. People in parked cars yelled at him constantly and shook their fists. "One way! One way."

"I only goin' one way," he drawled. "I ain't goin' two ways."

In Miami, I spent most of the time in the motel with the kids while Walt went car shopping. It had to be another American car, of course. Never in my life have I liked big cars. The next day we hitched on a little trailer to hold our stuff and headed for Grandpa and Grandma's house in Takoma Park. Dad was by now chairing the Religion Department at Washington Missionary College. New England had become part of our history. Few of us had the opportunity even to visit there again.

Now, just one week after leaving Jamaica, we'd suddenly become detached from our familiar lifestyle. Sadly it had all happened two years earlier than we expected. So now we had to steadfastly turn our faces northward.

The monuments were beautifully illuminated, and the kids woke up to see our nighttime approach to the city. Influenced by Sabbath School pictures they'd seen of the New Jerusalem, they watched in awe. "Are we in heaven?" they asked softly.

Well, hardly. This was Washington, D.C. Again.

CHAPTER 16

In and Out of the Ivory Tower

Once again we were home to Grandpa and Grandma's house—but unsettled. Dad had an appointment at the Ohio camp meeting, so he and Mum were away for most of our first week in Washington. Walt took off for Michigan to explore our possibilities at Andrews University. He wanted to add a BTh degree to the MA that he'd earned last time he'd been in "The Ivory Tower."

Being on Permanent Return with twelve months of salary ahead of us, we had a few job offers. At least, for one year, we would "come cheap." These invitations included an academy teaching post in the Midwest and the pastorship of the Ottawa Church in Canada. Both of us, however, had set our minds on graduate study. Indeed, I was really eager to get into serious English studies. The autumn leaves couldn't fall too soon for that to happen.

For a while, the bare essentials of living occupied most of my time. We'd said goodbye to our beloved Gwen. I knew that it was high time for the kids to be weaned away from the maid-service regime. It took endless patience to sell them on the idea of picking up their toys, sweeping the floor with their new little brooms, and helping with the dishes. Their consolation prize for all of this required labor was a tricycle and a doll "currage" (carriage) for Lorna.

Lorna always loved sorting the laundry. She loudly identified each garment, right down to the last pair of socks and underwear, which she called "aprons for the tummies."

Even though I abhorred cold weather, in a perverse way I now looked forward to four seasons again. A tweed suit? A woolly sweater? Sounded pretty good. At long last, I had an excuse to go back to knitting, a favorite hobby of my lifetime. While I supervised the kids, I started a sweater for Lorna.

Our post-overseas service always concluded with extensive medical examinations. It turned out that I would be heading for major surgery. This now accounted for my years of "diminished endurance."

"Do I have to have it right now?" I couldn't bear the thought of laying myself up just as I was on the verge of beginning my Masters degree in English.

"Not necessarily," the doctor replied. "But I believe you'll find that you'll want to have it done in a reasonably short time."

I walked out muttering. "No, not now. We can't. School opens at Andrews University next week." As usual, I wouldn't give up. Nothing domestic, medical, or academic was going to stop me from getting a shot at Graduate School.

I have to say "nothing" advisedly. Actually, back in 1950, when I'd graduated with my Bachelors of Arts degree, I had a GPA of about C+. At the time, I didn't much concern myself with that score. I'd had a pleasant enough trip through college, had made friends, written scripts and generally been a co-ed. I'd studied just enough to graduate without undue embarrassment.

When my job offers involved elementary teaching and other unsuitable occupations, I thought, in passing, of going to grad school immediately. Boston University, however, told me promptly and in no uncertain terms that my grades simply weren't good enough.

Instead of being devastated, I happily went off to my teaching job in Canada. Thereafter came marriage, mission service, and now children. For the past twelve years I hadn't really had time to think about going back to school. My years of college teaching in Jamaica, however, had given me, as it were, the "taste for red meat." Now my desire for study and research seemed to have no limits.

Once at Andrews, I interviewed my future mentor and friend, Dr. John Waller. Yes, we agreed, I should be arriving with at least a 2-point (B) average. "We'll give you provisional standing for the first semester," the Chair of the English Department told me. At least I was in!

As the Michigan winter loomed ahead of us we were allotted a large, very old Victorian house in Berrien Springs. University-owned, it was kept for transient families like us who were trying to re-establish themselves back on home base. We dug into our barrel of winter clothes, bought a few pieces of second-hand furniture, and distributed our few belongings through the cavernous rooms.

Having already lived under every imaginable kind of living conditions, I don't know why I disliked that house so intensely. It was dark and smelled moldy. When we sat down to eat in the kitchen, none of us ever seemed to be quite warm enough. The kids occupied two enormous, empty bedrooms upstairs, and it took nightly efforts to get Lorna to stay in her bed. "But, I'm scared," she whimpered.

Walt's and my downstairs bedroom was small with a disproportionately high ceiling. With mustard-colored wallpaper and heavy, faded green drapes it looked—and felt—like a viewing room in a funeral home.

After a month, we were all busy enough but very restless. Somehow, the house seemed to be dying, and we couldn't find life-support either for it or ourselves.

Walt had always wanted to own rather than rent houses. He looked forward to any day when we might be able to actually do it. Apart from our last eight months in Newfoundland, we'd never owned a piece of property.

The James White Library, Andrews University, Michigan. Warm in summer and sheltered and ice-covered in winter, these broad stairs led Dorothy into real intellectual adventures. Walt had already been into graduate study, but here she hit her stride in research and writing, for the first time.

Within a week, he'd found us a little house over on Greenfield Drive, within walking distance of the university campus. We bought it on the spot. It had the conventional three bedrooms, but the master suite had been converted into a rentable studio apartment. We immediately found tenants, a couple younger than ourselves and without children. Their rent helped us in a major way to meet our mortgage payments.

That left one bed and bath for us, plus a tiny room for the kids. Fortu-nately, they looked upon their bunk beds as a privilege and not a handicap. While the sound-proofing was rather poor, the lightness and simplicity of it all was truly uplifting. In the spring when the red climbing roses around the front door burst into bloom, we knew for sure that we'd made a right choice.

Another decision followed closely on our moving into the new house. With both of us in full-time studies, we made an offer to Gwen Robertson, daughter of one of Walt's older sisters. Would she like to come live with us and help with the kids and go to college? Would she? We sent her a plane ticket, and she was in Michigan to start classes within two days. Walt roughed-in two rooms in the basement, one for her and one for our books and our ever-busy typewriter. The arrangement worked well for all of us. It seemed that we just got on well with Gwens!

Knowing that I had only one year to finish my degree, I threw myself into my work. I had a retreat on the top floor of the James White Library, a little carrel all my own. Underclassmen and lesser persons had to congregate around the conventional library tables. In contrast, we grad types merited this precious privacy. I was buried among books and actually loved writing term papers. I hesitated to admit to this abnormality and never spoke of it aloud.

By Thanksgiving time in November, however, my mind-over-matter vow was failing. I started hemorrhaging to the point where we had to cancel our planned visit home to Washington. (Mum and Dad, instead, drove up to Michigan.)

I then realized that I would have to deal with my problem. Early in December I checked into the hospital in Niles and had the hysterectomy. Gwen took charge of the kids, and my husband stood by me. On the first day a blizzard blew in, but Walt was allowed to sleep on the floor beside my bed.

Semester exams were coming up in mid-January, and I had a lot on my mind. After all, I hadn't forgotten that I was a probationary student. Kindly classmates, teachers and other friends had to be aware of my concerns. Did I know, after all, whether I was graduate-student material or not? I had absolutely no track record to give me hope.

I got out of the hospital just before Christmas. Lorna was glad enough

Dorothy did all of her graduate study the hard way—*after* the arrival of Larry and Lorna. Together, in front of their little Michigan home, the three of them displayed her new M.A. degree.

to see me, but Larry—who'd told us that he would be a doctor—sat for hours on the bed asking me where my tummy hurt and examining the many bruises on my arms and hands. His inquiry ended only when someone hauled him off to eat or sleep.

I had a friend who worked in the registrar's office. She and her Seminary-student husband had tragically lost all four of their children in a house fire. Now she put all of her energy into helping other people. For the ten days that I was in the hospital, she sent me a personal note and a little memento every day.

The time came when I had to go to the registrar's office and pick up my grade slip. I waited at the counter while my friend looked for my report. "You know," she said, "I knew how worried you were about being in the hospital and then immediately having to take the final exams. So I didn't sleep much last night, thinking about you." She fished the envelope out of the file, smiled, and pushed it across the counter toward me. "Now I wish I'd just slept."

Shaking, I pulled out the report. An A in every class! Now I knew. I could do graduate work after all! Never again would I be on probation. Tears welled up in my eyes, and I had to rush out of the office.

When I sat in Dr. Frank Knittel's class in Middle English, I realized that I was the only one in the room who didn't know German. A distinct disadvantage! We had to memorize selected lines of the Prologue to "Canterbury Tales." Earnestly desiring to get the right pronunciation, I asked Walt to listen to me and correct my errors.

One night he interrupted my recitation with a yelp. "Don't say that!"

"Don't say what?"

"That word! What if the renters hear you?" That's when I, in my naïveté, learned that Chaucerian language is ripe with all of those four-letter words that are said to pollute modern speech today.

While I could praise all of my professors, I can never say enough good about John Waller. I loved the way he read poetry. His classes spurred us to maximum performance. Especially his course in research methods. We seven class-members didn't actually write a masters thesis, because, at the time, it was felt that the library resources in English were insufficient to support such an undertaking. Instead, at the end, we had to leave four major term papers on file, each of which we'd polished to a blinding blaze of intellectual excellence.

Dr. Waller also asked us to choose a topic that we might be interested in researching. We were to work up an outline and then prepare bibliography cards for every source that we could possibly use. Whether or not they actually existed in our library didn't matter. We weren't writing a thesis. Just toiling for a whole semester as *if* we were. We filed our cards in shoeboxes. Each card had to have the exact prescribed information, correct down to the last comma. Slowly we filled our boxes.

At the last seminar we had to submit our massive bibliographies. As we were fiddling with our cards, a great cry of pain went up from one of the men. "Look here! I didn't put in the name of the publisher on this one." He was waving the card about just as our professor walked into the room. "What can I do?"

Our professor considered the omission. "Well," he intoned. "I would say, 'If you have a sword, lean upon it now.'" He had always been fearfully exact. "Of course," he went on, "I could fail every one of you." Anything less than a B is failure in Graduate School. We looked at one another in terror. "Before I would do that, however, I would have to leave town on the first train." He leaned back in his chair and looked around the table, smiling. We all exhaled and started breathing again.

To be sure, this was the most stringent class I ever endured. Yet, it remains one of the best bits of training I ever had. A few years later, when I entered doctoral studies, I made a surprising discovery. I had classmates who were far along in their studies. Some had almost used up the seven years we were allowed before all of our credits rotted and we'd have begin again. Their problem was not classes, nor even passing examinations. They simply had never learned how to document their work. They couldn't set up a bibliography and footnotes. As for me, I did it all automatically, with no loss of time and no anguish.

A thousand times, "Thank you, Dr. Waller."

School routines, of course, dictated how our household operated. We also made new friends. We enjoyed the University Church where my mother's only brother, James Rhoads, was senior pastor. True to his lifelong hobby, he cultivated an enormous garden. He kept us—and scores of other student families—supplied with vegetables. Every Friday afternoon, Uncle Jimmie and his full wheelbarrow made campus rounds.

In mid-winter Larry and Lorna had their fourth birthdays. In the spring, they became Bible boy and flower girl, respectively, at the wedding of two of our former Jamaican students.

In June of 1963, I graduated and marched down the aisle of Pioneer Memorial Church, clasping in my hand my new M.A. degree *(Magna cum Laude)*. Mum and Dad came up to Michigan for the event. Afterwards, Walt and Mum took the children home to bed, leaving Dad and me free to attend the reception.

Although not outwardly demonstrative, my Dad was always profoundly interested in me and my academic adventures. After all, he was the one from whom I'd inherited this passion for study. On that spring night, he and I walked home together in the starlight. Silence.

Then he laid his hand over my arm—which was already linked to his. Almost choking, he said, "Well, bless your boots and your socks!" Again my tears came. Coming from my dear, sometimes whimsical father, this compliment seemed like a trumpet fanfare. I couldn't have asked for more.

But we weren't finished yet. Walt still needed another year to finish his theology degree. That meant that I had to find a job, quick time. If not, our financial coach would very rapidly turn into a pumpkin. Our PR (Permanent Return) money was coming to an end.

At the end of the summer, Walt bought us a conventional and very economical "Beetle," a Volkswagen. One morning Walt took Larry, and I watched my two men set off for Alberta in our little black Bug. While they were gone, I stayed home, shifted my own gears, and got ready to be the breadwinner for the coming school year.

After its trans-continental journey, The Bug would become my transportation on my daily trip from home to my school in New Troy, some fourteen miles west toward Lake Michigan.

Yes, there were other teaching positions available, but in all I honesty I had to tell any would-be employer that I could work for only one year. That admission, of course, has never been the successful path up the academic ladder. Therefore, the potentially "better" schools had no interest in me.

Finally, I found a place in the small public high school in New Troy. It gave me the work I very much needed. The school's existence was more tenuous than I imagined. Just three years later it would merge with the nearby Three Oaks High School, and even the building would be demolished. For the year of 1963-1964, however, I would function as the librarian and teach Grades 10, 11, and 12 English.

Once known as "Weesaw," the township of New Troy had been founded in 1837. With a population of about 2,500 the little community stood on a branch of the Galien River, not far from the Lake and its dunes. Hard-working middle-class people, they were. More or less middle-aged too.

The offspring of these families were, not unexpectedly, obsessed with sports and all of the other interests of mid-20th-century teenagers. Probably less than 15% of them would ever get to college. With a high school diploma as a terminal degree, most expectations tended to stop there also.

For me this was going to be a vast, new education, replete with lessons not found in books. In many ways, I was oddly suited to the New Troy appointment. Yes, this would be better than Newfoundland, very different from Jamaica, and also a total inversion of my graduate school experience. Having grown up in a professor's house, I was far into adulthood before I realized that not everyone went to college. Nor should they even try.

My two years as a library staffer in college helped me set up the little one-room library. Because there were several tables available, I automatically became the supervisor of those so-called (somewhat visionary) blocks of time

Grandma Comm and Larry in front of the Volkswagen that Walt bought in the summer of 1963. Before Dorothy started driving "The Beetle" to her teaching job in New Troy in the autumn, Walt made a quick trip to his beloved home country in the Peace River District of Alberta, Canada, taking Larry with him.

designated as "Study Periods." At times the resistance to learning seemed palpable. I cultivated a couple of very bright girls, however, to help me. After I classified the books, they wrote the Dewey Decimal numbers on the spines. They even advanced to the point of helping to control the study intervals.

Occasionally I had amazing—sometimes touching—insights into the life-stream of New Troy. The Grade 10 Reader contained the Biblical story of the Prodigal Son. I presented the story to them in class and then asked them to re-write it, keeping the same characters and plot but transferring everything else into a 20th-century setting.

After class one fidgety little rascal stopped by my desk. I knew he was bright enough, but for most of the year I'd been happier to see him going rather than coming. "But, Teacher!" He fixed a blue-eyed stare on me. "I just don't understand the story. If I did something like that, my father would kill me. He really would."

I took it slowly. "You see, Tom, in the story the father represents God." As I went on to explain the parable, I could see that I was breaking new ground with him, all of the way. Eventually, Tom actually turned in a pretty good story, despite his limited comprehension of what a father could be.

Shakespeare's "Hamlet" was also in our book. I thought about it. It seemed a little too sophisticated for the likes of Tommy and the other Grade 10 kids. They just hadn't done enough living yet. So I substituted "The Merchant of Venice."

Ever since our first interview Tom often stopped by to speak to me. "Hey,

Shakespeare's keen," he told me one day. "I really like that dude." Indeed, the boy's grades improved vastly as the year went on. I wonder what happened to him.

Then another case came up. Having caught Bill cheating, I called him into the library to discuss his offense. "Copying from your friend is nothing but stealing. It's exactly the same thing."

He looked at the floor

New Troy High School, Michigan, in 1964. Dorothy spent a very educational year teaching there to sustain the family during the latter part of their second Study Leave. (Photo courtesy of Friends of Troy. See <terry@centeroftheworld.net>).

and said nothing. "If you were in the post office and you found that someone had left a dime on the counter, would you take it?"

"Well, of course." He regarded me with pity. "Who wouldn't?"

"What if it was fifty dollars? Would you take that too?" He said nothing. He was streetwise enough to know that this could have criminal implications.

"Er ... no! Uh, because you see ... ."

"Well why not? You'd be stealing both times. Exactly how much you took shouldn't matter, should it?"

So we worked through that problem. Bill too began dropping by to say something to me. I hope he has also done well over these past forty-seven years.

One spring afternoon, I was sitting at work in the library. I heard a stampede on the steps, coming up from the first floor. In a moment, a red-faced woman thrust her head through the half-door that opened into the hallway. She didn't even come into the room. "You gave my son an F in Grade 12 English," she bellowed.

I opened my record book. Shielding the other grades, I pointed to the evidence of his daily performance. "Well, you see how the year has been going."

She barely looked down. "You failed him and now he can't graduate," she raged. "You have to change his grade."

I had a fairly sharp appreciation of what academic standards should be. "I can't just do that … "

"It isn't fair!" I thought she was going to strike me.

What to do? "I will promise you this. I will speak to the principal about the matter." I watched her literally unraveling before my eyes. "In fact," I rose to my feet. "I'll do it right now."

Without another word, the distraught, weeping woman wheeled about and rushed into the restroom, directly across the hall. Too crazed to notice the sign, she slammed into the boys' room.

Grade book in hand, I headed down the stairs. I could only hope that that roaring female found the restroom full of boys. Maybe that kind of shock would defuse a little of her fury.

Downstairs I laid out the situation to the principal, Mr. Ongstad. He listened carefully. "But you know," he said at last, "this boy will never do anything but work on an assembly line and screw down bolts for the rest of his life. What difference does it make?"

Without further investigation, I was fully aware that the cause of the meltdown might remain unclear. I knew that the boy was negative and very lazy, but I couldn't know whether or not he actually had the capacity to do Grade 12 English.

I hadn't felt so inexperienced or young for a long time. I pressed ahead anyway.

"For my part, I cannot change the grade. I simply cannot reward non-performance, even with a D. And what about reputation? Should he become a bona fide graduate of this school?" The administrator stared at me intently. "If you tell me to change his grade, however," I hurried to add, "I shall do so, but only under your instructions."

He looked me so hard that I wondered if I'd gone too far. "I will let you know my decision in the morning."

I made my half-hour trek home over the pleasant country roads, just now bursting into bloom. I wondered. Was I supposed to come down out of my ivory tower (or whatever it was) and just go with the flow?

The next morning Mr. Ongstad personally sought me out. "I've thought it over," he said. "The grade will stand as it is."

For the moment, I felt somewhat heroic. Over the years, however, I've wondered about that failed high school senior. What kind of a life did he have? Was it OK anyway? I never found out.

On Friday afternoon, November 22, 1963, Mr. Ongstad stepped into my Grade 12 English classroom. Without preamble, he said. "Our President, John F. Kennedy, has been shot." The whole room froze. Not even those chewing gum could move a muscle. "He died just thirty minutes ago."

The principal moved on, making his classroom rounds. After a heavy, abysmal silence, I knew I had to do something. If questioned, I believe just about all of us can explain where we were and what we were doing when the news of the assassination broke. I took a deep breath and spoke of death and the shock that goes with it. I don't remember my exact words

To open class on Monday, I read a poem by Emily Dickinson, that 19th-century American visionary who so transparently wrote of Time and Eternity:

The bustle in a house
The morning after death
Is solemnest of industries
Enacted upon earth,—

The sweeping up the heart,
And putting love away
We shall not want to use again
Until eternity.

Those twelfth-graders, from our handful of honor students down to the most indolent fellow in the class, responded with a depth of feeling that we usually don't expect from adolescents. We bonded because we'd shared an unfathomable experience that would mark us for life.

Still, New Troy didn't give me a very easy year. After all, I went home everyday to my two four-year-olds and regular domestic chores that never eased up. Considering all that went before and has come after, however, my first year of public high school teaching became an essential part of my education. After all, don't all professionals aim to be all things to all people? Yes, the Ivory Tower is indeed a lovely place to be, but it can also become a prison.

As the summer of 1964 approached, we started wondering. We had to find work somewhere, and we were entirely on our own. As it turned out, we would be going home again. Home in a now familiar way. Walt would be Acting Chairman of the Department of Religion at Canadian Union College. After one year, I would be offered chairmanship of the English Department.

So, for the third time, "Canada, here I come."

CHAPTER 17

Canadian Union College, Again

Just as we began to dispose of our shabby little collection of secondhand stuff and prepared to head back to Canada, a serendipitous event occurred. Wilf and Annamarie Liske left Jamaica and came to take up their new appointments on the faculty of Andrews University.

My first thought was, "Oh, if they could only have been here for the past two years with us!"

The second, "What a good idea!" That was when they bought the little Greenfield house that we were vacating. True, they didn't occupy it for long, because they bought a more spacious, family-friendly house out in Eau Claire. Still Greenfield remained as a rental in our "joint family" for many years. Nor was this the last real-estate venture we shared.

Our road trip from Michigan to Alberta should have been straightforward. Walt drove the new Ford pick-up truck that his older brother Ben wanted brought out from the factory in Oshawa, and I drove our old Ford.

After spending a weekend in Toronto, our little convoy headed west. In the farm country a few hours out into the Ontario countryside, we were passing through a small town at a modest pace.

Suddenly, without warning, a car in our lane made a left turn. The vehicle ahead of me stopped. By braking hard, I didn't hit him. The guilty car disappeared over a slight rise. Behind me, however, the chain reaction rippled down the road. Walt and the new truck slammed into the back of my car. The car behind him crashed into the back of the new truck. And on and on until ten cars were locked together, end to end.

Larry had been sleeping in the back window of the car, and he landed on top of me in the front seat. In the truck, Lorna fell to the floor under the dashboard. Although no one appeared to be much injured (visibly), everyone was noticeably shaken up. We all stood on the roadside surveying the mess and thinking hard thoughts about the driver who caused it all. Walt and I were particularly vexed because the new truck had left the assembly line only a few hours earlier. Now both its nose and rear end were thoroughly banged in.

Several children issued out of the damaged cars. Mercifully, a couple of women from a nearby farmhouse came and ushered them all inside for cookies and milk.

Before the police arrived, on the opposite side of the road, a motor home swooped over the hill. Utterly fascinated with the devastation on our side, the driver sideswiped a car already parked on the shoulder. The entire right side of his vehicle peeled off as cleanly as you would open a can of beans. Its innards scattered along the road for a half a mile. Pans, bottles, books, shoes, boxes, clothes—every private thing in that family's life was laid out for the world to see.

By the time the police arrived, they had many interesting things to do. Finally, all of the crippled cars dispersed, being, as I recall, still drivable. We decided to return to the hospital in Toronto to get checked out. I'd begun to feel decidedly squeamish.

After the x-rays came in, the doctor asked. "Have you ever had a gall bladder attack?"

"I don't know. What's that like?" I replied.

"Well, if you have to ask, it's been OK. So far." Then I remembered that I'd been told after my other surgery eighteen months earlier, that I had gallstones.

I recalled asking that doctor why he hadn't just yanked them out too at the same time. "Too much to do at one time," he'd said.

Now as we limped back toward Alberta in our two damaged vehicles I began to feel decidedly unwell. In short order, I had a very clear understanding of what a gallbladder attack feels like.

We were scheduled to move into the house of the Hugh Campbells who were away on study leave. When we arrived on campus, the house wasn't quite ready, so we spent a few nights in the girls' dormitory.

On the first night, Lorna fell off the top bunk on her head and had to spend the night in the hospital. The presiding doctor, Wilf Tetz, turned out to be a familiar friend. In fact, back in student days in college, he and Walt had been roommates.

We had just managed to get ourselves into the Campbell house before the next crisis hit. Walt's older sister Martha in San Diego had died. She had succumbed to cancer, the disease that would ultimately decimate the Comm family. Overnight, six members of the family rallied and took off to California in our car.

I sat down among the packing boxes with the kids to wait. Walt didn't return for a week.

During that time, however, a very good thing happened. I couldn't possibly have foreseen the lifelong implications of the friendship that began there. Vic and Gem Fitch lived across the street. He was principal in the high school division of the college, and she was a highly talented musician. They had two kids near the age of ours.

Right there, it all meshed together, almost as if based on predestination itself. Vic had been in my Grade 11 English class fifteen years earlier, but the truly fine relationship we have now began that week. Food, kids, whatever. Gem helped, helped, and helped some more.

Meanwhile, I had increasing bouts of enormous pain. Unable to lie down, I spent most of the nights sitting up on the sofa. The same day that Walt returned from the funeral, I checked into the hospital. The next morning Wilf Tetz removed the offending gallbladder.

The following day he came in with a measuring tape that he laid along the incision. "Ah! Very good," he chuckled. "Only seven inches."

As these things went in those days, I was destined for at least a week in the hospital. As the weekend approached, however, I begged Wilf to let me go home. "OK then. But you're not to be up doing anything."

Rejoicing and obedient, I went home. By this time, Walt had arranged for another one of his nieces to come over from British Columbia and hold the house together for a few days. His schedule of teaching, of course, was already going full bore.

Gradually, I felt better and started reading books, and gathering strength.

The following weekend a very attractive concert was scheduled for the Jubilee Auditorium in Edmonton. The famous Russian pianist, Sviatoslav Richter, was performing. I'd heard of his virtuoso technique and vast classical repertoire and absolutely lusted after the privilege of hearing him.

I phoned Wilf Tetz, "Is it all right for me to go to this concert next Saturday night? I'd just be sitting most of the time."

Instead of discussing my post-operative condition, he asked for details about the concert. "Yes, it's OK to go, but only if you take your doctor with you." That was the kind of family doctor we had those many years ago. So Walt and I, plus Wilf and Anne, went to the concert. Together, we had a night out on the town.

Our niece, of course, stayed with the children. Unfortunately, the next morning we discovered that she'd been complaining to her family about our living arrangements. A hard worker herself, she believed that I was just being lazy—playing the piano, reading, and even sleeping. My being just a week out of hospital didn't seem to factor into her thinking.

Before the end of the day, Walt had put her on the bus back to her home in Kelowna. "It's all right," he told her. "We're able to get along now."

In due course, I made a good recovery from the surgery—but not before I'd provided Larry with entertainment. He still maintained his often-expressed intention to become a doctor. I couldn't even wear a band-aid, however inconspicuously,

Few campus administration buildings have been more iconic than that of Canadian Union College, Alberta. Walt spent seven years here as a student, and Dorothy lived here at three different times in her life. Together they returned in 1964 to serve on the faculty.

without his inquiring into my health. He always required a complete case history.

About the same time he came up with another practical idea. He'd heard about one of the young faculty couples having a new baby. "If we cut our big car open," he asked, "could we get a baby car out of it?" Considering the state of our old Ford, I thought it could have been a useful idea, if we'd figured out how to do the job. If only we could rear a little car to adulthood what a deal of money we could save.

Meanwhile, I settled down into a brand new luxury, that of staying home. Just mother to Larry and Lorna. Something I'd been cheated out of in Michigan, and, to a large extent, in Jamaica.

By mid-winter, however, we were getting cabin fever. After a month of sub-zero weather that kept the kids shut-in, they resorted to a lot of fighting. A physical, drag-out fight seemed to alleviate their frustration. We'd also inherited Campbell's cats. Possum and his irresponsible mother, Snowball, and they did a lot of fighting too.

How the children grew that year. They both put on a growing spurt that kept me at the sewing machine just trying to keep them clad. Lorna became obsessed with cleaning, always wiping away at something. More or less tolerable, until she started using Dutch Cleanser on the piano.

Larry wrestled with bigger ideas, his mind traveling in an entirely different direction. He made daily testimonials of love. "Mummy, you're purty." While he revealed a lack of artistic discrimination, his loyalty could never be questioned. His devotion was indeed encouraging. "I like you when you get old, and I like you now when you are new," he said. Many days I felt anything but new, but I wasn't going to contradict him.

Then came another stage of comprehension. One morning, Larry found one of Snowball's kittens, dead and frozen under the front steps. He struggled to understand the fact of death. In his brief experience of six years, he really didn't have any words for sorrow and grief. He had to make several starts before he finally declared, "If you got dead, Mummy, I wouldn't be glad either."

After a time, the cats just didn't cut it, so we acquired, Skipper, a twenty-five-pound Standard Pomeranian. He would become the first of generations of Pomeranians in the decades to come. Stocky and cheerful with a gorgeous, dense coat, he turned out to be exactly the addition we needed in the household.

Baby sitters weren't really part of my life, so the kids accompanied me on most of my errands. One day I took Skipper down to the vet in Red Deer for his inoculations. Lorna hopped all over the backseat, content that we were simply getting out of the house and going somewhere. Larry, on the other hand, spent the entire fifteen-mile drive figuring out how "dog doctors" carried on their business. Skipper himself just cast a philosophical gaze out upon the snowy fields that raced by the window.

Do dog doctors wear white coats? Do they have beds in there? Do they stick needles into the dogs' butts? This was a long conversation, but I tried to answer the questions as truthfully as I could. I had to, because Larry was not ever going to give up.

As we neared our destination, Larry became more and more agitated, and I knew that he still hadn't asked the Big Question. His excitement escalated to the point where he could hardly get the words out. I parked the car and opened the doors. Much agitated, Larry finally got it out. "Are dog doctors … " his voice trembled with the intensity of his need to know. "Are the dog doctors dogs?"

When a large police dog killed our Skipper one night, we all grieved. Immediately we brought home a tiny, blond Toy Pomeranian. Mitzi enslaved us all, including the Fitch kids, Lana and Shawn. The latter came over at least once a day to play with Larry, and he became one of the new puppy's most devoted attendants.

About this time, Gem Fitch was pregnant with her third child. Lana was excited about the prospect of a new brother or sister. So was Shawn, at first. As he considered all of the options, however, the four-year-old came up with a better idea. "Mummy," he inquired of his mother one morning, "could you make yourself have a puppy *instead* of a baby?"

What a stimulating mix it is for us women who have had to balance public careers with the nuts-and-bolts of domestic life! Often exhausting but philosophically astounding at times.

Even so, my days passed, and I felt myself drifting away from my own academic pursuits. At intervals, we made trips to Calgary. Walt was fighting hard to retain his permanent resident visa to the United States. He had secured it after so much effort, we thought, perhaps instinctively, that he needed to preserve it all costs.

Whenever possible, Walt's family visited us, and, from time to time, we drove out to lumber camps and distant farming communities to see them.

The weather was, of itself, an occupation. With the blizzards and the temperatures sometimes down to 50 degrees below zero, I found myself hugely consumed with clothes. Something I seriously resented. I was either layering the kids or myself with woolen pants, shirts and sweaters, plus hats, boots and mittens. Putting the stuff on and then taking it off. Then gathering it together and laundering it. After years in the barefooted tropics, I never could muster the patience to live with so many clothes. Out on campus, on bad days, you sometimes couldn't identify anyone unless you recognized their clothes. "I'll tell you who I am, if you tell me who you are."

Then, in January 1966, as promised, President Richard Fighur offered me the chairmanship of CUC's English program. The Department was a small affair—just two of us. My former student, Donnie French, became my partner. Our allotted space was cut off from the end one of the upstairs hallway in the Administration Building. True, we had a big arched window, but our work space felt a little like the notorious Gulag. We industriously painted the room, but it still was what it was. I taught my first course in summer school.

During my year at home I'd considered (more than once) teaching in public school where I could have made $8,000 a year. A very attractive possibility. Then we could easily have paid of the last of our debts. Always trained to offer my service to the church first, I dismissed that dream quickly but not permanently.

In May Dad and Mum paid us a visit. They'd decided on leaving Washington and retiring in the hills above St. Helena, in the environs of Pacific Union College, California. Dad and Uncle Len bought eight acres if prime land. It's too bad that they couldn't have capitalized on that investment. Instead, in a short time, they turned around and sold it, for the same price.

Left. After years of island living, Walt bought a travel trailer to explore the vast open spaces of the Canadian West. Right. We encountered bears and other wildlife.

Dad, however, never recovered from the Great Depression. The beautiful real estate just couldn't comfort him. "I only want," he'd say, "to sit down and look at my bank book and see where my money is.

In the fall of 1965, Larry and Lorna, wildly excited about starting school, trotted off to Grade 1 in the campus elementary school. With their new lunch boxes and books, they couldn't have been more pleased.

Soon, however, the first of our series of storm clouds arose. Admittedly, Lorna and one boy in the school, had what today might today be called Attention Deficit Hyperactivity Disorder. Instead of working with the problem, the teacher simply ordered them out the door. Through no fault of his own, Larry got swept out with the other two.

We took them to kindergarten in downtown Lacombe. That solution was a poor one. The kids were too advanced for kindergarten, and they were smart enough to realize that they'd been rejected. Sadly, neither one of them ever really liked school again. My own disappointment for them has never really gone away either.

For the next three years, however, we consolidated wonderful friendships and somehow endured the Alberta weather. By Grade 3 Larry and Lorna had happily arrived in the classroom of Edith Fitch, Vic's very capable sister. At least, some of the wounds began to heal.

Then, subtly at first, I could detect history repeating itself. In a frightening way. Very early spring was when annual letters of hiring went out to faculty members. That year (1967), the college suffered a financial downturn, and the new president brought in a professional visitor to advise. I'd known from my Dad's experience many years previously that this man's decisions were erratic, severe, and final. For Canadian Union College he called for cuts in faculty positions

In due course, Walt received his letter, giving him work in the Religion Department, albeit in a reduced capacity. I received no letter at all.

After a month, the Great Advisor had left campus and gone on to wherever those people go. I went to the president's office and sat down where I could look at him directly across the desk. "I've received no letter. Do I have a job here or not?"

Long silence. He looked down, "Well, er ... ." He shuffled some papers on his desk. "We thought you wouldn't need the work so much because you have your husband to provide for you."

I bit my lip as a painful flash of *déjà vu* hit me. I had heard that line before, in a place 3,000 miles away. I paused, waiting to assemble the fragments of my anger into one manageable pile. "So, I have no work? Is that final?"

"It's final," he replied. I didn't look back as I walked to the door. In fact, I don't believe we ever spoke again for the rest of the school year. Oddly, I can't recall anyone else's being fired that year, so I suspect that my dismissal was settling an old political account that had nothing to do with me directly.

Now I knew exactly what I was going to do. In less than a month, I final-

The Comms' road trips ranged from (left) the Belloy church where Walt grew up in the Peace River County to (right) Moraine Lake on the Banff-Jasper Highway.

ized three plans. First, I applied to teach in the new Lacombe Composite High School. Really new! The mortar between the bricks was scarcely dry. Within days, I signed a one-year contract. Now we'd have a little extra money.

Even more boldly, I applied for (and received) a $10,000 scholarship to start doctoral studies at the University of Alberta in Edmonton the following year. (This largesse would even be extended over a second year.)

Thirdly, I picked up a contract teaching job for that same University. I became a Sessional Instructor in American Literature, with an evening class once a week in Red Deer. Acceptance, achievement, and even some money. Once more, I'd have them all. A really comforting and encouraging turn of events in my life.

Another couple of months passed. Our college president went elsewhere. As soon as his replacement, P. G. Miller, arrived, he sought me out. "We have no Chair for the English Department. We want you to come back and resume your work here."

I betrayed no emotion—I hoped. I happened to know that the College had longstanding accreditation problems, in part because virtually none of the faculty had earned Canadian degrees.

"I'm sorry, I've already signed contracts with the new high school and the University of Alberta. Naturally, I must fulfill them." Then, I made my strongest point. "Since I am already out, I have decided that when I finish my doctorate it might be quite helpful to this college. Besides, the government is paying my way, so the degree will come free."

The big man looked down at me with ill-suppressed scorn, "Well, I see that it will be good for you, but it won't do us any good." He turned on his heel and walked off. As it happened, I never again had any kind of conversation with him. I had laid my plans carefully, however, and I wasn't going to give them up on a whim.

Inevitably, I became increasingly distant from campus affairs. The one thing that did not deteriorate was our friendship with Fitches and the way our children loved to be together.

My year at Lacombe Composite High School served its purpose. Indeed, the spanking new school had a good deal to be said for it. Nobody seemed to be in need of rescuing. Although one suave 11th-grader announced his intention of writing a term paper to prove that "God is dead." I persuaded him that he had neither experience nor resources to undertake that piece of investigation.

As they came and went, I'd overhear kids' conversations. One day I heard two 10th-graders leaving my English class and earnestly discussing the steps they

With the chairmanship of CUC's English Department, Dorothy found herself back in the very same classroom where she had begun her teaching career fifteen years earlier.

would take to get involved in the stock market and get rich. No slackers, that pair.

The adult class in American Literature was particularly rewarding. One night it had been announced that Edgar Allan Poe's "The Pit and the Pendulum" would be on television later in the evening. We dismissed early so that we could all plow home through the snow and view it. "Next week," I said, "compare the movie with the original story. Decide which one you prefer, and be ready to tell us why."

The Poe story is inherently laced with terror and horror. In the usual Hollywood manner, these features were overdone to the point of the ridiculous. I felt pleased with the analyses that the students made and the reasons they gave for preferring the printed page. To be sure, this was the kind of teaching I really liked to do. I longed to find a permanent place in this part of the Ivory Tower. I felt that I truly belonged there.

As these plans formulated, my life-picture came into focus. One night, parked in the snow on a side street in Edmonton, Walt asked me. "Do you really want to do all of this work for a doctorate?"

I looked across at him. "I really do. I have the feeling that it's something I *must* do."

"Well, then, I shall do all I can to help you get there." Then, oddly, he added one more sentence. "And if someday I'm a not around, it will be something very good for you to have." Broad-shouldered and incredibly strong, he looked, as usual, indestructible. I said nothing, but the day would come when his word would prove to have been prophetic.

My Dad had been forced to stop short of his own doctorate, but he had endless interest in what I was doing. He loved nothing better than the exchange of ideas. He wrote: "Sometimes I think there's two of me/ A living soul and a PhD." Then he inquired, "Do think you can do this without losing your creativity?"

I assured him that I could see no threat. "I'm somehow just made to do research." I believed that I could avoid "academic desiccation." I truly understood, however, that the condition exists. During one summer school at Michigan State University I had one such dreary professor. He survived only because graduate students are largely self-motivated. Anyone else would have probably have been driven to desperation and would have attempted a lynching.

I began my study year (1968-1969) very carefully. The university advised that two years should be spent in class work. For some reason not clear at the time, I decided to do it all in one year.

Pleasures of home. Left. Lorna and Skipper. With Dorothy at the University of Alberta two days a week, Walt skillfully managed the household for the winter—kids, shopping, two horses, the dog, and all the rest! Right. Always time for dear friends. Gem and the rabbit, Dorothy with Vic Fitch, Jr.

I left home before dawn on Monday morning, arrived on campus and went immediately to either library or a class. I didn't leave the library until it closed at 11 p.m. Then I drove over to a cousin's house in North Edmonton, sat around long enough for a hot drink and a bit of chat. After that, I went to sleep in the basement. Tuesday was exactly the same, except at the end of the day I drove the sixty miles south to home.

The rest of the week I resumed the basic household chores. While the kids were at school, I worked on my own assignments. Our electric typewriter hardly ever cooled off.

Like some European models, the University of Alberta required that the candidate, upon arrival, know the area he/she wished to research. Immediately, then, the student had to choose a full roster of classes to support this decision. He also had to find a faculty mentor for the studies ahead.

The University of Alberta, Edmonton, Canada (founded in 1908), lies in a bend of the North Saskatchewan River. Dorothy was often rooted down in the Cameron Library.

I sensed that in the PhD industry a major rule-of-thumb would be to choose an area where no one else had been before. That way, at your dissertation defense you had a chance of knowing at least something that no one else in the room knew. That ruled out the "regulars," like Shakespeare, Wordsworth, Dickens, and so forth.

I decided to go into 18th-century English Literature simply because it is a difficult period. That keeps many people out of it. Someday in the job market it might give me an edge. Specifically, I proposed to examine Britain's first propaganda campaign, the anti-slavery movement. I felt sure that it had been reflected in the literature and stage plays of the time. (Indeed, it was.)

When winter really set in, commuting to Edmonton became challenging. No cell phones, so when I headed out across the black ice and snow-drifts, I was strictly on my own. Many nights when I returned to the university parking lot after some sixteen hours' absence I couldn't find my car. It was often totally buried under snow. Since other graduate students were working a schedule similar to mine, there would often be as many cars in the lot as there had been in the morning. Even now, forty years later, I feel the violence, the pain, and the long ache of the terrible cold.

In early March Mum and Dad came to visit us. Of course, I took Dad with me to the university. He attended my classes, met my professors, and explored the library. I watched his keen pleasure in all that was going on. At the seminar table, his sharp blue eyes flitted from one student to another, not missing a single nuance in the discussion. No question, I had to be his daughter.

For everything, I loved him with endless devotion.

One cold afternoon—it could hardly be called spring yet—he and I hiked out together around Lake Barnett. We talked of just about everything a father and daughter could explore.

Suddenly, with a catch in his throat (which he tried to disguise) he said, "Well, if I lost Mum I can't think what I'd do. I'd just be a mess."

"Look, Dad." At that moment I became Daughter the Caregiver. "Whenever either one of you is left alone, you will have a home with me."

I can't recall that we said much more, but suddenly a kind of understanding warmed us as we walked through the frosty fields.

When the day came that my parents headed their car south again, I sadly watched them go. Still, we were all excited about happy days ahead. Along with Uncle Len and Auntie May they were heading off on a trip around world. First, Hawaii to see Dad's old friends there. Then New Zealand where both couples had strong connections. Next to the family spread all over Australia. Dad hadn't been home in many, many years. Afterwards would come Singapore, India, Europe, Great Britain, so forth. They were going off, happy as four teenagers.

By the time Dad and Mum reached California, however, a crisis loomed. My sister Eileen was going into extensive back surgery. I knew that the means existed for hiring help to look after her four little boys.

Dad phoned about a change of plans, but at such a distance, I couldn't understand the dynamics of the situation. "Mum's going to stay behind to take care of the children for a few weeks," he said. "Eileen hasn't asked for it, but ... " his voice trailed off.

I protested. "But this trip is so important. How can you ... ?

"No, we feel that we have to do this." A little more chat, and we hung up.

I didn't know that I'd never hear my Dad's voice again.

Short letters from Hawaii and New Zealand indicated that Dad had great pleasure in meeting dear people from far back in his past. Later, however, Uncle Len revealed that in the midst of reunion with old friends, Dad sorely missed Mum, though he tried to hide it.

Finally Mum did arrive in Sydney and the foursome resumed their original itinerary, beginning with a week at Manly Beach. Then they worked their way across Australia to Cottesloe/Perth, Western Australia, where both Dad and Uncle Len had been born.

Meanwhile, Dad began having some gastric problems that put him into the Royal Perth Hospital for tests. "You need gall bladder surgery," the doctors advised him.

To be sure, this was not a new ailment in the family, and those of us who had been there had recovered without incident. Dad elected to travel on to Singapore. Something he felt that he needed to do. Youngberg Hospital was well staffed, and the surgery could be done there. Then, he could recuperate among friends. If Uncle Len and Auntie May wanted to go on, the four could reunite in India.

Back in the old Singapore surroundings Dad and Mum wandered the old familiar campus, shopped in Change Alley, ate *murtabak* and fried bananas again, and revisited the waterfront. On Sabbath he preached in the Southeast Asia Union College Church. Predictably, his sermon was on his lifelong, favorite theme. Even today, when you open his tiny, worn travel Bible that he always kept with him, it falls open naturally to I Corinthians 13, the mighty "Love Chapter."

In 1968 Gerald and Len Minchin gathered their seven children from all over the world to celebrate their joint 40th wedding anniversary. It was the last time that the two long-bonded famlies would have a complete reunion with not one missing.

In the College Church that day he must have felt that he had come home. Our old house pressed in from the left, as he walked up the steps into the remodeled assembly hall. For five years our whole family knew every inch of the campus. This, however, would be Dad's last sermon and just three weeks later, long-time friend, Don Roth, would conduct his funeral in that same room.

The next day, he checked into the hospital. The surgery went as expected. Still, days passed. He hadn't been released from the hospital. Being on the other side of the world, however, I felt no sense of alarm.

Sunday morning, May 11, 1969, I was puttering around the kitchen getting breakfast. Mother's Day! Maybe I should be thinking of something a little special.

The phone snarled at me. Eileen was on the other end, sounding like a voice from the spirit world. "Dad is dead!" she croaked.

When I could draw a breath, I just screamed. Again and again. I had never done that in my life before. Instantly, Walt and both of the kids crowded around me, all wide-eyed.

Don Roth in Singapore had called Eileen. Yes, he was taking care of

Left. An evening in Perth, Western Australia, with high school friends from Darling Range School (now Carmel College). Front row (L-R). Leona Minchin, Gerald Minchin, Millie Dawkins (beloved teacher of them all), Len Minchin, May Minchin. [The last photograph of Gerald Minchin, 1969.] Right. The grave of Gerald H. Minchin, 1901-1969), in the Chinese Christian Cemetery at Jurong, Singapore.

Mum and all of the funeral arrangements, along with everything else that needed management. A post-operative pulmonary thrombosis had snatched our Dad away.

Eileen and I decided not to bring Dad home. Some of the happiest years of his life had been in Singapore. That seemed the proper place for him to rest. Without a word of discussion, Walt and I agreed on one thing. We had to be in Los Angeles to meet Mum when she arrived home. Indeed, we would head south that very night.

Our little old Studebaker served us well enough day by day. "But," Walt said, "it has to have a major overhaul before we can drive as far as California."

In shock and pain beyond belief I just sat on my bed and stared at the wall. I didn't want to see anyone or talk to anyone. With one exception. I phoned Gem Fitch. Very few words were said. "I am coming over right now," she said

I still remember looking out the window, frozen to my bone marrow. She got out of her car with a box of Kleenex under her arm and walked into the house. Sitting on the bed together the two of us clung to one another and wept for a long, long time.

I can't recall that we said anything much. Those who instinctively back off from heavy grief experiences because they don't know what to say need to remember this: Actually, it's not primarily about the words. First and foremost, only love can really comfort, and my dear little Irish friend Gem knew that.

Eventually, she pulled us together somehow. She knew Dad quite well, so she had her own loss to deal with. Looking at Larry and Lorna she said, "I'll take them home with me for the rest of the day." At just ten years old, they'd been straying about the house, totally unable to cope with the upheaval. They too needed a place to anchor themselves down. "And they'll stay with us while you're gone," she promised.

Walt took our ailing old car to a garage in Lacombe. That same day, he covered his classes, and notified the President of our situation. I spent the rest of the day wandering about the house too much in shock to figure out what I needed to pack. As yet, I hadn't come even close to thinking of living in a world without my beloved father in it.

Vic Fitch had been away all day. As soon as he arrived home, both he and Gem came over. He stood over me, a crumpled, wordless heap on the sofa. "We have it all worked it. You'll take our car to California, and yours will be perfectly all right for us to use here." I could barely wrap my tortured mind around the idea.

They would lend us their new car. Only recently they'd bought an eighteen-month-old Meteor, two-door hardtop. And we would take it on that long journey and put on all of those miles? I tried to say something but only sank further into misery. "No, no!" Vic put in. "This is the right way for it to be." To have such empathy is an enormous spiritual gift. I've never forgotten that scene.

So it was, about midnight Walt and I began our journey south. Under normal circumstances I would have done my share of the driving. As it was, for almost 1,700 miles, I lay in the back seat drifting in and out of lucidity. At one moment, I'd feel normal, almost able to assess the situation rationally. Then, with no warning, a *tsunami* of grief would inundate me. I suppose that we ate some food, but I remember nothing of it.

Walt and I, Roger and Eileen, along with Auntie Norma Youngberg, were there to meet Mum. When she emerged from the jet-way at Los Angeles Airport, after the long flight from Singapore, she looked ashen, shrunken, as if the last bit of life had been drained out of her.

She fell into our arms, and the next phase of our changed lives began.

By this time, I realized that Eileen hadn't yet made the emotional journey I'd endured while we drove down from Canada. Still in shock, she couldn't look at the pictures Mum wanted to show us from the funeral. She could barely hear when Mum talked. So it was my part, at the moment, to look and listen, as much as I could.

We'd been in Eileen's lovely Pacific Palisades home less than two days when Mum fell over a step and broke her leg. This disability, of course, compounded everything else that was going on.

Our connections with Canadian Union College had been fraying out for some time. Walt had been talking about going into Public Health. This became an obvious possibility, now that we were already in Southern California. Moreover, I actually had finished all of my doctoral studies and was now free to carry on my research anywhere I wished. So this must have been why I had chosen to rush all of my university class work into one year instead of the regular two.

Once Walt had visited the School of Public Health in Loma Linda, we made our decision without much delay. In the back of our minds lurked the idea that this might be the way back into mission service. Also, we could give Mum a home where she could be surrounded by other family members. That would be a significant help in her first year of widowhood.

It now remained only to return to Canada and make the move. Once again, we had to cut our ties there. Personally, I'd already gone 95% of the way in accomplishing this separation. For me, the only hard part left was leaving a handful of friends and family—with Vic and Gem Fitch among those at the very top of the list.

Admittedly, the Future looked hopeful. In contrast, the immediate Past had opened up a great chasm of grief behind us. In between—at Present—we walked a narrow, uncertain trail. Alone and without work, our whole family would now have to live within the confines of my Canadian scholarship money.

And after that … ?

CHAPTER 18

Adrift, One More Time

Leaving Mum in the care of my sister Eileen, Walt and I turned north once more. First, we returned Fitchs' car to them. (As they would always say, "Our car saw California before we did.") We reclaimed our kids. Walt resigned his already-diminished position. We toured the house and decided what we would sell and what we could keep. Out in the field, Walt's beloved horses Comancho and Flicka grazed in the frosty grass, unaware that they were about to be sold.

Walt's penchant for buying rather than renting often made me nervous, especially since we were—once again—going off salary. Sometimes these affairs worked out all right. Other times not so much. Instead of renting a U-Haul for the journey south, he bought a moving van. So we left Canadian Union College as we'd arrived four years earlier, in tandem. Walt and Larry went in the truck, and Lorna and I followed in our shabby old Studebaker.

Again my equilibrium was shaken when Walt decided that we should buy a house in California. "But we're going to be here only a year, at most," I wailed. Like my Dad before me, real estate ventures truly made me come unglued. Nonetheless, the house we found was a very good one. Indeed, among the best we ever lived in. Grand Terrace looked down on San Bernardino valley and across to the mountain range beyond.

Although gnawing worries still vexed me, we pulled our big truck up into the driveway and moved in. We couldn't help loving the place. So far, so good.

From the outside it looked hardly as interesting as a warehouse. When you walked through the double front door, however, you stepped not into a house but into a large grassy courtyard, rimmed by a shaded curved patio. A double garage stood at the left and to the right a long house extended to the back of the property. At the front we had four bedrooms and two baths. At the far end was one more bedroom and bath for Mum. In between lay a wide-open kitchen and family room, paralleled by a large, fire-placed living room flanked by bookcases.

Rusty and Mitzi, our Toy Pomeranians, had the run of the house. When we lost Skipper to an accident, we replaced him with a pair of adorable puppies who worked their way into the very heart of our family. Unlike the horses, who had to be left in Canada, the little dog-couple went everywhere that we went.

Walt and I moved our big twin desks into the second-largest bedroom. After all, study would be our main occupation for the coming year.

Daily, we taxied Larry and Lorna to their Grade 4 classrooms at Loma Linda Elementary School. We adults discovered far into the school year, that our arrival in our tasteless Studebaker caused the kids a certain amount of suffering. Their classmates went home in Cadillacs, Porsches, and such. As usual, I was grateful for whatever transportation I had and required little more than that the wheels would go round. By and large, the "Auto as Status Symbol" has always been lost on me. Although the kids didn't really complain, it nettled me to think that our humble but serviceable car should be an object of embarrassment to them.

Before Walt disposed of that hulking moving truck he picked up an assignment to move a Loma Linda doctor's household goods back to the east coast. Again, I followed in the van that we'd acquired.

More or less along for the ride, came my cousin Ina (Madge) Youngberg-Longway, and one of her sons, Charlie, joined us. On the Loma Linda Faculty of Nursing, she was scheduled to attend professional meetings in New York and invited me to share the trip. We spent our days on the town. Our hotel room was deficient in several ways and gave us no particular reason to stay in it. I seized upon the opportunity to wander around bookstores while Madge attended meetings.

As we traveled the subways, my cousin decided to conduct a small social experiment of her own making. As we passed down into the sooty, dark passageways, we received the tokens that the shriveled little men hunched up behind the tarnished brass bars, numbly shoved out at us.

Being more of an extrovert than I, Madge descended upon one man in a cage, all sweetness and light. I suppose in the past forty years, no one had ever said a word to him. "Oh, my!" Madge exulted. "What an interesting job you have here." I thought the fellow's eyes were going to pop right out of his head. "All these people going by all day! Don't you just love watching them all?" She really knew how to lay it on!

We picked up our tokens and paused for one more moment to be sure that he wasn't going collapse in shock. His eyes, glazed over, followed us down onto the platform. His mouth hung open, but he never uttered a word. "I hope you have a really nice day," Madge threw back as we rounded the corner.

I don't remember exactly what happened to the moving truck. I had no attachment whatever to it and was glad to see it cleared out of our driveway. Walt must have sold it while I was in New York, because we all came home in the van. I only hoped that we'd somehow broken even financially, but I could never be sure.

In 1969 the Comms moved away from Canada for the last time. Walt and Larry with the truck that carried our household to Southern California. Dorothy and Lorna followed them all of the way south in the old Studebaker.

As soon as our family routines were established, I rushed back into the Ivory Tower. I set myself up in two places. My main center was The Graduate Library at UCLA (University of California Los Angeles). Daily I spent hours ranging among the book shelves and reading miles of microfilm, including twenty years of the *London Times* newspaper.

Eileen's husband, Roger, was a professor there. Although the large campus provided me with ample research possibilities, he sometimes made me wish for my Canadian university, snow, ice and all. One day he accompanied me to a specialized library in his building. When the elevator stopped and the doors opened, I stepped forward to board it. The doors closed on my right foot while the passengers within stared past me glassy-eyed. No one offered to hold the door for me.

Backing off, I said, "You know, at my home university, people would hold the door for you when they could see that you were halfway on."

Roger looked down at me, a little bored. "No use bothering about that," he replied. "You're never going to see any of those people again anyway."

I said nothing. It was a small matter. Within myself, however, I felt grateful that I didn't have to bear that kind of burden. People always matter, whether you ever see them again or not. Maybe California was too big, after all.

As I had done in Alberta, I drove into Los Angeles for two days each week and spent the intervening night at my sister's lovely cliff-side home in Pacific Palisades. Considering our long years of separation in the past—as well as many more distant ones yet to come—we thoroughly enjoyed those late-night visits.

I also studied at Huntington Library. Secluded in back rooms never open to the public, I spent long days reading 18th-century stage plays in manuscript and exploring generations of documents that pertained to the rather ambitious dissertation project I had undertaken. Set amid gorgeous gardens and galleries, Huntington provided me with lovely digressions whenever I gave myself permission to go outdoors to eat a sandwich or just to rest my eyes.

In my long-range effort ultimately to outwit my examiners in

During her doctoral research year in Southern California (1969-1970), Dorothy worked at Huntington Library and UCLA. Afterwards she spent every possible moment at her desk. That's where Rusty and Mitzi also took part in her studies.

my final defense, my project began with Britain's Abolition Movement (1740) and ended with the Emancipation Act in 1833. This hot political issue had ground its way through Parliament and society in general for fifty years. Certain that it would have been reflected in the popular press of the times, I tracked every black character I could find in poetry, stage plays, and novels.

With the instincts of a bloodhound, I very quickly struck pay dirt, and my enthusiasm enabled me to produce almost 1,000 pages of "stuff." The University of Alberta actually would have settled for 300 pages, but, as usual, I couldn't stop! In the end, I dumped the prose works, bringing the paging down to about 600. (I secured special permission for this excess.)

My faculty mentor, Dr. Hank Hargreaves, was spending this year in England. When a mail strike threatened our channels of communication, he and I worked out a deal through the Canadian Embassy and its diplomatic service. I wrote chapters and sent them to London. He critiqued them and returned them to California.

On the first exchange, he commended my diligent research and careful documentation. A published author himself, he then added, "I suppose it's too much to ask that it be interesting too."

Aha, I thought, if that's what he wants that's what he'll get. To be sure, there was a great deal of human interest inherent in the field. I abandoned the stereotypical academic stuffiness and cheerfully went on to supply narratives and art illustrations.

Actually, my study year became so productive that I knew that with just a little more push, I could finish my dissertation before we shipped out overseas again. When he returned from London, Dr. Hargreaves advised, "Just wait one more year." It turned out that the University really didn't want anyone skidding through in just two years. I needed one more year to fill out the expected, minimum three-year program.

During that single year we were most pleasantly situated among family. Roger, Eileen and boys came out to visit on weekends whenever they could. Mum's sister, Norma Youngberg, and our nonagenarian Aunt Blanche, were accessible in Glendale. My cousin Yvonne Minchin-Dysinger and family lived in Oak Glen, up in the hills above Yucaipa. Down in Loma Linda her parents,

Uncle Len and Auntie May Minchin, lived in retirement. Never in my adult life had I been so close to so many of my family at one time.

We notified the General Conference administrators of our willingness to return to mission service. Our kids were still young enough to be portable. Even at this beginning point, however, we agreed that when they finished high school we would "bring" them home, not "send" them. Whatever that might involve. For the immediate future, we could, once more, look forward to work and a couple of paychecks a month.

Our first offer was to teach at the Korean Union College near Seoul. My first response was "Way to go! The Far East again!" For lack of experience, of course, Walt couldn't understand how deeply I was attached to the Orient. After all, it was the very essence of my childhood. Yes, the West Indies had given us eight rewarding years. I now realized, however, that all the time I'd been subconsciously waiting to go back home to the Far East.

One morning, an administrator from the General Conference came to visit us. He spoke highly of the work awaiting us in Korea and left us several books to introduce us to the culture. Our teaching would have to be done through translators. I knew the language to be a very difficult one, and our

True bred-and-born Canadians, Rusty (left) and Mitzi the Blonde (right). They were the devoted Pomeranian couple that lived with us and each other for seventeen years and parented many children. Mitzi survived the loss of her Rusty by only three weeks.

prospects of really learning it seemed slim. I considered the irony of my just finishing up my doctorate and then teaching English at the elementary, second-language level. Not wishing to appear elitist, I held my peace. Still, I couldn't help hoping for a little more scope.

Meanwhile, our visitor looked around our house speculatively. "Of course, you will want to sell your house before you leave."

Is that what we wanted? Retaining it, I gathered, would mean that we would somehow have divided interests. Why? A little cursory investigation over the years since has revealed that many people in overseas service had a house (or two) waiting for them when they finally came home on Permanent Return.

In accordance with instructions, however, we did put our Grand Terrace home on the market. Happily, it did not sell. As it would turn out, eight years down the road, keeping it as a rental while property values kept rising would enable us to survive our re-entry into American society. Thus, instead of arriving in our usual threadbare, poverty-stricken condition we then would have a negotiable piece of real estate to get us on our feet again.

Meanwhile, for months, we faithfully studied the Korea books. A brilliant culture, to be sure. In fact, I had almost talked myself into being content with the way that I would have to teach English there.

Then, overnight, everything changed. In the summer of 1970, we were appointed to Philippine Union College near Manila. Our new boss would be Todd Murdoch, an old friend from Canada.

CHAPTER 19

A Significant Journey

When we celebrated my sister Eileen's birthday on September 13, 1970, we did it with a good deal of fanfare—and for good reason. It occasioned a vast family gathering. This, for the foreseeable future, was our last day in the United States.

Our decision to go to the Philippines and our trip there became one of the most significant transitions of our lives. Of the "Bamboo House Living" we had done up to the present time, this journey turned out to be the climax of it all. What followed was a curious—almost chaotic—mix of elements at work in our lives. The humdrum of everyday responsibilities lived out amid exotic travels. A new kind of career security atop the cultural changes. Spiritual growth and parenting. And much more.

Also, Mum was traveling with us. The Far Eastern Division had agreed to count her as a member of our immediate family. Thus, I was able to keep my last promise to my Dad. I would care for her for the rest of her life.

Walt and I had long since learned the wisdom of leaving home the day before a scheduled departure. Moving halfway around the world is, after all, a major undertaking. This buffer zone of time, however, made it possible for us to be delivered to the airport the next day, appearing relatively sane and in control of ourselves.

It was 9:00 a.m. on the 14th before we finished stuffing the last of our leftovers into the storage space we'd carved out for ourselves in our garage at 11815 Arliss Lane, Grand Terrace. After Walt nailed panels of plywood around the area, the incoming renters could have nothing to complain of. Other than that the double garage had virtually become single. The only item we left in the house was our lovely Canadian Nordheimer piano. It could have benefited nothing from being stored in the garage for several years.

When Bill and Yvonne Dysinger picked us up to take us to Eileen's place, we left our Grand Terrace home actually looking quite "put together" for our upcoming week of trans-Pacific travel. At noon, the whole host of our Southern California family had gathered at an expansive Swedish smorgasbord in Santa Monica. Together, we filled the entire center of the restaurant.

Upon congregating at Eileen's home, Roger and Cousin Wanda Knittel took all ten children down to the beach, leaving the rest of us to relax and visit on this, The Last Day. Theirs was a truly courageous and benevolent gesture, and they deserved Purple Hearts at the very least. Mum had ordered in a very large and beautiful birthday cake. We sampled it as we sat on the patio gazing out to the ocean that we were to cross in a few hours. When the beach party returned, the rest of the cake completely disappeared from view.

A week earlier, the dog-loving Todd Murdoch family had taken our Pomeranians, Rusty and Mitzi, to the Philippines. Indeed, our beloved little dogs were already in Manila awaiting our arrival.

After we said the first round of farewells, we made one more survey of our twelve pieces of luggage. With some effort, we were able to shed a little more junk. Having deposited our six wired-up kids into bed, we five adults just sat down and looked at one another. Instinctively, I tried, on that Last Night, to register and store up every image and memory for use in the years to come.

Although our tickets booked us through on Japan Air Lines, a little juggling the next morning got us aboard something new in the air, a 747! Larry was particularly enthralled as we stood at the window in Los Angeles Airport staring at Continental's "Proud Bird with the Golden Tail" that would take us to Hawaii. No forecaster stood by to tell that starry-eyed eleven-year-old boy that thirty years later he would be working in avionics for Continental Airlines at that same airport, LAX.

One more glimpse of Eileen and Kevin waving to us out at the far edge of the crowd, and then we were swept forward as more than 300 passengers surged down the jet-way. We were shown to the Bouganville Room, and buckled in, nine in a row. In a moment, we roared off through the smog and on up into the clean, sunny air at 35,000 feet. Unable to remember our return from the West Indies eight years earlier, Larry and Lorna were totally enraptured with it all. New, even to Walt and me, were the stereo music, movies, and martinis (!), plus the attention of fifteen stewardesses.

This, our first visit to Honolulu, effectively broke the barrier between continental America and the East. While high-rise apartments and hotels obliterated some of the traditional landmarks, we did walk the beach of Waikiki at sunset, past the Moana Hotel (home of Robert Louis Stevenson). We admired the colorful *muu-muus* parading the streets and watched some *hula* dancers. At a bazaar, Walt and Larry bought father-and-son matching Hawaiian shirts. Finally, friends treated us to a truly

Now the Southern California desert was given up, having been preceded by the Canadian Rockies and Michigan woods. To say nothing of friends and family.

excellent Chinese dinner. Remembering Singapore, I recognized that meal as being genuine. Not like some eateries back home that misguidedly call themselves "Chinese." The Honolulu streets even had that faint tropical odor that forecast things Oriental. With a sigh of relief, I realized that it would be a long time before I would have to feel cold again.

The next morning we resumed our Japan Airlines itinerary. Although the DC 8 seemed small compared to the "Proud Bird," Japanese artistry precluded any comparisons. The stewardesses wore red-and-purple-silk jackets, splashed over with silver Birds of Paradise. Damp, sweet-smelling hot towels offered on-going refreshment during the seven-and-a-half hours it took us to reach Tokyo (3,871 miles distant). The food was exotic, and we picked our way through pickled turnip and cold rice wrapped in seaweed.

For the first time ever, we flew into the sun, traveling at a speed of about half of the earth's revolution. In the old days when it took a month to cross the Pacific on a ship, no one could understand what it is like to be, literally, trapped in light. Indeed, three hours into the flight, the sun stood in almost the same position as when we'd soared out over Diamond Head.

The geography of the skies over the Pacific has never, ever, wearied me. Finally, that day, the great columns of dazzling white cloud began to look eerie in the slowly developing sunset. They became grotesque shapes in gray, pink, and purple. Dark, sinister mountains and valleys, with mists and swirls of fluff about their shoulders, reared their stolid heads in silhouette against the blazing orange sunset. The cloudy floor below us appeared illusively solid. More black masses moved past my little window as the plane began to fall behind in its pursuit of the sun. One sensed the vast loneliness of a single, man-made machine, solitary above the landless reaches of the Pacific and under the infinitude of the heavens.

Finally, we oozed into Tokyo through smog that could match Los Angeles any day. Before we reached immigration two charming members of the airport's "Greeting Service" paged us, labeled us, and delivered us to the new friends who were waiting for us. In a little Japanese station wagon, we crossed twenty city miles to the compound of Tokyo Sanitarium and Hospital. Ablaze with neon lights and astir with hundreds of vigorous, well-kept little cars, Tokyo emanated prosperity.

Our single day in Tokyo kicked off at 6.30 a.m. with a hefty Japanese breakfast in the Sanitarium cafeteria. In addition to conventional granola, corn flakes and boiled milk, we faced: Egg soup (hot), gluten (cold), rice,

Family farewells in Pacific Palisades, California (September 14, 1970). Left. The solemn adults. Right. The "Ten Cousin Line-up," fresh off the beach. Ranging from the tallest to the shortest: Lorna, Kevin, Edwin, Glenn, Larry, Wayne, Bryan, John, Tim, Janelle.

potatoes, noodles, raw cabbage, pickles and mayonnaise. In addition to chopsticks forks and spoons were provided for the unskilled and impatient. For me, however, the discovery of *nashi* was the primary pleasure. A cross between apples and pears, this fruit is indigenous to both China and Japan. Again, at hand, little trays with tightly rolled hot towels. That custom came close to *nashi* in importance.

The names of the Tokyo train stations were given in both Japanese and English. Other than that, no concessions were made for the linguistically impaired. The streets were nameless and numberless. Nonetheless, one had only to stand on a station platform holding a city map and looking confused. Someone instantly stood at his/her elbow offering assistance. The people were the epitome of courtesy.

A ride in a taxi was also a good way to go. In the ebb and flow of the streets, one could only think, "Well, when the crash comes, this isn't my car that's going to get it."

At the Meiji Shrine we spent most of our time in the royal garden that Emperor Meiji had prepared for his Empress. We found a large pond absolutely seething with carp (giant goldfish). Dotted with water lilies and surrounded by willows, the pond attracts many artists, all trying to capture Nature at a magic moment in time.

The Oriental Bazaar could have tempted even a non-shopper like me. The dark corners and alcoves harbored ancient vases and jars, lanterns, lacquer work, woodcarvings, dolls, and rainbows of silks and umbrellas. Beautiful, beautiful things. Heaviness of luggage and leanness of purse, however, prevented our making any purchases.

From the Mitsukoshi Department Store we saw, albeit from afar, the moat-encircled gardens of the Imperial Palace. Ten million of the Emperor's subjects live in closely packed, tile-roofed shops and houses. Even this far into the democratic 20th-century Japanese royalty still enjoy tangible remnants of their former glory.

In the evening we walked the streets near the hospital. At 9.30 p.m. storefronts stood open under a blaze of neon lights that were almost as large as the shops themselves. Commerce was highly compartmentalized, separate stores for handbags, china, pots and pans, toiletries, fruit and vegetables. A single banana could be had for US$5.00.

Amid drizzling rain and smog in the morning we saw that the demarcation between public and private life was barely discernible in Japan. Above an ornamental fish-and-flower shop, the proprietor (almost within arm's reach) contemplatively buttoned on his spotless white shirt. Beside him a thin woman fried *tofu* pieces while her husband arranged rice cakes in front of their tiny delicatessen. A young woman helped her two round-faced little imps choose ices out of a little glass cupboard. All the while, spruce businessmen strode purposefully toward the train station to take care of the vast obligations of 20th-century Japanese business interests.

Meanwhile, all five of us put ourselves into the hands of Japanese hairdressers. A memorable experience! Walt and Larry were served in a diminutive shop where the preliminary rites were administered by a girl. Then a non-English-speaking young man took up the serious business of shampoo, massage, and haircutting. Mum, Lorna I went a few steps down the street to a beauty salon where we were served by three lovely girls. Among them all, however, not one word of English. We had two latherings, anointing with various sweet-smelling lotions, plus vigorous scalp and arm massage. To this day, I ask beauty operators for a "Japanese Treatment." Then, I have to explain what that means. Sometimes, they almost get it right. Even so, I can never forget Tokyo itself.

Having come so close to living in Korea, we had requested that our itinerary should include Seoul, just so that we might understand what we'd missed. Struggling through the maelstrom of Tokyo traffic, we arrived a little late for our two-hour flight to Seoul. Korean Airlines, however, seemed to be laboring in some kind of organizational chaos, so we just joined the enormous line-up of home-going Koreans, laden with mountains of luggage. Finally, we all departed—only an hour late.

The weekend in Korea first brought us to the Servicemen's Center, where we met many student missionaries from the Language School. At the Center we were surrounded with reminders of the situation of a divided Korea. You can look up the valley to the pass through which the Communists came twenty years ago. They're expected again. The wartime midnight-to-4 a.m. curfew still prevails. In the school across the compound little boys in uniform spent the whole of Saturday in military training. The overseas workers here kept little caches of U.S dollars with which they could escape should a crisis arise.

Actually, we didn't get out of the strong American environment until we went out into the countryside to see the College. Situated in a wilderness setting it was approached by a tortuously narrow road. The fine property had the ancient tombs and images of Buddhist kings that created a kind of mythical atmosphere. Upon visiting with the lately arrived English teacher, however, I felt a new surge of relief that our lot had not fallen here, after all. The language was, indeed, a very real hurdle

There was nothing quite like mission service in the 1970s to wean people away from materialistic attachments. At Dr. Rue's Orphanage, for example, we saw anew how much "things" complicate the lives of Westerners. Although the buildings were very artistically designed, they were completely bare of furniture. In the *kimchi* cellar we saw the huge earthenware jars, buried for months at a time. *Kimchi* is, to me, a particularly odious kind of sauerkraut, bolstered with garlic, pepper, and salt. Along with rice, it is the staple Korean diet. To each his own. I've never yet been able to come to terms even with German sauerkraut.

Seoul traffic was, as the Newfoundlanders used to say, "the head yet." Lumbering old buses and strange three-wheeled cars monopolized the streets, and people constantly darted out from between them. I could not possibly enumerate the number of frights we endured in a single morning. School children bounced out almost under the front wheels, and then went on their way, laughing. "Hah!" Walt remarked. "Made it again." It must be some kind of national sport, seeing how close one can come to being killed without actually quitting the world.

Truly, the Seoul driver's besetments were legion. A man on a bicycle carrying a fifteen-foot ladder. Another on some kind of a bike conveyance bearing two or three twenty-foot lengths of iron pipe. Other bicycles laden with bales of stuff were weaving among the lanes of traffic. Innumerable over-loaded carts contended with trucks. Vehicles just moved along, sheering by each other's fenders and occasionally exchanging paint.

"Lanes of traffic," of course, must be understood in context. Marking of traffic lanes on the streets would have been a gross waste of labor. Directional signals were likewise deemed unnecessary and inhibiting to self-expression.

We spent an hour in the Bandu Hotel Arcade, moving from shop to shop, trying to overcome the temptation of beautiful Korean arts and crafts. To say nothing of the blandishments of smiling sales girls, each one certifying the excellence of her lacquer vases, her brightly costumed dolls, or her brassware. Along with the rest of us Walt was quite taken with their shy, genteel salesmanship.

By happy coincidence, we found Chairman Cheung Won Sung. With a considerable amount of effort we located him through the Seoul telephone directory. It had not a syllable of English in it. Cheung used to teach at the Malayan Seminary in Singapore, when Dad was the school principal there (1936-1941). Now he owned two construction companies and was a man of great wealth and substance in Seoul.

Most cordial, he came to meet us at Korea House. There we saw some exotic folk dancing—in gorgeous costume and to the music of ancient Korean instruments. Cheung brought two of his cars (with chauffeurs) to accommodate our baggage. He would have brought another two or three, had we'd needed them. His hospitality simply knew no bounds. His wife was a dainty little lady in a flowing Korean dress of turquoise silk, tiny matching *komashin* (slippers with turned-up toes) on her feet, and an ivory fan in her hand.

They entertained us at a Korean feast. Lest you think it was merely dinner in a restaurant, I must digress a little here. According to Korean custom, we left our shoes at the door (Our overseas workers in Seoul have also adopted this tidy custom.) We entered a little room looking over a tiny, private garden. The windows were framed in an elaborate wooden latticework. We sat on the floor, facing our host and hostess across a long, low, black lacquer table. Mum sat between Cheung and his wife, as guest of honor and thus as part of their family. Four alert young men waited on us. While they were very polite to us, they stood in utter awe of Chairman Cheung whom they obviously knew.

We each had our own chopsticks and bowls of rice and soup. Then came an absolute avalanche of food. I counted at least twenty-nine dishes set before us. With such a variety of foodstuffs, we could, with grace, avoid such things as one long, lean fish. It stared up at us with a hollow eye and grinned at us with a full mouth of teeth. Shredded herbs garnished his gaunt ribs. On the other hand, the deep-fried seaweed tasted quite good. My ignorance and lack of vocabulary prevent my detailing all of the rest of the meal. Suffice to say that it was an adventure in dining that we could never forget.

At the gift shop, Cheung bought Lorna a lovely Korean doll in a purple dancing gown. Larry received a stone statuette of Admiral Yi Soon Shim, a national hero from the 15th-century. (He invented ironclad ships to repulse a Japanese naval attack on Korea.)

Then we ladies were ceremoniously helped into the Mercedes, and the men followed in the Toyota. As usual, the airport was very crowded. As Westerners we called forth some attention. Chairman Cheung, however, attracted far more interest than anyone else in the terminal, receiving bows and greetings on every side.

Upon our arrival in Hong Kong a representative of the Astor Hotel met us. The beds looked very good, and we rolled in without ceremony. Unfortunately, being short, they didn't feel quite as luxurious as they appeared. Then, a green-uniformed bellhop brought in a steel pitcher of water. Once more, we tried to impress on the kids with the necessity of not drinking tap water from here on in. It had taken real diligence to keep the idea before them in Seoul. No point in getting sick before one's time. Water-borne ailments have always been a major problem of living in the Orient.

With our hotel located in the heart of the Kowloon shopping paradise, we didn't have to go far a-field in the leisure hours we had that morning. The purchase of a cassette tape recorder, headphones for our stereo set, a watch for Larry, and a few minor trinkets quickly consumed both our time as well as our small store of money.

By noon on Monday (September 21) we were airport-bound on a bus— twelve passengers plus luggage crammed into a space intended for six. In the East, every time the wheels turn, it *has* to be a paying trip.

Aboard PAL (Philippines Air Lines) we scarcely had time to doze, it seemed, before the first of the lush, green Philippine islands began to look up at us through the clouds. A marked contrast to our previous stops. A sea of tiled roofs punctuated the modern high-rise apartments in Tokyo, Seoul, and Hong Kong. Now we saw rice paddies, green fields, and a few scattered villages.

Manila, however, carried its own kind of frustration. The immigration process moved along pompously and inefficiently. Eventually, however, we were released to the multitude waiting to honor us with good will and leis of *sampaguita*—very fragrant little white flowers.

What a huge group of people had gathered at the airport to greet us! Nearly all of the overseas workers, the Union staff, Philippine Union College faculty, plus national workers from both the College and the Union. The English and Bible Departments and the Graduate School were fully represented. There, in the middle of the throng, were our dear little Rusty and Mitzi, in the arms of Todd and Jean Murdoch. Happily Mitzi had not imposed on the hospitality of her hosts by delivering her puppies before we arrived.

The compound on which we were to live offered much more than we expected. It was a walled-in, fifty-acre oasis, in the midst of a teeming Manila suburb, Caloocan City. Its gates were manned by uniformed, pistol-bearing guards. The sight of ample, tree-shaded lawns and of the goats and *carabao* (water buffalo) grazing at the edge of a tiny rice paddy created a surprisingly rural atmosphere.

The house to which we had been assigned was a high yellow box topped with a steep green roof and seven-foot wide eaves. In addition to colorful shrubs, the yard boasted palms, flame trees, mango and banana trees. We fell in love at once with the sweet frangipani bushes (temple flowers). Inside, dark paneling lined the walls and the floors were stained mahogany. Closely barred, the high windows were a concrete reminder of the questionable honesty of some of our neighbors on the other side of the compound walls.

We felt confident, however, that when our household stuff arrived (one, two, three or four months hence), we'd be able to make a comfortable equatorial home. Nonetheless, trying to exist without a minimum of household equipment (not even a car) created a kind of physical limbo, albeit temporary. Meanwhile, the campus hostess, Carolyn Rawson (wife of the college business

Left. The *jeepney* in the dense Manilla traffic symbolized the new world we had come to live in. Right. At any given time one might see literally *anything* coming in or going out of the gate of Philippine Union College (1970).

manager), had our beds all made up for us in the huge, empty house. We crashed upon them without further ado.

We started out, of course, in the social vacuum one feels upon moving into a large community of total strangers. Our first week on campus, however, filled our lives with no end of new realities. We were wined and dined twice daily in the homes of our fellow-missionaries. We toiled through the intricacies of immigration. Each of the five of us was fingerprinted about sixty times and came away literally coated with indelible purple ink—from head to foot. We made our first trip to a fabulous air-conditioned supermarket and also to the smelly, sultry local market at Balintawak. Mitzi produced another pair of puppies, the delivery of which kept us up for an entire night and entailed a journey clear across the city to the veterinarian at 3. a.m. In due course, we gave one of them to the Murdochs just to say thank you for all of their kindnesses.

Walt and I attended our initial round of committees (Academic Standards, Graduate Council, and departmental meetings). Walt's teaching was deferred one week to allow him a chance to regain his equilibrium. Mum was introduced to the Child Evangelism program, and then she went shopping for the beautiful hand-embroidered dress material for which these islands have been so justly famous.

Two-and-a-half months late Lorna and Larry started school, becoming the sole representatives of Grade 5 in the little overseas mission school. (Since the local elementary schools functioned in Tagalog rather than English, this little classroom existed for the benefit of international families). We also attended our first Sabbath services in the enormous, airy CA (the College Auditorium). It seated 4,000 and there we saw a large proportion of the 1,700 college students among whom we would work. (The high-school students met in a separate church service.) The CA had no enclosing walls. We worshipped close to the weather, sun and rain. Also, huge flights of birds joined in the hymn singing or performed *a cappella*.

We visited the Philippine Publishing House, the largest in the Far Eastern Division and situated on our compound. We also started to screen a long procession of applicants for the job of "house girl" and "yard boy" at our place.

Preparation for communion service for so many people in the CA had its own hazards. White bed sheets covered the tables and pie and cake tins served as plates. The first time we attended, we found that the pastor had streamlined proceedings by having the eighteen deacons remain within the

Above. An island of tranquility amid the chaos of the city, the campus of PUC was dominated by the CA (College Auditorium), an overgrown "Quonset Hut." Above right. On a smaller, human scale one could find students studying in the library. Right. Or, between classes, lingering under the big mango tree by the gate.

Left. The Comms relinquished their first campus home. A traditional, Filipino-style house, it was designed to catch passing breezes in the debilitating Manila heat. Right. Instead, they took this smaller, single-level one because it offered a tiny storeroom in the garage that could serve as a bedroom for Larry.

congregation during the taking of the bread and wine.

This measure saved time, but there was still one thing wrong with the plan. The designated wooden benches had been marked with white chalk with the words "Deacon Only." Handsome in their *barong* (embroidered) shirts, the men all finally reached the front of the CA, standing with their backs to the congregation. The seats of all of their pants were emblazoned with the words (in reverse lettering) "Deacon Only."

The sultry heat of Manila was all that it is rumored to be. Happily, dress was casual. Suits for the men seemed to be obligatory only on the platform at church services. We didn't resist the siesta habit which permits the casting off of as many garments as desired and the cooling and drying of one's clammy skin under an electric fan in the afternoon.

Outside the city limits, we had no telephone service. We decided that even that could be a pleasant arrangement, once we got used to the idea.

I truly believed—at least hoped—that we could learn to stop hurrying for a while. At least, we determined not make the mistake of the man described by the witty Englishman, Rudyard Kipling:

It is not good for the white man's health
To hustle the Asian brown,
For the white man riles,
And the Asian smiles,
And he weareth the white man down.
At the end of the fight
Lies a tombstone white
With the name of the late deceased,
And epitaph drear
Reads: "A fool lies here
Who tried to hustle the East!"

Indeed, the East does remain another world and, in some respects, another age. We were just opening to the first chapter of a book that we would study for the next eight years.

Somehow, our arrival in Manila did give us a sense of security. Here we were, two middle-aged people, with a pair of about-to-be teenagers. Within a matter of days, I would have to face my forty-first birthday. But that was all right. I didn't care. Also, with Mum living with us, I didn't have to have long-distance concerns about her wellbeing. Indeed, returning her to the Far East proved to be good for her. She now saw herself as picking up Dad's work near to where he had laid it down the previous year.

The Night-blooming Cereus is a huge, white orchid-type tropical flower. It blooms for a couple of hours, just one night in the year. Within our first week at Philippine Union College we were given one. Truly, its performance certified the very warm welcome that we received on campus.

For years, we'd been here and there, as well as the next place. We'd been in and out of the Ivory Tower. We'd worked hard and somehow stayed afloat. Now a new phase of life began. Even within the first days of our new assignment, I felt the calming effect of just knowing that we had "a place" in the scheme of things.

As if to force me into still further submission, I fell flat into bed with the flu a week after landing in the Philippines. Loss of sleep and the stress of travel finally laid me low. Exhausted, I had nothing to prove, so I just stayed in bed until I felt like getting out of it. My teaching responsibilities wouldn't begin until the next semester.

At night, I savored the fragrance of the frangipani flowers. By day I could stand on our front steps and look out over our lovely campus set amid Manila's dense urban sprawl. I could see a lovely stand of bamboo down near the carabao wallow. I felt a profound air of familiarity. One more term of overseas service, and life in the Bamboo House here would become just about the most satisfying tenancy we had experienced yet.

The Far Eastern Division of Seventh-day Adventists. The years in the Caribbean had assuredly been good ones. For Dorothy, however, returning to the Far East was, indeed, "coming home."

CHAPTER 20

We Arrive

Our arrival at Philippine Union College in Manila in 1970 started out quite predictably. This, after all, was not our first overseas assignment.

We expected that clearing our goods out of customs would, naturally, take some sleight-of-hand skills. Therefore, we were grateful for the services of Mr. Bulajan, a capable man employed by the Mission for dealing with the vagaries of customs and immigration. I was astonished—no, horrified—when I discovered that virtually no business could be transacted anywhere without bribes. I vowed never to give in to that practice—a stand that I would, on more than one occasion, regret. For the time being, however, Mr. Bulajan knew all of the right moves and when to make them.

Meanwhile, our family of five (Walt, me, my mother Leona Minchin, Larry and Lorna) had settled into one of the old two-story, three-bedroom houses on the college campus. Additionally, we had two student helpers, Beth and Melita. The girls instantly fell in love with our Pomeranians, Mitzi and Rusty. We bought an old Peugeot car. It seemed relatively roadworthy, though it had suffered some abuse at the hands of inadequate mechanics. Larry and Lorna entered fifth grade in the on-campus elementary school. Walt had started teaching. I was reading some M. A. theses and doing other tasks preparatory to entering the English Department when the second semester began. A slot had been prepared for us, and we dropped into it.

We immediately discovered that the Manila streets existed in a perpetual state of crisis. They offered little consolation for nervous drivers or persons feeling squeamish about sanitation. No lines were painted on them, so masses of vehicles oozed through, five wide in a space sufficient for two lanes, at the most. No traffic lights were to be found and only a few stop signs. City traffic would influence our lives in ways that we could not possibly foresee at the beginning.

The first time I drove into the city, Dr. Irene Wakeham (Chair of the English Department) was with me. When I automatically braked at the first stop sign, she cried, "Oh no! Don't stop here. Someone will hit you from behind." I was puzzled. Irene, however, had lived here for twenty-five years. What did I know? I would have to modify my understanding of road rules. I could see that.

The *jeepneys* added to the color and complexity of street scenes. We all came to see them as the very essence of Manila. The new bodies fitted over an old jeep chassis looked like something from Coney Island. No amount of fanciful designs, icons, names, color, chrome, and ribbons was spared. A Mercedes bumper would be yoked with Ford tail lights and topped with a silver stallion and a grass fringe, all on a single vehicle.

Take one example. The windshield was small (about 10 by 36 inches). Into that space a remarkable amount of material was crammed. Across the entire top hung a tin fringe. At first it appeared to be made out of red bottle caps and silver-and-green beer can rims. Actually, it turned out to be a string of ornate little crucifixes. Above this was a long, chipped (but highly decorated)

A formal family portrait in Manila (1971). We had had just enough time to fit ourselves out in the elegant embroidered clothing which is a hallmark of the Philippines. Seated: Lorna Comm, Walter Comm, Larry Comm. Standing: Dorothy Minchin-Comm, Leona Minchin.

mirror. This enabled the driver to see his passengers and get his 20 centavos (about 3 ½ cents) fare from each one. A gilt-framed picture of the Holy Family occupied the middle of the mirror. A large crack ran down the center of the windshield and was covered with wide tape. Superimposed over that was a picture of a cherry-colored Virgin, "Our Mother of Perpetual Help—Pray for Us." All things considered and given the very real hazards of the way, that seemed to be a wise request.

On the right side of the windshield, almost completely obstructing the view, were signs announcing the services for which the vehicle was available. It covered various Manila suburbs—Santa Cruz, Blumentritt, Quiapo, and Monumento. In the same area were at least five certificates, full of fine print, seals, and signatures. Also a "No Smoking" sign. The driver himself bought and used a smoke from a cigarette boy. The lad made his sales by bouncing in and out between the cars caught in the traffic jams. Lacking sufficient capital to lay out for a full pack, people often bought just one cigarette at a time.

Finally a border of paper seals decorated the lower part of the windshield. All of this left the driver with a rectangle of no more than 6 x 12 inches to see through. Perhaps it's as well not to see too much here, I concluded.

We had been in the Philippines less than three weeks when I went down into Central Manila in a *jeepney*. I had to round up some textbooks for the course in Classical Literature that I would be offering in the second semester. A helpful young man from the business office went along to help me find the best bookstores.

Jeepneys, however, are not constructed for the comfort of the Western frame—at least not my kind. My head grazed the wooden roof, and my knees almost touched the bench on the opposite side. The hard back of the seat caught me in a most unlikely spot. So much for spatial problems.

Passengers disembarked and boarded through a rear end-gate, usually while the vehicle was in motion. People seemed to know instinctively where there was still a four-inch space to squeeze into. Thus two seats might accommodate three or four people apiece. Five or six per bench was the standard load. While a *jeepney* might carry six passengers in reasonable comfort, as many as twenty might be seen piling out of one.

Whether from the driver's lack of visibility or from a temporary loss of nerve, I don't know, but about halfway home we had an accident. Our *jeepney*, a yellow number with red scallops, sideswiped a red one flying multi-colored steamers. A few chrome strips got torn off both of them, but there was little commotion. In Jamaica all of the passengers would have piled out and probably have shouted one another deaf. Here, however, the two drivers simply walked around a bit and exchanged a few commonplaces in Tagalog. Then they got back into their *jeepneys* and drove on. The passengers paid scarcely any attention at all. Although life moved forward to the squawks and squeals of car horns, the people expected little courtesy. They remained relatively mild and easy-going amid the chaos.

The spare tire on the side of our conveyance was so smooth that you could actually see your face reflected in it. Pink streamers flying from every prominence also reflected themselves in the shiny rubber. As might be expected, a *jeepney* rides as if totally devoid of springs or shock absorbers. Holes in the street (as deep as six or eight inches) also contributed to the hardness of the way.

Although downtown Manila is by no means surgically clean, it is negotiable on foot. Only twice in our peregrinations did we have to pick our way through a garbage heap. There we shared the narrow path with a transparently thin white cat. It completely lacked the blasé air of self-confidence common to his kind. Perhaps the loss of his tail, which appeared to have been chewed off about two inches from his posterior, undermined his confidence and gave him actual wrinkles across his forehead!

One of my students inquired, "Do people use *jeepneys* in other cities?"

"No," I replied. "I never saw one until I came here." She could not conceive of an urban economy surviving without them. Obviously it couldn't here. Very few citizens can afford a private car.

While the weather was almost unbearably hot, great shade trees made our campus a park-like oasis within the teeming city of Manila. Indeed, after fifty-eight days' residence we felt quite adjusted. Actually, fairly normal. That, however, changed very suddenly.

Although our freight shipment from California had recently arrived on

Manila streets have always been a paradox. Left. A boulevard in Makati. Right. A street in Blumentritt.

the *Golden Bear*, we had unpacked very little of it. We were about to move across the fields to another, newer house. The "newness" did not interest us as much as the fact that there was a small, windowed storeroom off the garage that could be made into a bedroom for Larry. We planned to change houses the very day that the record-breaking typhoon hit.

Shortly after our arrival, my mother had joined Irene Wakeham on a three-week farewell trip around the Far Eastern Division. On the afternoon of their return, Walt and I went to Manila Airport to meet them. They came in from Saigon on Vietnamese Airlines. (Yes, the war was on, and they'd heard the bombs falling.) This trip was the first real responsibility we'd laid on our recently purchased "new" car. It looked all right, but it had internal disorders that we knew not of.

About halfway home the Peugeot showed alarming symptoms. Almost as if it had endured some kind of battlefield trauma itself. Walt stayed by the ailing vehicle, and we three women took a taxi home.

We arrived on campus just in time to get Irene Wakeham to her farewell party. The festivities were pretty well finished by the time Walt arrived. He'd left the Peugeot to spend the next few days in a garage.

The next morning (November 19) the Main Event began. We woke up very early to a gray, cold (that is for Manila) world, visibility about nil. Soon after Larry and Lorna went off to school, with raincoats and umbrellas. The latter would prove no defense whatsoever against what we had coming.

Everything around us then fell into a kind of nervous agitation. The radio announced the maximum typhoon warning, Number 3. Up in the treetops on the second floor we felt rather like the Swiss Family Robinson on a bad day. The house, however, had been standing since the 1940s so we were not, at first, unduly anxious. The girls had some food cooked—enough for a couple of meals.

Because this was our fourth typhoon since our arrival, we had made some preparation. Since none of the windows in the house fit well, Walt nailed most of them shut. Even then, a steady gale blew through the house. We used every towel in the cupboard, first packing them around the windowsills and then mopping up the floor. The water we couldn't control leaked downstairs. "Our book boxes are soaked," Walt reported. "Some of the stuff down there is actually floating."

Eyes dark with fear and ears and tails flat, the little dogs crept around under the furniture and kept trying to find a lap to sit on. A thunderous crash and the big mango tree in the back yard went down, flipping its roots some twelve feet in the air in a gesture of despair.

Even at the best of times we had no telephone service. On this day we

Left. A colorful leftover from World War II, the *jeepney* is indispensable to transportation in the Philippines. Its decoration is limited only by the imagination of the owner. Right. A tricycle mounted on a motorcycle is also a product of fantasy and has equal rights on the road.

could only look out the windows and guess what was happening to our neighbors. We saw books and papers blowing from the far end of the campus and wondered what had collapsed over there. Flying debris shot through the air, barely clearing the beaten down banana trees and shrubbery. Electricity came and went, so I had both of my typewriters set up, the new electric and the old portable. Thus, I recorded our day as it passed, minute by minute.

In shock we watched the plight of our nearest neighbor to the left, the Philippine Publishing House, standing naked. One wall of the warehouse collapsed, exposing tons of paper and supplies. The rain drenched the hundreds of bales of paper while the wind fiendishly tore off the wrappers. Half the roof was gone, and, with every gust, the other end lifted several feet. Suddenly, one more blast, and it broke free and catapulted out of sight.

Meanwhile, the roof of our house kept tugging at its moorings. We huddled away from the windows and prayed.

Then we saw Raymond Woolsey (the Publishing House editor) dash across our front yard. He held a child in each hand, hauling them home to the graduate apartments behind our house. The kids were flying, stiff and horizontal. If he'd let go, they'd have vanished as the warehouse roof had done.

We knew that our kids were in the nearby classroom, but we desperately wanted to get them home with us. Walt stripped off everything movable on his person and went to get them. As he ran across the yard, he could barely keep his own feet on the ground. Soon we saw the three of them scrambling up the front steps, Lorna barefoot. The wind had blown the shoes right off her feet.

Larry had declared the last typhoon "exciting." The show we were now watching, however, was more drama than anyone could have sanely asked for. This typhoon would be pronounced the "worst since 1882."

An hour and a half into the tempest, we endured a weird intermission with amazing atmospheric effects. The air settled into a heavy stillness, and a band of clear air formed on the southern horizon while the north remained black.

A hundred-foot section of the fifteen-foot-high compound wall had collapsed. Through the great hole we could see the clutter of poor little brown houses in the *barrio* on the other side. One had disappeared altogether leaving only rubble behind. It looked like the aftermath of a nuclear attack, but the end was not yet in sight. Knowing that each phase of the storm would be about equal length, we waited for the next act to begin. (With any luck the curtain might fall about 3 p.m.)

Once more the pressure built up, and the rain blasted back in, falling in cataracts. We returned to the ground floor trying to get our boxes above flood level. One of our bedroom windows blew in. We sopped up pails of water. What we couldn't catch soaked down onto the boxes downstairs.

When darkness came, we had no electricity. I had one very large decorative candle that my sister Eileen had given me last Christmas. We spent the evening in its light. Who would have thought that a candle born in the California desert would have come to this end.

We gave supper to a family of ten Filipinos from the *barrio.* They had lost everything. We dragged in mattresses from somewhere and made beds for them on and among our packing boxes. Then we went upstairs, flung ourselves onto our own wet beds, and went to sleep.

The next day turned out to be cloudless and violently hot. We had no electricity, no water, and no car. Our one tiny radio with a feeble battery kept us in touch with the world. We tried not to obsess about having a shower or even finding a cool drink.

So the cleanup began. It did so in that almost automatic way that it does in places that are accustomed to violent weather. When disaster comes infrequently, people seem to be less able to cope with it.

The college administration now laid on a heavier-than-usual security detail. Looting and theft were to be expected. Precautions also had to be taken against typhoid and cholera. What little water we could get had to be boiled and preserved for drinking. Power lines hung like streamers from poles that leaned crazily this way and that.

The Blanco family had arrived to join the college faculty even more recently than we had. Just in time for the typhoon, in fact. Walt and Jack Blanco rounded up a party of graduate students and went to work chopping up fallen trees. The only tools they could find were axes. My big-footed con-

Left. The gateway to Philippine Union College appeared normal enough. Right. Then you realized that the guards who checked you were armed—and for a good reason.

tribution was to lend a young man my good leather hiking boots from Canada. When he brought them back, they were a sad exemplar of the utter ruination of our campus and of all of the tribulation we'd passed through. I could never wear them again.

I looked at the lovely, park-like community, now a heap of rubble, and thought, "When shall we ever recover from this?" I had forgotten that in equatorial lands even a fence post can sometimes burst into green life. Just three weeks later on December 9, campus life had begun to appear fairly normal.

Then the next disaster struck. That morning an ominous column of black smoke billowed up over one side of our compound. Classrooms and offices emptied instantly as hundreds of students and staff members converged on the east gate.

By this time, we had been having water and electric service three times a day—for just two hours at a time. This moment was an "off time," so when the fire broke out there was no water to save the houses. Twenty-three staff families lost whatever the typhoon had spared them. Of the 200 homeless people, half of them were college students who had nothing left but what they had taken to school with them that morning. Thankfully, no lives were lost. People just had cuts and bruises from flying debris.

Once more the whole campus formed itself into a disaster team. They collected money and clothing, prepared meals, and found homes for the destitute. By this time we had moved across campus and fitted ourselves into a rather small house. After the fire we took in a student, Rodolpho, far from his home in Northern Luzon. He slept on a mattress on top of our trunks in the garage.

By the time Christmas 1970 came around, we decided that we'd earned a few days in Baguio. In the weeks since our arrival in Manila, we had already done an enormous amount of "hard living." We wanted to see something outside of the teeming, steaming city.

Of course, our somewhat sickly Peugeot had long ago come home from repairs. Now we had to believe that the car would somehow get us up into the mountain resort that we had heard so much about. Leaving Beth and Melita to take care of the house—for better or worse—the five of us wedged ourselves into the four-passenger car. Mitzi and Rusty came too, but they really were very small dogs.

The countryside offered us a pleasant change. From the rice-planters, knee-deep in the mud of the rice paddies to the crowds lounging around the *sari sari* stores in the *barrios*. The little brown huts were giddily decorated with Christmas decorations, mostly made out of colored construction paper. Bamboo fences, bushes and rocks along the roadside were festooned with drying clothes. We looked on a new world. Or, more correctly, a new part of the old world that we were learning to live in.

We shared the road with motorized bicycles with sidecars, tricycles, and fancifully named buses. One "Philippine Rabbit" bus passed us, the

The campus of Philippine Union College was an island of tranquility amid urban chaos.

Fernando Norte became Larry Comm's good friend. He, along with other students, kept our lawns and gardens tidy.

windows packed with curious faces staring at us. Up on the roof, among the bundles and baskets, a goat was tethered. Unquestionably, he was well placed. He lunched on the market produce around him. Unbelievably tiny ponies drew decorated *calesas* (carriages) on unpaved roads.

The final thirty miles took us up into the mountains in a scenic series of switchbacks and hairpin turns. The city of Baguio at the top is at an elevation of almost 5,000 feet. Its relative cleanliness and spaciousness surprised us. This, of course, was only the first of many trips we'd take into the cool mountain community. Headquarters for the Far Eastern Division had been here, temporarily, before the offices moved to Singapore in 1936. The four remaining buildings (two of them duplexes) looked down over a terraced lawn with pine trees. The banks of red and white poinsettias made a very seasonal addition to the landscape.

We were barely into our cabin, however, when the other responsibilities of Christmas fell upon us. We were to have at least a dozen groups of carolers every night, each trying to outdo the others in volume and agility. The Bontoc women danced in their colorful, hand woven skirts and jackets. Old men beat out rhythms on paint cans or cracker tins. Occasionally a guitar or a real violin showed up. In any case, we had to pay for each performance, and our supply of small change was soon gone.

We met Student Missionary Philip Payne and girlfriend Pam Frost from Southwestern Union College in Texas. After the recent ordeals of the typhoons and fire, we had come to respect the work of student missionaries. Many of

Left. Within days of our arrival on campus Typhoon Yoling (1970) severely damaged the Philippine Publishing House that shared our compound. Right. It uprooted giant old trees and tossed the wounded warriors aside, frail as houseplants.

them left home as materialistic middle-class Americans but really "found themselves" amid the challenges of working overseas. Over the years, we learned to value any program that gave young people such a zest of living and such singleness of purpose.

This first trip to the mountains confirmed my interest in the work of the woodcarvers. With nothing but hand chisels they carved dishes, tabletops, and all kinds of animals. Their finest work, however, was reserved for their animal, the *carabao* (water buffalo).

In general, domestic creatures in the Philippines were woeful specimens. Dogs and cats were expected to be self-supporting, subsisting on grass and garbage. Only the *carabao* really prospered. He lived among them, intimately, working for them, furnishing transportation and (once in a long while) steaks for a feast. He slowly plodded about his tasks, apparently able to absorb nourishment from the mud he rolled in by the rice paddies. Owning a carabao was the equivalent of having a car. When he gazed at you, however, it was with strangely inexpressive eyes.

We bargained for three calf-size, carved *carabaos* for 200 pesos. (We could have bought a live one for P400) In the tourist traps in Manila these would have cost P150 apiece. I loved those three beasts. I could see the muscles, bones and tendons and could almost expect to feel warm flesh and blood to the touch of their glossy wooden skins. The dark grain in the acacia wood gave just enough variation to call to mind the mud with which the *carabao* is usually encrusted. Fortunately the Blancos came up to spend the weekend with us. They kindly took two of our cattle back to Manila with them.

On Friday we were invited to a pig roast. The neighbors behind our cabin roasted a whole pig to eat at midnight. Impaled on a long pole from stem to stern, the pig was slowly rotated over the fire with loving care for five hours. "You are Seventh-day Adventists," one man said." I know. Otherwise we would invite you to join us."

We appreciated the gesture. But no thanks. The spectacle of the unhappy pig with his forelegs folded resignedly across his chest, his shiny skin crackling in the heat, and his sightless eyes unblinking in the smoke. Not an attractive prospect. "And he's stuffed with rice, vinegar, and garlic," the man went on, trying to entice us to celebration.

Leona Minchin immediately identified herself with many mission projects. The motto of her life was always: "I don't want to miss anything." Very soon after her arrival, she set off on a Far East Tour with a friend, leaving Manila Airport en route to Singapore.

Along in the early hours of the morning the pig-eaters really got merry. Presumably they partook of something more stimulating than just the poor old porker.

Early Christmas morning another party of Igorot women came begging. Specifically they wanted something to drink and had their cups with them. All we had was boiled water—which, of course, was of no public interest.

The most lovely bells, however, rang through the night. Never heard them more beautiful. In Europe through the centuries past bell-ringing has virtually been one of the fine arts. So this was part of the islands' colonial heritage.

At church the Christmas services went forward in English, Ilocano, and another dialect. Everything that Walt and Jack Blanco said had to be translated at least three times. A spindly Christmas tree had been made out of bamboo, wrapped in cotton wool and decorated with colored construction paper.

The pulpit however was a wonderful specimen of craftsmanship. The grain had an unusual "cloud"

When we reached the "Baguio Lion," we knew that we were nearing our destination, high up in the mountains. Built by the Americans in 1900, Baguio became the "Summer Capital" of the Philippines.

effect. The piano, on the other hand, was an ancient, hollow-chested thing with a nasal voice. An elaborate hand-crocheted bedspread with long fringes covered the less comely parts, making it more worthy to stand near the pulpit.

The instrument was played with great gusto, however, and the choir provided all that could be wished for in music. The congregation really sang. Filipinos are very musical, as we had come to see at the College. All one needed to do was stroll out about the campus in the evening to hear singing. There were several boys' quartets who did most of their practicing, it seemed, as they walked to and from their work appointments.

By Monday the 28th we absolutely had to return to Manila. When we reached the coast, however, we turned off to a beach at Bauang to swim and have lunch. We still had this kind of thing in our blood from the Caribbean. The surf, however, was too high for snorkeling. Even so, coconut palms on miles of beach before us and a clean blue sky above made the stop worthwhile.

Our dogs went wild chasing each other up and down the beach. Lorna lost her fins, and Larry almost lost his glasses hunting for them.

From a shy little boy I bought a rusted old pie tin full of shells for one peso (16 cents). Unlike anything we'd taken in the Caribbean. Judging from

Baguio was our perennial getaway, a cool, fresh escape from Manila. Left. At Christmas time the then unspoiled little city turned itself out in extravagant decorations. Right. The pine trees and the roadsides ablaze with red and white poinsettias easily propelled us into the spirit of the season.

the smell, some of the mollusks had only lately quitted this world.[1]

We took our time down the coast looking for other beaches. Every time the car stopped dozens of children mobbed the car. Mitzi and Rusty were the center of attraction—probably the only Toy Pomeranians in the Philippines at the time. Some people speculated that they were a new kind of monkey!

By 2 p.m. we headed back to Manila in earnest. We needed to get through the Huk country before dark. The Huks were the Filipino Communist guerilla army, and we had no desire to meet any of them. All of the way home, the countryside was popping with firecrackers. Hundreds are killed and maimed every year, for these homemade devices can be as lethal as a hand grenade. Indeed, some of them *are* grenades.

For this, our first Christmas in the Philippines, the Gensolins[2] sent us a specialty of the season, *ubi*. A kind of spread made from sweet potatoes, it was a pretty shade of lavender. With it came *suman,* sticky rice mixed with coconut milk and sugar, wrapped in banana leaves and baked. (In Singapore, we used to call it *pulut.)*

Altogether the conventional sleigh bells and holly wreaths existed on another planet. From the exotic to the trivial, this would be our kind of Christmas celebration for years to come.

At our cabins we were visited by Left. "Carollers," and Right. Igorot dancers. In both cases, we were expected to pay for our entertainment.

Sadly, one commonality would remain. We reached home, however, to find poor little Beth in great sorrow, having not slept for three days. One of her brothers had died the day before Christmas. He had been ill with terminal kidney disease, so his death was not unexpected.

The burial, however, became rather bizarre. Unfortunately, the family owed the hospital 2000 pesos for his treatments. So the authorities halted the funeral until they got their money. Although we weren't on hand to help, our college president, Dr. Ottis Edwards, calmed the crisis.

Left. *Carabaos* (water buffalo) are the staple animals of the rural Philippines. Owning one is roughly the equivalent of having an automobile. Right. The skilled woodcarvers in Baguio create many things, but they are at their best when they produce *carabaos* in acacia wood.

We all live on the edge of a great sea of heartache, as wide as the world. In places like the Philippines, we were learning, the pain is just much closer to the surface than we had previously supposed.

Notes

1 Ultimately, I donated our rather large shell collection to the Natural History Museum at La Sierra University, Riverside, California. Over decades, it was gleaned from both the Caribbean and Pacific

2 Dr. Amador Gensolin was the campus dentist. Dr. Leonore Gensolin was Chair of the Filipino Culture Department and was very active in the affairs of the international students and faculty at Philippine Union College.

CHAPTER 21

A Couple of Milestones

Within our first year in the Philippines, I passed two life-changing milestones. The first was very physical while the second was wildly emotional. At the same time, both were spiritual.

When we arrived in Manila, great unrest already prevailed, and the surface of our life on the college campus was often agitated. For one thing, the extreme poverty of the people ultimately caused riots. Amid this desperation communist elements (the Huks) arose. Then, in January, 1971, just as we were recovering from the December typhoon and fire, the *jeepney* drivers –15,000 of them—threatened a strike against a rise in fuel prices. City life ground to a complete halt.

One night Walt came home in a taxi, the Peugeot laid up for repairs—again. He had been up near Huk country that day. No public transportation was supposed to be operating, so the jittery driver turned off his meter and covered it with his hat. Then, he asked Walt to sit in the front seat, so that car wouldn't appear to be a taxi. We were all very glad to see Daddy home safe that day.

About the same time, one of the cashiers at the bank advised me to lay in extra food before the strike. There seemed to be a kind of morbid urgency that some blood must flow and something must burn before satisfaction would come to the land.

President Ferdinand Marcos was one of the wealthiest men in Asia, and it was hard to find anyone to say a good word for him. It was believed that he had become so at the expense of his own people. In a single week that January, two plots to assassinate him were uncovered.

Because university students were heavily involved in the disturbances,

Philippine Union College received threats. Classes could be suspended for days at a time. Moreover, "get tough" elements surrounded our campus. I spent those unexpected holidays grooming my doctoral dissertation for its final defense. (I faced a journey back to Canada to defend my academic efforts.)

Our television set had been stolen off the Manila dock when we arrived months earlier, so we had only radio news. Reports of demonstrations in the Quezon Bridge area were like listening to the sound track of a Western movie with all of the gunfire. Announcers managed, however, to project suave, even elegant, control: "We shall now continue to report of the pandemoniums which have been happening here this afternoon."

Having weathered the threatened-but-failed revolution of January 25, Anne Figuhr[1] and I accepted the Gensolins' invitation to go shopping in Quiapo the next day. As we three women were walking back to the car, we passed a mob of some fifty people on the sidewalk. They were all looking at a poor man sitting on the curbstone, head in hands. He had a large hole in the top of his head. The blood streamed over his face and shoulders and ran into pools around his feet. As if a gallon of red paint had been emptied over his head! I was amazed that he could even be sitting upright. No one made a move to help him. With all of the unrest in the city, Mrs. Gensolin hurried us forward. No time for mercy. At least not from us foreigners.

That scene proved to be a prelude to our own little drama. Dr. Gensolin was not at the car when we arrived. "I think I know where he is," Leonore said. "Be back in ten minutes, after I find him."

"I know a music store." Anne pointed down a narrow side street. "Let's go there while we're waiting."

With Anne at the cash register trying to pay for some sheet music she'd chosen, I stood gazing out on the street. Or, more correctly, the alley. It always took a while because every transaction in this country required a handwritten receipt, a cash register notwithstanding.

Suddenly, with no apparent preliminaries two men started fighting. One in a white tee-shirt had the other—in a yellow tee-shirt—pinned under his arm and was virtually wringing his neck I thought it was simple domestic affair, until I heard terrible strangling noises coming from the Yellow Shirt.

From a doorway directly opposite the music store, a woman rushed out and tried to tear the two men apart. By now a large company of spectators had assembled, and two men tried to help her. After enormous effort the combatants were separated. The Yellow Shirt shot down the street and was seen no more. The woman, with her dress half torn off, along with the two men, finally forced White Shirt back into the doorway, bracing their bodies across the entrance to keep him inside.

During all of the time not a single word had been uttered. Westerners are accustomed to seeing fights proceed with screaming, kicking, biting, swearing and so forth. This was a cold, methodical, controlled struggle. Naked hatred in its most elemental form. Chilled to the bone, I knew I'd never before seen such raw, primitive anger. The Western temperament probably can not quite build up such a reservoir of wrath as the Asian can. We tend to dilute our emotions with bluster and talk.

Only the woman and one of the peacemakers remained in the doorway across the street. The affair appeared to be over. Certainly it had nothing to do with us. I stepped out of the door, Anne right behind me. I had gone no more than three paces when the crazed man reappeared. Flinging the woman aside, he strode out into the alley, brandishing a stout *kris* (a dagger with a wavy-edged blade).

Anne and I froze where we stood. The man came straight at me, his wide black eyes fixed on mine. I didn't feel frightened. (That came later). I could only think, "This isn't happening to me. But now I am going to die."

Shuffling back a step, I muttered to Anne, "I guess we'd better go

Even with urban Manila trying to climb over our compound walls, the campus of Philippine Union College had a few very lovely little beauty spots that we prized.

The old Spanish city, the burgeoning modern capital, or the open-air markets notwithstanding, the Quiapo district is one of the most dense centers of Manila commerce.

back inside." That had to be the master understatement of my lifetime. There was no rush, no sound, nothing. Just the ghastly, slow-motion unfolding of a horrible event.

Then it happened. When the White Shirt got within about five feet of me, he stopped short. His face went blank, and he turned aside. It was as if a curtain had dropped between us. We were completely out of both his sight and his mind. He turned up the street, *kris* still poised, looking for the Yellow Shirt.

Meanwhile, the alarmed clerks were removing an expensive guitar from the show-window. They pulled Anne and me back into a storage room at the back of the shop. We could still see White Shirt prowling back and forth in the street. "Is there a back door here," we asked the clerk. "So that we could get out onto another street and return to our car?"

"We have none." We waited for an unmeasured length of time.

Finally, one of the young men said, "I will accompany you to the car. If he comes again, I will place my body before you and protect you." Truly a noble offer, but we assured him that we would not take that risk for him. Nor for ourselves either.

It seemed that time had passed into eternity itself. The young man reconnoitered the street. "Someone has pulled him inside," he reported, pointing up the street in the direction that we had to walk. The people who had at first taken refuge had now come back into the street, and we did likewise.

As we sprinted to the car, we didn't glance at any doorway. No one knew

Manila has always been fire-prone. Left. One day Manila International Airport was there. Right. The next morning it had burned to a blackened skeleton of itself.

which one White Shirt had been pulled into. Near the car we met Gensolins, "We were so frightened," Leonore cried. "We thought you were lost!

We weren't lost, but we were badly frightened. I knew that we had been spared by Divine Intervention. I could explain it in no other way. Thereafter, I could know every day—for the rest of my life— that "Life is sweet." Sweet no matter what. It took me almost a week before I could sleep without repeated nightmares where I saw the White Shirt coming at me with his *kris*.

The riots abated, at least temporarily. It was not typhoon season. We went into the city very rarely—and the children almost not at all. Life took on the appearance of normalcy, whatever that might be. Some days after I finished grading papers I even had strength enough to work on my dissertation. The on-going disturbances caused the serious re-emergence of the Communist Movement. Eighteen months later Martial Law would be introduced.

By the end of that autumn of 1971 I had reached my second "milestone."

When we had left for the Philippines in September of 1970, it had been with the understanding that I would have to return to Canada to defend my dissertation at the University of Alberta. My first year of teaching at Philippine Union College, therefore, had been a frenetic mixture of classroom and committees, writing and rewriting.

My faculty advisor, Dr. Hank Hargreaves, had been on sabbatical leave in England that school year. Because of a mail strike that dragged on and refused to resolve itself, I had communicated with him circuitously, through Canadian diplomatic channels. While I was grateful for the connection, I had had, all in all, a highly stressful school year.

Then, for six weeks in June and July (1971), Mum and I toiled away, wholly consumed with the labors of completing the revisions in my dissertation and retyping it. All 545 pages of it. (The bibliography alone occupied twenty-two pages.) No question! It was overkill. On July 15, 1971, we shipped it off to Canada to be duplicated and distributed to the examiners.

By this time Leona and Norman Gulley had arrived to join the PUC faculty (July, 1971). That I should live and work for years in the same place with my cousin Leona seemed beyond all probability. But there we were. While we were perennially busy, we spoke often of a time when we would start "living right." That is, we'd goof off somewhere and just have fun doing nothing. Well, it was an ideal that we always kept before us, even if we seldom made good on it. For me, I was happy every morning when I looked across the campus to that old house and knew that my dear Leona was in it.

For Mum's sixty-fourth birthday Gulleys and we took her to the *"Jeepney Restaurant"* in the upscale district of Makati. Together we ate a delicious meal in a booth made out of a radiantly colorful *jeepney* body. Moreover, it seemed the proper way to celebrate the fact that my dissertation had been dispatched. Therefore, let no one scorn the humble *jeepney*.

One never expects to have family nearby when on overseas assignment. When my first cousin, Leona Minchin-Gulley arrived at PUC in 1971, we indeed rejoiced. Clockwise around the table: John, James, Leona, Sharon, Sonya, and Norman Gulley.

For the past ten months I'd lived like the widow in the Old Testament who had the barrel of meal and the cruse of oil. She got up every morning and found her needs supplied for the day. Now, utterly exhausted, I had limped through the first nine weeks of teaching in the new semester. Then I got up one day and found nothing available. So, I had to submit to the orders of our doctor. I stopped work altogether.

I left for Canada on September 12, just about a year from the day when we had come in for our first term of service in the Philippines. Immigration processes for leaving the Philippines were, as usual, onerous. This time it required twenty-one signatures and thirty-one fingerprints. A kind of diversion, I suppose, but anxiety still paralyzed me.

The day before leaving Manila I had to stop by the Union office in Pasay. As I passed Amy Sherrard's door, she called out to me. "You look terrible. What's wrong with you?"

"When I started on my doctorate, it was a private affair, but now everyone in the whole Far Eastern Division is tracking me." I collapsed in a chair and admitted to my fears. "I'm so tired. And I'm just plain scared of that examining committee."

Amy gave me a level look, befitting her position as an experienced nurse. "Oh, pull yourself together," she replied. "You don't have to worry. Just remember that when those men get up in the morning they have to put on their pants one leg at a time, like everyone else."

My mind told me to let go and laugh. Instead, I murmured a faint goodbye and left Amy's office.

I knew that the possibility of flunking one's orals at the University of Alberta was terrifyingly real. Unlike U. S. universities where a candidate passes many tests and milestones on the way to a

Leona Minchin's typewriter never cooled down. In the end, she endured the typing of six complete drafts of the 600-page dissertation.

doctorate, many Canadian universities operated on the European plan. Having conducted your research any way you wished, you could only hope that your preparations would be adequate. In the end, the defense of my research would be a single life-or-death event.

Back in July I'd shipped the dissertation off to Canada with some ceremony and with a vast sense of relief. Now, just hours away from flying home, I fell into despair. I felt myself staring potential failure in the face, eyeball to eyeball.

My mother and my nephew Kevin accompanied me on the journey. Kevin had spent the last three months living the "Philippine life" with us, and, for his sake, we visited Hong Kong, Taipei, and Tokyo so that he could extend his Orient experience a little bit further.

Our stopover at the Ginza Hotel in downtown Tokyo was particularly soothing to my frayed nerves. We were shown to a huge, air-conditioned room on the tenth floor where the shutters were sliding panels of straw and parchment. The décor was a delightful mixture of traditional and ultra-modern. Fine matting covered the walls, and a folding screen separated Kevin's bed from Mum's and my twin beds. Unlike the usual soft and too-short beds in Hong Kong, these were long and firm. A pair of slippers awaited us at each bed. The bedside table offered two books—the New Testament (on the bottom) and the Teachings of Buddha (on the top).

The bathroom featured an *ofuro,* a small swimming pool of almost-boiling hot water. A fascinating change from Manila's perpetual program of cold showers. Ice-cold drinking water was on tap at the wall. Other facilities included a Finnish sauna bath. Also, the Azuma Bar, said to be complete with "charming Bunnies and mood music." We chose to sleep instead!

We arrived in Los Angeles on September 16, in the morning. The yellow smog had crept out nearly half-an-hour's distance at sea to meet us. The purity of the atmosphere in mid-Pacific had certainly been one of the attractions of the whole trip. Although Kevin had had a really high summer, he was pretty excited to see his parents and three brothers again.

I arrived back in Alberta on a Sunday night. The city of Edmonton bloomed up a bouquet of bright lights on the prairie. I took four days to relax and visit with friends and family. Dr. Hargreaves, my mentor, had no particular chores in mind for me, so I did not present myself at the University until the morning of the examination.

Hargreaves entertained the external examiner from Ontario and me at lunch. We ate at the Faculty Club, overlooking the North Saskatchewan River with its banks ablaze in autumn colors. To my great amazement I found that Dr. Booth, the guest, had, like me, grown up in Singapore. Indeed, at the same time as I was there. He was the son of a banker. Who could have guessed in those far-off pre-war days that we would one day meet on the other side of the world. And on such an occasion! Although I had little appetite, I still took a piece of apple pie in honor of Walt. He absolutely doted on apples, and they were an impossible luxury item in the Philippines. Meanwhile, Dr. Hargreaves did his best to discuss anything in the world except the forthcoming examination.

At 3.00 p.m. the most intense, exhausting experience of my life began. Three of the examiners were English experts. Another professor came from the Department of History as a specialist in revolutionary movements. The one lady-professor on the committee was absent, having just given birth to a baby two days earlier. Actually, I considered that a good thing, because women have a way of being very hard on one another in certain high-stress circumstances.

The opening shot was fired when I was sent out of the room while Dr. Hargreaves went through a little ritual: "If there is any just cause why this examination should not go forward, speak now or forever hold your peace." With that formality over, I was recalled to sit at the seminar table before the firing squad for the next two-and-one-half hours.

At one stage the Great Ones began arguing a point among themselves. I sat quietly letting the academics go to it, relieved to have the break. As I looked around the table, Amy's comment sprang into my mind: "When they get up in the morning, they have to put their pants on one leg at a time, just like everyone else."

Tight as a bowstring and saturated in adrenalin, I almost strangled myself. There arose in my mind that ludicrous domestic view of the professors getting dressed in the morning. It almost catapulted me into hysterics. What if I had

 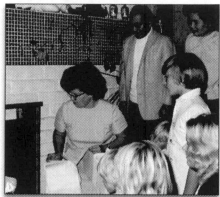

Left. With the final version complete, Walt returned the rented electric typewriter while Dorothy carried the manuscript to the Post Office for mailing to Canada. Right. The PhD now safely in hand, Dorothy officially burned the working copy of her dissertation in Eileen's fireplace in California before returning to Manila.

started laughing at that inopportune moment! It took every ounce of strength I had to stay in control.

Finally, I was sent out of the room again to await the final verdict. It seemed eternity to me, but in reality I think it was not more than four or five minutes. I opened a window in the hallway of old Assiniboia Hall and leaned out into the fresh, late-afternoon air to cool my over-heated brain. I took in some long, slow, deep breaths.

Then, Dr. Hargreaves appeared at the door, all smiles. He shook hands with me with gusto and led me back into the room. "I want to introduce our Department's newest PhD." Very formally all of the gentlemen stood and welcomed me into fellowship, as it were. Too exhausted to register any feeling, I sat down. My mind told me that it was all over, but my body and emotions refused to respond in any way.

At the fashionable hour of 10.00 p.m. that night, at the Hargreaves' home, I supped with the committee members and their wives and other members of the English Department. I was amazed at the number of people who seemed to know all about me and my overseas teaching assignment. Happily, I had brought *pasalubong* (traveler's gifts) with me. I presented the Hargreaves with a pair of Philippine, hand-carved *carabao* bookends and a horn vase. To be sure, without his excellent guidance I could never have survived.

For the next week I basked in congratulations while I toiled over corrections—mostly typos. This, after Mum and I had literally bared our bones trying to produce a perfect copy. After passing through the hands of nine readers, the document had to be made as error-free as was humanly possible.

No hand-made alterations allowed. The University of Alberta is very proud of its dissertations, and there was even some debate about what typewriter I should use to make the corrections. Back in Manila we had typed the original on a German Adler typewriter. (Happily they decided not to send me back to Manila.) I spent fourteen-hour days in a little office assigned to me. There I scratched with a razor blade, erased and re-typed. It took three days for the binding to be done. On October 4 I delivered all fifteen copies to the English Department to be certified.

Then, I officially bowed out.

An original building from 1912, Assinaboia Hall housed the English Department of the University of Alberta, Edmonton, Canada. In this classic old residence Dorothy sat in seminars and finally met her examining committee in 1971. (Photograph from 1941, courtesy of the University of Alberta Archive, #72-58-1629).

After three years of close communication, I felt quite nostalgic saying goodbye to Hank Hargreaves. I had learned so much from him. "Now be sure to keep in touch with me at Christmas," he said, "and at other times too.

Without a continuing relationship with one's graduate students, teaching in a university like this can become like working in a sausage factory, you know."

In the years since, considering my friendships with my own students, I decided that Hargreaves had stated the case very aptly.

My weekend with Vic and Gem Fitch at Canadian Union College took an ironic twist. With that Canadian degree now firmly clutched in my hot little fist, I was offered my old position in the English Department. Of course, the then-president, had had nothing to do with my wilderness experience at the College three years earlier. Yes, as I had once predicted, I could have helped CUC toward accreditation. Now, however, I belonged in the Far East. Moreover, I would happily return there with never a backward glance. Nonetheless, all things considered, it was nice to have been asked!

The only real regret that I had at this point was that I had dreamed that Dad would share this academic victory with me. He was so passionately interested in my literary studies. He would, indeed, have felt that my completion of the doctorate was a fulfillment for him also. That final sharing, however, had been denied to us.

In due course, as I sat in Edmonton Airport awaiting my flight to Vancouver, I knew that I had come to the end of an era. I had a heady sense of liberation. Never again would I have to work at anything so doggedly. From now on I could make more of my own choices. An utterly intoxicating thought!

The plane came in from Toronto, three hours late. Once aboard, I found myself sitting next to a distinguished man who turned out to be an executive of the Imperial Oil Company of Canada. He read the financial news, spoke knowledgeably and expansively of world affairs, and pointed out to me the various river valleys where he'd flown with geological survey teams. He was amiable and smartly groomed. Altogether impressive!

When we landed in Vancouver, I invited him to disembark ahead of me. "I have already missed my plane to Los Angeles, so it doesn't matter." Besides I was encumbered with a lot of luggage, including a shopping bag containing two extra copies of my massive dissertation.

As he stepped across in front of me, I perceived, to my utter astonishment, that there was a great gash in the seat of his pants, from "stem to stern." It revealed a rather broad expanse of blue polka-dot shorts underneath. So, he too had put them on "one leg at a time!" Although he was obviously unaware of his condition, I felt no need to discuss such an intimate matter with him. Therefore, with great dignity, he proceeded out into the air terminal.

An airport limousine whisked me away to a fine hotel. Since Air Canada was footing the bill, I took advantage of the bounties of Guiseppi's Dining Room, just off the lobby. It was dark, expensive, and elegant in shades of red. Great ranks of silver and stemware sparked in the candlelight, while romantic guitar and violin music drifted out over the polite and officious labors of the little Italian *maitre d'*. Still, very tired and very tense, I just let myself wallow in atmosphere. I found the menu a little mystifying. Because I was unable to determine the exact contents of Soggioco Alla Griglia, Osso Buco, Florentina al Ferri and so forth, I settled for spaghetti. Nonetheless, it turned out to be one of the tastiest meals I've ever had.

Even more important was an evening visit from Floyd and Fern Penstock. They were just then severing connections with the British Columbia Conference in order to accept a call to take charge of two schools in Bangkok, Thailand. We talked for hours. Service together in the Far East indeed bonds people. Beyond that, the conversation occasionally strayed back to our student days together at Canadian Union College, to say nothing of our early years together in Newfoundland.

I went to sleep that night gratefully and vigorously aware of how rich my life was. Academic success, yes, but I was not destined to isolation in the top of the Ivory Tower. Heaven had blessed me with family and friends, all of the dearest and best kinds. Besides, I had been given a marvelous opportunity for service, as well.

Although fog delayed my flight to Los Angeles the next morning, when the Western Airlines plane took off, it climbed heavenward like a homesick angel. The sun rose over the graceful heads first of Mt. Rainier and then Mt. Hood. Dark ridges marked the valleys far below us with pools of mist lying in them. The somber evergreen forests were spotted with patches of autumn reds. As we glided in for a landing in Portland, Oregon, we saw fields of fat, yellow

Left. When Dorothy returned from Canada in November, 1971, she arrived on campus to find a welcome sign on the college gate. Right. Her colleagues created a real "academic festival" for her home-coming, presenting her with a "Happy Doctoring" cake.

pumpkins, bright in the golden morning light. The color scheme blended with the stewardesses in their orange micro-mini dresses, flaunting tanned skin, and long, bleached-blond hair.

A few days later, I embarked alone on my long trans-Pacific flight. Kevin was in California again and Mum had decided to stay home with the family for another five months. Only twenty-one passengers on the China Airlines 707 flight. That meant that we all had three seats apiece where we could get some serious sleep.

For the first couple of hours, I entertained myself with Richard Armour's *Going Around in Academic Circles: A Low View of Higher Education.* (I'd picked it up in the UCLA bookstore.) It spoofs everything and everybody in the university world from bottom to top and back again. After my heavy, often agonizing, labors of the past three years, I enjoyed it immensely. In the privacy of my three seats I laughed to my heart's content.

Then I noticed that the young Chinese steward paused to look at me curiously as he passed up and down the aisle. Who knows? He might be thinking that I was on some other trip, in addition to the one from Los Angeles to Tokyo. I didn't care. I still had a good deal of stress that I needed to get out of my system.

I arrived to an uproarious welcome back in Manila. From family, friends, faculty, students and dogs. I made a point of telling Amy Sherrard, however, that her effort to cheer me up had nearly blown my oral examination for me. I'd almost fallen into hysterics when, at a critical moment, I recalled her saying that no one is smart enough to get their pants on both legs at the same time.

Out on the College compound a banner hung across the entrance gate welcoming "Dr. Comm" home. Yes, I was home again. I had the doctorate in the bag!

Notes

1   Our next door neighbors Richard and Anne Figuhr had lately arrived on our compound. He became Dean of the Graduate School. She, a gifted musician, taught organ and, for her own pleasure, had started working on a Masters Degree in the English Department.

Having finally cleared the last of her postgraduate hurdles, Dorothy donned the regalia of her profession (PhD in Eighteenth-century Colonial English Literature). The degree was awarded in absentia, November 20, 1971.

CHAPTER 22

Our Island of Retreat

Queen of the Night

Unquestionably, the park-like campus of Philippine Union College was an island of retreat—almost of tranquility—within the seething city of Manila. Even so, the need to move the College into a rural setting prevailed for many years. Years of planning, hope, and defeat. Finally, the move did come in 1978. The life of the school—its students, faculty, talents, and aspirations—all transferred to the lovely hillside property down in Silang. Nothing but the dirt we had lived on was left behind in Caloocan City. When the property became a cemetery, somehow the sequence seemed to be right—symbolically.

Nonetheless, when we arrived in Manila in 1970, the city-bound compound offered much more than we expected. It was a walled-in, fifty-acre oasis with ample, tree-shaded lawns. Goats and an occasional *carabao* grazed at the edge of a little rice paddy in the middle, creating a surprisingly rural atmosphere. The gates, however, were manned by uniformed, pistol-bearing guards.

The traditional house to which we were first assigned was a high yellow box topped with a steep green roof and seven-foot wide eaves. In addition to colorful shrubs, the yard boasted palms, flame trees, mango and banana trees. We fell in love at once with the sweet frangipani bushes (temple flowers). Inside, wood paneling lined the walls and the floors are darkly stained. The high windows were closely barred, a concrete reminder of the questionable honesty of some of our neighbors on the other side of the compound walls.

The newer house to which we moved was on the other side of the campus. "American style," it was smaller and was, relatively, poorly ventilated. Still, in addition to the conventional three bedrooms, it had two bathrooms

Left. As for relief from the heat, we would have done better in one of the old traditional two-story, Filipino-style houses. Instead, we fitted ourselves into a one-level that would have suited a less equatorial climate. Right. The College's "Philosophy of Work" program fostered gardens and helped everyone push the threatening city a little further away, at least in their minds.

and a little room for a study. Best of all, there was a tiny storeroom in the garage. Hardly bigger than a twin bed, it had a standard-size window and became Larry's bedroom.

Within the first week, Walt and I attended our initial round of committees— Academic Standards, Graduate Council, and departmental meetings. Walt's teaching was been deferred one week to allow him a chance to manage his jet-lag. I, on the other hand, had a few extra weeks while my predecessor, Irene Wakeham, finished off the first semester.

Acquaintance Night came in July, at the beginning of the new school year. With 1700 students and 200 faculty and staff, obviously not everyone could shake hands with everyone else. Freshman enrollment was limited to 400—for the simple reason that the College didn't have facilities for any more. Therefore, the freshman were the selected ones. I watched those hundreds of shy, smiling faces. Then the hands. Some were petal-smooth. Others were rough and hard from work at home in the *barrios.* Ruefully I thought of all those kids back home who value a college education at virtually nothing. These Filipino students would soon be coming through our classrooms. I began to understand where they were coming from.

The College never did have a church building on the Baesa Campus. Lack of material assets, however, never had the least effect on the hospitality and friendship that enfolded us into college life there. Just three days after our arrival the Registrar brought us a treasure from her house. A flowerpot containing a Night-blooming Cereus, just ready to "perform." This huge, white, orchid-type flower blooms for just a couple of hours, one night a year.

Flowers do, indeed, "say it," anywhere in the world. About the same time, the Gensolins gave us an undistinguished-looking little gray root. "Plant this under your bedroom window. It is a *Dame de Noche* ('Lady of the Night')."

We did so, and then promptly forgot about it. Even when wandering tendrils climbed the wall and poked long, exploring fingers into the jalousie windows, the bush was still so unprepossessing that we gave it scant attention.

That is, until one night, six months later, when we came home after dark. The powerful fragrance stopped us in our tracks. It could not have been more arresting if you had just smashed a gallon jar of the most expensive French perfume on our verandah. Our Dame de Noche had blossomed into tiny, greenish-white flowers. By day the bush retreated into odorless anonymity. No amount of sniffing could extract even a whiff of perfume. After dark, however, our whole front yard was enveloped in an explosion of sweetness. We went to sleep nightly like the mythical Lotos-eaters, drugged with the fragrance of paradise.

Soon after our arrival at PUC we screened a long procession of applicants

Left. Under martial law great efforts were made toward the "beautification of Manila." The needs were indeed great, and the painting flower pots on the street was pleasant enough. Right. We would have given higher priority, however, to the piles of garbage that defaced the city. Accumulations of trash like this cropped up all over Manila. They never went away.

for the offices of "house girl" and "yard boy." Beth was the first. She remained with us from our first to last day in the Philippines and became "head cook." (My mother added to Beth's repertoire by teaching her how to make excellent whole grain bread, Australian lamingtons and a few other family favorites.) Then we had Lolita, a capable little girl who came to us out of the northern mountains (and a Catholic convent school) in 1971. Last, we took Zeny from the south. All three girls did, indeed, become members of the family—our true Filipina daughters. In return for their loving, faithful work, we gave each of them a college education.[1]

From the start my mother, Leona Minchin, carved out a place for herself in the College community. She worked with the Child Evangelism program. Her involvement with the evangelistic Voice of Youth programs took up a great deal of her time, especially when she went on extended "jungle jaunts" with groups of the college students. She negotiated with the local Bible Society to get translations of Scripture out to the villages. Early on, she instituted— and campaigned for—the Gerald Minchin Scholarship Fund. As long as she lived, she wrote journals describing her project and its results. Designed for would-be ministerial students, the Fund enabled a large number of young people to earn their college degrees. Thus its benefits have extended to the present day.

The sultry heat of Manila was all that it is rumored to be. Happily dress was casual. Suits for the men were obligatory only on the platform at church services. Even that changed after Martial Law forbade Western suits and substituted transparent *barong tagalog,* the elegantly embroidered shirts of *jusi* (banana fiber) or *piña* (pineapple fiber) fabric.

Nor did we resist the siesta habit which permitted the casting off of as many garments as desired and the cooling and drying of one's clammy skin under an electric fan. (That is, whenever the electricity worked.)

Although Walt taught classes in Religion, his major contribution was the establishing of a new Department for Health Evangelism. Fresh out of Loma Linda School of Public Health with his MPH degree, he had the interest and the right connections at Loma Linda to promote the establishment of a new, ambitious curriculum.

The fieldwork of Health Evangelism often kept him on duty almost around the clock. For instance, he conducted a Five-Day Plan to Stop Smoking at Clark Air Force Base. Running concurrently with his summer classes, it required a four-hour (round trip) drive to that U.S. Base to meet with the fifty-six enrollees each evening. They were a determined, we're-here-for-business group of military personnel.

One night I went with him. A young woman who had been smoking four-and-a-half packs a day reported that she was now down to only ten cigarettes a day. Clearly she would not be one of winners in that round. Still, Walt made appropriate congratulatory sounds.

Another woman complained, "Well, you've done it again! First, you tell us no tea and coffee, then diet, and now no alcohol. I know! Tomorrow night you'll tell us 'No sex.'"

Walt laughed. "You come and see. You'll find out otherwise. There are lots of good things left."

One of the chief staff officers at the Base hospital, a medical doctor, was also in the group. "Here I am a patient, not a doctor." Nonetheless, Walt turned some questions from the floor over to him, and he answered them very fully and intelligently. In so doing, he made quite an impact on the group. "All of this makes me feel pretty stupid," the doctor admitted. "I know all of the medical reasons, and yet I'm here trying to get help for myself."

Meetings like these were good for Walt's graduate students when he took them along to learn the techniques. To accommodate the hundreds of inquiries that came, Walt had another session less than three months later at the Air Base.

On the other hand, my duties kept me close to campus. Teaching English in the Philippines produced challenges different from those I had faced in the West Indies. Fortunately, I had eight very capable teachers in my English Department. I believed them to be the best in the entire institution, although I was careful not to speak loudly of the matter. Even so, decades later, colleagues still describe them as "the cream of the crop" on the faculty at that time.

As usual in any foreign country, aberrations of the English language kept surfacing. One of my first experiences occurred in the CA at the time of

A student missionary (Ross Decker) from Andrews University trained PUC's "Gymnairs," a very creditable acrobatic team. Left. A ladder display. Right. A boys' routine.

Summer School Registration. One of the teachers, Bienvisa Nebres, showed me a note she had just received from the Business Office: "Please allow Kathryn to pass Station I. She has saturated the promise."

"What does that mean?" I asked in amazement.

"Well, that's what the Diction Class does to them," Bien sighed. "In the Diction Class everyone concentrates on vocabulary building. That's all." Having learned an exotic array of words, of course, people desire to use them. There and then I decided to abolish the Diction Class and find a better way to approach the English language next year.

Our inter-office memos sometimes carried their own kind of syntactical interest. For instance, for years, PUC had had security problems. Early in 1971 we were afflicted with junk peddlers, along with newspaper and bottle buyers, coming within our compound walls. As a result, some equipment had been stolen from the Motor Pool (machine shop). A memo from the Business Office read, in part:

"If teachers are interested in selling their junks they should do it outside the gate. We would like to encourage our department heads to keep those junks and request Mr. Palafox to do the selling of these junks, if not at the gate then probably they can bring it directly to the junks stores. We hope that the incident has taught us enough lesson in order to be more prudent in our ways."

As a department chairman I got 1% higher salary than I would otherwise receive. Now I could see why. This reimbursement came to pay for my looking after my departmental junks. Three months later were we still having trouble. Another note:

"Please gather in one place at your vicinity broken chairs, tables, tools, pieces of wood, boxes and whatever junks you have. . . .Let us make our buildings within this week neat looking, with more space for up-coming junks."

The thought came to me: "Why don't we just keep the junks we already have." Besides, if I were to clear my office of all the junks in it (typewriter included) the place would be stripped bare. Truly, working overseas, you learn how much stuff you can do without.

Still, everything was secondary to the exhilaration of watching self-discovery at work in the classroom. That first moment when a student hears himself or herself make an intellectual breakthrough! Surely, that is every teacher's grandest reward.

At Philippine Union College I taught a course in American Literature. Not because I was qualified but because there was no one else to do it. Indeed, in my actual heritage, I am barely even a bona fide American. Still, I enjoyed the day that we discussed Benjamin Franklin's "Way to Wealth" from *Poor Richard's Almanac.*

I wanted to see how well the students could bridge the cultural gap. "Look at this sentence, I said: "Now I have a cow and a sheep, everybody bids me good morrow." I went on to explain the concept of agriculture being a mark of prosperity. I well knew that in this country there were thousands of people who owned nothing. "Now can you put Franklin's statement in a Filipino setting?"

One boy's hand shot up. "Now I own a carabao and a goat, and all of the people say to me, 'Good morning, Sir!'" He and the rest of the class laughed in delight at their success in re-interpreting the wisdom of America's Old Sage.

To be sure, the students at PUC were as smart as those anywhere else. So often, however, their English languished for lack of use. Moreover, they had very little real experience in literature.

In my early years in the Philippines I worked steadily on developing a textbook for Biblical Literature.[2] The subject had been a favorite of mine for many years. While there I produced the first edition, conscripting both Walt and Mum to put the book-syllabus together. Actually, my mother put more than fifty unpaid hours on the job. Over the years I came to rely on her efficient secretarial help in many, many ways. To the point where I could not be satisfied with the services of any ordinary secretary. By and large, when a fast job had to be done—and be done right—it was up to "Me or Mum."

In my second year at PUC I created my first multi-media program. The first of many more to come. Finally, I found the intersection where three of my passions could meet: My fascination with photography and art, a desire to write, and a love for music. I took 300 pictures from Canada that had been lying around for twenty years, wrote a script, and shaped up a twenty-five minute program for the college students. It was a small preview of many more scripts to come for the use of the Far Eastern Division.

At age thirteen Larry got his first vehicle. Sometimes he took Lorna for a ride. His excursions were confined to the College compound, of course.

Reaching into my picture resources I prepared several bite-size programs for my classes in the Humanities. On one occasion I took a program on ancient Greece to Manuel Quezon University.

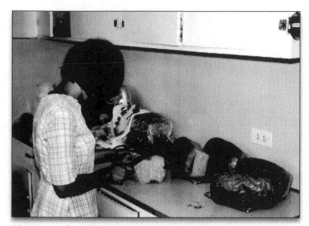

No one in the whole campus community made better bread than did our Beth (Siapco).

Since they had been teaching Arts and Humanities without any audio-visual aids, my simple little demonstration aroused more interest than it probably deserved. From this small beginning I started down an inter-disciplinary path that intrigued me throughout my professional life.

Our social life on the compound was divided into two distinct parts, equally satisfying but literally worlds apart in style. As a group of generic *Americanos* we observed Christmas and Thanksgiving. For one day we laid aside the *pancit, lumpia* and fried bananas and tried to create an actual Stateside kind of meal. Then once a month we tried to get together for Bible Study,[3] prayer, and discussion. Supper followed and usually featured an aggregate celebration of the birthdays for the month.

Sometimes we went to considerable effort to reconstruct Western traditions. One Christmas Shirley Kehney hosted the whole group (some forty people). She had a ping-pong table with a white sheet and red streamers, set out under the big flame tree in her front yard. We had real Irish potatoes, properly mashed. That took some effort in a land of rice.

Dottie Edwards brought in a large pot of gravy. The steam, however, had vacuum-sealed the lid. Gordon Bullock gallantly offered to assist in its removal. The said lid came off with a pop and plunged into the gravy which shot up in a spectacular geyser, inundating about one-third of the table, as well as a few of the spectators.

"Well, I quit playing Boy Scout," Gordon sighed heavily as he retreated to a chair in a secluded spot.

"Oh, don't worry about it." Shirley smiled cheerily. "If I were an ideal Far

Eastern hostess I would do something worse. Like emptying the rest of the gravy over my head. Then you'd feel better." Truly, Oriental courtesy actually does call for that much dedication. It's wonderful

On that occasion our family's contribution to the meal was Australian (steamed) Christmas pudding with coins in it. The Zacharys, newly arrived from Mountain View College that day, were with us. Being Canadian, Jim entered into the spirit of the thing and had three helpings. He collected seven of the coins.

Then we had the other component of our friendships. Many weekends we entertained student groups. Included would be any guests who happened to be on campus. One Sabbath the Gulleys and we hosted all of the members of the Religion Department and Seminary, plus new church members from the Health Evangelism meetings.

As usual, we used the ever-serviceable ping pong table draped with a king-size bed sheet. We parked it on the parched grass under the mango tree in our yard. We expected forty to fifty guests. Actually 125 (conservative estimate) came. Leona had a great heap of spaghetti and sauce and baked beans. I had three large carrot roasts and two jello salads. Also, we'd laid in ten

The early days of the Seventh-day Adventist Seminary (Far East). Faculty and students.

dozen buns. As our official drink mixer, Walt declared that he had made eleven gallons of punch. Beyond all of that, the Indonesians brought *gado-gado* and the Koreans came with fried rice and seaweed. Even then, we had barely enough food.

No matter. High, good spirits and warm fellowship prevailed. More than one guest wanted to know, "Why can't we do this every month?"

Oriental hospitality and the zest for entertainment made this part of our lives a joy, despite the extensive responsibility. Our efforts were rewarded with unforgettable, wholehearted enthusiasm.

One Saturday night, on the lawn between our two houses, Fighurs and we entertained our counselees (students to whom we had been appointed as faculty advisors).

Just before refreshments, we sent them off in two competing groups on a scavenger hunt around the campus. Among the items required were such things as: One live frog (a whole basketful of big, horny critters was gathered up in the first five minutes). A green feather. (The cage of our lovebirds was ransacked. I suspect that our poor little Romeo had a couple of his feathers plucked). A goat hair (one team lugged in a whole goat, just to be sure of an adequate supply). The final trophies were Ross Decker and Dave Buxton, our two student missionaries. They came willingly enough to join in on the ice cream.

Series of student missionaries brought a variety of inspiration to the campus. Ross Decker made a unique contribution—modeled on a similar group at Andrews University. His training of the "Gymnaires for Christ" culminated in a Saturday night performance in Luneta Park down by the bay in Manila.

He and his team handled the usual setbacks with the equanimity of long-experienced performers. A half-shell roof covered the stage of the modern little amphitheater. The audience, 4,000 strong, sat on stone benches in the open. First, the college bus that carried the students and their equipment broke down. The old bus looked handsome enough in its new coat of paint, but its internal disorders kept it periodically disabled. Fortunately, the collapse occurred within walking distance of the arena in Luneta Park.

Then came the rain. The young people immediately prayed about that,

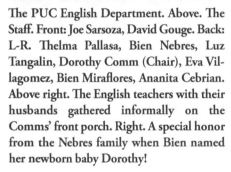

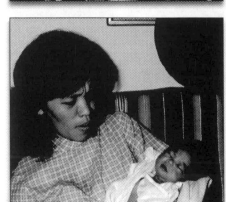

The PUC English Department. Above. The Staff. Front: Joe Sarsoza, David Gouge. Back: L-R. Thelma Pallasa, Bien Nebres, Luz Tangalin, Dorothy Comm (Chair), Eva Villagomez, Bien Miraflores, Ananita Cebrian. Above right. The English teachers with their husbands gathered informally on the Comms' front porch. Right. A special honor from the Nebres family when Bien named her newborn baby Dorothy!

and it stopped. In fact, it held off for about three-quarters of the performance. By that time, however, the spectators were so engrossed with the show that most of them stayed on, rain or not

Indeed, the students looked handsome in their jumpsuits, hot pink for the girls and purple for the boys. Both wore brilliant, psychedelic print silk blouses with long, flowing sleeves that enhanced their graceful movements. The tumbling, pyramid building, and other stunts were interspersed with songs and short testimonies. All in all, the Gymnaires presented a fine witness to "high level living."

A couple of fellows behind us, dragging away on the cigarettes, kept uttering little grunts of surprise and approval, especially when the agile girls bounced across the stage. The message was clear enough. The audience could see that most of the spectators were in no physical condition to accomplish such feats of balance, precision, and endurance.

Socially, our family differed from all of the rest of the campus in one respect. This, indeed, provided us with a distinct third element of companionship. Leona Gulley and I were first cousins. More than that, our two families had grown up so close together as to be almost indistinguishable. "Cousin" fell far short of reality. To all intents and purposes we were sisters.

One day Leona and I went shopping in Cartimar. Hazardous as it could be, we both prized the independence of doing our own driving.

"I'll wait for you at the car," Leona said as she turned to the door.

Amazed (as people always were), the saleslady asked, "Did you drive your car into the city."

"No," I replied, "my friend brought her car today."

The woman looked at me sharply. "Is that lady only a friend?"

"Well, no," I admitted. "She's my first cousin."

"Hah! I thought so!" This discovery delighted the saleswoman. "I knew because you both have the same face."

So much for keeping secrets. We had been found out even by a shopkeeper on a back street in Manila! We truly prized this family privilege, rarely awarded to people in foreign service.

All in all, despite our sometimes

Left. Norman Gulley taught a class in Eschatology. Below left. Dorothy's Biblical Literature class (Graduate School).[2] Below. Small graduate seminars (like Victorian Literature) sometimes escaped the classroom and met more comfortably in the Richard Fighurs' patio.

vexing problems, Philippine Union College gave us two rewards: Work with a future and enriching friendships.

Although the dreams of moving the College campus to a rural area were not realized during our years there, we had surprisingly lovely diversions.

To mention one. What enabled our city campus still to be an "island of retreat" was the way the rains came. They cleansed the air and gave us a little respite to the intense heat.

At the time, I frequently digressed in my journals to describe wonderful storms.

Imagine lying in your bed (in a solid

With our very international population, potluck dinners on campus opened up amazing food adventures for everyone.

concrete block house) with the shrubbery lashing the open windows, flashes of lightning clipping off chunks of darkness, and, over it all, the thunder rumbling along in a heavy, counter-bass. The rain splattered off the wide eaves, rushed down the rusted gutter pipes, and orchestrated a steady beat on the sidewalk. With the whole world so beautifully alive, you could never be annoyed at waking up at 1 a.m.

A grand show—those monsoon rains. None of your indecisive, drizzly fog stretching out for gloomy hours and days. No solitary, tentative raindrops making dust balls in parched brown earth. Sometimes it all came so suddenly that the sun didn't have time to hide. So it just kept on shining through the curtain of golden green and silver rain.

I liked to remember how King David caught the spirit of it all. Standing atop Mount Herman watching a storm blow in across the wilderness, he burst into poetry. Hearing the majestic thunder, the "Voice of the Lord," he cried:

The Lord breaks the cedars of Lebanon. . . .
The Voice of the Lord flashes forth flames of fire.
The Lord shakes the wilderness
The Voice of the Lord makes the oaks to whirl, and
Strips the forests bare,
And in his temple all cry, "Glory!" (Ps. 29)

One summer, my nephew, Kevin Eckert, came to stay with us at PUC. In his passion for tropical weather I found a true, kindred spirit. One clear night we dragged chairs out on the front lawn under the *santol* tree to watch a celestial spectacular. Behind us the full moon made light sparkles on the palm tree fronds. In front, in the direction of Manila Bay, were curly banks of moonlit clouds, shot through with flashes of lightning. No sound! Just an endless fireworks display. Lightning came in streaks, in balls, in fans. ... What a show!

On another perfectly clear night the stars hung overhead, while a cloud-bank of thunderheads lay along the western horizon, just above our coconut palms. At one moment the lightning slashed through and illuminated the whole landscape, and at the next jagged spikes punctured the clouds.

Another text pounded itself into our minds: "As the lightning comes out of the east and shines unto the west, so shall the coming of the Son of Man be" (Mt. 24:27). When that happens, it won't be just spasmodic flashes but a continuous, escalating illumination that climaxes in a fantastic intensity of light. A blaze that will slay some of earth's watchers and transform others into immortality.

Approximately once a month the overseas work force met together for Bible study, discussion, and supper.[3]

Multiple celebrants with 50th birthdays called for real festivity. Left. We ate the main course at Gulleys' house. Right. Then the "birthday kids" got their cake at Comms' house.

True, Philippine Union College was still enmeshed in Manila's congestion, slums, and violence. Yet, our campus-island gave us more beauty and more comfort than, perhaps, we could appreciate at the time.

One night the three Seminary professors showed up in almost-identical embroidered gray shirts. We called them the "Grey Friars." L-R: Walter Comm, Arnold Wallenkampf, and Norman Gulley.

Notes

1   Beth Siapco became a college librarian (unmarried). Lolita Mamaril, a registered nurse, worked for many years in Saudi Arabia (married with two sons). Zeny de la Roca (married with one daughter) earned her doctorate and now serves as a professor in Naga View College in Bicol.

2   See Dorothy Minchin-Comm, "A Study Guide to the Bible as Literature and Art." (La Sierra University, 4th ed. 2000), 243 pages. Although this class has been widely taught in Adventist colleges, the Church has never produced a textbook.

3   In December, 1976, I served as moderator. We had a series of studies on the twelve sons of Jacob. As each one brought in his and her findings on the characters, an interesting line of thought evolved. See Dorothy Minchin-Comm, *Gates of Promise* (Review & Herald Pub. Assn., 1989)

CHAPTER 23

Matters of Mission

Walt's and my assignments at Philippine Union College looked quite straightforward on paper. I was Chair of the English Department. Walt was a professor in the Seminary with an emphasis on Health Evangelism. We both carried a full teaching loads and taught in the Graduate School.

It was the other appointments that spiced up—and often over-filled—our lives. What with public meetings and follow-up visitation Walt was away more nights a week than he was home. Then he had preaching appointments on the weekends. At times, it seemed that he worked eight days a week.

In addition to traveling with him, I produced the campus paper and edited MA theses and other writings, as required. Moreover, Leona Gulley, and I were the only two women on the compound who would drive a car in Manila. Therefore, I often acted as a tour guide, chauffeuring visitors for sightseeing and shopping in the Old City. Within our first year our campus friends had introduced us to the many historic landmarks in Manila, so I had ample training for the job. Visitors came our way in an almost constant stream.

In fact, my role as Purchasing Agent/Chauffeur/General Guide to Metro-Manila continued throughout our Philippine years. With this opportunity for observation and research, I felt free to comment upon tourists. Ultimately I constructed a five-point checklist for evaluating them.

The **Activists** are enthusiastically in touch with Life and insatiably curious about what they see. They hail every new experience with zest. Having an intelligent sense of the past, they buy a real education with their travel dollars. They tend to bypass the prescribed tourist sites and want to see life as it is really lived in the land.

The **Sheep** jet around the world and dutifully "do" all of the prescribed tourist things. From the windows of air-conditioned buses, they see only what is prepared for foreign eyes and purchase. They flit in and out of souvenir shops, stocking up on loot and snapping pictures left, right, and center. Then they rush on to the next item on the list.

The **Nervous Nellies** are unnaturally preoccupied with food, sanitation, sleeping conditions, heat and cold, dry and wet. Although they may not always verbalize their doubts, you quickly recognize that they are busy measuring everything by what they left "back home."

The **Pre-Programmed Travelers.** These include women who know precisely which placemats will match their china. The men who know exactly which embroidered caftan or capiz shell lamp to take to their wives. Again, there are men who have no idea what to buy for the women in their lives. They only know that they must take home *something*.

The **Been-Theres.** These blasé types who have already seen it all and have no further capacity for adventure. Travel has simply become a bore and a chore.

These attitudes were not necessarily right or wrong. They were just the ways that people related to the challenges of travel and the demands of being in a foreign country.

Of the many guests I served, I enjoyed none more than Dr. Siegfried Horn. On the eve of retirement as Dean of the Seminary at Andrews University, he did his last formal teaching in the Far East. His intensive course fascinated our whole campus.

Most of the men-folk had been his students back in Seminary. Well aware of his international reputation, we women held him in awe. Naturally, we all addressed him as "Dr. Horn."

He, on the other hand, very much wanted to be one of us. "Call me Siegfried. Please." But we kept forgetting.

He threw himself into everything with enthusiasm. A gifted storyteller he entertained us on every trip. He would sit on a hemp mat in the back of the van telling stories of his life as a struggling student in Germany and then as a prisoner-of-war in World War II.

One day, Walt and I, along with Gulleys and Zacharys, took him down the Bataan Death March Road and across to the island of Corregidor in a *banca*.

We stopped for a picnic lunch. "Do have another sandwich, Dr. Horn," someone urged.

He stopped in mid-sentence and fixed a professorial frown upon us all. "I told you, the name is Siegfried," he would intone. Many times he showed us how very human a great scholar can be.

Back in the City I was the one who showed him around Manila. He manifested no interest in the usual commercial tourist sites. Instead, I took him to Intramuros and Fort Santiago (dating from 1571) and other historical sites. There the Spaniards executed the Philippines' national hero, Jose Rizal, in 1896. At Nyong Filipino he saw model villages representing the various regions of island culture. Then we went down to the 200-year-old Bamboo Organ in the church at Paranaque.

I also was asked to prepare Siegfried's farewell gift from the College. I bought a finely carved wooden box. After several hours of investigation, I turned up quite an impressive collection of postage stamps. Each portrayed a significant person or event in Philippine history. Then I wrote historical notes to accompany each stamp and packed it all in the artsy little box.

There was no possible mistaking Siegfried's delight in the box and its contents. He was thrilled. I can't remember any other tour-guiding job that I ever did in the Philippines that I enjoyed more than the hours I spent with our very personable Dr. Horn.

Barely on our feet after the depredations of Typhoon Yoling, Walt and I visited two country churches for the first time in early 1971. Along with a carload of students we drove out into the province of Pampanga. Only seventy miles out of Manila, but the people in Manibaug spoke their own language. A number of other students had preceded us. Indeed, many of our young people regularly spent their weekends visiting rural churches.

The local elder told us that they saw visitors only once in a couple of years. Moreover, Manibaug didn't even have a scheduled pastor. Instead three lay preachers kept things going. Walt's sermon, of course, had to be translated.

He learned immediately that he had to avoid any kind of idiomatic expressions.

In the afternoon we went on to Baliwag and another church. In the feverishly busy town square we saw an enormous statue of Rizal. He had an angel whispering in his ear and dead bodies lying at his feet. As the Abraham Lincoln of the Philippines, Rizal was an intellectual revolutionary whom the Spanish executed. All schools (including ours) were required to teach a course in the life and teachings of Rizal.

We drove home in stifling heat and through long rutted roads bristling with soldiers. The big treat of the day, we thought, would be the chance for a cold shower. But that wasn't it. It was Valentines Day, and our neighbors, the Gensolins, sent over a cassava cake shaped like a heart. Saturated with coconut milk and baked in banana leaves over an open fire, it was delicious. From the very start we understood that our greatest reward lay in the companionship of the people among whom we had come to live.

Those church visits, however, were mild compared to some that would follow. In the month of April, 1971, we were really inducted into off-campus travel, making three onerous but very educational journeys

Left. Marion Blanco shopped at Tesoros, a conventional store in Manila's tourist district. Below left. More difficult—but certainly cheap and practical—would be shopping in Divisoria. Below. In that same market one might purchase a bra straight off of a jeep on the open street.

Dorothy found Dr. Seigfried Horn to be one of the most interesting tourists she ever took sightseeing in Manila. Together they looked over his farewell gift, stamps featuring Philippine history.

The first took us to an island off the east coast of Luzon where Walt preached the baccalaureate sermon for Polillo Academy. Our party[1] left campus at 3.00 a.m. for the bus terminal (an open cattle shed). The "bus" had a plywood body built over a truck chassis. The aisles were crammed with bags of rice, produce, and unidentifiable junk.

Somehow we scrambled aboard.

Just one block down the street, the bus broke down. The wrecker hauled us back to the station, and we transferred to an "express" bus. Forty minutes later we departed again. Five minutes out, we had a flat tire. We relaxed while the driver smoked and waited for some kind of enlightenment.

Finally, our third departure, thirty-five minutes later, propelled us into Manila's morning rush-hour traffic and mercilessly hot sunshine. By this time an uncounted number of extra passengers had joined us.

For the next five-and-a-half hours we jolted over mountain roads of the Sierra Madre, little more than the width of the bus. At the numerous stops, passengers disembarked through the windows. The rough benches bruised us black and blue at every point of contact, elbows, shoulders, knees, ankles and rear ends.

We staggered onto the pier at Infanta for the second part of the journey. The flat-bottomed boat awaited us. It was about sixty feet long, full of splinters and peeling paint. We boarded over a gangplank twelve feet long and eight inches wide. Down below we found ants, flies, and cockroaches the size of field mice. We chose to stay up on deck where the cool sea breeze soothed us.

We reached Polillo two-and-a-half hours later, joining two Japanese logging ships anchored in the harbor. I can't remember ever being so tired in my life. The top of my head seemed about to lift off. I was so disoriented that I felt that I was in two or three bodies, going several directions at once. Our hosts, the Estuita family, opened their comfortable home to us. I almost wept when I saw a real bed awaiting us.

The weekend was very full. Typhoon Yoling five months earlier had reduced the academy buildings to a pile of rubble. Classes had been meeting in the church. People were living in houses that had no roofs, doors or windows. Just a few uprights with torn nipa mats for walls. No electricity, as such, but at special "high moments" the occasional generator kicked in

Graduation was a huge event, and the entire town turned out in a fiesta mood. On the elaborate printed program, Walt saw himself listed as the "Ass Professor of Theology."

"Well," he mused, "at least I know where I fit in." While I supposed that I had simply come along for the ride (and what a ride), I found myself speaking extemporaneously at the afternoon meeting.

We had been welcomed, fed, and honored in every conceivable way—including a swim on the reef on Sunday morning. Monday morning, Walt, Gil Fernandez and I were carried in three tricycles to the wharf where an exu-

Public transportation was to be shared by all. Left. A bus parked in the market place in Tarlac. Tethered on the roof, among the produce, a goat helped himself to lunch. Right. Waiting to get on the ferry to Marinduque Island, we watched a pig being boarded. He shrieked all of the way, aware, perhaps, of his destiny.

berant crowd had come to see us off. We had had three days not only to get acquainted with our colleague, Gil, but also to partake of our first sampling of the hospitality of the Philippine countryside. Stunned by seeing the hardships and courage of the people, Walt and I promised to send 1,000 pesos back to help with the rebuilding of the school.

Back on shore in Luzon, we waited for three hours in the rain. No one seemed quite sure when the Manila bus would come in. Eons of time later we reached home. I dressed Walt's abrasions on his spine that he suffered from the bus bench. Then, I went to bed for the next three days, stricken with fever and vomiting.

I got up just in time to fly to Cauayan, Isabela Province, the following Friday. Walt had another baccalaureate address at Northern Luzon Academy. We arrived in a little two-engine jet-prop plane, and the whole school administrative staff was there to meet us. Two weeks earlier we had mailed them a letter announcing our exact arrival time. It had not yet reached them, so they had all been waiting there in the little barn-like terminal for almost four hours.

A 1953 Model Ford carried us away to the school. At one stop a cluster of little boys sprang up around the van. They danced around it, patted it, and murmured endearments to it. You would too if you had never ridden anything but a *carabao*. Or, if you were lucky, a tricycle.

On Sabbath morning we arose to a magnificent breakfast (the only meal we had that day). Oatmeal, hot chocolate (cold), pancakes, rice, gluten steaks, *pancit,* two dishes of vegetables swimming in coconut milk, three kinds of bananas, two kinds of melon, and star apples. Plus a few other incidentals.

It was a fiercely hot day, and Walt preached to a packed auditorium. More than a thousand people banked up to the walls and standing in the windows.

Then we rushed to the airport in the jeep from Cagayan Valley Hospital. We had to be back in Manila for PUC's graduation Sunday morning. Needless to say, we anticipated the comfort of the flight as opposed to the plywood bus trip of the previous weekend.

It was not to be. For the first time, we were caught up in corruption. A lot of delaying action and much Tagalog chatter went on around us. The agent

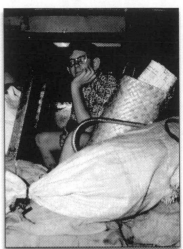

Above. The bus from Manila to Infanta (and on to Polillo) was just a box, all hard angles. **Top right.** Wedged into his seat, Larry surveyed the cargo in the aisle. **Bottom right.** Dr. John Scharffenberg exited the bus the only possible way, through a window.

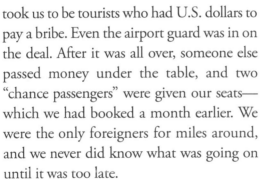

took us to be tourists who had U.S. dollars to pay a bribe. Even the airport guard was in on the deal. After it was all over, someone else passed money under the table, and two "chance passengers" were given our seats—which we had booked a month earlier. We were the only foreigners for miles around, and we never did know what was going on until it was too late.

So we rattled on to Santiago and the bus station. A day earlier I would have thought that I could not possibly endure another bus trip. But we did. The conductor gave Walt and me his own seat, a little iron box twenty-eight inches wide (I measured it). Thereafter, we had an unusual amount of time to visit with each other. Our bus bruises from the Infanta trip had barely healed, but, at least, the new ones were grooved into different places.

We rode the 300 miles to Manila over mountainous, rutted roads with cliffs hanging over green abysses. After a while, the sun set, and we couldn't see the precipices so well. That helped.

We left the bus on the north side of Manila. By taking a *jeepney* and then a taxi we made it home shortly after midnight. Mum and the kids received us with vast relief. We had no way of notifying her that our plane seats had been stolen from us. Ottis and Dottie Edwards brought supper over to the family. "Don't start worrying about them for at least two days," they advised. "Anything could have happened." And so it had!

The next morning we attended our first PUC graduation for 154 seniors. I wore Walt's "disposable" masters gown and a hood from the University of the Philippines. (I had not yet earned my own academic regalia from the University of Alberta, Canada.) Walt, on the other hand, looked almost papal in the theology gown that had once belonged to my Dad. It always pleased me to see him in it. Carrying on of a family heritage.

It was utter madness to start out on another trip before we could even get our exams marked and the grades into the Registrar's Office. Walt had long ago, however, committed to help in the launching of another series of meetings with Public Health emphasis. This time it was to Masinloc, in Zambales Province, six hours' drive up the northwest coast of Luzon.

At least, we could travel in our own car, such as it was. This time we would be in control. Or so we thought.

About halfway to our destination, we heard a rattle and a thump. Our muffler had just dropped off. Plunk! Walt picked it up, cooled it off in a nearby *carabao* water hole, wrapped up the remains, and stowed them in the trunk. Then we roared off through the hills and down to the lovely palm-ringed shoreline of the China Sea.

At our second river crossing, the bridge had been taken out by Typhoon Yoling. A barge attached to cables towed us across the 150-foot expanse of water. We were moved by sheer brute force, with a tiny man laboriously cranking a wheel.

We found that the "Better Living Tabernacle" had been pitched on the edge of Masinloc's town square. Living conditions were, however, very primitive. Not a "comfort room" in sight.

One of the girls (my student of the past semester) explained, "Oh,

Visitors usually wanted to see Corregidor Island in Manila Bay, and we followed the Bataan Death March Road to get there. Upper left. The pale marble figures on the War Memorial commemorate the horror of that World War II event. Upper right. Children played on the Bataan Beach while we negotiated for *bancas* to take us across to Corregidor Island, visible on the horizon. Lower left. The shark-infested crossing from Bataan to Corregidor. Lower right. The unique "blood rocks" from the beaches of Corregidor are a natural memorial to the hundreds of soldiers (both American and Japanese) who perished there.

ma'am! You cannot be comforted here."

"You've been here for two days," I replied. "What have you been doing?"

"We went down to the beach," she said. "When it's low tide, you can walk out far."

So that's what we did too. The managing evangelist remarked, "It is good for the students to learn that this is what the life of a minister means." Denying everyone a designated comfort room, however, seemed to me unnecessarily rigorous.

Nonetheless, the pastor's wife prepared a delicious supper for the whole crowd of about fifteen people. She did it on a single-burner primus stove.

Then everyone was off for the evening meeting. Without previous warning, I found myself telling stories to the big gangs of kids sitting in the front rows at every meeting. As it turned out, I told children's stories wherever kids were congregated.

They were everywhere by the dozens and the scores. They poured out of every house whenever we passed through a town. Unlike my mother, I did not do children's stories well. Indeed, I never felt at ease with an entourage of kids swarming around me. Instinctively I knew that I belonged in the college classroom. When I lived overseas, however, I had to force myself to do this— as well some of the other unusual tasks—when we were out "on the road." I could only hope that my ineptness was not too obvious.

By the evening meeting in Masinloc, Walt had developed a vicious throat infection and could hardly croak. With his translator, Pastor Leonas, coming through loud and clear, he got through his public health talk. Considering the wild intemperance of these past days of travel, it struck me as ironic that we had observed so little of "private health" but remained out on the road talking about public health.

The students begged us to stay one more night, but with summer school about to open, we decided to drive back to Manila that night. The nationals always feared having us traveling about the provinces alone—and probably with reason. Jun Rabanes came along with us for protection.

Through the night we roared (without muffler) into several checkpoints that were usually unmanned in daylight. Each station was alive with men and guns. One fellow came out to inquire very closely into our affairs. He ended up asking for money "to buy vegetables." A rather unlikely story. We had no money because we'd spent our last on two big baskets of mangoes at

Walt Comm and two of his colleagues (Delfe Alsaybar and Rick Salamante) discuss plans for health evangelism in Metro Manila.

the Masinloc market. He turned his flashlight into the back seat where Rabanes was pretending to sleep. He abruptly stopped his inquisition. "Just go." He waved us on.

We reached home at 3.00 a.m. and found Larry and Rusty sleeping in our bed. Happily the water was on. (It seldom was during the night.) We luxuriated in the cold shower and then fell into bed. Never underestimate that privilege. We determined not to leave home again. At least not for a week or so.

As Walt's health evangelism students scattered around the country, mission trips became longer, and increasing numbers of baptisms called for careful organization. The "Mission to the Mangyans" became a major undertaking for the College. Indeed, it was a center of interest when the Tri-Division Education Council was held at Philippine Union College (November 2-5, 1972).

For that occasion student missionary, Marilyn Bito-onan, brought Chief Abraham and about twelve Mangyan children from the Mindoro mountains. They trailed her around the campus like the Pied Piper. The kids had never seen the sea or a boat. Although they arrived in G-strings, enough clothing had been collected by the weekend to dress them. Busy ladies made clothes for them all out of the feed sacks donated by the College Poultry Department.

The meetings concluded with the College Music Department doing themselves proud in Saturday night concert. The Ambassadors sang Philippine folk music, dressed in a variety of costumes from the 18th-century Maria Clara gowns to the peasant garb of the rice planters.

During that time, we had two guests, Drs. Gordon McDowell and Eric Magnusson, both from Australia. I took them to their off-campus appointments. Martial law was new and at high tide. On Sabbath Magnusson preached in one of the small city churches. It happened to be in an area where President Marcos' New Society people were tearing down shacks along the canals. Part of the poor little church happened to be within the twenty-foot "demolition range." Magnusson could barely make himself heard with people tramping across the tin roof overhead. "And the congregation just sat there as if having the church pulled down during the service was the most normal thing in the world," he exclaimed.

Upper left. Sign for the Loma Linda University sponsored a health evangelism project in far-away Agta, Polillo. Upper right. (L-R). Dr. John Scharffenberg (supervisor), with Lorraine, Rae, and Marilyn, arrived in a tropical downpour. Center left. Rae Lynne Ward accommodates a little helper in showing the villagers how to become self-supporting with their own gardens. Center right. A student flushes a newly constructed, prize-winning "jungle toilet." Lower left. The Toilet Building contest followed the creation of a model toilet for the new station. This was the first time the villagers learned about sanitation. (They found it restrictive.)

Left. The hikers rest under a rock on the long climb up into Mangyang country, on the island of Mindoro. Right. Chief Abraham was proud of his role in the changes that came to his village.

Sunday night we took some of our guests to the Sulo Club. I slowed down at an intersection. "There's often an open manhole about here," I remarked. Indeed, it was open, just visible in the smoky lights. "Pedestrians have a tendency to steal the heavy metal lids and sell them for scrap iron," I explained.

Magnusson fell silent, and then he shook his head. "Manila is so real, you just have to believe it, don't you?" That, I thought, was a good way of saying what is otherwise indescribable,

At the end of the month our whole family went to Mindoro for a "Mangyan Follow-up." The flight to San Jose, Occidental Mindoro took only forty-five minutes, as opposed to a sixteen-hour boat journey. (In bad weather the voyage could take three or four days.) To our astonishment we saw no beggars or thieves in the town. All in all, it seemed to be a healthier society than in Manila. The population of 75,000 as opposed to Manila's millions helped too, of course.

Mum, Lorna and I stayed in the simple home of Pastor Cudanin, leaving the long mountain hike to Walt and Larry. I had an excuse, for my recent bout with hepatitis still lay upon me. Warm hospitality enfolded us into the family.

At sundown worship on Friday evening we were inducted into a new custom. Upon rising from prayer, everyone says to one another, "Good Morning," "Good Evening" or "Happy Sabbath." With natural cheerful grace, each child kisses the hand of a parent or older person, bows, and presses the hand to his own forehead.

Built of raw wood, the house had a kind of "receiving room." It contained one very old, rejected church bench and a small desk. It also served as the pastor's study. The kitchen contained a table, two plain benches, a gas hotplate, and a big earthenware pot for drinking water. We slept in the only bedroom. We could lie on the floor mat and watch the chickens under the house through the widely spaced two-inch slats.

The large windows had heavy wooden shutters propped open with bamboo poles. Because there were few inside walls to hinder its movement, the wind stirred all through the house. Privacy is not a commodity in great demand in much of the Orient .

Bathroom protocol in the Cudanin home was carefully observed. The room was a six-foot-square cement-block enclosure at the front of the house, under a couple of Australian pine trees. You sloshed water over yourself from the buckets of water that you had filled at the pump. Since the wall was barely shoulder high, you could watch the traffic on the street. (Unfortunately, over the weekend, some visitors had mistaken the bathroom for a toilet, so that night we had to bathe like nymphs in the starlight under the banana trees at the back of the house.) The actual comfort room (toilet) was a high cement castle in the back yard. It could be reached only by a narrow, steep ladder. The appointed place for brushing teeth was under the *kamasali* (tamarind) tree by the kitchen door. Considering how cluttered our lives are, living a while with the bare essentials was a kind of a tonic.

My assignments in San Jose began with prayer meeting. Many times, at my desk, "large thoughts" pass through my mind. Sometimes I have the fleeting notion that it would be nice to make a sermon on one of my ideas. Then, I remember what dour old Samuel Johnson wrote 200 years ago. "A woman's preaching is like a dog's walking on his hind legs. It is not done well, but one is surprised to find it done at all." That night I talked about one of Christ's neglected little parables, yet one of the richest: "I am the Alpha and the Omega" (Rev. 1:8, 11). Such occasions made me entertain the idea of some day writing a devotional book. Maybe.[2]

Meanwhile Walt, Larry, Pastor Cudanin and two young men had set out Wednesday afternoon on the three-day journey up into Mangyan country. En route, they picked up two guides—a little Mangyan man and his wife, clad in dirty G-strings, their mouths fire-red with betel nut. At the foot of the mountain the guides assured them that Sandok Talahib was just "three shouts" away. Measured by time this proved to be about two hours. Fortified with egg sandwiches, biscuits, peanuts, raisins and malted milk tablets, they hiked in the rain along a winding riverbed, through thick jungle. Despite the rugged terrain, they found the landscape beautiful.

Upon arrival Walt discovered that the student missionaries (in just one year) had already built a substantial little bamboo church, seating 100 people. Everything had been done by sheer manpower. Not even a *carabao* had been available. The visitors slept in the storage shed, bedded down atop bags of rice and bulgar wheat.

The energetic, young Chief Abraham (now a church elder) had made his village blossom like a rose, both spiritually and materially. The fifty-three Christians in his now-disciplined community were clean and wearing clothes. (Bathing had never been part of Mangyan culture.) They stood apart from the rest who suffered from severe skin diseases. Walt testified that he couldn't help thinking of the early Christians at Antioch in the days of the Apostle Paul.

Friday afternoon the hikers returned. Larry seemed to have grown an inch taller in the time he was gone! They surprised the rest of us at the beach. I had just returned from White Island. It was a little coral atoll some 500 feet long and a fifteen-minute *banca* journey from shore. Early in the day it wore a lovely hairnet of morning-glory vines.

Church the next day was a lively gathering. They had no musical instrument, so whenever music was wanted everyone just burst forth into song together. Two pretty little teenagers pinned primroses on all of us, the visitors' token.

Chief Abraham had returned with the hikers. By now he had become quite a "man of the world," having made two trips to Manila. He had learned a little Tagalog and a couple of words of English. With energetic sign language he made it clear that he wanted a souvenir from Walt. It turned out to be the green visor-cap he'd worn on the hike up the mountain. We autographed it, and I took a picture of Walt planting it on the chief's round little head. Abraham went off grinning. "The hat," he announced, "has a spirit. When the white man Comm goes back to Manila, I can be the doctor in the mountains."

Then there were other "souvenirs." Walt gave Bais, one of the laymen, his leather belt. He bestowed ten pesos apiece on the two pack-carriers. (The Mangyans seldom saw any money.)

The goodbyes came hard. "We just hope the plane doesn't come," the pastor and his wife whispered.

It did, of course, and we got back home just in time to start our second semester classes the next day. That time we had no ill effects. Although the Mindoro mosquitoes ate us alive, we faithfully took our quinine and hoped for the best. Certainly we didn't need to add malaria to our medical records just then.

Our off-campus journeys did not always take us to churches and the venues of public evangelism. I particularly enjoyed going down to PUC's little sister school, Naga View Academy, in Bicol.

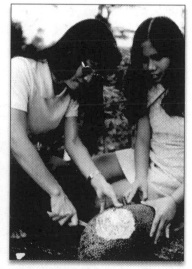

Left. Naga View College's truck regularly broke down, but the students doggedly walked back to campus. Right. For a treat during a rest-break two girls cut into a jackfruit for the summer crew working on the new Administration Building.

Very remote Tirad View Academy, Northern Luzon. Left. Our shy, city-bred van negotiated the dry riverbed. Right. Faculty housing at TVA. Pioneer conditions prevailed.

My first visit called for the writing of a couple of publicity articles as the new school was soon to attain junior college level. Mum and Larry went with me. Although the one hour flight was relatively predictable, the journey was by no means uninteresting.

The Principal Rick Salamante met us in a Ford Combie that the Union had purchased from US Clarke Air Force Base. Although it had some transmission problems, its youth had been partially restored with a fresh coat of blue and white paint. It still had the unfortunate habit of sucking up clouds of dust through the exhaust and coating the passengers gray.

When Salamante showed us their other vehicle, we had to agree that the Combie was "much better." We looked reverently at an ancient two-seat pickup truck. Its body had a tooled metal look and was covered with rust and peeling paint. "We use this one for marketing." Our host remarked. It sat by the maintenance shop, like a dying patient forever in the doctor's waiting room. "Somehow it keeps going," Rick said. Any ordinary bystander would surely have given it up for dead.

Our guest room was a gray, cement-block chamber at the end of the Administration Building. Three cots stood under the wooden slat windows, and we had a doorless bathroom to the side. Vines grew through the holes in the wall. Passing snakes and lizards used the facilities also. Salamante brought us three mosquito nets. "Our mosquitoes here are very fierce," he admitted.

We went swimming at a beautiful little pool below the school property. Set in a cluster of bougainvillea bushes and fed by a freshwater spring, it was a good place to beat the heat and dust.

Then we met Zeny de la Roca, who ultimately came to PUC as one of our Filipina daughters. She cooked our meals and tried to serve us food she thought we were used to. We assured her that we were very gifted rice-eaters. The regular dessert she served was *buco*—coconut pieces, pineapple and raisins afloat in coconut milk.

I interviewed many hardworking students, all with a fine "small school spirit." Their stories of stamina and hope inspired, so the articles were easy to write. When I was asked to take Friday night vespers, I decided to give the young people a new look at "The Last Supper." That iconic painting is to be found all over the Philippines, though not exactly true to every detail that Leonardo da Vinci put into it. We found a print large enough so that I could interpret the characters and make a devotional talk out of it.

I was amazed at the enthusiastic audience response to the symbols and body language in the picture. At the end, Rick Salamante rushed forward and grasped my hand. "Thank you so much. Now I understand." Bright-eyed students clustered around him. "I must get a copy made for our dining room right here," he declared. "Now that we understand the picture, we must have it. I'll sell another cow in order to get it!" he promised.

Our Naga friends took us sightseeing on Sunday. When we hiked on

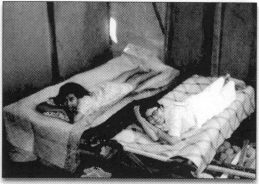

Left. Manila Center for Evangelism, Walt preaching and Pastor Acosta translating. Below. Students arrange their sleeping quarters behind a church in Masinloc.

Mt. Isarog, Larry helped Grandma down the trail. I recalled the days when he was such a tiny little spider of a boy. Grandma loved cuddling him. Now he'd grown to such a hefty fellow. We both depended on his strong arm that day. Then we went on to see Mayon volcano, the most perfectly symmetrical cone in the world.

For Dorothy presentation of the "Last Supper" in the cavernous CA, Nilo Palma painted a reproduction that was 15 feet wide. No problem.

Finally, we departed Naga Pili Airport, completely encrusted with Naga dust! I don't believe even one of Naga's new garden rakes could have been dragged through my hair. When I got home, I shampooed four times before the water came clean. No matter! This was just one of the additives to my regular schedule that gave me the most rewarding job in the world.

Notes

1   In addition to Walt and me, the group departing from the PUC campus was made up of Gil Fernandez, professor in the Religion Department), a male quartet from the College, and Mrs. Marion Simmons, Associate Secretary of Education at the Far Eastern Division office in Singapore.

2   See Dorothy Minchin-Comm, *Glimpses of God* (Review and Herald Pub. Assn., 1998.)

CHAPTER 24

Running with the Footmen

It is not good for the
white man's health
To hustle the Asian brown,
And the white man riles
And the Asian smiles,
And he weareth the white man down.
At the end of the fight
Lies the tombstone white
With the name of the late deceased;
And the epitaph drear
Reads: "A fool lies here
Who tried to hustle the East!"

Rudyard Kipling (1865-1936)

Being programmed always to do our best, Walt and I habitually aimed to "run with the horsemen" rather than "the footmen." It grew naturally, no doubt, out of our Western background and Christian commitment. We wanted to get things done. To get them done right. Preferably, we wanted them to be done now. Overseas living, however, demanded adjustments to these expectations. And stuff happened every day.

So, we accepted the fact that it was going to take longer to accomplish any given task. Beyond that, however, lay an assortment of unheard of hindrances. Obstacles that utterly defied the imagination. That's when we had to forget the horses. We only hoped that we could keep up with the footmen.

One of our first out-of-the-city journeys, in 1971, was a case in point. It occurred before President Marcos subjected his country to martial law. At the time there was but one stretch of four-lane divided highway, just north of the city. A toll road, of course. At the entry toll booth we found that the money-collectors were on strike. A company of soldiers surrounded the car to scrutinize us and the three student passengers in the back seat. Then, with a smile and a bow, they waved us through.

Twenty miles later when we reached the exit tollbooth, however, we found that those people were not on strike. "Where is your ticket?" A sinister-looking fellow in dark glasses trained his sub-machine gun on us. "You can not pass."

A fierce, rapid-fire exchange in Tagalog ensued between the students and the armed guards. Finally, he-of-the-dark glasses lowered his weapon. "Go, then," he growled. We drove on, grateful that we were not alone that day.

Driving in Manila traffic was a nightmare any day of the year—with the exception of Easter. On "Black Friday" it was believed that God was dead, and the streets would be virtually empty. Otherwise the city was crowded to the point of implosion. Downright claustrophobic. Manila literally closed in on both body and spirit. No wonder plans had been afoot for decades to move Philippine Union College to a rural locations. That desire never waned.

Meanwhile, we learned to live with what we had. One Saturday evening we, along with the Lee Wilsons, were entertaining some friends visiting from Okinawa. We took them to the Sulo Club in Makati. It was one of Manila's best showplaces, featuring a good restaurant, along with Filipino music and folk dancing.

A classic traffic jam in Cubao threatened to make us miss the whole show. Four lanes of traffic headed north on a two-lane street. The other side was being paved, but no one had been able to co-operate with that restriction. Consequently, we sat in a total dead-lock, breathing exhaust fumes for at least half an hour.

Lee walked up to the intersection to survey the situation. Needless to say, not a policeman was in sight. With his encouragement, the two drivers, in a noble gesture of self-sacrifice, finally backed up and enabled the traffic to move. I remembered episodes like that from Jamaica, but I had never seen Filipinos face off quite so doggedly.

Occasionally the drama on Manila streets provided sheer entertainment. During one flood season, we had spent three hours negotiating what should have been a forty-five-minute journey. One lane over from us we saw a little white van bearing a roof sign: "The Great Dr. Tito, One of the World's Greatest Fortune-tellers and Magicians."

The rest of the drivers sat resignedly in their cars like zombies, eyes staring dully ahead. A distraught figure in a flowing Arabian headdress with a bright, triple-buckled band kept leaping in and out of the van. In a fury he searched the hectic street for a means of escape. A large picture of the doctor mounted in the back window confirmed the fact that this was, indeed, the great man himself at the wheel. No doubt, he was en route to some performance of international consequence

Such a pathetic little scenario. If the mighty Dr. Tito were a fortune teller why could he not have foreseen the traffic jam and kept out of it? Or, failing that, if he were a magician why didn't he forthwith remove himself from the situation altogether? To be "one of the greatest in the world" and yet so victimized? One's heart could just bleed for the poor man!

Traffic trauma inevitably magnified the cross-city trek we frequently made to the airport. That confusion was doubled with the virtual impossibility of having telephone communication, whatever the circumstances.

Consider the day that our friends, the Gilbert McLarens, returned from a month's vacation back home in Australia. (At the time he was the main doctor at the hospital in Saigon, Viet Nam.) Since Walt was otherwise occupied, I agreed to take our feeble little Peugeot and make the airport run. Mum and I and the two kids set off at 4 p.m. The Qantas flight was due at 6.p.m. We ought to be able to get there in time, right?

I had driven about a mile from the campus when a fire broke out in the huge Balintawak Market. In moments it exploded into gigantic proportions. I was caught up on an overpass when a *jeepney* (as usual) cut across my path. Once stalled, the car would not start again. With the black smoke rolling over us, several *jeepneys* emptied themselves, and crowds of people stood on the bridge watching the fire.

"Look, Mum!" I said. "You and Lorna walk down to the highway and get a taxi and go home." They could at least tell Walt where I was. I kept Larry with me.

Deluded, I actually believed that if I could get the car off the bridge, I might still make it to the airport. When an amiable party of men agreed to

The Sulo Club was a favorite place to take visitors for an elegant ethnic meal and folk dancing. Left. Planting rice. Right. Celebrating the Spanish heritage.

push me backwards, I got the
car going. By this time,
however, the traffic was a solid
pack. Nonetheless, I was off
the bridge and facing
downtown. The heat from the
fire and exhaust pipes became
overwhelming. Moving an
inch at a time, we covered
about a third of a mile in an
hour-and-a-half. All the side
streets and alleys were now

Formal recognition of our cousinly connections. (L-R). Dorothy and Walter Comm, Norman and Leona Gulley (1974).

plugged. As yet, not a policeman to be seen anywhere.

Then one showed up, replete with red stripes, brass buttons and a gun.
He appeared to have no interest in the present situation. "Can't you direct
some traffic here," I pleaded.

He looked upon the undulating mass of humanity as if he'd been struck
by a really novel idea. Perhaps he could do something. Within another half-
hour he had actually loosened up the gridlock, and I was able to ooze through.

I stopped at four different shops before I could find a telephone in operation. On the last try, after I dialed eight times, I reached the Qantas desk at
the airport. Yes, the plane was on the ground. In moments, Gilbert McLaren
was on the line. Surely, this had to be one of the most amazing telephone
achievements of my lifetime.

Before I could explain my plight, Walt himself walked into the air
terminal. He had taken a *jeepney* in Balintawak, run on foot for half a mile past
the fire, picked up a taxi on the other side, and had reached the airport!

I had no idea, of course, when I might get out of wherever I was, but now
it didn't matter that much any more. I was in a part of the city I'd never seen
before, and I couldn't recognize a single landmark. Dozens of vehicles stood on
all sides with their radiators boiling. I dared not turn off the Peugeot's engine,
or history would have repeated itself all over again. It took Larry and me
another two hours to get back to the campus.

I reached home just five minutes before Walt and the McLarens arrived in a taxi. Beth and Lolita had a good supper waiting. Larry was eager to eat, but I was too far gone in heat and frustration to participate. Being a doctor, Gil McLaren diagnosed my case as nervous exhaustion, and no one required anything more of me that night.

Sometimes our airport trips partook less of physical challenge and became, as it were, forensic.

On another occasion our Canadian friends, Ed and Ethel Heisler and their four kids arrived. After seventeen years of service in Inter-America, they were headed for Penang, Malaysia, where he would become hospital administrator. Because our friendship went back to early days in Jamaica, we were keen to have them spend a week with us, en route.

A letter had arrived the previous week to announce their arrival at 3.30 in the afternoon. Mum, the kids and I headed for the city in mid-morning. "I'll meet you at the airport this afternoon, after classes," Walt promised. Thus, we'd all be together for the joyous reunion of our two families after a long absence.

We reached the Manila Sanitarium for lunch. As we parked outside the cafeteria, Lorna pointed to the Union van parked beside us. "Look at all the American luggage."

Momentarily, I thought David and Leona Gouge had arrived. They were our new elementary school teachers. Six months of summer vacation had been

The little Baesa Elementary School served the mission children and others who could not attend the local Filipino schools which (at that level) were not conducted in English.

too much. Even the kids were beginning to feel that perhaps life should have a little more structure and were looking forward beginning school soon.

When we walked into the dining room, however, we stopped short. Behold, there sat the whole Heisler family, already working through their rice and *pancit*. After the first joyous greetings, we discovered that there had been the usual breakdown in communications. The plane had actually come in at 9.30 a.m. After two hours fighting off taxi drivers and other entrepreneurs who profit off the ignorance of tourists, Ed got a telephone call through to the Union office. Ben Sumicad, the Assistant Treasurer, had gone out and picked them up.

Our next problem was how to get in touch with Walt and tell him not to come to the airport. A frantic hour of trying to get a call through to the College ended in total failure. So we loaded up the Bedford van started out for Caloocan City and PUC campus. Because of the recent floods, travel time had doubled and even tripled.

I could envision Walt wandering about the ruins of the newly burned-out airport, not knowing what had happened. There never seemed to be anyone there to answer a question on any subject. Then he'd spend the rest of the day in taxis, trying to figure it all out.

Still, I couldn't think of anything else to do. We reached Cubao where the road had degenerated into a kind of rock quarry. The Bedford van's frame groaned with the strain as we jounced through the great holes. As we inched

Left. Grade 8 graduation at Baesa. (L-R) Larry Comm, Lorna Comm, Sharon Gulley, Julie Gouge. Right: Lorna received her diploma from Gordon Bullock (Board Chairman) and her teacher, David Gouge.

along, Ed asked, "Has Walt changed since we saw you last?"

"Not really," I replied. "He has a mustache now, but that's about all that I can think of."

Larry was sitting behind me. "Watch the other side of the road," I told him. "Daddy might be in a taxi going to the airport about now."

Suddenly a joint cry rose from Larry and Mum, "There he is!"

Walt, however, had not seen us.

In a Filipino maneuver, I pulled across three lanes of traffic. At home it could have earned me a traffic ticket and perhaps a jail sentence. It signified nothing, however, in Manila. I stopped in a side street.

Now what to do? "Ed, run back and try to stop the taxi." I figured his long legs could cover the ground most efficiently. It was nearly a quarter of a mile to go, but, predictably, the traffic was at a crawl.

Trouble was, Ed hadn't actually seen the taxi and didn't even know what color it was. The spectacular sight of a lanky *Americano* loping down the center strip, looking into each vehicle on the way, brought all activity in front of Farmers' Market to a halt. Now all he had to do was find that man with a mustache.

Meanwhile, a policeman had stopped the traffic on that side of the street in order to deliver some admonitions to a *jeepney* driver and also to Walt's taxi driver. They had run interference with one another. Being thoroughly engrossed in this immediate matter, Walt was wholly unprepared to see the door burst open and have a flying figure fling itself in upon him. His first reaction, naturally, was that this was a hold-up, and he was being robbed.

The taxi driver accepted the whole thing as just another exhibition of Western imperialism, I suppose. He meekly made a U-turn and came back to the spot where the rest of us were all standing on the street corner, following the drama, as best we could and cheering on the principals.

It would be hard, I think, to match again such accurate timing. Even amid the pandemonium that is Manila? Hardly!

Cars brought no one any joy in the Philippines, not even to an auto-fancier like Walt. None of us could afford anything but almost derelict old wrecks. Just to keep them going constituted an almost-constant crisis. By the end of our first term of service he had the care of our ever-frail Peugeot. Also, the Gulleys' Peugeot had plumbing problems. They often had to carry a thermos jug of water to supply it with drinks. Then our Bedford van, in constant "general" service for the campus, developed a kind of chronic asthma before it finally went out of our lives. It declined because Walt couldn't find time to tend to its ailments as promptly as he needed to.

In addition to the chaos of Manila traffic, shopping itself could be treacherous. In this arena we operated at four levels: Vendors on the street, the open markets, small emporiums, and Greenhills. The last was actually a supermarket. A good one and a model for the future.

The amazing little Chinese shops stood halfway between the clean and lovely Greenhills Supermarket and the open *sari-sari* stores. Near the campus we had Cesar's Emporium. Stacked to the ceiling with stuff, it was a small, dark, windowless shop. Rows of bags of rice, pop-bottle boxes, and egg crates at the front give the entrance the appearance of full military preparedness. Inside, small, doll-size grocery carts were provided. The aisles were so full of people and heaps of foodstuffs, however, that we couldn't move the tiny carts around. Therefore, we had to carry everything in our arms. We could approach the refrigerated counter only by climbing over heaps of cartons and baskets.

Still business was very brisk, any time of the day or night. Its being Chinese- owned explained a great deal. The most progressive businesses in the Far East are (still) Chinese. Amazingly, in the midst of the madness that was Cesar's we could find some of the most surprising commodities. Like Danish cream and the biggest selection of Swiss chocolate I've seen outside of Switzerland itself. Also dairy products from Australia and New Zealand and much more.

We had to learn what we could and could not expect to do in each of these places. From time to time we

Having chased down the taxi in Cubao, Ed Heisler and his son Bruce posed beside a particularly flamboyant *jeepney*.

Although Walt loved playing cars, he did sometimes weary of the tasks. Left. He had to keep our Bedford van going. Right. He also serviced the two Seminary vans. Their fresh paint-jobs belied their chronic internal disorders.

women went to Divisoria Market. It had been a Manila landmark for more than 400 years. We could find the same goods as were sold in the tourist areas of Mabini and Makati—for half the price.

Just parking the car in Divisoria, however, constituted a supreme trial. So much so, that I sometimes went down there by *jeepney*. (A decision not to be taken lightly.) Then, one day, I discovered a parking lot within just three blocks of the center of the market. Near one of the *esteros* (canals), it occupied about an acre, shaped like an irregular pentagon and enclosed with a composite fence made of stone, corrugated zinc roofing, wood, and cardboard—all assembled in a highly abstract design. Unpaved, the ground resembled a rocky beach more than anything else. Nonetheless, it provided actual space for parking.

At the entrance a large sign was painted on the wall: "The Manila Parking Lot." A somewhat extravagant claim, I felt. Below was the cheerful announcement: "Open fur bussines." In finer print further down appeared a telephone number and the name of an attorney who was apparently the owner and promoter of the enterprise. Inside, a uniformed guard and a parcel of idle youths awaited the coming of customers.

A truly great discovery. I returned to the Manila Parking Lot and gave them "Bussines" for many months to come. Having actually located a parking place in Divisoria, I hoped that even Walt would find courage to come again.

He did not. Actually, I think he never recovered from his first visit to the roaring, seething hotbed of commerce which has always been Divisoria.

To succeed in places like Divisoria one had to under-stand the art of bargaining. Something that I detested. I never became good at it, and, whenever I could, I studiously hunted for others to shop for me. My good neighbor, Dr. Lenore Gensolin, gave me my first lesson in Divisoria. Her bargaining techniques were truly educational. She picked

Shopping in Divisoria market was physically taxing, but what beautiful bargains were to be found there!

up a fine piece of embroidered *jusi* (banana fiber) fabric. "How much?"

"Twenty-eight pesos, Ma'am."

My colleague opened her eyes wide with astonishment. "Aaah! ... #i5%65jfgi0& (flood of Tagalog)!" she cried. "Fifteen pesos, nah!"

The saleswoman stirred uneasily. "Twenty-four," she muttered.

At this Dr. Lenore smiled charmingly, patted her on the arm, and rattled off some more Tagalog. Her tone of voice implied, "Now, of course, you don't mean that! Really, for shame! Let's start again." In a little aside to me, she explained, "I am bargaining for twenty pesos!"

To the proprietor she said, "#(&E98fnj. . . Fifteen only, nah!" A little more give and take while I awaited the outcome. Presently, Lenore announced, "She will let us have it for twenty pesos."

Smiles all round, business transacted, and everyone happy. The sales-woman, of course, never expected to receive twenty-eight pesos, and only a tourist would have given it to her.

Bargaining, I came to understand, is an inborn gift. Young Zeny de la Roca, one of our "adopted" daughters, knew all of the right moves too. Coming in from a country trip we stopped the Bedford van at a roadside fruit market in Tagaytay.

The 14th birthdays. Left. Lorna invited the entire singing group, the Ambassadors, to her party. Right. Larry stuck to his school friends. Front. Fernando Norte, Victor Gouge, Larry, John Gulley, Lee Wilson. Back. Lorna, Laurie Wilson, Sharon Joiner, Sharon Gulley, Julie Gouge

Very attractive and alive with personality, Zeny left the fruit vendors in a glassy-eyed daze. When they woke up and counted their money, they probably didn't know what had hit them.

Because, again, the negotiation took place in fast-paced Tagalog, I couldn't tell exactly when the defenses of the vendor began to collapse. The doomed fellow had shown us a large banana stalk. "Four pesos and fifty centavos."

Registering utter astonishment at such blasphemy, Zeny climbed out of the bus, talking all the while in low, forgiving tones. At the same time, however, she was cynically examining the fruit at close range. She gave him another opportunity to redeem his reputation. The sunbeams danced in her long, wavy, raven-black hair. The vendor said, "Four pesos."

At this point, she adopted a now-let's-be-reasonable tone, and the agitated dialogue continued. With everyone in the bus laughing and offering advice and with a group of interested bystanders gathering, the poor fellow lost all confidence in his produce and distributed a dozen "sample" bananas for everyone in the van.

Ultimately Zeny bought six or eight pineapples and three big stalks of bananas—with three more pineapples thrown in for *kumsha* (extras)

Thus we departed with the back of the bus loaded with most choice fruit and with our purse only very slightly depleted. We left the vendor in good spirits, smiling and waving goodbye.

In this land of devious business prac-
tices, it takes one Filipino to reduce another
one to his lowest common denominator.
Whenever we took our girls, Beth, Zeny and
Lolita, to the market, they did their best work
when we kept ourselves completely out of
sight.

Even when Walt and I were alone, we
usually got better-than-tourist prices. That is,
if we could stand the physical assault. One
day, on our way home from Baguio, we
unwittingly became involved in a "Great
Pineapple Riot." Pausing in the town of
Calauan, we were besieged by pineapple
vendors. Boys boarded the van fore and aft.
They thrust pineapples in at all six of the
windows crying, "I am here, ma'am!" "See
me!" "This one very sweet, ma'am."

The Bamboo Organ in Las Pinas,
Paranaque has always been a special
tourist destination. Built by Fr.
Diego Cere between 1816 and 1821,
all of the pipes are bamboo, except
for the horizontal trumpet stops.

Actually, we acquired thirteen of them, and they cost only fifty *centavos*
(eight cents) each. But not before we suffered abrasions on our hands and faces
as the rough pineapples were thrust under our noses. One kid dropped his
two pineapples on the floor and then clung to the moving van as Walt tried
to maneuver the vehicle out of the middle of the street. One thing you had to
say for them, they really believed in the product they sold.

Actually, I admit to a fundamental abnormality. Unlike most other
women, I do not like shopping. With one exception. I do love Oriental arts—
silk, embroidery, painting, lacquer, jade, ivory, wood carving and all of the
rest. Because those things fascinated me to the point of addiction, I never
minded taking visitors to those kinds of stores.

To that end, over the years, I cultivated a little store in downtown Manila.
Owned by a gracious mother and daughter, the place stood right next door to
Tesoros, a very large tourist destination. My guests and I always received a fair

Our three Filipina "daughters" whom we sent to college while they lived with us. L-R. Beth Siapco, Lolita Mamaril, Zeny de la Roca.

price, however, without the pain of bargaining. Because of my loyalty, every year I received a very nice Christmas present, usually something of my own choice.

One day I was in the shop alone when a tourist bus pulled up outside. Forty or fifty Americans surged through the door. "You just wait over there." The older woman motioned me to the back of the room.

So there they were in Hawaiian shirts, shorts exposing knobby knees, cameras slung around their necks. They shouted at the proprietors, who spoke impeccable English. They believed, I suppose, that if you're in a foreign country and you talk louder you'll be better served, whether the "natives" know English or not. The crowd lumbered around among the showcases like a herd of cattle, bellowing their comments to one another. The ultimate "Ugly Americans," I mused as I shrank back into the storeroom. I didn't want in any way to be connected with them. Through it all, the two Filipina ladies were the epitome of grace and courtesy.

In due course, after buying a considerable amount of stuff, they all piled back onto the bus and were taken away. They had "done" the Philippines, I suppose.

I returned to the front of the shop and picked up the embroidered table-cloth I had chosen. At the counter, I had no eye contact with either of my friends. I did detect the faintest hint of a smile, however, when one of them murmured, "And your price is … " I realized then that for the very same item some of the tourists had paid four times what I did.

Whether you ever master the fine points of bargaining or not, it is never safe to assume that you have had the "last word" in any foreign country.

Thus, the daily tasks of getting from Point A to Point B and the keeping

The girls kept our kitchen filled with tropical food supplies. Left. Beth grated coconut. Center. Bargaining for pineapples and papayas on the roadside. Right. Also we grew our own papayas in our own yard.

of food on the table challenged us. The pressure never let up.

Once we gave up on the horses and just ran with the footmen, we avoided a great deal of stress. But not all of it, of course.

CHAPTER 25

The Demands of Survival

Asian House Gecko

Everyone suffers discomfort simply from living in what we call the "human condition." In the Third World, however, all of these things—whether the violence of the weather, disease, or political unrest—are magnified. Moreover, the solutions to the problems are often hard to come by. In fact, they may be altogether unreachable.

The year 1972 produced a larger and more varied parcel of problems than we had ever faced before.

It began in mid-May when I succumbed to what appeared to be severe stomach flu. The campus doctor set me up with intravenous drip to counteract dehydration—always the first line of defense in the tropics. Hopefully, I'd make it through without hospitalization.

My private nurse, Cousin Leona Gulley, slept with me the first night to manage the equipment. "I am sorry to take your roommate away tonight," I told Norman.

"Oh, that's quite all right," he replied. "I've got someone else." That's when I learned that Gulleys have been chasing a "dragon" around their house for several days. A huge lizard, many sizes larger than the little geckos that live in our houses all of the time, he had, thus far, eluded capture.

Actually, living with lizards was usually not difficult. Dozens of the little gray ones skittered across the ceilings and up the walls. They hid behind pictures and in curtains. We had a system of peaceful co-existence worked out. They minded their own business (eating insects) and we tended to ours. When a new crop of babies came out, they were tiny and black-skinned, almost transparent in their fragility. We considered them gracious houseguests—in contrast to the snakes and enormous cockroaches that could fly.

The current problem was that Gulleys' dragon was reported to be fifteen sizes bigger than our usual lizards. After a week, he was still at large. Meanwhile, I remained intensely unwell and went off the hospital before I could hear the end of the dragon story.

I spent the next seven days in Manila Sanitarium and Hospital. In a way, I might almost have thought that I was on vacation. An air-conditioned room, spacious, and decorated with colors instead of the usual dead white. My sheets were blue with white flowers. My last hospital incarceration had been in Canada where, as I recalled, the beds had been made up with bleached sail-canvas.

A competent doctor, attentive nurses and hosts of concerned friends and colleagues, yes. We were to learn that such gastro-intestinal illnesses were a constant threat, often ending in trips to the hospital. The problem simply went with the territory.

Then we had more exotic complaints that felled us from time to time. My mother was one of the first to go down with H-Fever in early July. Hemor-rhagic Fever is mosquito-borne and closely related to Dengue Fever. It culminates in what looks like a rash but is actually the rupturing of tiny blood vessels. A tropical disease, it becomes especially prevalent in the wet season. Heaven knows, we had plenty of wet that year. Actually, we had three typhoons the week she went into the hospital. July and August broke the records for storms and floods in 1972. Mum returned home in time for her birthday on July 24, but it took her many more weeks to recover.

With the whole city awash, floods crumpled the already broken pave-ments. The trans-Manila journey from the College campus to the hospital became an epic undertaking.

One night as we came home from the hospital, a truck loaded with steel pipes leaped out of the downpour and crossed the median. Although Walt braked the van down to less than 10 mph, a forty-foot pole blasted through the windshield. It exploded into a million pieces. Just another six or eight inches forward, and Walt and I would both have been decapitated.

In shock Lorna scrambled out of the back seat screaming and stopped a taxi. All of us van passengers returned to campus while Walt waited on the street for the police.

Rainy season spared us nothing. **Left.** For days at a time the rain poured off the roof in spouts. **Center.** Larry and Lorna played under the eaves, and we all took showers out there at night. **Right.** Walt and Larry ditched the back yard to keep the floodwaters out of the house.

Our neighbor, Dr. Conrado Jimenez, the campus doctor, came to the house immediately. He was still digging the glass out of my legs when Walt and the police arrived. They had with them the truck driver, now under arrest.

Suddenly the room was full of people crowding around the bed. The policeman wanted a statement from me. He began his investigation with wanting to know my mother's maiden name. The glass extraction was still in progress, and by now I had five holes in my leg—not wide ones but deep. Besides, I was rather shaken up and in poor condition for bureaucratic nonsense. In a word, I considered the officer just one too many people in my bedroom. Mercifully, Walt took him away, and I didn't see him again.

I got up the next morning wondering if there could possibly be anything left to go wrong in our world. There was. It turned out that the Union Office building in Pasay (right beside the hospital) had burned down in the night. When we visited Mum the next day, we saw the blackened shell, a skeleton standing in the flood waters. We heard that the firemen refused to start work until they had haggled over a price. They were offered 2,000 pesos, but apparently that wasn't enough. So the entire building was lost.

One of Mum's nurses speculated, "Maybe we aren't living right." If that pharisaical theory were true, our beleaguered family was doomed, for sure. Indeed, our recent afflictions seemed to be vastly out of proportion to our wickednesses.

This philosophy, however, proved to be widespread. Reyes, our little typewriter repairman, held the opinion that this horrific weather was punishment for the person who broke off the head of the Santo Niño image in the Quiapo Church.

Meanwhile, the storms raged on. I stood on our front porch where the sun was shining. I watched a slightly opaque, silver wall of water move across the campus. It hit our house like a nuclear bomb. Then, in less than five minutes the sunshine broke through again.

One time, it rained for thirty-two days and never once stopped. I had never seen anything like it, and I was no stranger to the tropics. Torrents of rain shredded umbrellas and flooded the lawns. Larry set a bucket out in the back yard and collected four inches of rain in four hours. When the water came to within an inch of our doorsills, Walt and the kids dug a ditch across the lawn to divert some of the flood.

I waded ankle deep over to Fighur's house. "Well," Anne asked cheerfully, "who has the pattern for the ark, so we can start building?"

"I don't believe anyone has had any special instruction for this emergency, have they?"

"Oh, dear," She paused in mock surprise. "Well, we won't be able to get any gopher wood here anyway. Dick already inquired." On days like that, if you didn't laugh, you would have to cry.

One of the typhoons broke the neck of the papaya tree that my nephew Kevin had planted. It stood bravely out there in the downpour, however, with a crown of bright young leaves covering its wounds. I remembered how plants back in our homeland died quietly in the autumn, spent the winter in the grave, and were resurrected in the spring. Here they would be murdered in a typhoon and in less than two weeks vibrant new growth leaped forth again. The papaya tree had to be a parable of our own lives. Through all the days of endless rain, trees, and lawns remained a mass of living green.

Soon other consequences became apparent. Food shortages escalated.

We struggled to town to lay in a 100-pound bag of rice and two bags of flour. Fresh produce disappeared out of the markets. Snakes became a problem. They traveled in "herds" looking for dry ground. We found very poisonous brown cobras and banded kraits much in evidence.

Ironically, throughout the deluge, we often had no water in the taps. Habitually, under cover of darkness we took our showers during rainstorms, outdoors under the downpour coming off the eaves of the house. No great hardship really. Inside we had no water heater, so cold showers were all we had even in the best of times.

We simply had no way to keep anything dry. In the house the walls and floors "sweat" moisture. Books and shoes took on a coating of green mold that might have produced a fortune in penicillin, if we'd known how to harvest it.

For two months our journals and letters home spoke of nothing but the rain. I had to apologize. All I could say was, "We hope you're not bored. We aren't. We have no time to be."

By the end of August Shirley Kehney was just recovering from her bout with H- Fever. About the time she got out of the hospital Barbara van Ornam entered with it. Multiple illness began to run parallel with the violent weather.

One day in mid-September I was working at my desk when a flash of pain in my back took my breath away. I might as well have been stabbed with a *bolo* knife. I assumed that I was now also one of the chosen victims for H-Fever. I was alone, the rest of the family having gone off to the airport to meet our incoming new family, the James Joiners.

Instinctively, I made some long-range plans. I cleared my desk and took some galley proofs I'd been working on over to the Publishing House. Then I dragged myself home, crashed on the bed, and sent Beth to call Dr. Jimenez. He arrived about the time that Walt and Mum returned from the airport. An injection temporarily broke my fever that, at that moment, stood at 104. Unfortunately it straggled on for the next week, ranging from 101-103.

Finally, Walt had to haul me across the city to the hospital, an almost incoherent heap of misery. I had hepatitis, gastritis, and a kidney infection. I had a hard time accepting the fact that all of these things had befallen me at one time. Just H-fever alone, I thought to myself, might have been a good deal after all. (Our family, the Gulleys, plus all of the house girls received gamma globulin shots, so that they should be safe from hepatitis.) Walt being much occupied with the public health ventures he was inaugurating, Mum was the one who sat by my hospitable bed for many, many hours.

After a week in the hospital I achieved normal liver function and was released. Hepatitis, however, leaves you with an indescribable tiredness that no amount of rest or sleep seems to cure. I just kept hoping that I'd wake up some morning and feel alive again. My days were all the same, however, the doctor speaking darkly of six weeks of rest. Or maybe twelve weeks. I would be debilitated for some time to come.

Meanwhile I assessed my blessings. I was still alive. I read many books, my dogs snuggled up around me, the while. My cousin Ina Longway sent me Tolkien's trilogy, *Lord of the Rings*. "I have only one regret," she wrote, "that I can never again have the thrill of reading the books for the first time." (It turned out that she had read *The Rings*, all 1,500 pages, eight times!) I now had the time to read the whole set in less than a week, without interruption. Being familiar with Norse epics, mythology, and British folklore, I enjoyed a marvelous reading experience.

Food became a tedious chore because I had no appetite. Being threatened with intravenous feeding, I tried to remember some good food. Like the time when Jack and Olivine Bohner brought apples from Australia and made apple pies. Like the time that Dottie Wilson found sugar somewhere in the sugar-

Left. One night the office of the North Philippine Union Mission in Pasay burned. Right. The very next morning workers, unfortunately accustomed to city fires, were tearing it down to make room for a new building.

less (pre-martial law) Philippines and made me a batch of her superior potato doughnuts. Then Beth prepared some *puso*. That precious banana blossom that came off one of our own trees. Divided among the seven of us, of course, we each had only a very modest serving. Still, I ate it, and it helped me back toward a normal diet.

In all my years of living in the tropics I was visited regularly with painful ear infections. Soon after my first hepatitis event, I had another episode. I made a series of visits to the office of Dr. Lim. A specialist trained at McGill University in Montreal, he kept two offices in the most elegant parts of Manila. He had patients to match.

I was duly grateful for his expertise, painful as the treatments had to be. All conversation in the office proceeded in English, that being a symbol of real "class."

One day as I waited, a dignified, very glamorous Filipina came in. She was accompanied by her son, five or six years old. Turned out in a spotless white suit, he stood dutifully at her knee, his round little face the very essence of innocence.

The doctor's assistant computed test activity at an instrument panel that would have done justice to the Houston Space Center. Dr. Lim studied the results intently. "Your son has perfect hearing, Ma'am," he said. "There is no problem."

"Oh, I am so thankful." The mother's relief was obvious and genuine. "I was so worried."

"Yes," the doctor continued. "It is only you that he does not hear. He has just tuned you out,"

Everyone in the room laughed, even the discomfited mother herself.

The doctor patted the little fellow's well-groomed head. "No, we will not have to remove the ears." He smiled down at the boy. Then, he frowned, "Yet."

Clearly anxious, the boy looked back at the doctor as his mother led him out the door.

All of which forces one to a difficult conclusion. A high level of medical service is actually available in many parts of the world. That is, for people who can pay for it. In places like the Philippines where the "middle class" is weak, where the gap between wealth and poverty is very great, the sharp contrast is accentuated. It is, in fact, deplorable. More than once we availed ourselves of good medical services. At those times we were profoundly aware that thousands of Filipinos were born, lived, and died without ever seeing a physician.

We could even provide our little dogs with preferential care. Mitzi regularly delivered her pups between midnight and 3 a.m., well past the curfew hour of Martial Law. In fact, it took special permission from the presidential palace at Malacanang to tend to her needs.

In addition to the one that went to the Todd Murdochs, another went to the Gordon Bullocks. They called her Tiki (Indonesian, *tjantik,* "beautiful"). Some others went to our eager Filipino friends. (It appeared than no Pomeranians had ever been seen in the Philippines before.)

Finally, when Mitzi delivered triplets by Caeserean surgery, we decided that ten litters and twenty-one puppies had been enough for one little five-pound dog, so we had production halted at that point. The three so-fragile little mites (two female, one male) weighed in at 70, 75, and 90 grams. Walt and I had an hourly schedule, feeding them with medicine droppers. Their poor, patient mother was befuddled because they yelled all of the time. Within a month, however, they became a lively little gang.

Miss Hernandez frequently came from Bocaue to sell us embroidered fabrics. After waiting more than a year, she finally was able to buy the little blonde from Mitzi's last litter. "I will name her Girlie," the lady told us. She was fairly dancing when she arrived in a Volkswagen van to take the puppy home. "The *jeepney* isn't good enough for her, you see. So I had to hire a car."

Medical concerns and exotic tropical diseases were not the only hazards we faced. Sometimes much more mundane affairs overwhelmed us. The Manila climate of itself could be unspeakably oppressive. Exhaustion sometimes felled me like a blow to the head. One day I was teaching my three-hour graduate seminar in Victorian Literature. We discussed Tennyson's "Lotos Eaters." The smooth, rich language itself was a kind of opiate, and I dismissed the class an hour early, simply because I couldn't continue in the unrelenting heat.

One afternoon, Mum and I came home from errands in the city. We

Manila did not lack for modern buildings. The problem was that squatters' shacks would spring up around them, almost overnight.

trundled along in the Bedford van in what felt like hell fire itself. Secretly, I resented the ratty Bedford. What a glorious thing if it had air-conditioning! I didn't dwell on the idea for long, however, because I knew that we did well to keep it running at all.

That night, indeed, I felt that I'd had a slight heat stroke. I kept thinking that a trip up to the Baguio mountains would have cooled our fevered brains nicely. We hadn't been there for almost a year. . . .Thus ran my disjointed imaginings.

Indeed, our work was a constant round of public responsibility, and we often had to "live beyond ourselves." Although the demands seemed everlasting, their fulfillment brought us huge satisfaction, and that kept us going. Occasionally one longed for just a little "aloneness," being overcome with people fatigue. Lacking air-conditioning, in the main, we picked up other ideas for relief. The airlines of China, Japan and Korea, for instance, taught us how to soak towels in ice water and wrap them around our necks

Still, climate and personal health were not all. Certainly not! Enormous social and political challenges existed, and they called for long patience and considerable ingenuity. All of that came to a head when President Ferdinand Marcos declared Martial Law on September 21, 1972. (That was the night I had entered the hospital with my first round of hepatitis.)

Marcos promised the country *Bagong Liponan,* a "New Society." By early 1973 he had a new constitution in place that closed Congress, allowed him to rule by decree, and established a nightly curfew. At first he strictly controlled the media. One newspaper functioned, and foreign magazines were banned. After three weeks a few radio stations returned to the air, and three television channels re-opened. Marcos' political opponents who survived went into exile.

Since martial law was not lifted until early in 1981, we lived under this government for the rest of our days in the Philippines

The creation of the New Society started off with some rather dramatic effects. Some garbage was cleared off the streets. Health services improved, Corruption in public offices came under scrutiny. Even the *jeepneys* were urged to keep within traffic lanes. Some of the canals were cleared and squatters' shacks on the banks were torn down. The authorities confiscated fifty gambling machines, crushed them with steamrollers, burned them, and dumped the remains in the Pasig River. Miraculously sugar reappeared on the supermarket shelves. A minor point, but interesting.

What affected us most was the closing of the schools and colleges, and universities were carefully examined. These restrictions, along with the weather, made havoc of our first semester at Philippine Union College. Although we might have been safer than at any time since we had arrived in Manila, it was hard to know how the whole business would finally play out.

Over the years, martial law failed to transform the country into another Garden of Eden. Thievery, for instance, never really slackened off. That first year we lost two bicycles, Lorna's and mine.

Then came the case of Fernando Norte, a student who worked on our yard. When he had received 200 pesos from home, he went down to Santa Cruz to buy new pants and shoes. (He had only one pair of each.) Three gang-sters held him at gunpoint and took his money. He came back too heartsick even to talk about it. At least, he still had his life. Larry gave him a pair of his pants, and our weekly discussion group took up a collection to get him outfitted before the new school year began.

Robbery occurred in many other forms—in ways

Rusty and Mitzi's puppies were in high demand. Quite possibly they were the first thoroughbred Pomeranians to arrive in the city.

still meshed in with the government.

One day, as we were inching along Roxas Boulevard, a little Coca Cola truck slammed into us. Damage to the hulking Bedford was inconsequential, and the little Toyota got a curled fender. All quite trivial. Upon discovering that they had collided with foreigners, however, the occupants of the truck determined to make some money. After three hours of police "investigation," it became clear that we were supposed to come through with a bribe.

Even though we had long since accepted the fact that bribery was simply one of the occupational hazards of overseas living, I fought through to the finish line. I couldn't help myself.

The policeman in charge sat with his feet elevated on the desk top among his papers and no less than four telephones. He was getting a complete manicure from a little girl in a smart pantsuit. She applied the metallic pink nail polish with earnest concentration. This scenario made me all the more determined not to submit to fraud.

After huge effort, I got a phone call through to Gordon Bullock at the Union office. "We're on our way to jail," I told him.

"Congratulations!" I caught the edge of real concern under his usual jovial manner. "How did you manage that?"

Ultimately Gordon connected with our insurance company, a New Zealand outfit to which we could look with a hope for some efficiency, and, above all, justice. If we had this much trouble when someone hit us, what would be the fate of the unhappy foreigner who himself hits someone! (That was an eventuality awaiting us in the not-so-distant future.)

Given the prevailing conditions of Manila traffic, an accident was inevitable. It had never been a case of "If." Only "When."

We got back to our campus home about 8 p.m. that evening. As we drove through the gate, we saw eight or ten students strolling down the road toward the College Auditorium and choir practice. In perfect harmony they were singing the rather elaborate anthem, "Bless the Lord, O My Soul." Their voices drifted out on the night air. We forgot our wounds and knew that all was well.

Bureaucratic red tape can be exasperating anywhere, and the coming of martial law in the Philippines only intensified the misery in that far flung island nation.

A journey Walt and I made to the island of Palawan was a case in point. Today threats of terrorism have complicated all airport departures. Our frustrations ranged from the fanatical (in Manila) to an attitude akin to that of the *carabaos* (in the provinces). Who cares?

During our pre-boarding baggage inspection, the guard had no interest in our cameras, but he eyed our little red water container with suspicion. "Why do you want to carry water with you?"

"Because when we go to the provinces we sometimes get sick," we humbly replied. "We need to carry a little water to use before we prepare other water with the chemicals that we must use."

He considered this an unlikely story, so he detained the whole crowd while he poured some of our water into his hand. He smelled it and tasted it. Finally, we boarded the little twin-prop plane. His conscientious investigation made our departure only one hour late.

Palawan Island, as it turned out, gave martial law little upon which to feed. In the town square children romped around the inevitable Rizal monument while *carabaos* and goats were feeding nearby. Down on the muddy shore, among the fishermen's huts the boat builders worked. Life was unsophisticated, slow, and un-commercialized. We didn't see a single machine gun. I did, however, observe a policeman sitting by the roadside languidly reading the newspaper that contained the usual account of Marcos' latest orders. At the time, we found the situation quite relaxing.

Upon arrival in the Philippines everyone had to expect the wasting of at least two days being fingerprinted and documented. Departures were equally difficult. We discovered that even applying for a simple visa could drive one beyond the outer limits of sanity.

Early in 1971 we started planning for the arrival of two of our nephews, Kevin Eckert (my sister's son) and Brian Robertson (Walt's sister's son)—both minors. They were to come to the Philippines for the summer.

Gordon Bullock advised us to "get someone from the travel agency to go with you. It would take weeks for you to try to do it yourselves." Forthwith,

From time to time, Martial Law, in quest of the "New Society," closed colleges and universities. The hundreds of students on our little compound never caused a disturbance, but we were often frustrated in trying to meet our academic obligations.

Mum and I started out at 8 a.m. on a Thursday morning. Our first stop was at the Ministry of Foreign Affairs. At that point our guide deserted us, and we saw her no more.

During the rest of the day we made twelve more stops, each one inept and exasperating in its own unique way. We threaded our way through inner and outer offices, among lawyers, secretaries, and other persons with altogether inscrutable identities. The "Recorder" was but one case in point. Near the end of the day we were exhausted and near hysterics, laughing at the pomposity of all of these pointless procedures.

Appearing at first to be a deaf-mute, the Recorder flipped through a pile of papers by a typewriter. "Where is your typist?" I asked.

"I don't have a typist." He started pawing through his papers at top speed and wouldn't even look at me. "Come back this afternoon—maybe."

I clearly understood that "this afternoon" was a euphemism for "tomorrow" or "next week. " Or maybe until the next batch of typists graduated from some business school. Remembering how we had recently lost our plane seats at Cauayan Airport, I realized that this was probably the moment for a bribe.

Nonetheless, I decided to stand my ground. This was the second day I had spent on this case. Now we had only four more offices to go. "I will not leave this office today until the papers are completed. Moreover, it is impossible for me to leave my work at the College for another day. Besides, the visas have to reach Los Angeles today."

At this point, a miracle occurred. From somewhere, in about fifteen minutes, there appeared a typist in a mustard-colored satin dress. I requested the Recorder's permission to talk to her. He refused either to look at or speak to me. So I walked past him and sat down with the girl. I went over every detail of the case.

One of the most incomprehensible facts turned out to be that one boy was American and the other Canadian. In the first round of documents Brian was listed as a U. S. citizen. On the next try, both boys appeared as Canadians. It was early afternoon when the men and the secretaries returned from the fatigues of the lunch hour. I wrote out a statement to define this unusual difference—Kevin was American and Brian Canadian.

The last step was a trip to the "Code Room." From this inner sanctum a cable requesting the visa would be dispatched to the Philippine Consul in Los

Angeles. We took the elevator up three floors, walked through a maze of corridors, and then down at least four flights of stairs to a small hole in the wall. When the door opened, an angry face greeted us, for we had broken in upon a game of checkers. "The cable will be sent within two hours," one of the players snapped.

We could do no more. So, that was the day that was. I reverted to a concept upon

Gordon Bullock and Walt confer during a social evening. A "man of many parts," Gordon had the oversight of everything from our financial and immigration crises to controlling the outbreak of head-lice in our Baesa school.

which I have meditated for my whole life. These jobs in immigration, customs, and law. Is it a certain kind of person who chooses that kind of work? Or is it the job itself that makes them "that way" after a while?

In any case, Kevin and Brian arrived on Monday, June 14, 1971. Two blond heads appeared at the back door of the plane, and then the two boys strode down the steps with all of the aplomb of the most seasoned world travelers. The shrieks from our kids on the observation deck bought a quick response from below. Suddenly the two boys, ran furiously for the gate. Walt

Left. Arrival at Manila Airport (June, 1971). Two more earliteens joined our household. (L-R). Larry Comm, Brian Robertson, Kevin Eckert, Lorna Comm. Right. With his usual love for gardening Kevin planted a papaya tree. In a very short time, he and Brian could stand in its shade.

talked his way past the barricade to help get them through customs and immigration.

Then we all jammed into the little Peugeot. (At that time, the Bedford van had not yet entered our lives.) The kids didn't stop talking for the whole hour-and-a-half it took to get home to the campus. Lorna traded rooms with Larry. Now she slept in the storeroom, and the three boys crammed themselves into the little front bedroom.

Meanwhile, we had another on-going difficulty that really never improved. Emotionally all of us overseas workers became inordinately dependent on letters from home. If the local administration cared about international mail half as much as we did, we would have had delivery twice a day! We found the vagaries of the postal service very distressing. They were made all the more vexing because we really didn't have a telephone service. Not in the usual sense of the word.

Over Christmas, for example, we received no mail for more than a week. The problem had at least four components. Firstly, there was only one key to open Box 1772 in the Manila Post Office. Sebastian [not his given name], the mail carrier had it. Glum and moody, he rarely spoke to anyone. Even some of his own countrymen agreed: "Sebastian is not nice."

Moreover, he kept mail at his house, if he didn't feel like going to the office. We often waited from Saturday to Tuesday for Friday's mail. Thirdly,

The College *jeepney* that Sebastian drove had internal disorders and could be laid up for days in the Motor Pool. Moreover, Sebastian had no mailbag. He carried everything loose on the seat beside him, fluttering in the breeze.

The man had many other tasks, so the post office box downtown could remain unharvested for many days. Perhaps he had to take ladies to Divisoria. Or drive the school bus. Or go on an errand to Naga Academy (a twelve- hour trip, one way).

Dick Fighur once wrote a cunning letter to the Administration proposing "postal reforms" that would, he declared, "boost the morale of overseas students and staff." He even went so far as surreptitiously

Leona Minchin visited our mailbox in the Administration Building. No one could put a price on the value of receiving letters from home.

securing a copy of the post office box key. When some one of us used the key, we did so very secretly. We usually found Box 1772 stuffed beyond its limit. The little door popped open and the box would belch out an ankle-deep pile of mail. Nothing, however, really worked. Computers, email, texting—indeed, all social media—and the internet remained many years in the future.

Along with the physical challenges we faced, we had a list of emotional hazards with which we had to live. Two stood at the top. First, the lack of communication. Second, we required a super-human amount of patience just to move us from one day into the next.

Frail as the structure of the Bamboo House may appear to be, those who live there learn profound lessons. Many go on to develop strong characters. Residents work, cope, and survive. At the same time, they enjoy! Often they begin the days with the energy and lift of the lark's song rising.

Still, they know, perhaps instinctively, that another phase looms on the horizon. When Larry and Lorna became certified teenagers, Walt and I knew that we had only a few more years to live in our Bamboo House. We had just one more major move to make. Permanent Return to our homeland. Giving up overseas service was not a happy choice. We would gladly have remained abroad until retirement overtook us, if such an option had been available.

Moving into The Gazebo, however gradually, brings significant change to everyone. At first, we still fly high. Then, slowly and imperceptibly, we begin to lose altitude. Next, our descent gathers velocity. Finally, it takes every ounce of strength we have left just to maintain our living space. Thus we adjust to the last earth-bound home that our hearts can occupy.